With Love, from Colorado

Rebecca J. Fisher

withlovefromCO@gmail.com

A NOTE TO THE READER:

This novel is fictional and the characters are not meant to resemble anyone. Any similarities of characters to actual people are unintentional. The depiction of Hope House is also fictional, but loosely based on Hope House Colorado which is metro-Denver's only resource providing free self-sufficiency programs to teen moms, including Residential, GED, and College & Career Programs.

A special thanks to: my intrepid father, Bill Fisher, for facilitating my second act in life; my sister, Temple Genung, for her keen editorial eye and unflinching emotional support; my brother Garth Fisher for his graphic design expertise on my photo and website logo, my friends Julia Hedges for cheering me on throughout the entire writing process; and Pauline DeVries and Kati Nybakken for their editorial support. Thank you, Kerri Munro, for illustrating and designing the book cover. Lastly, a heartfelt thanks to Ibon Izurieta for being a loyal co-parent and for-life friend.

Table of Contents

Chapter 1: The Golden Ticket

Chapter 2: The Interview

Chapter 3: The Wait

Chapter 4: The Meeting

Chapter 5: The Intake

Chapter 6: The Team Meeting

Chapter 7: The Truth

Chapter 8: Gael

Chapter 9: Marcus

  Five Star #1

  Five Star #2

  Five Star #3

Chapter 10: The Hideout & The Hotline

Chapter 11: The Interview

Chapter 12: Real Here Now

Chapter 13: One Degree of Separation

Chapter 14: Convergence

Chapter 15: Small Group Work

Chapter 16: The Visit

Chapter 17: The Clean Up

Chapter 18: Bliss To The Rescue

Chapter 20: The Rescue

Chapter 21: The Aftermath

Chapter 22: Sleep Tight

Chapter 23: One Step Forward

Chapter 24: Sunday

Chapter 25: Accountability Partners

Chapter 26: Monday

Chapter 27: Barbara's Hideaway

Chapter 28: The Deal

Chapter 29: The Summit

Chapter 30: Monday Night

Chapter 31: Bitter Pills

Chapter 32: Tuesday

Chapter 33: Gala Night

For Naia & Zoe – may you always stay as thick as thieves.

Chapter 1: The Golden Ticket

Nova felt embarrassed with aging. It was supposed to be a process, yet it took her by surprise. Logically, she knew that it's a glacial evolution, one gray hair at a time, but emotionally it was a shock. She realized that she looked very 46 after work redundancies had left her without a job last month and put her on the interview circuit again. It was just so much easier a decade ago to persuade a search committee when she didn't feel self-conscious about her personality being indelibly stamped on her face. It was also simpler when she actually wanted to work a 40-plus hour workweek. However, at this midway point in her life, it was far more difficult to muster the enthusiasm to jump on the career treadmill again.

Anger and depression permanently indented lines above her upper lip. Puffy eye bags revealed how she didn't cope well with stress and was – more often than not – hung over each morning. Wrinkles multiplied seemingly overnight and subtitled her every expression. There was nowhere to hide anymore. The conspiracy of muscle memory and less skin elasticity seemed harshly unkind to a woman who had given so much of herself to her late husband, two grown children, and career as a nurse practitioner. The inevitable shift of fat drooped her eyelids, waddle, and eventually her smile. The affliction of aging amplified a naked, vulnerable feeling that she couldn't seem to shake, so after Nova lost her job, she packed up and sold her house in Saratoga Springs, NY. *En route* to a last-chance-life in Denver, CO where she promised herself to be *the best Nova I can possibly be*, she pulled off interstate 76 to a westbound rest stop in Ogallala before the Nebraska-Colorado state line.

Nova reflexively stretched her pale arms with emerging 'maturity' spots high into the air toward the cloudless, sunny sky and yawned as soon as she got out of her Jeep. *Three hundred days of sunshine a year, here I come*, she mused. Four days of driving on highways full of Mack Trucks left her nerves jittery and muscles tight. Her right hand reflexively rubbed the small of her back as she beeped the SUV locked. No other cars were in the parking lot. *Alone.* A few empty picnic tables sat useless outside the small cement structure. Nova glanced at her Fitbit to check the time. *Four o'clock. That's about all it's good for these days,* she sighed. At this rate, Nova calculated, she could be in her new apartment before 6pm. *Good. Almost there.*

Inside the public restroom, white walls made out of painted cinder blocks housed three stainless steel stalls. Nova's line of sight was immediately drawn to contrasting bright red graffiti on the wall of the last stall without a door. Curious, she walked closer and saw a message. "With love, from Colorado" was written in large curly letters above an arrow snaking down to a small stainless steel shelf. Nova's eyes focused on what appeared to be a golden piece of paper the size of a movie ticket or bookmark. She immediately looked over each shoulder and inside the other stalls. *Is this a practical joke?* she wondered searching for a camera. *Is it a prize?* She quickly grabbed the golden ticket and shoved it into her rear jean's pocket before anyone could walk in and catch her with it.

Once Nova was back inside her Jeep, she locked the doors and retrieved the ticket. It was thick stock paper and gold on both sides. The black lettering swirled like an ornate wedding invitation. One side had a company name, "Bliss," and on the back was a website, "blissout.com/79458212." *Bizarrely specific.* This was the first time Nova had smiled in four days.

Heading southwest from Keenesburg to Brighton and then through east Westminster and into downtown Denver, the sea of copycat houses morphed into a skyline of cranes and ever-taller apartment buildings. After parsing the Internet for an apartment, Nova had rightly concluded that they are pretty much the same. All the new apartment buildings in Denver had a decent gym, an outdoor pool, shared office space, a shared 'guest apartment' for visitors, a shared dining room and kitchen for hosting parties, communal grills and pavilions, and one parking space. Nearly all of the buildings were pet friendly and seeking Leed's certification to denote how environmentally conscious they were. Urban life was deliberately organized like a box store: no matter the building, clients knew exactly what to expect.

The key difference, at least at Nova's financial level, was location. She would have paid nearly the same rent if she had wanted to live in any other new apartment building in popular Colorado cities like the Tech Center, Cherry Creek, Boulder, Denver, or Colorado Springs. Suburban life would have been cheaper, but ideally, Nova wanted a walkable life. In upstate NY, a car was required on a daily basis. The grocery stores, work, library, and post office were all not less than a 15-minute drive from her house. She had had enough of it. Enough mowing the lawn, enough shoveling snow, and enough of the four month long gray, cloudy winters. Downtown Denver held the promise of more than a modern apartment. It meant sunshine, anonymity, good public transportation, a thriving arts community, and plenty of food options, all without needing a vehicle.

Nova's new home was a pricey, 890 square foot, single bedroom 'urban apartment' on the sixth floor of the new Cadence building near Union Station downtown. As soon as she closed and locked the front door behind her, she texted her mom that she had arrived "safe and sound," and enabled the hotspot on her cellphone. Anticipation made her feel giddy; *what is this website?* She opened her MacBook Air on the gray and white, granite kitchen counter and typed "blissout.com/79458212" into the browser.

"This site is only intended for those 18 and older. Are you 18 or older?" was written on the screen. "Hello", she sang happily at her laptop. No pictures, no navigation, no company name, just the question with hyperlinked words "yes" and "no". Nova clicked "yes."

What appeared next made her stomach drop: the word "Congratulations." A full-bodied, African American, female voice that reminded her of Oprah Winfrey said, "Congratulations and welcome to Bliss." After three seconds, the word dissolved into the background. *I've won something! What did I win?*

The next screen was the Bliss homepage. *Where is it? Denver?* Nova scrolled down to the bottom to see the address: 43 Dharma Road, Boulder, CO 80301. She copied and pasted the address into Google maps and pressed the return button. *How far of a drive?* She typed in her new home address and found the result to be 44 minutes. *Okay, not horribly far away.* Nova then scrolled up and pressed the triangle to begin the video. *What is this place?* Tranquil jazz music played and then the same deep voice came on again.

Welcome to Bliss – your discrete, private oasis.

I like the sounds of that. Images of all kinds of women in a gym appeared. There were close ups of women of color laughing, broad shots of Asian women in red boxing gloves kicking and hitting a punching bag, and elderly Latinas with gold, cross necklaces wrapped in white towels chatting at the edge of a Jacuzzi.

> We are a unique, multiservice company in the business of supporting women. Bliss was created by women for everyone who identifies as a woman. We have spent the last ten years developing Bliss into the kind of retreat that focuses on adult women of all backgrounds. We offer an individualized, curated experience that guides you to your best self and maximum happiness.

In contrast to the wide variety of female clients in the advertisement, Nova noticed the complete absence of men. It was a bright and colorful, modern retreat with a bar, relaxation rooms, prayer rooms, and rooms for group exercise classes. Women were depicted coaching other women in the gym and at the pool. Female massage therapists were kneading clients' shoulders on a massage table, and female servers were setting down drinks in front of businesswomen. Nova watched and tried to make sense of it all. *Why would they have a bar at a gym? Why would they have prayer rooms at all?* she puzzled.

> So if you need some tender loving care, some time to focus only on yourself, some motivation to get back into shape, or want to achieve unconditional self-love… if this is you, then visit us in Boulder today! Let's co-create a genesis to your best self!

Tacky ending, Nova thought. She made an online appointment for the next day and received an autoreply email within 30 seconds that read: "Thank you for making your appointment on Wednesday, April 17, 2019 at 11am. Please bring the golden ticket with you. In order to get to know you better and offer you customized support, our intake interview lasts approximately 20 minutes. Please plan accordingly for your first visit."

Plan accordingly? How can I plan for a retreat about my happiness? A genesis to my best self – LOL! Nova smiled and bent herself down so that her fingertips touched her toes and remained in this position alternating the stretch from her left to right sides. The knot in her lower right back felt slightly less inflamed. In fact, the irony wasn't lost on her; *of course I can't plan because I've never actively planned my happiness. Of course I have back pain because I sit too much and don't exercise enough. My waist has extra inches of fat because I drink too much! This was your design, Nova, no one else's. Take some responsibility for once.* Nova was too young to feel hopeless and too old to lie to herself anymore. If age had given her any gifts, it was that of honest acceptance.

Nova walked her hands out onto the floor into a downward dog yoga position. Then, she curled up into child's pose with the right side of her face lying on the tiled floor blankly staring across her empty apartment. Her phone dinged that she had received a text message. *It's just mom.* Nova didn't move.

Chapter 2: The Interview

The crane operator roughly yanked the heavy wooden library chair away from the worktable. The loud protest of chair legs grating against the marble floor drew an irritable glance from the female cop pacing the 3rd floor of the Denver Public Library. *Excuse the fuck out of me, officer*, his thought spat out as all 200 pounds of his bulky, five-foot-nine frame plopped down onto the seat. He spread his legs wide to free his swollen scrotum and tossed his yellow hard-hat to his left on the table with a louder-than-necessary noise for the benefit of his new friend. Her facial expression reflected her lack of amusement to which he responded indifferently by running his stubby fingers through his ultra-short silver-gray hair.

As if swimming the breast stroke, his pudgy hands dove forward and then swept apart to his far left and right until they braced the table's corners. He looked around. *Black, female cop at 10 o'clock, homeless tweaker at 1, book shelves behind, a white, skinny, bearded homeless vet at 8, and high-ceilinged hallway entrance at 3.* A single bead of sweat travelled down his tanned forehead, meandered around his right eyebrow and then down the side of his round face. He quickly wiped it off with his left hand, and then wiped it against the thigh of his dirty jeans. *Keep your eyes at 3,* he told himself.

As he white-knuckled the edges of the table, he saw a classy-looking woman enter the great hall and strut toward him. *This has to be the one*, he surmised. She looked as out-of-place as he did among the regular library patrons. His mouth suddenly felt parched, his tongue thick and useless. Her gate was revealing. He scanned her from her shoulder-length straight dark brown hair, down her long neck, pale-pink dress-suit, her perfectly natural breasts, hips, and long legs with high-heeled shoes. *Open toed. Apple-red nails.* Her style of walking wasn't the hippy-sway of a kid wanting to draw stares. Although, she did seem younger than he expected. *No*, he surmised as he processed her erect spine and puffed out chest. *Swagger. She has swagger. She's satisfied. That there is a satisfied woman*, he remarked to himself.

"Are you David?" she asked, relatively sincerely, in a clear, educated, Midwestern accent before she sat down.

"Yeah," he growled more than said as he looked around suspiciously. "You Nefertiti?"

"Yes, call me Nef." Without making any noise, she gently lifted the chair directly across from David and pulled it out to sit down. "I believe we share a friend in common."

> While some folks find it hard to believe that unrelated people would interact, I don't. I have seen it happen many, many times because I help make it happen. That's our job. No, it's like our vocation or a calling. It's community building really. I'm Chaya – but I'm not shy, like not at all. That's just how my name sounds, but with a silent "c". I'm a ginger, Jewish girl from Brooklyn, NY as you can tell by my accent. Nice to meet you! I work the front desk and counsel clients at Bliss. Betts and I go way back.
>
> You see, serendipity – coincidence – all of that shit is rare. Why the fuck would anyone risk leaving their catacomb these days? Honestly, in our 21st century echo chambers, we are all so goddamned insulated that it is a mother-fucking miracle that anyone communicates anything of import with anyone else in the non-virtual world. What happened to fighting and fucking? Why has

> the celebration of life been boiled down to simple folk pleading on a podcast, "How do I get debt free?" Better yet: why do we listen to them and feel like we want to ask the same damn question? Everyone seems to be so focused on their indentured servitude to the machine-we-call-capitalism that they forget everything else like joy, raising hell, skinny-dipping, not owing a goddamned penny to any-fucking-one, and living their passion. The singular drive today is to just *make it through* – make it through the next hour without a drink – the next day, without yelling at my kid – the next week, without binge-watching 10 fucking episodes on Netflix – the next month, without running out of money – the next year without gaining ten pounds. Without. Without! Wouldn't it be nice if someone were there to take care of *you*? To focus on *your* needs for a change?

"Is this real?" David leaned back and crossed his thick arms over his chest.

"Legitimate? Very much so, David. I can assure you."

"Stop using my name... please."

Sensitive or angry? Nef squinted her eyes discerningly. "I didn't mean to offend."

"I know the trick about how using someone's name makes them relax and divulge more information. No, you want something else, and I'm not sure I'm buying. This here is just a reconnaissance."

Okay, he's nervous. That makes sense. "Buying?" *Ha!* Nefertiti half-laughed at his expense. "Honey, wrong side of the counter. Let's not waste any more of each other's time. Let's just get down to business, okay? I'm sure you want to know the details as much as I want to know why Betts thinks you're a good fit."

"I'm listening."

"To start, we aren't here. You never met me. I never met you. It just IS, without questions. That's how this works. Some people have needs and wants. Others, AKA you, have answers. Tell me... are you a solutions kind of guy?"

David noticed that she didn't parrot his name at the end of her question. *Good girl. You didn't use my name. You can follow orders.*

> What's Bliss you ask? We give women answers. Solutions. A way out. A fix. We're an exit from the mind-numbing tedium of the routine they pass off as life. "Another day, another dollar!" Fuck that. Another day is another opportunity to look in the mirror and say, "wake the fuck up, asshole." It's another opportunity to reach out and stretch your reaches, baby! 'Stretch... Your... Fucking... Reaches,' is what I preach. This is our job. We're community builders. Bliss connects people, people just like you who are seeking solutions.

"By the look on your face, I think Betts didn't give you the run-through." Nefertiti took a deep breath and exhaled. Leaning forward, she interlaced her pedicured fingers.

David focused his mind. "I don't know what you folks think a 'solution' is. You have some fancy words to mean fancy things, but I know what I know."

"What, exactly, do you know?" Nefertiti's response was genuinely inquisitive.

"Betts told me what you all do. Said you're looking for – for – you know – 'companions'. Lots of lonely women out there who will pay handsomely for –"

"So you get it," she interrupted looking around at the general possibility of being overheard. "The very, very, basic gist of it, at least. We all have jobs. My job is to see if you are a PRO. I mean, if you meet the PROS – the Preliminary Requirements Of Suitability."

David massaged the bridge of his nose to his forehead with closed eyes and then let his fat hand drop to the table. "Well, I'm here. What do I have to do – to prove – my 'PROS?'"

"There's no need to worry. The first part is a simple word game. Nothing more." Nefertiti opened the clasp of her small sequined purse and removed a pair of thick, black, Gucci reading glasses. Slowly, she rested them on the end of her nose and returned to her purse to extricate a small piece of paper. "Ready?"

"Right now? Do I need to write? I don't have a pen or –"

"Just say what comes to your mind. Don't over-think it. I'll say a word; you tell me what you think."

"Can I say more stuff or you just want a one word answer, or what?"

"I don't care about the length of your answers, David. We all have jobs. My job is to say a word, and your job is to tell me what that word means to you. Ready?"

"Yeah, okay."

"Cunt."

"Jesus H. Christ!" David loudly whispered. His hand smacked the table flat as if it killed an errant mosquito.

"That's what comes to mind?" Nefertiti prodded.

"I think you should warm me up a bit first, darlin'. Jumping right to the end without… it's harsh. Give me a different word. I'm no prude, but I'm a gentleman at heart."

"So, you feel uncomfortable."

"You're damn straight. Shit, lady. Like I said, I'm far from prude, but have some decency here. We just met, and we're in public."

"Decency."

"Dignity. Even if I come to work for you – or Betts – and that's a big 'if' – I'm not a piece of meat. I'm a person. I want to make women happy, but I expect –"

Nefertiti's face was as serious as the stark, naked truth. "You're selling your body. That might be your job, should you be chosen. You don't get to have expectations beyond safety, privacy, and a fat wallet. Next word: Cock."

"That's my word. I go from 'cunt' to 'cock?'" David asked exasperated.

"Yes, 'cock'. Go."

David rolled his eyes. "Stupid. As in: This… Is… Fucking… Stupid."

"Thank you. Next word: 'Vulnerability'."

David shook his head from side to side and snorted air out his nostrils like a mad bull. *Absolutely ridiculous. This test is such bullshit. What a waste of time.* "Look, lady. I'm sure you're real nice and all, but this might not be my thing. You know, Betts and me, we go way back. Back before you, that I know. I think she was tossing me a bone by bringing me into her little enterprise. She knows – who I am – and she accepts me for who I am – and she is someone I can truly call a friend, so I'm trusting her here. But you – this stupid test – I just thought…"

"You thought what, David?"

David did not like hearing his name. "Honestly, although I do construction work and look rough around the edges, I feel like this job may tug at my heart a little. You said the word 'vulnerable,' and I thought of my heart. It's not like I can't compartmentalize, I can. And of course I love sex, but I feel like I'm under a weird, blurry microscope here."

Nefertiti smiled. "Good job. Shall we move on?"

David readjusted his weight on the chair in surprise, then wiped his parched mouth with the back of his right hand.

Nefertiti spoke as if she was reading a list of groceries. "Be creative. You knock on a door. It's a nice hotel, upscale. The peephole turns black. She's looking at you. You wait. She finally opens the door. Average looking, average age, average everything. You have no reaction. Completely neutral. She's not overly shy, nor scared, nor happy. You walk in. She shuts the door. You look at each other. Go." Nefertiti sat back in her chair with her arms crossed around her chest.

This is an interview. Keep it together. You need the money, David coached himself. "Well, I would identify myself, I guess. I would want her to know that I'm with Betts' company. What's it called? 'Bliss'? So it's like she ordered milk from Safeway, and well, this here is Safeway knockin' at your door, ma'am. I'm the milk. I'm safe. I would keep talking too. Not that she needs to be put at ease, but that it's the right thing to do. I would say that I want her to know that her safety and comfort and care are my utmost privilege to ensure tonight. That my name is whatever, I'd tell her something specific and short – easy to remember, Ted or Sam or Mac – something neutral and general like that. And I imagine that I should mention boundaries and ground rules, 'cause I think that if I say mine, then she ought to know I'm gonna respect hers too.

"So, I'd say my name, my rules – and then – and then I'd say that, with her permission, 'I'd like to sit down on the bed, and I'll just wait for her to let me know how to proceed.' And then I'd do just that. Sit down and wait. And when she comes to me, I'd see if she didn't want to say anything. 'Cause I know some want to talk and some don't, so I'd leave that up to her, I guess, but I'd watch her and study her carefully, and if she didn't say anything, I guess I'd stand up and go to her with my head down low, looking down at the carpet."

"Go on."

"Well, I guess I'd reach for her hands next, and I would squeeze them. And every step of the way, I'd be looking at her to see what she likes and what she doesn't. The things that excite her and the things that don't. You just have to see how they respond, ya know? And I would go with the flow. I mean, I think I could. I think I have a good idea about maybe how it would go – I think."

"Let me give you a common scenario and you tell me what 'you think'."

"Okay."

"Woman A, a first timer, is embarrassed about the size of her waist or her ass or what-have-you. It doesn't matter. The point is that she feels somehow unattractive. No one has had sex with her in years. She's obviously self-conscious. What do you tell her so that she is comfortable getting undressed?"

"I'd tell her that most men don't care about that frontal 'magazine' angle. Our eyes aren't taking in the overall picture. We're far more focused on a different angle than she realizes. I'd tell her not to worry about it, and then I'd ask her permission to show her – to prove it to her."

"Okay. Good enough. We can work on that – help you with your approach." Nefertiti dug into her small purse again and produced a silver colored, flat, plastic hotel key that looked like a credit card.

"Really? I passed?" David was pleased.

"Well, not entirely. We still need to 'kick the tires' so to speak. Betts got your medical paperwork, so you're good to go for the next part. This key opens room 210 at El Teatro on the second floor. Go in and take a shower. They have a great shower, by the way. Use the robe. When you come out of the bathroom, you'll meet Celeste. Celeste gets off on giving BJs – why, I have no idea – but she does. Shower again. Thoroughly. Again, when you leave the bathroom you'll meet another lady. I'll call her Sharon. Sharon wants you to make her beg for it. Shower again. Lastly, and this is only if you make it this far, you'll get to meet 'fun girl.' If at any time you or the others want to stop, just say 'stop.'"

David was thankful that his growing hard on was hidden underneath the table's surface. *Hot damn!*

"One other thing: we have cameras in the room so we can evaluate your performance."

And, it's gone. "No, I never agreed to being recorded."

"We aren't recording, just watching from another room. Streaming in real time. And don't get fancy. This isn't about hitting certain numbers or endurance. It's not a porn scene. The goal here is your partner's satisfaction. Any questions?"

David tapped his index fingers on the table like snare drum sticks as he inhaled. *About a million.* "Betts will be watching?"

"Yes. Is that a problem?" Nefertiti, now having met David, wondered where Betts had met *Mr. Ordinary. C'mon, Betts,* she silently admonished her favorite boss, *He's not at our level!*

Betts has built this company from nothing, into another kind of nothing. We couldn't be seen before because we didn't exist, do you know what I mean, lady? Chaya doesn't exist. Now, today, we can't be seen because no one wants to be seen. No one. Understand the difference? We're here, but we're not. It's like magic. But we are super real, though, ironically. Everyone has a job and gets a paycheck. Betts is the CEO. I have a lot of direct contact with the clients, and there are many more who keep our clients safe, anonymous, and happy.

Nef, she's a recruiter of sorts; she has a very special knack for picking the right ones and sussing out the useless ones. Knows how to read between the lines, that one. There was a different girl before her, but she didn't last long. Focused too much on the looks. Everyone had to be super-handsome which just made all the clients even more self-conscious. So Nef, she's your girl. She's amazing at her job.

Nef will find you your Bradley Cooper in *A Star Is Born*. She will get that shit, hunt it down, and spit it out from her mouth on your bed like a cat with a dead mouse. That girl's instincts are unreal. Imagine Bradley – I mean, imagine THAT. Imagine you're Lady Gaga and you're so fucking talented, way more talented than this homeboy. But he stretches his reaches. He's an actor and yet he pushed himself way past his reaches as a musician. And then you have Lady Gaga who is a master musician, pushing herself way past her reaches as an actress. I mean – that's acting to me: when I forget that this is Lady fucking Gaga, and I am her because I feel the love for Bradley. She did it. She did it for me, and it doesn't matter any stupid Oscar or not. She did that. She made us all be her and want that flawed and perfect partner to just smile at us like he smiled at her, and admire us the way that he admired her. But I digress, as I often do when I'm high. And I'm very often high. Sorry, you didn't come here to listen to some speech about the greatest fucking singer that ever lived. Sorry. Let's get back on track.

Celeste and Sharon work here too. Betts hired them once business hit its stride. If you ask me, privacy and scale-ability are the secrets of our success. Celeste inspects them, shall we say. Sharon, now she's unique. She's a black belt and former marine. You wouldn't know it to look at her, but she could kill you clean – three different ways – in less than ten seconds. She's perfect at her job. Sharon helps 'em calibrate just-the-right degree of… touch, pressure, electricity, what-have-you, and she runs security too. Oh, lady, you have no idea how good your life is about to get.

"Well, look at you, Cowboy. A bit rough around the edges, aren't ya."

"You must be Celeste. I'm Cal." David extended his chunky hand to the 40-something attractive woman in front of him and started making mental notes as fast as he could. *Real auburn hair color. Expensive, soft fabric. Pastels. Covered, not much skin showing. Loose, tasteful pants, un-tucked blouse, big black glasses. Hair to her shoulders. Shakes hands square and strong. No jewelry. Direct eye contact. Shoes off. No nail polish. She's a straight shooter.* "I heard what you like. Is there anything else I need to know?"

Celeste smiled. "Why what a pleasant surprise, Cal. You're exactly as Betts described."

"What? Clean? They forced me to take a shower." David joked dramatically wiping down the front of the white, terry cloth robe from his shoulders to waist. She chuckled lightly in response.

"I mean that she said you cut-to-the-quick," Celeste replied.

"When I can, I do." David focused on her lips. "What else did she say?"

Celeste shrugged. "Just that you're doing her a favor."

"She's too generous, as always. She's doin' *me* the favor actually – word on the street is that I'm gonna get my dick sucked real good today. Would you know anything about that?"

Celeste smiled again, but this time her genuine surprise was revealed. *He's witty?*

"I'm gonna go over to that chair." David stepped very close to Celeste, close enough to smell her *Cashmere Mist* perfume, and pointed a fat index finger across the room. "I'm gonna sit down and spread my thick thighs nice and wide for you."

However, before David could move, Celeste responded. A little assertive talk, and that's all it took. She was easy. She had always been easy with funny men. That's why she loved this business. "Wait." Celeste leaned in and kissed David's lips long and passionately. Their tongues danced in circles until he ended up in the armless chair, just where she wanted him.

"Get up." Celeste giggled as she removed her glasses and laid them on the bedside stand. "I want to do something."

David stood and stepped away from the straight-backed chair with a curious grin as she situated it to face the end of the bed.

"Okay. Now you can sit," she announced.

David remained standing and asked, "What you got up your sleeve, girl?" He gently reached in through her hair on the back of her head and pulled her in for another kiss.

Celeste rubbed her nose against his. "I'm hoping that under that robe there's a big, hard cock for me to suck, Cal." She parted the terry cloth and reached for him.

"This one? Right here?" David teased by hitting her hand with it like a happy dog's tail.

Ha! "You're fucking mine." Celeste put her palms on his shoulders and gently pushed him down into a seated position. "Sit."

> Every woman is different, right? Different positions, different body parts, different timing, different ways of cumming – there is no 'one model'. The pros we hire and train know that. They have an instinct for it, don't worry. And of course we teach them what they don't know. That's why they are so successful in this business. They get filthy rich, by the way. The

other kind of pros, the ones on film, are the opposite. They have a formula for the masses – the fucks who haven't a God-damned clue what they want. None of that shit makes sense, if you ask me. They Google their fetish word and then are surprised when the results show nothing more than exactly the search word. Sex, love, orgasms, relationships, it's not a one-size fits all. It just isn't. If you don't know your particularities, then that's a problem. You have a problem. You've got to know what you like and don't like, but also be open to the occasional surprise. You feel me? That's where Bliss comes in. We have a step-by-step plan to help you know what you want and get you what you want. Gymnasts don't learn a double handspring in one day, am I right? Similarly, you need to ready yourself for each consecutive step. Chance, as they say, favors the prepared.

David had had his share of women going down on him. Some might even say that he had had more than his fair share and therefore was technically very qualified to make the following declaration when his manhood was nearly choking Celeste: "Holy universe, I'm in a black hole."

Knowing that David would cum shortly, Celeste, whose job was to inspect David, began her work by pulling away.

"What?" David's body was still purring like a German, racing-green Mercedes. He looked down to see Celeste disengage, wipe off the edges of her mouth, and reach down for a small bottle of lube. *Where did that come from?* She pointed her right index and middle finger out flat, facing up and doused them with the viscous liquid. Then his eyes drunkenly followed as her left hand grabbed each one of his legs and pushed them to brace off of the wooden bed frame behind her. Before he knew it, he was repositioned for a new test.

Teasingly, she licked and sucked his tip a little and then bargained, “You want me babe? Wanna fuck my face?”

God, yes. Yes, I do, he communicated by repositioning his hips.

“Well, then it’s quid pro quo.” She deftly rubbed the gel onto David’s anus and inserted the tips of her fingers slowly and gently.

David smiled. “You think your fingers are the first, girl?” He wrapped his hands gently around her head and helped her feel his rhythm and depth. His ability to use words was replaced with holding his breath. He swirled down rapidly into the suction of the black hole.

Celeste was checking off a list in her mind: *He’s clean, funny, allows me to take the lead and able to lead as well; he’s a good kisser (unrobotic, playful tongue), and willing to let me explore his body. Good*, she thought as she feasted and downed and sucked and fucked. She felt him suddenly bear-down, so she let her fingers slide into place. *Atta boy.* Celeste deep throated his dick while pushing at his ass a few times. *Let’s see.*

David grabbed and pushed against the seat of his chair to put counter pressure on his legs pushing against the end of the bed and raised his waist into the air, banging her face and moaning.

Celeste, still fully dressed and on her knees, released her mouth to focus on giving him a double hand job. Like slowly playing an accordion, she moved her hands in harmony: *Out. Now in slowly, oh, so slowly... Now – out a little. Now – in deeper. And hold. Wiggle the fingertips. And hold. And wiggle and hold. Now – out a little.* The closer he came to the edge, the harder her right hand vibrated like a bass speaker inside of him. "C'mon, baby," she cheered him on to the finish line. "I want you to cum, so I can cum. I need you."

David followed her command through incoherent snarls. Celeste felt the suction cup of his jellyfish-ass floating on her two fingers and his throbbing, veiny cock in double-ecstasy.

+ + + + +

"Sharon, hi." David emerged from his second shower that day to see date number two. *Petite, black hair, muscular. Neck muscle. Strong. Mole, right cheek. Tan. Hawaiian? Thai?* He pushed his hand out to shake and gauged her pulse, muscle strength, eye contact, and risk level.

Sharon lowered her gaze to the floor and flicked her neck to the right to move her hair over her shoulder.

"Hey!" David's mind continued to take notes in order to pass the test. *Not too strong, acting coy, neck-flash with a smile, quick eye contact, then looked away.* He wondered where the camera was. *Hit all the basic points*, he told himself. "We can talk about boundaries and safe words. I know a little bit about what you want, but feel free to let me know. I want you to be very satisfied." *Is she faking it? Bluffing?* David remembered what Nefertiti said, "Sharon wants you to make her beg for it," so he psyched himself up. *Call her bluff! Call this bitch's bluff!* Just to fuck with her, David lifted his right hand and touched, then fondled, then pinched her left nipple through her shirt. "When you say 'stop,' I'll stop."

Instead, Sharon's nostril's and long erect nipples shouted 'go, go, go!'

Slowly, David shifted behind her, reaching around like a hug from behind to feel her soft skin under her t-shirt. No bra, perfect. He cupped her small breasts and then pulled both of her nipples outward which made him harden. He let it just barely graze her buttocks.

Sharon felt her clit swell. *Fuck!* She admonished herself. *You piece of shit. Get back in control.*

David was not fond of her coy act, and told himself whatever he needed to hear to pass the test. *Don't trust her. Make her cum. She needs to learn not to fuck with me.* David leaned in to her ear and whispered his command matter-of-factly, "You're going to cum right now through these sexy little tits, or you have to leave."

What? That's unexpected. "Okay, but I need to brace myself." Sharon walked over and sat upright on the bed placing her hands flat under her buttocks. "I'm ready to show you what a good girl I am now."

"You better be." David stood in front of her and pulled outward on both of her long, ultra-hard nipples through her shirt and heard her obey him perfectly; she came, and wasn't faking it. He was never so hard. It took him an extra beat to process what all had just happened. *It's not every day that you act like a baller and the universe gives you a Happy Ending. This just never fucking happens.*

Sharon caught her breath. "Holy fucking shit. You're not bad," she declared with surprise.

David chuckled, "That's good to hear," and walked into the bathroom where his dirty clothes laid in a pile of filth in the corner. From his pants he quickly pulled out his brown leather belt. As he stood to walk out, he caught himself, naked except for an open white bathrobe with a belt in his hand, in the full-length mirror. *Fuck, yeah.* He strutted out and handed her his belt. "Take off your clothes and think about where you want me to buckle this." He walked back into the bathroom, shut the door, and made her wait longer than she wanted to wait.

When David reappeared, he pushed off his robe to reveal his stiff cock and walked over to the bed where Sharon was seated. To her left was the belt wrapped in a small looping circle. To her right was a black ribbon she must have brought. "I know you want me to fuck you, Sharon. In fact, you want me more than I actually want you. I can walk away right now. I probably should. I should walk away from this whole interview. Is that what I should do? Walk away?"

Sharon was thrown off her game a little. Very few men have the gusto to give her an orgasm in the first five minutes of meeting her. *And where is this going with the belt?* She hoped that this train was still stopping at her station. "No, stay. I want you to."

"For what? To make love? To fuck you? Is that what you want?"

Half hearted, she replied, "I do. I mean it. I want you inside of me."

Lie. Tease her into submission. Pass this interview. "Time to buckle up in case of a bumpy ride. Where's it going, babe?"

"Here." Sharon pointed at her upper-thigh as close to her crotch as possible. *You need to earn it, bitch*, she chided him in her mind.

"Okay. Go ahead. Put it on," David instructed with a slight smile.

Sharon slowly unraveled the belt, then looped it through the buckle so that it made a circle. She stepped into the circle and pulled it up to her high-thigh and closed it hard just inches below her hairy, black triangle.

David's hard on nearly touched her, but he didn't want to yet. Instead, he leaned into her ear. "You think you're so smart, huh? I can still give it to you even with your legs belted closed. Maybe that's how you like it." David kneeled at her feet with a thud and reached for the black ribbon on the bed and symbolically tied her wrists together in front of her with a bow. He smelled her pussy, which was right in front of his face. Then, with his big right thumb, he reached for her clit inside her mound and pulled the skin straight up an inch to expose it. *Beautiful flower bud. Stunning.* Without thinking, his tongue and lips lunged for her. It only took seconds before her legs bent, and she fell onto the bed in ecstasy.

David pushed her onto her left side in the fetal position. He hastily grabbed a pillow and shoved it under her waist so that the height was an optimal height as he measured by the level of his dick to her ass. He shoved her around like a doll until the position was perfect: the tip of his cock was kissing her wet labia. *Your sideways ass and cunt belted closed are so inviting.* David smiled. He grabbed his penis like a hose and parted her lips with his hips moving back and forth, back and forth. If she moaned, he would rub up against her clit and then quickly go back down to her labia again. He loved just putting himself right at her door with an ever-so-gentle push. *She still has to beg. That was the test.* She was so wet, he knew the answer, but asked anyway to give her what she wanted – the control of what would happen next. “Do you want my cock, babe? Do you want this? Right here?”

“Babe, yes,” she admitted with a lingering /s/ sound.

Dave thought that she sounded a little more authentic that time. *Progress. Good girl.* Rub. “What’s that?” He feigned deafness.

“Yes. Please fuck me,” she semi-pleaded.

Standing behind her meant he had to slowly find the right angle. *Slide up to the clit. Rub. Slide down. Find the give and push a little more inside. Oh, shit. Back out. Push in a little! Oh, no. Pull out.*

For Sharon, there was no more acting. The tsunami was coming. “Oh, babe. Go, go, go! You pass!”

David heard the magic words and faithfully discharged his duties as deep as he could and as hard as he could. He made her cum in her g-spot, a climax so warmly satisfying and long that she felt like a recharged cell phone.

David towel dried his face and then wrapped it around his waist and exited the bathroom. *Two down, one to go.* He wondered, *who is this ‘fun girl’?* And then he quickly stopped in his tracks realizing that he wasn’t alone. “Betts?”

✦ ✦ ✦ ✦ ✦

“Chaya.” Desiree admonished her as if a mother were scolding her child. “Chaya! What in God’s name are you going on and on about? Loose lips sink ships. And to a client no less!” Desiree was far enough behind the welcome window that Nova could not see her, only hear her. Nova could tell right away that this was the voice of a large, black woman. "You have got to be out of your mind! A smack upside your head is what you need."

Chaya sat in front of Nova with a window separating them as if Nova was paying for cigarettes inside a gas station. There was only enough room for money or ID cards to be slipped back and forth between them in the hole.

Nova could not see anything else except a closed door on her left and a closed door on her right. The smell drifting through the hole was unmistakable. *Holy crap. She's high. That explains a lot.* Chaya was the first person that Nova encountered as she entered the front door of Bliss. She just opened the door, took two steps inside to the 'welcome window' which was not welcoming in the least, and said 'hello' to the red head who then proceeded to unleash a stream of consciousness at Nova for ten minutes straight.

"I know! I'm sorry! I smoked too much at break," Chaya admitted to Desiree. "I'm too high right now!" She turned to Nova and said, "Parenthetically, these are the hazards of living in Colorado." Then she turned back to Desiree. "But in my defense, she has the golden ticket." Chaya pointed toward Nova in the foyer.

Desiree was circumspect. She walked over behind Chaya and the window to take a look out at Nova. "Can we get some ID, please? And the golden ticket?"

Nova pushed her NY state driver's license and the gold card that she had found the day before through the little opening. "I made an appointment online."

"Well, well. 'Nova Gambino,'" Desiree read aloud. "That's a strong Italian name."

"Don't mess with this one," Chaya joked, "or you might get popped."

Nova rolled her eyes and cursed her uncle. *Fucking John Gotti.*

Desiree quickly glanced at the schedule on the computer in front of Chaya. *A match! This is her.* In a new, sweet tone, Desiree properly welcomed their newest asset with a big wave of her hand. "We've been waiting on you, lady. C'mon in." She pressed a buzzer that sounded loudly as the door to Nova's right unlocked.

Chapter 3: The Wait

Once through the foyer of Bliss, Nova entered a luxurious waiting room. Three other women were seated and thumbing through magazines or their cell phones. The video that Nova had seen online was playing silently on a wide screen television on the far wall. Instead of narration, there was soft jazz music coming through the speakers in the ceiling, and gurgling white noise from a rose quartz fountain in the corner. Nova realized that the whole previous conversation with the crazy woman with tons of freckles and long, unruly, red hair had not been heard inside this very soundproof waiting room. *This design is very intentional,* Nova realized. She looked up and read a framed sign in the center of the wall in front of her, '*Who are you to decide wherein properly inheres my bliss?'*

The room was thoughtfully decorated in muted colors, Restoration Hardware style, with straight-backed crème colored chairs, a gray stone coffee table, and fluffy, textured accent pillows. If the target was to exude money, they hit the bulls eye. Strangely to Nova, there was no front desk and no clear exit. In fact, as she glanced around, she registered that none of the four doors had handles. *Fire hazard.*

Intrigued, Nova sat and rested her backpack-style purse on her lap. She tried not to stare at the three women, but it was impossible. One fit and skinny white woman with her hair pulled back into a ponytail was dressed in yoga clothes and had a gym bag at her feet. Another was seated on the bench under the widescreen television and looked like an elderly, Japanese woman in a tennis outfit with a visor. The third was probably in her late 20s, early 30s. She had Asian features, a plaid schoolgirl mini skirt, tall black boots, and purple dreadlocks. *Wow,* Nova thought, *we are a beautiful, motley crew, aren't we.*

Each of the four doors in the waiting room had a unique, distinctive design. The threshold that Nova had just crossed was the most common style of a white door with six rectangles as decoration. In contrast, the distressed, arching wooden door on her far right looked like someone had stolen it from a European church. It had long, black, steel hinges, which gave the illusion of growing metal weeds across the front. The weeds encircled a large sign in the center that said, "Women only. No men allowed." *How about that!*

The large, golden door to Nova's immediate right was definitely Arabic. She noted the outwardly expanding small, blue rows of tile around the doorframe and how the two doors that opened outward from the middle were rounded on top. The metalwork on the face was a geometric feat of multiple stars made of rays from other stars. *Exquisite*, Nova admired. *But why such different doors?*

Confusion, at this point in Nova's life, was welcome because it was unscripted, and if it was unscripted, it meant life could get better. She had grown tired of having all the answers. She recognized that this meant her life had been very boring and very predictable. Like repeating the same day over and over again, she had learned to perfect her routine and increase efficiency. Year after year of telling her kids where their stuff was around the house, years of knowing her late husband's medicines and amounts and how often he needed to take them, years of barking orders and training medical support staff in the clinic had all been enough.

About two years ago, she had started playing the game of pretending to not hear, not notice, and not know the answer. She stopped anticipating everyone's needs, stopped giving advice and answering questions, and started letting friends, family, and coworkers make mistakes or figure it out on their own. She could help folks stay on course, obviously, but she was tired, and her efforts over the last decade went unappreciated. Her good intentions seemed to have been boiled down into an essence of enabling. This was the unexpected consequence of her love. So when the tipping point had been reached, she mentally disengaged from it all. The catalyst was her adult son pressing her button with the snide comment, "Get off the cross, mom. We need the wood." *That's it. I'm done.*

This specific moment, however, this confusing moment where doors only open from the outside, and where Nova couldn't quite figure out how such different women could come together for a common purpose, made her feel alive. She didn't know what would happen next. *Is this a brothel like the red head alluded to? Is it a gym with a tennis court? A pool? Why are those staffers so happy that I found the golden ticket?*

A distinctive sound of a door being unbolted from behind loudly clicked, and the fourth, thick steel door at the far left end of the room opened. A wave of phones ringing and people talking suddenly filled the waiting room. There stood the large black woman that Nova had seen moments before. "C'mon in, Nova."

I feel so alive right now. As Nova walked over, she secretly wondered where the Arabic door led. She guessed that the "women only" door opened into a gym or women's locker room, but mystery engulfed the possibilities behind the Arabic door in her imagination. Desiree handed Nova her license and golden ticket back, shut and locked the steel door, and opened her wide, pink palm to shake.

"Hi, Nova. I'm Desiree. I'm the Director of Client Development here at Bliss. Sorry to make you wait." Desiree was a curvy, black woman with a haircut so short and a spine so straight that the clients knew she meant business. No one gave her trouble except for Chaya, and that was tolerated by choice. Desiree's black dress hugged her coffee skin in all of the right places, and not less than ten gold necklaces laid like a shimmering metal scarf around her bosom. She sported large hoop earrings to match too.

Nova reached out her pink knuckled, blue veined hand to shake. "Hi." She quickly deciphered that they were in an office reception area.

Redheaded Chaya came out from behind the front desk to shake Nova's hand too. "Chaya. I'm the Operations Coordinator. Can I get you some bubbly water? Perrier?" she asked Nova as they shook vigorously.

Nova scanned Chaya's blue t-shirt that said, "No is a full sentence," and thought, *aren't you under-dressed, Ms. Operations Coordinator?* "No thank you, I'm good," Nova politely refused. *Really? You're high as the stars. I'm not gonna trust anything from you.*

"But where is your water bottle? You're new to Colorado; I insist." Chaya pressed on.

"Yeah, I got here yesterday," Nova confirmed.

"Well, you now live in the 'mile high city,' where carrying something potable is a must. I'm gonna get you one of our signature bottles and fill it for you. Be right back." Chaya turned and left Nova alone with Desiree.

Nova relaxed and asked Desiree with a laugh, "Is she always so… intense?"

"Yes. She spews angry, cynical rants most of the time and especially when she's high, but there's a place for that here at Bliss. She's a good motivator with many of our clients. Many have a healthy sense of outrage against the universe, so she gets on well. Walk with me. Let's go to the intake room."

Nova didn't move. "Sorry, I'm a nurse practitioner, and when I hear 'intake' it sounds like I'm checking in somewhere clinical. Forgive my resistance, but I don't even know what this place is." *Seriously ladies, this can't be a surprise.*

"Oh, no. Sorry. You're right. We can find a better term that is more clear and doesn't make women think of clinics or hospitals. See? You're helping already. No, this is just us trying to get to know you. You can leave any time you want. It's just right down the hall here."

I can leave any time I want? The fact that you have to say that out loud is a problem, people. Nova thought the best of confrontation and instead – lied. "I don't know why I'm being so ambivalent, I'm sorry."

Chaya returned and so did the smell of pot on her clothes. "No go, eh? I'll tell you why." She handed Nova a metal water bottle with a white exterior and the brand Bliss stamped on it in blue. "You don't know us and yet we're treating you like we know you. This seems strange, but I can tell you that we are genuinely happy that you are here. You think it's an act; we must be selling something or have some ulterior motives, right? But this friendly affect is our job as well as who we are."

Really? That's what you think? How am I the least naïve person in the room right now? Nova paused for a moment, then shared another lie: "You nailed it. I'm sorry, you both are very kind, and I'm genuinely intrigued by this operation and the golden ticket, but I think I should trust my instincts and go," Nova tried to hand the water bottle back to Chaya.

"Keep it," Chaya responded with a smile. "I left my first time too. I wasn't used to people being nice to me for no reason either. Desiree, remember how long it took me to come here? I used to think that I didn't deserve to be in a place like this."

Desiree nodded her head. She knew exactly what Chaya felt. "Mmmm hmmm. Like life is supposed to be about us giving, but not expecting anything. Like we have to earn kindness. Thank you for reminding me how far I've come."

"No problem," Chaya responded.

Oh my God, these two are such... Nova lowered her head. *Stop being an asshole,* she admonished herself. "How about this. Can I just get a tour today, and then I can come back for the intake another day?"

"Absolutely," Chaya replied. "Good middle ground. I like that about you. You don't scare easy and are solutions-oriented. That's gonna be really helpful. Let me take you around."

"First floor only," Desiree stated firmly.

"Yeah, yeah. C'mon. I'll show you the locker rooms and the gym." Chaya and Nova walked down to the end of the hallway that formed the letter "T". The large tile on the right side of the floor that filled the hallway to the right was Santa Fe stucco. The tile on the left side hallway was completely different and reminded Nova of the shiny

Arabic door in the waiting room. Ornate Moroccan tile in greens, golds, Indigos, and blues stretched and shimmered in the opposite direction.

"Wow, that's so beautiful," Nova reacted.

"Too bad we're going down here then, huh?" Chaya teased as she pointed to the right.

Nova smiled wryly. *I'm in a real bordello!* "It's still on the first floor. Desiree said I could see the first floor."

"Oh, so now you're interested," Chaya teased. "You want to see some action, don't you?"

Nova snorted and shrugged coyly. "My imagination is just running away from me, I guess."

"Tell me, do you really think that we have secret little peep holes or two-way mirrors and watch our clients?"

"No. Maybe?" Nova shrugged again.

"Let me tell you something you already know: We would have been out of business a long time ago if we didn't earn and keep everyone's trust. Now, I'll give it to you that some women want to be watched, and others prefer to watch as their experience. As general practice, though, no way."

Nova blushed. "Got it. I really wouldn't mind seeing more though."

Chaya could see Nova's excitement and slight embarrassment. There was a time not so long ago when she had had the same reaction. Growing up a Hasidic Jew in Crown Heights in and of itself was not especially detrimental to her psychological well being. Chaya had a sense of place and purpose. She was grounded in her faith alongside an abundant number of friends and family who loved her. They tethered her positively until she left for college.

Up until that point, her modest clothing and ponytails were non-issues. Praying was normal. All of the women surrounding her spent their valuable time teaching her about navigating the highly delineated separate spheres of the sexes, the basic *Chumash,* holiday traditions, prayers to recite, prized recipes, not to mention the piano and violin. If teaching is an expression of love, then Chaya was well loved. However, if teaching is inculcation into subordination – as she later believed once she entered college – then she was propagandized.

As with many teenagers, testing the boundaries of her religion took the form of testing her parent's household rules and openly questioning contradictions of the Jewish faith. Their final argument was over a *sheitel.* Tradition dictated that once she was married, Chaya must either wear a wig called a *sheitel*, shave her head, or cover with a scarf. Although she was single, Chaya loved her billowy red curls and absolutely refused on principle. Her parents, being devout, cut their daughter off financially hoping that she would grow out of this rebellious stage faster. However, it backfired. Word spread and little by little the community shunned Chaya in, at first, small ways, then more outwardly rejecting her conversations and friendship. Within months, a community of aunties, friends and family suddenly treated her like a gentile. Wounded and lonely, Chaya withdrew all of her savings and headed west to Colorado where she met Betts.

"Everything okay?" Nova asked as she saw Chaya pause momentarily and then come out of a short trance.

"Sorry, I was just thinking about growing up in Brooklyn, and how it's not easy learning to love your body. Making friends with it.

Building trust. Leading it gently toward happiness." She tapped her head with her index finger. "Lots of noise from my parents up here, you know what I mean?"

"I do, I absolutely do." Nova joked, "You've gotten your MMR vaccine, haven't you?"

"Of course," Chaya smiled. "That was one of the first changes I made. I will not be patient zero! Okay, golden ticket winner, let's take a real tour of this place."

Nova grinned, "Really? I'd love that."

"Follow me and prepare to get blissed," Chaya invited as she turned in the opposite direction toward the indigo tiled hallway. "On the other side of the building is our gym and spa. Those areas are fairly standard, so let's skip them. But on this side, this is where the bliss happens."

Full of curiosity, Nova followed Chaya down the long, gently lit hallway with no windows. At the end, it branched out like four spokes on a wheel. They stopped and stood at the four hallways as Chaya pointed out their names. "These are the Ute, Arapahoe, Pueblo, and Cheyenne wings, named after some of the indigenous tribes of Colorado." Each hallway had a different color and style of tile. "Down the Ute Wing we have our earth, wind, fire, and water themed rooms. Then down the Arapahoe Wing we have three different cave-rooms, which are super popular. Do you wanna check one out?"

"Sure," Nova replied. *How intriguing!*

"This one is called Cave 2," Chaya said as she pulled a white, plastic card out of her back pocket and held it up to the reader on the wall, which beeped its response. She walked in first and held the door open with one hand, while pulling a curtain back with the other.

"Why do you have the curtain here? It's like a medical office," Nova judged as she walked through into a Santa Fe-red room with very authentic looking faux rock walls and arched ceiling.

"Pretty cool, huh?" Chaya said proudly. "The curtain is just an added layer of privacy if people order room service." She shut the door and said, "Watch this." She played with the light dimmers to find just the right amount of brightness to accentuate the curves and darker corners of smaller, further inset caves. "So this is one of our cave rooms. As you can see, we're trying to evoke the feeling you get at Moab or the Red Rocks Amphitheater. Have you been there yet? Betts and Brock debated with the size of the inner cave for the bed. Is there enough room for movement? Yet, is it small enough to feel like you're in a cozy womb?"

Nova chuckled. "That's what you should call it; call it 'the womb room.'"

"Nice idea," Chaya agreed. "Much better than boring 'Cave 2.' So, all of our rooms have a theme like this one, but then more services or items can be added *a la carte* depending on individual requests like flowers, a wet bar, a toy bar, particular types of linens, fragrances, music, the list goes on and on."

"I seriously had no idea that something like this existed for women," Nova admitted.

"Oh, there's a lot more. We have luxury naughty chambers, a Game of Thrones suite, a Hollywood Red Carpet After Party loft, Steampunk Victorian Gothic quarters, a Roman Bath, an Observation Deck with one-way mirrors, a Zen Balance Indoor Garden, and our newest is the Ninja Warrior playroom."

"So what about the Game of Thrones room? I love that show," Nova requested.

"Sure, I can show you that, but then we should probably get back to the main office before Desiree comes looking for us," Chaya replied.

Chaya and Nova walked down a new spoke in the wheel of hallways lined with blue and orange Mexican tiles all of the way to the end. Chaya unlocked the door, opened it, and dramatically drew the metal, chain-link curtain to the side. The room was as large as a residential great room with a high ceiling and a tall triangle shaped window with black geometric designs. In front of the window was a replica of the dark gray Dragonstone throne where women fantasized they were white-blond Daenerys, princess of the Targaryen dynasty and Queen of the Dragons.

"Wow!" Nova was stunned at the close approximation of the room to the set of the show.

"Although it looks rather stark and cold," Chaya explained, "I can assure you that this is one of our most popular rooms. We've actually augmented the experience quite a bit, so that now the throne is adjustable. We also cut out the middle of the seat as you can tell so it's the shape of a toilet for better access, and the carpet in front of the throne has three-inch thick padding."

"Why?" Nova asked thoughtlessly.

Chaya smiled. "Padding is to cushion the knees of our Specialists, of course. We've even had a small chamber orchestra in here to play medieval music to a few of her majesties. And our clients dress the part too. They look lovely. I wish I knew what all went on in here, actually."

"Cool. I didn't realize that pretending to be a queen was a thing."

Chaya elaborated further. "Well, I think the fantasy of commanding from a throne is not new to our clients. So many of them regularly digested princess stories as kids that it's not a big leap of the imagination when, as adults, they want a more powerful version of the same narrative."

Suddenly, Nova and Chaya heard Desiree's voice off in the distance, "Chaya! Get back here!"

"That's our cue," Chaya said as she gently pushed Nova out the door into the tiled hallway. Then, she lowered her voice to just above a whisper, "The secret to this place is giving it time to grow on you."

Nova wondered aloud, "like Kimchi?"

"Classier. Bliss is an acquired taste that you'll soon never want to live without."

Chapter 4: The Meeting

Brock was born Brock Jake Anderson in Bozeman, Montana to boring, upper middle class, white, Methodist parents in 1970. Brock ended up a happy bachelor at age 49 in Colorado much to the chagrin of said parents who preferred that he settle down back home. He made a good living working only when he felt like it and downhill skiing or mountain biking when he didn't, so there was never a reason to not call Colorado his home.

Brock was blessed with two unearned gifts that alone changed the trajectory of his entire life: his deep, rich voice and sultry, rugged good looks. When Brock told a joke, smiled, or tilted his head to the right a little, people felt dizzy like they were hanging out with a movie star. His dark hair with blue eyes and a square jaw made him seem all the more magnetic and magnanimous. The more attention that was given to him, the more he learned to cultivate it. Riding the ski lift with him left hundreds of straight women and gay men longing for more. Indeed, he had received so many phone numbers, indiscrete offers, and lurid invitations by age 27 that he realized his true purpose: to get paid for what he loved doing most, making people – and himself – super happy.

Betts helped Brock to more fully realize this God given potential after meeting him on a long chairlift ride up the face of Copper Mountain back in 1997. Always a businesswoman, she sized him up as they slowly soared over the fantastically tall snowy trees. When he spoke, the bass in his voice provoked the reptilian part of her brain to imagine him indelicately. That he was attractive in both build and face, could converse on a wide range of topics, had Cerulean blue eyes, and asked her thoughtful, open questions sealed the deal. She had to have him as an employee. *He will set the standard for Bliss.*

At first, Brock was flabbergasted at the proposition of being – in his words – a "whore." However, Betts had her God given talents as well, and before long Brock was persuaded to work with her.

Now, so many years later, with rusty brown and silver hair and a full beard, Brock was mostly a recruiter, but sometimes would make himself available to certain types of women if Nefertiti thought it was a good match. He had earned his stripes in the sex trade and could therefore decipher which college-aged men had a proclivity to behaving like responsive lovers and which didn't. He didn't consider himself a pimp, although he did get a portion of his new recruits' earnings. That was Betts' way: first the house gets paid, then the recruiter, then the Specialist. It's no different than selling makeup door to door or cutting hair in a salon. It was for this purpose that Brock walked around the Metropolitan State University art gallery in the Santa Fe Art District on a Friday evening: to scope out men with potential.

Brock sipped from a tall thin glass of champagne as he walked around pretending to look at the various exhibits. He had dressed in his usual garb that fit in with the hipster crowd: rolled up skinny jeans, over the ankle shiny leather boots, white t-shirt, bomber-style jacket, and a cashmere navy blue scarf. He noticed a man about his age but with a button down shirt, suit jacket, and tie. *Must be a professor*, Brock thought. Brock overheard him talking in a low voice to his wife, "I don't see the dean or the provost. I can't believe that we came all of the way here. I take time out of my busy life, and I can't even introduce you to the right people."

"No worries, honey. Let's just enjoy ourselves. Maybe they will come around later," said a white woman dressed head to toe in rose pink.

"We should just go," the man acquiesced defeat.

"Not yet. I'm going to check out those masks over there. I'll be back in a few," she replied and walked to the opposite end of the student exhibits.

Just in case he could recruit the woman, Brock followed her. She looked like a pretty typical client of Bliss – inattentive husband, in mid-life, was once very beautiful but now gives herself permission to not chase perfection, highlights or colors her hair, is manicured, and probably well-educated.

She walked toward the food table and put a cracker with smoked salmon into her mouth, then took a glass of champagne by the flute, and wandered over to the furthest exhibit. She read the name of the college student under the exhibit title and started chatting with the artist about the inspiration to hang seven different artistically styled masks with magnifying glasses in a circle around a sensual, very hairy, and very naked female mannequin posed sitting backwards in a blue kitchen chair. She was relaxed and smiling, inviting the gaze without self-consciousness. Attendees could walk up behind each hanging mask to view the centerpiece from a different angle. After five minutes, Brock saw the woman's husband walk over to her and join the conversation.

"Alex Grupe, this is my husband, Professor Zezza. Have you ever taken one of his philosophy classes?"

From about 20 feet away, Brock witnessed the handshake and then Professor Zezza's direct appeal to his wife to leave.

"Why don't you go get my jacket from the coat check, and I'll meet you at the door in ten minutes. I want to finish chatting with Alex."

"Oh wait! I think I see someone I know," Professor Zezza said as he quickly left his wife and pushed through the crowd toward the other end of the hall.

"Alex, I have to say that I love your work!" the married woman in pink flipped her dark red hair over her left shoulder.

Alex smiled proudly, "Really?"

"Of course I do. It's very 21st century. You're forcing me to interact with the art as I view it. I'm then part of the art. Love that! And I noticed that each of these magnifying glasses that you use as lenses have various strengths and highlight a different part of her beautiful body. It's just fabulous. Thank you for sharing."

Brock permitted himself to watch the woman more openly and walked a few feet closer. He moved directly across from her in the circle with his feet planted wide.

She moved her face against a black leather mask that had a zipper over the mouth and looked through it at Brock instead of the mannequin.

Aware she was watching him, Brock pressed his face against a highly stylized metal, death mask that had its mouth bolted closed with little jail bars.

They looked at each other with the masks and then, slowly, without the masks. "You're good with students," Brock complimented loudly from across the artwork to start the conversation off and then took a sip of champagne.

"I'm good at a lot of things," she cooed back.

Playful! How refreshing! Brock felt happy and intrigued.

"Hi, I'm Alice. Sorry, I didn't mean to sound flirtatious." *Hell yeah I did! You are beautiful. But I better give him a reason though.* "It must be the champagne talking. I've been in the industry for about 20 years, so I know this age group pretty well."

"Art or Higher Ed?" Brock held out his hand to shake. *She's so chipper and positive.*

"Higher Ed, and you?" Alice accepted his hand into hers. *This is no handshake*; they slipped into and held each other's hand. She didn't want to let it go. Something about his voice and laugh wrinkles around his happy eyes made her curious.

"No. Different industry and slightly longer than you." Brock winked to self-deprecatingly poke fun at his obviously older age. He squeezed her hand tighter and then let go. "And for the record, it's okay to flirt. Makes me feel young. Thanks for doing me the favor."

"I'm not that much younger than you, I'm sure," Alice complimented.

"Well I'm not about to ask a woman her age," Brock admitted. "So let's just assume I'm right."

Alice winked back as she said, "Since your being right is skewed in my favor, I'll give you the win." They shared a silent moment looking at the masks. "What do you think?" Alice refocused on the art.

"Uhmmmm…" Brock danced in his mind for an answer. Thoughts of kissing her crowded everything else out of his mind.

Alex, the student artist, was several feet away, but looked at Brock sheepishly and with curiosity. It was suddenly evident to both Brock and Alice that Alex was listening. They were being noticed.

"I think…" Brock announced toward Alex, pointing with a glass in his hand at a mask, "I think… I'm just trying to remember this guy, this photographer…" Brock's left hand found its way to his forehead rubbing it vigorously as if to say to the brain, *Wake up! Think!* "I think that you have an artistic eye." *Yes, I got this.* He turned and walked over to the student with intensity. "Your use of masks reminds me a bit of Ralph Eugene Meatyard, this American, black and white photographer who used to pose kids and adults in these gigantic, grotesque masks.

"In one photo, I remember, he had his wife and young secretary posing in the masks. Just those two. One is facing the camera, but the other is looking straight at the first one. Through the lens of the audience, however, you can't tell who's who, and you begin to wonder if he's making his wife look at his secret lover or making his lover look at his wife. I always wondered, what was the benefit of making them look at the other in such a distorted, ugly way? Was it to unearth dormant, raw emotions? Because, that's what I was experiencing as I was looking at Alice behind her mask – through my mask – just raw emotion. I was both the seeing subject and being seen as her object, yet disguised to everyone else. Well done. You did that." He offered his hand ceremoniously. "Good on you." Brock shook Alex's hand vigorously, and then the student walked away proudly to go talk to her classmates. Brock turned back toward Alice and gave her a sarcastically proud expression. "I'm good with this age group too."

Alice chuckled. "Well done." Her smile revealed that she was impressed.

They both took a sip of their champagne to slow the conversation down, to carve out five extra seconds to feel, and to process this off-script diversion. Their suspension of self-control tasted deliciously organic, like savoring slightly bitter, dark chocolate with sea salt until it melts away. In those extra seconds, they allowed themselves to chase milli-dreams: Brock visualized sitting in front of his fireplace with her by his side while she fantasized a passionate kiss from him. They lived, loved, and parted all within a second. The chocolate finally melted. And at that moment, as they woke out of their dream state and returned each other's gaze, they realized that they were secretly seeing the other and being seen by the other in public. It was love at first sight. Tempting fate, Alice did not walk away as a good wife should. She allowed herself to gaze at the smile wrinkles on his cheeks and into his blue eyes without faltering, and that's the moment she realized that he had just dreamed about her as well, and he was still smiling too.

In his smooth bass baritone tone of voice, Brock stated the obvious. "This will get complicated."

"Good," was Alice's honest reply.

Chapter 5: The Intake

Leah opened the second floor bedroom door wide to excited shouts from her three young children who sat upright in their beds: Max, Matilda, and Lola.

"Is the party over yet, Mommy?" Max asked.

"Mommy! We can't sleep!" Matilda greeted her.

"Stor-ee! Stor-ee!" chanted little Lola, her two and a half year old daughter.

"It's too late for stories. You should all be sleeping by now." Leah tried to sound stern and not smile as she peered dramatically at her watch, but the upturned wrinkles in her eyes gave her away. She forced herself to stand motionless another ten seconds before joyfully throwing herself down onto Lola and Matilda's bed. "Okay!" High-pitched giggles followed.

"Just one, Mommy, please!" Her six-year old son Max opened negotiations on behalf of all three children from a nearby bed. "Then, we'll go back to sleep."

"Promise?" Leah asked Max as she combed the disheveled blond hair out from in front of Matilda's green eyes with her fingers. She was willing to negotiate the small stuff with him because he was so bright for his age.

Matilda, the four-year-old, thought aloud while looking at her older brother Max for guidance, "We promise, right Max?"

"Yep!" Max promised.

Lola nodded her head in agreement as well and clapped her hands, then climbed onto Leah's lap.

"Yeah," Max agreed, "Tell us the one about you and Mom." He laid on his stomach while propping his head up with his hands. His auburn hair was cut short for ultimate Frisbee at school.

Leah pushed herself up so that she was sitting with her back against the headboard. She loved being surrounded by her sleepy, cute children. To lazily lounge around singing or story telling while little hands grabbed and poked and little bodies laid on and squished her was a boon that far surpassed any she had imagined before she had met Nefertiti. "Before I was born…" she started the story so familiar to her kids that they could recite it by heart.

"No!" her son corrected pointing at Matilda. "Before *she* was born!"

"And before *he* was born," Matilda pointed back at him.

"Oh yes, yes, yes. You're right. I almost forgot," Leah feigned her mistake as Lola settled into a more comfortable position in Leah's lap. Lola intertwined her small fingers between her moms.

"Before *you* were born," Leah gently touched her daughter's nose, "and before *you* were born," she pointed to her son on the other bed, "and before Mom and I were married, and before we bought the house, and before we kissed…"

"And before you held hands," Max recited.

"That's right. And before we held hands..." Leah raised the hand that Lola was holding into the air.

"And before butterflies!"

Leah smiled confirmation to Matilda, "You're so smart, sweetie. Um hmmm, and before Mom gave me butterfly kisses…"

"Give me!" Lola tried to open her eyes as wide as she could, to which Leah pulled her closer and kissed her forehead with her lips.

"Like this?" Leah pretended.

"No! Like wings, Mommy! With your eye lashes," Lola instructed.

"Oh, like this!" Leah pushed her right eye over Lola's right eye and blinked until she giggled.

"Before thumb wrestling Mom," Max reminded Leah where she had left off and ignored Lola.

"You got it, buddy. Before we thumb wrestled… when we were just friends…" Leah paused and exhaled for dramatic effect: "I broke up with her."

On cue, all three children heckled her: "Boo!"

"Bad Mommy! Boo!"

The littlest stood up on the bed and threw her body down dramatically.

"Yeah, BAD Mommy," a female voice laughed from the doorway.

Leah turned her head to see her beautiful wife leaning against the door jam. *Svelte, killer lips, and still sexy after three kids. How did I luck out?* she wondered.

"C'mon. Time to sleep," Nefertiti cooed as she approached her wife of ten years and gently ran her fingers through Leah's long black hair.

The impression of Nefertiti's touch remained like footprints along a shoreline slowly dissolving into the wet sand as she walked away. Leah longed for more.

"Awe, Mom!" Max whined.

"She's right. Give me kisses," Leah hugged Lola.

"Butterfly, Mommy," requested Matilda.

"Okay, are you ready?"

Matilda faced her Mommy and tried to open her eyes very wide as Leah turned her head slightly, cupped her face with both hands and placed her right eye over her daughter's. They both blinked several times.

Once all three were tucked in, kisses were blinked and the light dimmed, Leah cracked the door and joined her wife who was waiting in the hallway.

"Bad Mommy," Nefertiti giggled while ceremoniously wagging her index finger.

"I'll show you bad," Leah laughed as she grabbed Nefertiti's arms, pinned them high against the wall and pressed the length of her body against Nefertiti's. They playfully rubbed noses. "Did I really break up with you? How could I ever have done that?"

Nefertiti grinned. "So many times I stopped counting you *loca Mexicana*." She opened her lips and ever so slightly kissed and licked the middle of Leah's welcoming bottom lip.

"No hands. Now what are you going to do?" Leah playfully threatened.

"Oh no, I'm at your mercy," Nefertiti replied coyly.

As a mother cat roughly nudges her kitten during a tongue bath, so too did Leah force her kisses on Nefertiti's left cheek and exposed ear. Gentle nibbles to the ear lobe, however, were not enough to spark anything at the end of this long day, and that's when Leah yawned widely.

After mirroring the yawn, Nefertiti acknowledged defeat. "Me too. *Venga*, let's go to bed, *mamacita*." With that, she deftly disengaged. "Hey, and thanks for putting the kids to bed."

"My pleasure, babe. *Gracias* for cleaning up the kitchen for me." After a smooch of mutual appreciation, they proceeded down the hallway to their bedroom in hopes of a good night's sleep.

At sunrise, the noise and biological needs of their children served as their alarm clock. Nefertiti awoke as soon as she heard one of the kids going to the bathroom. Lola had just been potty trained, so Nefertiti quickly walked down the hall to see if it was her. "*Buenos días*, sweetie. Look at you, so grown up on the big toilet! Good job!"

Sleepy Lola hugged her mom and climbed onto the step stool to wash her hands.

"Should we go tell Mommy the good news?" Nefertiti asked as she kissed Lola's forehead.

"Yeah!" Lola yelled triumphantly and ran down the hall.

Nefertiti smiled. *Today is going to be a good day.*

✦ ✦ ✦ ✦ ✦

As a gym, Bliss was not as financially successful as its IRS filings claimed. Number one, there was too much competition from other chain fitness centers with top of the line trainers and new equipment. Number two, Bliss was only for women, so it had a more international and older vibe. Number three, Boulderites love being outdoors. This town attracts and keeps athletic alphas because of all the bike trails, proximity to skiing meccas like Vail and Aspen, and healthy farm-to-table eateries. These folks are repeatedly ranked some of the healthiest in the country despite all of the locally brewed beer that they drink. Therefore, creative accounting was a full-time, well paying job for Bliss' CPA and Director of Finances, Ying Jiang.

Ying was born and raised in Beijing, China and forged a new life in the US earning a master's degree in accounting, then interning with Elevations Credit Union in Boulder. It was in Boulder on Pearl Street where she first met Betts. Within the year, Ying took a job at Bliss and made it into one of the most fraudulent and profitable businesses in Boulder nearly rival to the pre-legal marijuana market.

Indeed, Bliss masked well more than half of its operations. Everyone had parts of their job that were public facing and other duties that were illegal. All applicants knew the truth before they accepted their jobs. Desiree managed the front office, but also on-boarded all new employees including Happy Ending Specialists and Happy Ever After Specialists – all officially known as 'Specialists'. Nefertiti and Brock recruited and trained them. Sharon and Celeste tested them. Sharon also doubled as head of security for the building, the business, and staff.

On the down low, Chaya was a 'counselor' who gently nudged clients toward the upper end, 'Happy' services. Simultaneously, she also managed the legitimate daily operations of the gym and spa, including the weekly, Monday afternoon leadership meeting. She was a loud and easily out-smarted semi-boss of the gym staff, but she did okay. As usual, she sent out an email request for agenda items Thursday of the prior week, but no one responded except Betts, so Chaya resorted to verbal harassment, which was in her wheelhouse. When Brock came in the front door at 8:15am, for example, she refused to buzz him through to the waiting room. Instead, she said, "You're late."

Brock smiled broadly and walked closer to the window that framed Chaya's poufy, red hair. As usual he read her shirt. Next to Ruth Bader Ginsburg's face were her famous words, "Women belong in all places where decisions are being made."

"No, no, no, pretty boy," Chaya scolded with her tongue and wagged an index finger. "You can't butter me up with your charm. You haven't sent me any agenda items for this afternoon."

"Good morning, Chaya. How's my girl?" Brock replied with his most patient attitude.

"Grumpy. It's Monday morning, and I'm not high. You come in late, you don't respond to my emails…"

"I'm sorry, babe. Are you still doing that cleanse? Because you gotta stop. Right now. It's not for you, or for any of us around you," Brock smiled at his own wit. "Just buzz me in, and I'll give you my talking points, okay?"

"What are you sportin', a backpack? You in college now, old man?"

"It's a satchel. All the cool hipsters have them."

"Jesus! When did counter-culture become so mainstream? See this is why I hate Mondays," Chaya whined. "Anyway, you got class today at 10:30," Chaya reminded him as she pressed a button behind the counter.

The door to Brock's right unlocked, and he pushed through to the waiting room. Then, he pulled out a card from his back pocket and held it against the small reader on the wall next to the metal door to enter the front desk office area. Resting his elbows on the counter, he leaned toward Chaya. "I'll give everyone an update on the newbies, okay? You happy?"

"Newbies, got it. Ying is looking for you."

"Why?"

"Because she discovered that you're syphoning off profits into your private, off shore bank account. How the fuck would I know?" Chaya accused with her tone and expression.

Brock shook his head and then said, "I forgot to ask, how was your weekend?"

Chaya's cloudy facial expression was immediately transformed. "So good. The Mile High 420 Festival was downtown on Saturday." Chaya dramatically clapped her hands and giggled a little. "Fifty thousand stoners, man, and not one single fight. Not fucking one. Next year you have to come with me."

"For my bud-buddy, anything." Brock and Chaya both dramatically pretended to suck on an imaginary joint and then gave each other a fist bump.

"Hiya, Brock," Desiree greeted melodiously as Chaya spun around back to the window to buzz in some clients.

"How are you, beautiful? Good weekend as always, I hope," Brock asked Desiree with a warm smile he reserved for his besties.

"A mixed bag. Went down to the ceremony about Columbine in Littleton. Twentieth anniversary. It was healing, but it's always emotional."

Brock's smile vanished. "Yeah, I caught some of it on CPR."

"Well, it wasn't all heavy, just the memorial." Then Desiree smirked, "I had fun too; I kept busy."

Brock chuckled devilishly at how Desiree had pronounced 'busy', "I bet you did, Ms. Alabama Shakes."

"Mr. Alabama Shakes kept busy too," Desiree joked back, thinking about how she and her husband danced themselves into bed Saturday night. *Rich times.* "How about you?"

Brock leaned in so that only Desiree could hear. "I met a woman this weekend."

"No way!" Desiree replied enthusiastically because she knew he met women every day of every year – he had just never mentioned it casually in a whisper before. Ever. She grabbed Brock's elbow and pulled him into the intake room where they stood in the doorway away from Chaya's range of hearing. "Tell me everything."

"Well, it was one of those moments when you're sure about something before you have any evidence, you know what I mean? I had butterflies in my stomach and everything. I think it's the real deal," Brock admitted.

"Oh my gosh, Brock. You fell in love?" Desiree covered her mouth with her hands in complete surprise. *This is not the Brock I know!*

Brock smiled with a lowered head and put his right hand over the bottom half of his face. "I can't believe it, but yes, I think I fucking did."

Cheering for him, Desiree did a quiet happy dance and spun around. "What does she look like?"

"She's white, a dark red-head, really elegant in this noble kind of way. I don't know, there's something unique about her long nose. Anyway, I can't stop thinking about her, what am I gonna do? Who is this? Not me! She's married. I have this job. Betts will want to run a background check. It's just impossible, but I have to do something. I have to see her again," Brock admitted.

"Of course you do, and you will," Desiree cheered him on.

"But I only have her number. Well, her first name and her number. Oh God, I sound pathetic, don't I? This is not me."

"Look. I know you have to prep for class this morning, so give me her name and number, and I'll do a little research for you. Don't tell Betts anything yet though. Keep it to yourself, especially that grin," Desiree warned him with her own knowing grin. "Everyone knows your smiles, and this one is gonna get you into trouble. Hide that shit. Leave it to me."

"Thanks, Desiree." Brock opened the contacts in his cell, and texted Alice's name and number to Desiree. "Let me know what you find out."

"Will do. So happy for you!" As Desiree walked back out into the main office area, Chaya was buzzing in Nefertiti. After ten seconds, she walked through the metal door.

"Good Monday morning, ladies," Nefertiti greeted.

"Good morning. How'd the potty training go this weekend?" Desiree asked.

"So well. This morning Lola went all by herself as soon as she woke up. Isn't that amazing?" Nefertiti held her right hand to her chest with pride.

Chaya clapped enthusiastically. "Oh, you and Leah can start counting down the days now. Soon you won't even have to wipe her ass anymore. That, my friend, is the beginning of normalcy again."

"Yep. You're exactly right," Nefertiti agreed. "Hey, at our meeting today, can you put me on the agenda with Brock about recruitment, and then I want to share some other new ideas for our online presence."

Chaya was typing as she responded, "Sure thing. I doubt Betts will go for it, but no harm in trying. You know you have an intake this morning, right? 9:30? The girl with the golden ticket."

"Why do I have her, why not one of you?" Nefertiti asked more than a little frustrated.

"Well, she came by last week," Chaya began, "and I was a little high at the time…"

Desiree interrupted, "Chaya opened her big mouth and told the lady about Bliss."

Nefertiti swung her judgmental glance back at Chaya. "You did what?"

"I know, I know I fucked up," Chaya played down the situation. "Don't get your panties in a ruffle."

"It's more than that, and you know it, Chaya," Nefertiti admonished. "Does Betts know?"

Desiree quickly jumped in, "No, and she doesn't need to know, okay? We think you should do it because you can speak to her in detail about our more 'advanced services', but don't scare her. You're good at easing people in. Ease her in like a new dick after a sex-hiatus."

Nefertiti shook her head disapprovingly at both of them. "I don't do dick, but I catch your drift. She knows about Bliss in general, is that correct? She just doesn't know the details."

"Exactly," Chaya agreed. "I gave her more of a list of reasons why women come here but didn't exactly explain how our system works."

"Thank God for that," Desiree interrupted. "Could you modify the intake so that it includes some of our 'next step benefits?'"

Nefertiti's eyebrows pulled to the center of her forehead as if a clothing stitch had been pulled too tight. "This is too early. She's probably not ready, but I get it. Happy Endings, then?"

"If I've said it once, I've said it a thousand times," Chaya strategized, "there's nothing wrong with a good old fashioned finger fucking. If you feel like she can't handle a lot of detail, just make it sound like our Happy Endings are the last service we offer. That will cover us in case Betts asks. What do you think?"

Nefertiti sighed. "Okay, fine. But no more getting high at work, you hear me?"

"Promise. Thank you," Chaya lied as she crossed an X over her heart. *Are you kidding me?*

✦ ✦ ✦ ✦ ✦

"Hi, Nova, I'm Nef. Nice to meet you," Nefertiti shook Nova's strong grip as she entered the intake conference room. *A rather plain-Jane,* Nefertiti assessed.

"Likewise." Nova was dressed in a simple gray t-shirt and jeans. She pushed her mid-length tan and gray hair behind her ears and then sat down.

"So, congratulations on finding the golden ticket," Nefertiti sang her enthusiasm and ended with a big toothy smile. "At Bliss, we put a golden ticket out there every so often to share our services with a broader audience. Usually people only hear about us by word of mouth. We don't advertise, so the golden ticket is our way to meet clients who we might not otherwise."

"Can I ask what this place is?" Nova tried to use a tone of voice that understated her obvious interest.

Nefertiti cleared her throat before she spoke. "Bliss is a multiservice company by women, for women. We have found that many women appreciate guidance as they develop into their best self, which means that our launching pad is a gym without mirrors. It's a women's only, very affordable gym so that clients can get in shape without feeling self-conscious. Research has found that about half of Americans are too intimidated to work out in a gym. They feel like they have to get in shape before they can even go to a gym to exercise next to super-skinny or muscular athletes.

"Our clients, in contrast, are less athletic-looking, so the intimidation factor is very low here. This is the benefit to being located in Boulder. Those who come to Bliss actively choose to come here for the feeling of acceptance and anonymity. In fact, there was even a correlation found in Turkey between women who worked out and women who owned their own businesses, so women's only gyms are all the rage there. Here at Bliss, exercising is only the first of several steps in becoming more of an agent in your own life. You look pretty fit. Do you workout?"

"Not ordinarily, but I'm a nurse practitioner, so I can get a lot of steps in on an average day just working. I quit my job in NY, though, so right now I'm between gigs. Anyway, Chaya showed me your gym last week. Does my golden ticket give me a membership there?"

"It sure does. You'll also have unlimited access to our next level, the spa, too. This is an area with three different pools: a large whirlpool with jets, a cold pool, and a hot pool without jets."

Nova smiled. Relaxing in a hot tub sounded like a real prize to her.

Nefertiti continued, “There’s also a hot sauna, wet sauna, a crystal room, and a mud room for detoxing.”

Yep, those are for me. “Wow, sounds amazing. I’m surprised that Chaya didn’t show me the spa last week.”

Nefertiti wiggled her right index finger ‘no’. “No, we can’t tour that area because clothing isn’t allowed. Everyone is naked in there. This setup is very inclusive of our immigrant and Muslim clients. Same gender nudity is very common in many parts of the world, like Korea. We have a lot of Koreans who come here regularly. However, if you’re uncomfortable, you can just go at the less popular times. Chaya can tell you when those are. Have you visited any nude spas or beaches or anything?”

Nova smiled remembering all of the naked people she has seen over the course of her career. “It’s funny because I used to be such a prude, so modest, but once I started doing rounds, that changed. When you’re in the medical profession, the body isn’t sexualized, it’s more like a riddle. My job was to find the answer to the riddle and fix or manage conditions.”

You know exactly what we do here then, Nefertiti recognized her dumb luck. *A nurse practitioner! She could come in handy.* “What is your specialty? If you don’t mind me asking.”

“Not at all,” Nova was happy to discuss her professional life. “I worked at a family practice for over 15 years, which is the front line basically, and so I’ve seen a very broad variety of non-emergency health problems, but I did a stint in the ER too, so I consider myself well rounded." Nova exhaled a deep breath. "Honestly, a hot tub sounds like heaven to me. I could care less about the nudity."

"Oh, I'm so glad. I just ask because you never know. You can also get a massage up on the second floor too. Did Chaya tell you that?" Nefertiti asked disingenuously, already knowing that Chaya hadn't.

"Really? Is that part of the golden ticket too?" Nova was beginning to feel genuine enthusiasm. Massages typically cost a dollar a minute. Even a one-hour massage once a month was not financially prudent with family obligations over the last decade. "I can't even remember the last time I had a massage."

"Well, you're in for a big treat, then. We have highly trained massage therapists that do: Swedish, sports, TMJ, neuro-muscular, you name it."

"Nice," Nova started wondering whom she should thank for the golden ticket when Nefertiti threw a curve ball into the conversation.

"And you can get a happy ending if you want too." Nefertiti forged on to reduce the dramatic impact of such weighty information. "You don't have to, but if you want, all that you need to do at the end when the massage therapist says 'Namastay,' just stay where you are under the blanket, put the eye covers on, and bend your knees up. That's the signal, and another massage therapist will come in and finish. Finish you."

Ha! Nova's smile embraced the full extent of her prize. *Oh my God, this is awesome!* "Wait, so is the second massager a woman or a man? A woman, right, because that's a women's only space?"

Nefertiti smiled in relief that this news was taken in the best possible way. No outrage, no threats, no storming out and slamming the door. She had seen it all over the years. Transitioning women from the gym to the spa was easy. However, the transition from the spa to the simple massage was a bit more difficult. Usually that was a matter of money, but many times the hesitation was that they were not ready to be touched by anyone even to sooth sore muscles. Even harder was the transition to happy endings. It was just not part of women's culture; it was taught as foreign and taboo. Happy endings were for men in Hollywood movies or for those who visited Thailand or Bahrain, not for women. Not ever. Nefertiti knew the range of possible reactions, so was pleasantly surprised by Nova's non-judgmental curiosity. "Personally, I'm biased. I think the women are the best, but clients just indicate their preference from the beginning and we make sure that they have what they want."

"When is the beginning? Right now? Like we start now? Today?" Nova stumbled over her words.

"Yes, Nova. It's time to customize your experience. Can I ask you a few personal questions?"

What is she gonna ask? "Sure." Nova tried to sound self-assured.

"Do you prefer men or women?" Nefertiti's pen was poised to tick the orientation box, then noticed Nova didn't blurt out an answer. Typically this question is like asking someone their birthday, so when she heard the pause, she followed up with, "…or neither or both."

"Both."

"Thank you. And what type of appearance and personality turn you on?" Nefertiti continued filling in the form.

"I was married. My husband passed away three years ago. Cancer," Nova stated plainly. All her excitement faded from her face. "We had two kids. They're grown now. If you had known my very masculine husband, you would assume that I would want a more butch lesbian, but actually I'm attracted to a balanced woman – a woman who loves her body, is not self conscious, a leader who allows herself to be led and protected sometimes, a woman who takes care of herself physically, who is capable of raw honesty, and who can carry a conversation."

Part of the family. Alright. "Let's move onto some procedures. The first 'happy ending' is really simple and straightforward so that we can understand the basics about you."

"What are the basics? What do you mean?"

"Biologically, for example," Nefertiti explained, "we need to know what we are dealing with. Some clients are transgender and in transition, others have had FGM or other surgeries, you never know, so we just confirm and make a note of it, even if that just means you're healthy and everything is in its original place. Then, there is the simple question of whether or not you can even orgasm."

"Well, doesn't the setting make it difficult, like it's an appointment at a business. How is that sexy? I don't know if I would be in the mood in that context."

"Okay. Good feedback. I'll make a note of that, but in our experience, when women know what will happen, when they know why it's a stepping-stone to an even better experience, and when they choose it for themselves, they just lay back and enjoy it. It's not the best orgasm in the world, I'll be honest, it's just a quickie hand-job, but it really is a great way to complete a massage. You'll be very relaxed;

you can just keep your knees up, eyes covered with an eye-mask, and imagine anyone you want at the other end of the table. You finish, he or she leaves, you never even have to know who was there. It can be a big deal for some, but it doesn't have to be. So, can you have orgasms, right?"

"Yeah, I'm alright in that department," Nova confirmed without a smile. She shifted her weight from the right to the left in her seat. "Back when I actually had sex, I'd have them in threes. Anything else?"

"Nope. Constellation level – good to know. That's what my boss calls a group of orgasms – a 'constellation' – God, she's got names for everything. So that's it. We're done. Do you have any questions for me?" Nefertiti asked as she pushed the form into a manila folder.

'Constellation-level' orgasms. That's funny, but let's get serious now. "Well, I hate to state the obvious, but prostitution is not legal in Colorado," Nova stated plainly. "Nor is it morally acceptable anywhere."

"Not yet," Nefertiti corrected.

"Why should I, even if I have won the golden ticket and everything is free, why should I put myself in a position where I'm risking my nursing license? What if I just happen to be here hanging out in the hot tub and then the place gets raided by the police, how does that make me look as a professional? What is my level of risk?"

"Usually, this is the point at which I tell clients to trust us, that Bliss has been around for over a decade, and that we all want to preserve what has been built. The staff are paid handsomely for their expertise and silence, even and especially the housekeepers, and we thoroughly screen all staff ahead of time. Everyone who works here has at least one other person on staff who personally has vouched for them. Clients vouch for other clients. We operate in a slow and methodical way so that if clients or staff want to move on, they can do so without any trace connection to us."

Nova read between the lines. "You said that this is what you *usually* tell clients. What would you say to me who isn't officially even a client yet?"

Nefertiti sat forward in her seat and leaned her elbows on the table. "We have a golden ticket backup plan: if a cop or someone 'un-blissful' finds the ticket and comes in, we never talk about our illegal services. However, since Chaya let the cat out of the bag already, I would say that you are in the unique position to be part of the future, Nova. Growing, distributing, selling, and using marijuana used to be illegal and unacceptable in many social circles, but now it's not; it's legal and shame-free. All kinds of people are benefitting from its medicinal benefits, even kids with epilepsy. I argue that there is also a growing wave of acceptance of sex work as legitimate and legal here in the US. Prostitution is legalized in many places around the world, but we want to do it American style: *private, safe, profitable, scalable, with emotionally present staff, intentionally focused on women,* and *consensual.*"

Holy crap! Nova recalibrated her mind a little. *This lady is serious.*

"Bliss – our trade – it's bigger than you understand. A very real need is being served here. We are just unique because we are all about women and women's happiness, not men's. We are also a niche market as compared to the porn industry. I can go on and on, but basically I would just ask that you try us out. Take it as slowly as you want, but give us a chance, that's all."

Nova reluctantly smiled at Nefertiti. "Thanks, Nef. I appreciate your honesty. I will hang around and try out your hot tub. I'm not persuaded about the happy endings yet, but I could use a little relaxation and exercise. Give these tired bones a wake-up call. Thanks for your time."

"Sounds good, Nova. Each at their own pace. Let's go back out front and get you a swipe card so that you can come and go as you please."

✦ ✦ ✦ ✦ ✦

"Welcome to Bliss, guys. As you know, my name is Brock, and I'll be your trainer for the next few weeks before you begin your residency." Wearing jeans, a linen button down, and an outdoor vest he bought on sale at REI, Brock leaned against a desk in front of three men who sat behind tables. "You'll learn everything that you never knew about women, their anatomy, positions, loving touch, various ways to kiss, psychological issues such as BDD – Body Dysmorphic Disorder, association, transference, sex and love addiction, avoiding STDs, all the details you need for this line of work which is complicated, but can be very fulfilling too.

"There are all kinds of jobs at Bliss, and we keep growing and growing, so keep that in mind for the future. This could be your stepping stone like it was for me. I started when I was in my late 20's and now I am a very successful, very happy, part owner of this place. I started like you will start," Brock paused and smiled broadly for effect, "by giving the best happy ending a lady has ever had."

The three male students laughed loudly.

"After I mastered that, I moved onwards and upwards until now I pick and choose what I do for work within Bliss. I always choose to teach this class though, because you guys are the best. You're at the beginning of what can be a very brilliant career. So before we begin, can we just go around the room and introduce ourselves? First names only, please. Let's start with you, David."

"Hey, I'm David, and I'm a crane operator. What else should I say?"

Brock wanted to build rapport, so he didn't push them to share very much. "What do you hope to get out of this profession or training?"

"Money," David laughed and the others laughed with him. "That's the main reason, but it's also like I'm sick of what I have been doing. Construction is hard on the body after a decade or two. I like the camaraderie with the guys, but I'm just ready to explore something new, something different. Something that's more my personality, you know?"

"And what's your personality?" Brock gently prodded further.

"I'm a nice guy, sensitive. I'm one of those guys who in high school the girls didn't want to date. I wasn't an asshole, so they weren't attracted to me, but I had lots of friends. Still do, but the married life was never for me."

"You need to be friendly in this biz, for sure. Thanks for sharing, David," Brock replied. "How about you Marcus?"

"Hi, I'm Marcus," a tall, muscular black man cleared his throat. "I'm here for my daughter, Gigi. She's four. My goal is to make enough money so that she doesn't have to go to a public school. I want her to learn Spanish like her mom who passed, and there's a private, Spanish immersion school in Lowry called the International School of Denver. I want her to go to kindergarten there this fall."

"I can help you with that! *Hola*, I'm Gael. It's a weird name for you probably. I'm Latino, obvs, and even though it sounds like 'guy el', it's spelled G-A-E-L, like Gael García Bernal. You know, the actor?"

As Gael seamlessly slipped into a Mexican Spanish pronunciation of the actor's name, the others shook their heads and shrugged their shoulders.

"*La Mala Educación? El Museo? Amores Perros? Y Tu Mamá También*?"

No response.

"Oh, c'mon guys! *Mozart in the Jungle*?" Gael sang as if placating to English speakers.

"Yeah, I know that one." "I loved that show," Brock and Marcus said simultaneously.

"*Dios mio*, guys. You have to get woke. New topic. What can I tell you about me?" Gael's long brown hair was tied above his head into a man-bun. "I like to play my guitar and dance, and I'm saving up to buy a tiny house, something on the Front Range. Right now I'm couch surfing, but hopefully in a few months I can rent an apartment."

"Thanks," Brock said.

Gael continued, "Oh, and you should also know that I've done this before. I didn't like having a pimp, so I'm hoping that this place is gonna be different."

"Bliss is completely different, Gael. There are no pimps here, I promise you. But, like any job, you do have a boss, and for now that's me. Okay. Let's talk about some ground rules. Gentlemen, we're going to discuss a lot of topics that are typically forbidden, so we need to support and trust each other. No shaming. We need to have each other's backs, okay? Not everyone makes it through training and has a high paying job at the end. It sounds like you three are motivated by money, and that's fine. If that's what makes you pay attention and focus, I don't care, but I do need you to take this class seriously. We will have fun, but the idea is not to make fun of each other or of the clients. Right now, you need to show me consistent improvement. Just like college or high school, we have a curriculum. You will have homework. You will be tested. Sometimes the tests will be on paper, sometimes on Celeste and Sharon. You need to prove yourself every step of the way. Any general questions at this point?"

Gael raised his hand. "We get paid during training, right?"

"Yes," Brock was not surprised by this question, which was typically asked on the first day. "You will meet with Desiree before you leave today and set up where you want your pay deposited. You'll have to clarify the rate with her, but I believe that it's $25 per hour for training."

Gael's expression looked happy, but David's did not. He raised his hand. "I can make more in construction. The rate gets better right? You said that you're paid well?"

"Yep. I'm paid very well," Brock admitted through a wry smile, "and you will be too if you put in the time and effort. Once you establish your clientele, you'll be paid by the service, not necessarily by the hour. After one year, you can easily make over $50K if you're working full time – and that's not an eight-hour day, guys – a lot less. That's the beauty of this work. You'll have some clients that pay ridiculous amounts of money because they want what you give. They want you, David. Not Gael, not Marcus, not me. They want what *you* do and how *you* do it and want to repeat how they feel when they are with *you*.

"The not-so-secret key about many of these women is that they are shockingly and ironically loyal. Most prefer to be loyal to their spouses or significant others, but they stray when they have to, when hope is lost. It's like they're grasping at straws to see if there is any fix. Similarly, if they are happy with you, they will stay and not shop around, so first impressions are absolutely the very best way to build up your client base. You're like someone who cuts their hair – once they have an attentive stylist that they trust to do a good job, they just book their appointments every six weeks, or every month, or every time that they are in town, you feel me?"

"Think big," David summarized. "Think long term, is what you're saying."

"Go big or go home, gentlemen, that's right," Brock confirmed.

Chapter 6: The Team Meeting

After giving Nova a swipe card, Nefertiti went back to her office and opened up her laptop. On one of the two wide screen monitors was a web browser open to her favorite Youtube vlogger named Sister Shuree, an African American life coach with broad shoulders, bright red lipstick, and cornrowed hair parted over her right eye. Below the video was the title, 'Sister Shuree on Conversation Fatigue' and '1,702,301 views'. *Holy shit, Marcus' sister is famous!* Nefertiti glanced at the time in the corner of her screen. *Fifteen minutes before the meeting starts.*

> Hey, hey, hey! This is Sister Shuree, your favorite life coach here to hold a guiding light over your path. Today, we have an email from Heather in Phoenix, Arizona who writes, "I feel like men talk too long, and I can't get a word in edgewise. I feel like there is some magical off ramp that others know about except me. This happens at work and in my personal life. What should I do?" Ladies, no one has time to listen to mansplaining or lecturing anymore. This is the 21st century. We busy, okay? We are too busy focusing on our health, our daily comfort, and giving time to those who actually deserve it. Oh, what's that you say? You don't focus on your health, Heather? How about daily comfort? Do you spend any time at all taking your internal 'comfort temperature'? No? Shocker! Do you spend time critically thinking about who deserves your energy and who doesn't? Well there's your problem then. Heather, you're so focused on others that you can't find the off-ramp because

you're not looking for it. You need to reprioritize your time, girl. Your health and comfort come first. You've got to stop making it so easy for these guys. Number one: stop giving them so much eye contact. Number two: stop nodding like a bobble head. Ladies, how can I be more clear? Active listening is only for the deserving; it is not our default.

At that moment, Brock wrapped gently on Nefertiti's office door.

"Hey, what's up?" Nefertiti paused the video.

"Who's that?" Brock asked looking at the screen.

"Marcus' sister. She's a life coach vlogger."

"Cool. Wanna get going to the meeting?"

"Yeah, I'll walk with you," Nefertiti responded by closing her laptop and shoving it under her arm. "How are the newbies?"

"Fine, so far. Only three though. Betts was hoping for five," Brock said as he held open a hallway door for Nefertiti to walk through first. This part of Bliss was off limits to the clients, and although it was the business end of the building, Betts had spared no expense in the design or interior decoration. The long hallway was carpeted with Japanese style gray and pink cherry blossoms with off-white walls. Lovely, mid-sized Georgia O'Keeffe lithographs hung every ten feet.

"This has always been a numbers game," Nefertiti replied as she swiped her badge at the entrance of the main conference room. "We're still on track with three. If she insists on boosting the numbers, we can bring that Arab lesbian back into the mix. She really was fine, just not my shade of red. I was a little concerned at her age and religion too. Maybe in the future."

As Brock heard the click of the doors unlocking, he grabbed both handles of the wide French doors and pulled them open simultaneously to a bath of natural sunlight. The far wall of the conference room was made of floor-to-ceiling reinforced glass and had an unobstructed view of Boulder Valley. *Always spectacular*, Brock thought to himself as he breathed in the ambiance. Hundreds of bristlecone pine, Colorado blue spruce, and Douglas-fir trees of the Great Plains sat in the foreground of the green Rocky Mountains. On either end of the picture windows were a medley of a dozen cacti in all different shapes and sizes and types of pots.

Nefertiti flipped the switch for the lights and the bar was illuminated at the far end of the room. In the center was a large oval shaped white table that easily sat five people on each side. Typically, no one sat on the ends, and everyone wanted a chair on the mountain-facing side of the table. She walked over to the head of the room and pressed a button to lower the screen.

Chaya entered and set her bottle of water and cell phone face down on the table and arranged herself in the swivel chair adjusting the height a little bit lower.

Within a few minutes, all of the leadership staff was seated at the table – Brock, Sharon, Desiree, Celeste, Chaya, Ying, and Nefertiti – all except Betts who Zoomed in on the big screen.

"Hi guys, how's everyone doing today?" Betts asked her staff. Today, she dressed business casual in a navy blue blouse that flattered her unnaturally curvy breasts. Her chest length black hair was parted in the middle and pulled back into a low bun at the nape of her neck. Betts' olive skin always glowed with a soft tan, which complemented the apple red lipstick on her full lips. Like a typical energetic

Boulderite, she was extremely skinny, agile, and strong. Rock climbing and bouldering kept her fit and lean three seasons out of the year while cross-country skiing honed her athleticism in the winter. The combination of her svelte body with brown eyes set wide on her face, high cheek bones, and long white teeth gave her a not-so-subtle power to attract attention wherever she went. "Okay! Let's get started," Betts declared. "Desiree, are you taking minutes today?"

"Absolutely," Desiree responded by typing in her laptop.

"Our first order of business," Betts began, "is deciding who is going to lead next Monday's meeting."

Brock raised his hand just enough to get everyone's attention. "I can do it." He looked up at the screen to see Betts' beautiful face. *My special girl*, he mused at the oversized Betts-head.

"Thanks, Brock," replied Betts from the big screen. "Okay. Let's talk about the new recruits. How many did you interview?" inquired Betts to Nefertiti and Brock. Betts was a better CEO working alongside Brock, one of the greatest loves of her life. Adept at compartmentalizing their relationship away from their business, they had become healthy accountability partners and trusted allies over the years. Compartmentalizing was not only prudent, it was selfishly satisfying. They both wanted each other without the entrapments of the outside world. Indeed, their intimacy on all levels stitched together more than a decade of carefully cultivating Bliss and a precious, honest, and open relationship.

"About 15 between both of us," Nefertiti admitted, knowing that their monthly yield wasn't as high as last year.

"You only netted three, right? What do you think the problem is?" Betts tapped her pen to the legal notepad in front of her hoping for a quick answer.

Nefertiti exchanged a meaningful look with Brock. "It's both supply and demand."

"Demand?" Betts questioned, "Are we down on sales?"

Chaya opened her right hand to interrupt Nefertiti. "I got this, Nef. Betts, folks are over stressed, more than usual, okay? The economy is great here in Colorado – we're still in the right location, don't get me wrong – but there are so many new transplants that the way of life here is going sideways a bit. Most people now are living paycheck to paycheck 'cause the rents have shot up, the commute has increased to an hour or more each way, the lines are longer everywhere, the schools continue to be really shitty, and the trails and dog parks are totally packed. In short, the local ladies have less time and less money nowadays. Everyone is hustling."

Now Nefertiti put her hand up to interrupt Chaya. "To be specific Betts, eight failed stage one and four failed stage two." Nefertiti briefly remembered a few of the failed test takers.

#1
"Just say what comes to your mind. Don't over-think it. I'll say a word; you tell me what you think."
"Got it," replied Bookworm.
"Cunt."
"I don't know if you've read any 14th century literature or not, but I love Chaucer's *Canterbury Tales*. They're in Middle English, so it's a bit of a slog at times, but they are laugh out loud funny and lewd – very progressive for the time. 'The

Miller's Tale', to be precise, is about this student who is renting a room from a carpenter and falls in love with the carpenter's wife. Chaucer wrote about how the student seduced her by catching her 'by the queynte'. Definitely before the 'metoo movement'. So etymologists don't know the exact origin of 'cunt', but one theory is that it comes from the Old English 'qwaynt' or 'coint' and is evidenced from that line in 'The Miller's Tale.'"
Nope.

#2
"Just say what comes to your mind. Don't over-think it. I'll say a word; you tell me what you think."
"Got it," replied Homebody.
"Cunt."
"Easy: 'pussy'. And 'pussy' makes me think of cats, and cats reminds me that I need to ask you if we will be done by 5pm because I need to go feed mine. That's 'happy pussy time' at my house, I'll tell ya. I'm an animal lover. I built these little catwalks on the walls for them to climb all around my parents' house. I have eight beautiful kitties, and if daddy doesn't crack that can by 5pm, daddy gets little brown presents on his pillow that night. So I'm leaving at 4:30, actually."
Nope.

#3
"Just say what comes to your mind. Don't over-think it. I'll say a word; you tell me what you think."
"Got it," replied Horney.
"Cunt."

"Oh, I love it when women talk dirty," Mr. Horney quickly stood and leaned over the table to kiss Nefertiti on the lips, "Say it again, fuck doll."
Nope.

#4
"Good. Thanks. Next word: Cock."
"I have one. That's a word I use. I'm not sure what to say, oh! When I'm fucking black chicks, I like to say, 'You like my white cock,' 'You wanna suck my white cock,' like that.
"So if we were fucking, what would you say to me?"
"Wow! Well, uh, what are you, Mexican?"
No.
"Uh, then I wouldn't talk at all, I'd just be like bangin' that sweet brown ass all night long. I love anal sex. I prefer it when they get all loose down there, you know what I mean?"
Deadpan his ass.
"After a kid? Know what I mean?"
Nope.

#5
"Really? I passed?" asked Rude-Boy.
"Well, not entirely. We still need to 'kick the tires' so to speak. Betts got your medical paperwork, so you're good to go for the next part. This key opens room 210 at El Teatro on the second floor. Go in and take a shower. They have a great shower, by the way. Use the robe. When you come out of the bathroom, you'll meet Celeste. Celeste gets off on giving BJs – why, I have no idea – but she does."
"'Cause they're fuckin' awesome, that's why! I love grabbing their hair and just ramming my manhood straight in. That's why I don't fuck

short-haired chicks, what am I gonna yank? Am I right?"
Nope.

#6
"Really? I passed?" asked Green-Boy.
"Well, not entirely. We still need to 'kick the tires' so to speak. Betts got your medical paperwork, so you're good to go for the next part. This key opens room 210 at El Teatro on the second floor. Go in and take a shower. They have a great shower, by the way. Use the robe. When you come out of the bathroom, you'll meet Celeste. Celeste gets off on giving BJs – why, I have no idea – but she does. Shower again. Thoroughly. Again, when you leave the bathroom you'll meet another lady. I'll call her Sharon. Sharon wants you to make her beg for it. Shower again…"
"Wait, hold up. How do I do that? How would I get, I don't know. Can you give me pointers or is that like, cheating? Like, usually I'm the one begging for it, not her."
Nope.

"And the competition is rough," Desiree added.

"What competition?" Betts asked in surprise. "There are brothels for men, but nothing like Bliss for women, is there? I haven't been away that long."

Brock's smooth, deep voice mitigated the message. "No, Betts. It's indirect competition. This is nothing new. The online porn just grows exponentially. You know how it is, they crank out more and more videos, live people who are very interactive…"

Betts interrupted. "But even if it's live and interactive, it's still not full-on, tactile, 3D sex. It's an independent, alienated form of sex, but it's no Happy Ever After!"

Everyone seated at the table was familiar with Betts' stance: why masturbate alone when you can have the real deal? "We think that it's time to adapt a little bit, Betts," Brock cautiously suggested. "Our new clientele are a bit more adventurous and digitally oriented, let's say. The younger GenXers and Millennials seem to need less handholding too. Yeah, there's still the Rom-Com crowd, but feedback indicates that more folks want cannabis Happy Every Afters and more options for LGBTQ, kink, and tactile-specific rooms."

Betts needed to brace her desk that was luckily off-camera. All they could see was her pausing. Thinking. *Again? Again with 'digital' sex?* "I've heard you over the years, okay? I acquiesce that there is a very real place for masturbation. But does it have to end there? That's my point that you guys are not understanding. When you can't get it any other way, by all means, enjoy toys, take risks, explore all of your amazing hidden thoughts, challenge yourself to unlock more doors and fly out windows… 90% of it… I grant you: an orgasm is an orgasm is an orgasm. Fine. But. That other 10%, in quality, is not one tenth of the experience. We all know it is so much more. If you can get off – in the flesh – with another consenting adult, if you have even a scintilla of a chance, you must reach out and grab it, and fuck it or make love to it or do whatever it is you two agree to do to each other. And that's what we do, guys. Don't forget that. We give them hope that they can jointly create art in real time – that they are more than the sum of their parts – that someone else wants to cheer them on to the finish line. That is not nothing. They deserve tactile, smelly, interactive, viscous, 3D sex! They deserve a heightened experience to counterbalance the pain in this world!"

Chaya broke the pregnant silence by whispering low enough so that Betts could not hear, "Brock, time for the unconscious bias training." She then cleared her throat loudly and joked, "So Betts – I guess an online, client-collective cum-counter is out of the question then, right?"

Chapter 7: The Truth

Brock parked his Tesla in the Auraria parking structure on the third level and walked down and over to the library. Newly renovated, the first floor centered around a twenty foot high media wall. There, in front of her infographic with statistics about sex slavery on the wall, was Alice talking to an audience of about thirty college students and professors. Brock's stomach dropped. Alice's office assistant told Brock that Alice would be at the library, but he had no idea why. Her straight, Autumn-red hair was loosely swept back, revealing her long neck. He noted that even from his distance, her light blue summer dress matched her eyes. Because there were no walls, Brock moved about ten feet away from the group and leaned on a two foot wide, white pillar in her peripheral vision. He scanned the crowd for her husband and found him standing behind the seats.

"Sex slavery is not bound by time, scale, or space. Throughout history, from the ancient Roman Empire to WWII Korean 'comfort women' to the present day Islamic State, rape has long been weaponized to maintain the institutionalization of patriarchy, hasten genocide, or dominate a particular ethnic population. Two infamous examples from the 1990's include the Hutus in Rwanda and Serbians in Bosnia who mass raped hundreds of thousands of women. That's just in one decade.

"It's estimated that twenty million women, right now, are out there somewhere being held against their will and forced to have sex with strangers – in other words, are being raped in epic proportions. Folks, *The Handmaid's Tale* is no allegory. It is reality today. Sex trafficking is 80% of all human trafficking, ranking it the second largest criminal industry in the world. In the US, it occurs in all 50 states, including Colorado in both rural and urban areas. Just to cite a more recent, local example, in October 2017, about 250 local, state, and national officers worked together to rescue 17 children. And guess what? Ten of the 17 were boys, so this leads us to the first myth: It's a myth that only girls are trafficked for sex. The vast majority are indeed, girls and women, but it's not exclusive to them.

"On average, kids start being trafficked at age 12. They are from all ethnicities, some are brought here illegally from other countries, but many are also local; they were born and raised right here in Colorado.

"Another myth is that all of these kids have been kidnapped. This is how Hollywood depicts it, right? However, in reality, thousands of American kids are recruited online – kids in situations that leave them vulnerable – like physical violence from their parents or guardians and drug abuse and neglect in the household – these kids are more easily recruited because they are looking for a way out. The recruiting propaganda includes making a kid feel like part of a new family. Tragically, about 10% of the kids in the Colorado sex trade are trafficked by their own parents, so this isn't an easy crime to solve.

"There are many aspects of the sex slave trade that foil law enforcement. First, there isn't one unique profile of a typical sex slave or of a trafficker, mind you. The myth is that only men traffick humans, but research has shown that not to be true as well. Women are often used as front-line recruiters because they have an easier 'in' with their peers.

"Second, we also can't assume that only educating parents and kids about online recruiting techniques will help reduce the problem either. We also need, as a community, to be vigilant about abusive and neglectful parents. Third, from a macroscopic, inter-continental perspective, the infrastructure depends on the coordination between terrorists, local criminals, and drug cartels. Typically, law enforcement doesn't fight crime as a hybrid unit like this. There are separate units focused on combatting separate limbs of this beast. However, without proper data synchronization, we will never strike a fatal blow to its heart.

"Here is the number on the screen for Colorado for Kids," Alice directed the audience's attention upwards. '1-844-CO-4-KIDS' was written in large text. "Keep this number in your phone contacts. If you see something, say something. Thank you."

Alice fielded questions for 20 minutes before the audience dispersed. Brock watched as she approached her husband and pecked him on the lips. Brock recalculated what he had previously assumed to be a dead marriage. *He looks like he genuinely admires her.* As they exited the library together, Brock caught Alice's eye. *Butterflies*! His heart pounded faster.

Holy shit! Brock's here! How long has he been standing there? Should I go back? Alice's stream of consciousness visibly disengaged her from her conversation with her husband.

"Honey, are you okay?" Alice's husband asked her once they were outside.

"Yeah, I'm just gonna go back and grab a cup of coffee from the café. I'll see you at home tonight, okay?" Alice smooched her husband, turned around, and ventured back inside, back toward an unknown adventure.

\+ + + + +

"How could this work?" Alice wondered aloud in a hopeful voice to Brock. *Please know the answer.* "I don't know what this is supposed to look like." Alice and Brock had walked over to the Auraria West station from the campus, taken the E line lightrail to Eliches, and sat next to each other on the cement steps on the far side of the bridge at the base of the theme park's parking lot. The roof over the pedestrian bridge provided shade from the searing, midafternoon sun.

Alice was so full of anticipation that she was hardly aware of how much she was sweating in the 85-degree heat. At first Alice had been happily married, then less happily, then unhappily married. It had been a slow decline. So slow in fact that she couldn't see any of her options anymore. Uncertainty in politics and the environment were enough to force her to not jeopardize her lifestyle. Also, financial security, social standing, and no drama were not nothing as well. They counted. A boring life is worth protecting in many, many situations, and so Alice persevered sexless for five years so far – the devil's trade off.

A satisfying marriage no longer seemed possible to Alice. *It's not a marriage when you're co-parenting roommates, is it?* Options were limited. An agreed-upon open marriage seemed highly improbable. Divorcing and downgrading her lifestyle was not an attractive possibility either. She felt stuck as if she was waiting for a broken traffic light to turn green. *Brock is the unknown factor. If he really wants me, I might be persuadable – but to what? Of course, that still doesn't mean I'm going to just drop Nolan. Nolan,* she lamented, *you're better than this. Why have you just let me go?*

Alice's thoughts then returned to Brock who sat beside her leaning his elbows forward on his knees and covering his mouth with his fists. *He's pensive! Why?* He wore expensive, 'breathable' athletic wear that easily doubled for casual summer attire. *Just tell me that you want me, Brock. Tell me that I have been on your mind all day. Tell me that you want to build a new chapter in life with me. Kiss me, at least. Tell me that you're feeling what I am feeling, but please don't make me deny our electricity or beg for your attention. I deserve to come first in someone's life sometime.*

"Alice, can I just share something without you reacting? I want to be transparent, but I need a few minutes to explain and for you to just listen," Brock began. When he had listened to her lecture at the library, he had tried to will himself to walk away several times. *She hasn't seen me yet! Just go! This is going to be more than 'complicated.' A relationship with Alice will be messy, guaranteed. A sociology professor who specializes in sex trafficking? What are the fucking odds?* 'Run,' he could hear Bett's voice in his head. 'For the sake of Bliss, just cut your losses.' However, when Alice passed by him in the library, and when their eyes met, he felt the pull of a highly strong addiction. Then when she returned back to him in the library alone, he had an outer-body experience. There was no way he would let go. In fact, he knew he would fight for her every day thereafter.

"I want to tell you about my dear friend and business partner, Betts." Brock started his story in a general sort of way. "Betts means the world to me, and I want you to know that she will always be a part of my life. If we move forward, like I hope we will, I want to be up front so that there are no surprises or failed expectations. I don't want to hurt you." Brock chose his words very carefully. "Betts and I have been through a lot together in the last 15 or more years. The lines between friendship, work, and love have been blurred. Beyond repair. She's like an organ in my body at this point; she's literally a part of me.

"When you meet her, you'll see how strong and powerful she is. Betts is like a force of nature that is very productive and innovative. Her flame burns bright. There's nothing she can't do if she sets her mind to it. But you know what? She's human. And I'm her safe place. I'm a part of her too. Do you remember playing those kid games like tag or baseball, when if you were touching one specific pole or a base you were 'safe?' No one could tag you out. I'm that for her.

"With everyone else she's 'tits up,' you know? Full of confidence, talent, beauty. On top of it all, she tries really, really hard. Most people float through life doing the minimum. They don't try and fail and get up and try again. When they fail, they just stop. They give up because it's hard. The truth is that it's all fucking hard. All of it; no one gets a pass. But Betts, she keeps right on trying until she gets it right. She's intrepid. But failing repeatedly can bruise you – bruise your soul sometimes. Motivating yourself to wake the fuck up and do something better day after day is not easy. So you know what? I help her relax and recharge, and I'm never going to stop."

Brock could tell that Alice was taking him seriously by the way she was listening to try to understand him. He felt so blessed that she was giving him the benefit of the doubt, so he continued. "Betts and I are lovers sometimes, but more often than not, it's all about Bliss. We have a job to do and lots of people count on us for their livelihood.

Sometimes we can go a whole year or more just as coworkers – completely separate private lives. That being said, does she want to hold my hand sometimes? Yes. Cuddle sometimes? Yes. Fuck sometimes? Yes. Does she have bouts of depression and need me to coax her out of bed? Yes. You see, she's got other people in her life too. We've never been exclusive, just really sensitive and aware that what we have works. It doesn't fit into a neat definition that you can study in a textbook though. Our relationship is simultaneously very fluid and solid."

Alice didn't want to judge him harshly, but her heart hurt. This was the very last commentary that she would have wanted to hear at the beginning of their friendship. *I'm always #2. No – stop the negative thinking*, she quickly reprimanded herself. *I owe it to myself to at least state my feelings.* "I'll be equally as honest with you as you have been with me, Brock. Thank you for that. I do appreciate your honesty. That takes courage. But, I feel like you're putting up a blockade before we even have given this a chance. I mean, we haven't even kissed, and I feel like I'm falling for you. I know I am, actually. I'm not a kid anymore, Brock. I know what falling in love feels like, and I think you feel it too."

"I do, Alice," Brock's smile reassured her. *God you're an Icelandic beauty.* Brock reached over and clasped both of Alice's hands. "I feel it, of course I do. I love this feeling."

"Then why do I have to deal with this information before I even have had a chance to get to know you? Are you in love with her?"

Brock suddenly felt deflated. Of course the answer to her question was 'yes,' but he was frustrated that Alice lacked the vision that he was capable of loving them both. *Be gentle. Answer her in a way she can understand.* "Yeah, sometimes. Our love in some ways gets stronger and more powerful over time because we just leave each other be. I don't try to change her, I just accept her. Always have. As is. But Alice, none of that has any bearing on how you have absolutely rocked my world. I've been distracted and unfocused for the last week with you perpetually on my mind. I have about a million questions to ask you; I want to memorize every inch of your body so that if you die in a horrible car crash and your head is squashed, I can still identify you by a secret tattoo or birthmark somewhere."

Ha! You fool. "That's creepy, weirdo." Alice playfully squeezed Brock's hands.

"Well, joking aside, I also daydreamed of us escaping to a cabin in Aspen and playing a game of chess this weekend… and maybe doing a few other things."

Now we're getting somewhere. "Then why don't you just shut up and kiss me?" Alice invited with a smile. "Why all of this?"

He lifted her hands to his mouth and kissed them a few times.

Alice leaned in, but instead of kissing her, Brock looked intensely into her eyes as if he was thinking about whether or not to say something more to her.

There's more. Now Alice felt deflated and dejected. *Of course there fucking is. This is my God damned luck. I can't just find a lover who actually wants to fall in love and have crazy sex, can I! No, I have to find the hottest guy in the state who does not even want to kiss me. Wonderful. Now I'm gonna have two sexless relationships.* "There's more, isn't there." Alice didn't bother hiding her disappointment. She pulled her hands away from his and crossed her arms in front of her chest. "What is it – you two have a kid together? You're married?"

Brock hesitated again and tried to buy time by uncrossing Alice's arms and kissing her hands. *Please let this go well,* he prayed. *Please let this go well.* He briefly remembered one of Marcus' sister's vlogs:

> QUESTION: Dear Sister Shuree, Radical honesty or compartmentalization?
>
> ANSWER: Love requires radical honesty, always. Compartmentalization is easier and more convenient, though.

Alice sighed. "Just say it." Her voice was flat as she steeled herself to hear the answer. *Over before it even began. My stupid luck.*

Brock took a deep breath and looked straight into the hazel of her eyes. "I'm a whore, Alice. I've been part of the trade for about 15 years at a company named Bliss in Boulder."

Alice's eyebrows instantly stitched themselves downward. "What the fuck? Are you joking?" She was stunned.

"This is why I wanted to tell you before we became involved intimately. You need to walk into this with your eyes wide open." Brock felt a strange mixture of emotions. *Is the truth worth risking her walking away? Is dishonesty worth keeping her?*

Alice stood with her hands on her hips and walked down two steps where she faced him directly. "So you have sex with men for money? Like a real, real whore?" *I cannot fucking believe this!* Alice was progressive and obviously understood the difference between a person choosing to sell sex versus being tricked and enslaved to do so, but *this just doesn't add up. He looks and acts like a normal guy!*

"I do and have done a lot of different types of work over the years, but it's almost always with female clients. Not men. And I hardly sleep with clients any more. I'm old." *Usually that joke lands well, but not today. Be serious,* he coached himself. "I recruit, I teach, and I manage Betts. I help implement our vision of what Bliss should be."

"Are you healthy? Are you HIV positive?" The questions in Alice's mind were numerous.

"I'm quite healthy according to my last stress test for the old ticker here," Brock pointed toward his heart. "The only drugs I do are pot and alcohol, and I've always practiced safe sex. No HIV or any STD or unwanted pregnancy – ever. I'm cautious to a fault. Present moment excepted."

He thinks it's not cautious to be with me? Alice tried to summarize what she was hearing to make sense of it. "So, you used to have sex with women for money, but now you're more behind the scenes. You teach the younger sex workers."

"That's what I do, yes. I also own a fair percentage of the business. Betts has the majority, but I'm comfortable financially." *Where is this conversation going to land?* Brock generously gave himself 50-50 odds.

Alice was still processing this information as she walked back and forth on the stair in front of him. "Is there any non-consensual sex at Bliss? Does everyone choose to work there of their own volition?"

Brock smiled a little in relief. *There's my girl.* "Everyone is paid well above minimum wage. Bliss is completely the opposite of what you research, Alice. We pay our taxes. You would like my coworkers. They are political and funny, and they all have this *joie de vivre*. They just want to help women improve their lives in a safe, private, consensual, sexy way. You see, unlike sex-slaves, we have a mission that we all believe in."

Neither of them spoke for a minute. *Such a highly improbable situation!* Alice stood with arms crossed over her chest and her back to him looking toward the amusement park. Brock waited patiently for the verdict. *Alice is either gonna walk away angry or... C'mon, girl. Fight for me too.*

Alice turned around to face him. "Brock, I educate students, and I donate money to rescue women from this life."

"Which is amazing and very, very necessary work, but once the slaves are out, once they've recovered, once they settle into regular, normal life, Bliss is the place that rescues them from the second 'problem with no name.'"

"Oh, you're going there?" Alice could not believe what she was hearing.

Whoops, Brock kicked himself. *I'm so dumb!*

You've got to be fucking kidding me. Alice could not help but argue back. "You think that your work is at the level of Friedan? *The Feminine Mystique* reflected a nation of unfulfilled housewives. What do you think is going on in the States right now? You think that *this* is our biggest problem? That we aren't getting enough dick? That may be my personal problem, but..."

"Please don't belittle me or my work. Do you know how broken and physically deprived some of these women have been over the years? I can give you example after example of how after a few years at Bliss, these women have totally reprioritized their lives and are poised for success professionally and personally. Did you know that

Boulder has a very high percentage of female CEOs? Did you know that they are in the top ten best paying cities for women in the entire country? Do you think that all of this is a coincidence? Physical health, sexual agency, prioritizing themselves and other women first – this is how we rescue women. And it takes time and it's hard. We're in it for the long-term, Alice, not some quick fix."

A part of Alice was genuinely impressed and on board, but she was skeptical. She couldn't not be herself, so she finished her peace. *God have mercy on us.* "Then answer me one last question, Brock. I just need to know. Do you personally profit by recruiting 'whores' or 'controlled bottoms' or whatever you call them?"

The light in Brock's eyes disappeared. *Power off.* Jaw clenched, his gaze lowered to the cement in anger.

Answer me! "Do you personally make money when one of your boys fucks one of your clients?"

Brock sat silent. *Flatline with the universe. Let her go.*

Alice expressed both her anger and hurt. "How does that NOT make you a pimp, then Brock? Tell me how you justify it, because I can't right now. What a hypocrite I am for falling in love with someone like you."

Someone like me? Brock felt like a defibrillator had just resuscitated him. "They are not controlled, they are trained and well paid."

"That's fucking bullshit and you know it. They are inculcated and persuaded with money – possibly drugs or something else, I don't know – but they come from a part of society who is not mentally healthy. It is just not healthy to want to sell your body and open yourself up to such high-risk situations. That's how you pick them out of a crowd, isn't it? You look for the weak ones who are easier to control."

Brock's hands, mirroring each other as if he were praying, pushed against his lips and nose. "This is bullshit," he said softly to himself. He stood and turned to walk back up the steps.

"A little too on the nose, aren't I," Alice sneered at him. *I'm so pissed at you right now!*

Brock spun back around and shuffled down five steps to meet her in the eye inches from her face. "No, Alice, you're actually quite wrong. Do you want to know what kind of guy I'm looking for? What type of increasingly rare guy can pass all of our tests and screening? I'll tell you."

Alice met Brock's blistering stare.

"Bliss recruits mature men who can actively listen and empathize with women. They need to demonstrate self-control and respect boundaries. They must love women to the point that they want to cheer them on. They need to admire women's success as a reflection of their own success. There's no height or physical requirements other than good sexual health. The key characteristic is empathy. Without that, all of the rest is bullshit. And how is me being paid so different than you being paid? Huh? It sounds like your entire career has been built on studying the slave trade. Not me. Not one fucking dime of black market money is in my bank account. Not one dime." He was nose to nose with her.

Alice struggled to respond. *We're both hurt.* "I'm sorry. I went too far." Alice stated nervously.

Brock quickly dove his hands into her red hair on both sides of her skull and drew her mouth onto his. *The feast.* His tongue felt thick and needy for her. He tilted her head in every direction that their tongues wanted. Inside where it was warm and wet – that's where he urgently had to be. They pushed and pulled and filled each other's open mouths with suckable love until they were out of breath.

"Holy shit," Brock reacted. He pushed his right hand down beneath his shorts to readjust his throbbing cock to a more forgiving angle.

He has a hard on for me! Alice was genuinely surprised and instantly reached down to touch his bulging mass through his shorts as if to make sure that her eyes were not deceiving her. "You've gotta be kidding."

"What?" Brock was anxious about her reaction.

"I can't believe that you have a hard on for me. I don't think a man has reacted to me like that in many, many years."

Brock relaxed and feasted on her mouth again.

Alice was entranced and kept her hand there for a few minutes, but then wasn't sure about next steps. "You feel so good right now, but I have to leave."

"Why?" Brock was desperate.

"I don't trust myself, I'm sorry. I don't know what will happen next," Alice admitted.

Brock reached down to his dick and jumped a little to calm it down. "I can't walk around in public right now. You better go, because if you stay, I'm gonna... You're too fucking sexy, Alice. Go now, because I'm just about to grab you."

Upon hearing that he wanted more from her, Alice's clit swelled to the point it hurt. She reflexively reached down and pushed it inwards like an unselfconscious child.

Oh, fuck! Brock knew what it meant when a woman tucked in her womanhood: her clit was swollen and ready. As forewarned, he lunged into her arms and kissed her slowly, but fervently. Then he turned her around so that his chest was against her back. Off in the far distance, they could both see a family slowly walking toward the stairs up to the pedestrian bridge. Brock tucked his left arm around her waist and turned her toward the railing and wall. He pressed his hard cock against her ass and moved his right hand over her dress to give her vagina a little squeeze.

Uh! Alice double-fisted the railing to steady herself. Her clitoris and hole pulsated as his hand pressed up on both.

Brock whispered an order in her ear, "Cum for me baby." His middle finger tip found her clit and he pressed gently in a circular motion. "Oh man, you are so sexy. I can't wait to be inside you. I want to suck on these lips… yeah, I feel your luscious lips down here… I wanna suck them." His fingers circled deeper and wider. "I want to lick them with long strokes." Even though his hand was above her skirt, once he felt her hole widen, he pushed inward just enough and repeatedly through the surface of her upside down tunnel.

The verboten nature of Alice's tryst in public in conjunction with the sheer joy of someone simply wanting to have sex with her made it so easy for her to cum.

As soon as she did, Brock whispered "Good girl," in her ear.

I am. Despite her feminist politics, there was something stimulating about those two words: 'good girl'. A sudden craving to please him kept her turned on. *I like being your good girl.*

Brock turned her around to hug her as the Mexican family climbed up the stairs chatting in Spanish and passed them unaware of what had just happened. They leaned up against the railing behind her and softly tried to catch their breath.

"I can't believe that just happened," Alice declared in hilarious surprise.

Brock grinned at her with his Hollywood smile. "You have to start believing, my lady. This is only the beginning of us."

Chapter 8: Gael

"Just say what comes to your mind. Don't over-think it. I'll say a word; you tell me what you think."

"Got it," replied Gael.

"Cunt."

"That's kind of a lewd word for me. I don't use it, personally. I hear some guys use it when they're pissed at their girlfriend or something, but it's not really me. I prefer 'pussy'. It's like come of age, right? It's been re-appropriated out of the swear-words-pile into NPR and BBC permitted language. I swear, every time I heard them talk about the band "Pussy Riot" on the BBC two years ago, I laughed my fucking ass off. That accent with the word 'pussy' totally did not mix. You could even tell from the tone of their voice that they were hesitant, not like a huge deal, but I could tell that they didn't want to use the word.

"Then, do you remember at the 2017 Women's March how thousands of these gray haired, older women – who would never, ever have used the word – suddenly knit themselves those pink Pussy Hats overnight? They were motivated! Like fucking karate ninjas they whipped out their needles and knit that shit in one night! Even if you gave me a year, I couldn't do that; they're amazing.

"So, you know what I did? As we were marching, it was like my mission to ask as many of those women that I could – I played stupid, right? – 'What's that hat called, sister? It's great! I want one!' I just loved how they gave themselves a reason and permission to say 'pussy' – probably for the first time in their lives! And every single one of them smiled with this shit-eating grin on their face and told me, 'It's called a Pussy Hat.' Seventy year olds! Eighty fucking year olds! Saying 'pussy' like a gangster. Like, 'That's right. You heard me, son. I said 'pussy', and I like it. And I'm gonna say it a hundred more times if I want to because I can. Today. I can. I can today.' *Ha!* Oh God, that was one of my all time most memorable moments. Long overdue for those women. Hell, for all of us, really."

Pass!

+ + + + +

"Find everything alright?" the male cashier asked his muscle bound customer dressed in worn jeans and a faded Harley Davidson t-shirt.

"Yep," John took out his wallet as the cashier waved his groceries one by one through the sensor. Twenty feet directly in front of him past the line of empty grocery carts was the Customer Service counter with a long line of working class folks of all different ethnicities. Some waited to buy cigarettes, and some wanted an RTD pass. Others, like the guy at the counter with a man-bun who drew John's attention, were getting their paychecks cashed.

"Paper or plastic?"

"Plastic." John kept his eye on man-bun. He witnessed the Customer Service cashier lean in and whisper something to the guy as she handed him a stack of cash. *This one could be ripe.*

John's cashier swiped his bakery bag of muffins. "I'm guessing that isn't flour all over you if you're buying doughnuts."

"Nope. Puttin' up sheet rock over on Sundown."

"Starting or ending your day?"

"Got the nightshift. Pays time and a half. I'll sleep when I'm dead."

"Big job?"

"73 sheets."

"Thought that was a young man's game," the cashier joked as locals sometimes do with each other.

"Shit, I was too old 10 years ago, but they keep paying me," John replied scratching his bushy beard with his fat fingers.

"Taping too?"

"The works."

"Power to ya. That's back breaking work."

"It's no joke. This is the best I'm gonna feel all day," John smiled and tracked man-bun who had just walked out of the store over his cashier's shoulder.

✦ ✦ ✦ ✦ ✦

The first weekend after being hired and taking classes at Bliss, Gael received his first paycheck. Since he didn't have a bank account, he went to the King Soopers grocery store on Table Mesa Drive and cashed it at the Customer Services desk. *Eight hundred dollars cash!* He still didn't understand why Bliss had to take out taxes when his work was illegal, but he wasn't about to complain. He hadn't earned this much money in a week ever.

The female clerk behind the counter realized that she had just given a good-looking, possibly gay, Latino guy with a man-bun a large amount of cash, and he was grinning ear to ear. *What a target,* she thought. She leaned in so as to not be overheard, and in a low voice said, "Wipe that grin off your face. You in public, stupid. Take a look around you, and go to the bathroom and hide it somewhere good."

Gael didn't think that he had been so revealing to warrant such help, but he knew it came from a good place, so he thanked her and walked directly to the bathroom where he decided to put the cash in his tube sock around his ankle. He washed his hands and spoke to himself in the mirror while dancing the floss, "Eight hundred fucking dollars, *guëy*! Who's your *papi*? I'm your *papi!*"

Because the Soaring K truck stop in Aurora had gotten clean in the last several years, Gael decided to just check out a more local spot on back roads off Route 36 heading west where truckers would pull over for the night. He parked his car a few blocks away and sauntered over toward a lamp post where there was enough light for him to be seen by the truckers at 11:20pm but not so much that anyone could identify him in a line-up. He walked a few steps, then did a little swivel. He only had to wait five minutes before a passenger-side door opened. Gael jogged over and climbed up inside.

Gael had no more than sat down and made eye contact with the trucker, than his door opened again from the outside. *The police!* He couldn't turn around quick enough before two sets of hands forcefully grabbed him and yanked him down and out onto the hard street.

A fat, white, beer-bellied man on the street lifted his right thumb up to the trucker and said, "Thanks, Jim. You get two freebies."

Gael heard the door slam shut as it drove off. He tried to get up, and the white man grabbed him under the left arm and the black man grabbed him under the right. Even though Gael was almost six foot tall and of medium build, he realized by their strength that he would have no chance fighting them off, so he begrudgingly allowed himself to get yanked along. They brought him into a building at the end of the street that had all of the windows covered up.

From a block away, John the sheet rocker witnessed what had happened and watched in the shadows as two large men dragged man-bun through the door. *That's my money; I saw him first.*

Gael was beside himself with worry. *Holy shit! Talk to them!* "Hey, hey, hey guys, I didn't mean anything. I'm sorry! Just forget about me. I can just go and never come back! I won't tell anyone anything. I was never here!"

They yanked him down a corridor of rooms without doors and with dim lights. The smell of pot mixed with patchouli incense hung in the air, and he could hear a man grunting through sex somewhere. Gael lost the ability to walk when he saw in the first room on his left a teenager in her bra and underwear passed out on a mattress on the floor. When he was forced along the second room he saw a large, dark skinned man thrusting into the ass of a skinny, white boy. Gael's heals dug into the carpet to stop. "No way!"

"Shut the fuck up, boy. You gonna see Nick," the big black guy named Terrance yelled as he continued to yank, foot by foot, Gael down the hallway.

Gael was in full panic mode as he passed two more rooms without doors. Both had one black girl, both barely clothed inside. "I'm sorry! I'm sorry! What did I do?"

The last room at the end of the hall was Nick's 'office'. Nick was the local pimp who turned out homeless teens for protection against guys just like him.

+ + + + +

"Brock!" Gael shouted his whisper into his cheap, pay-as-you-go phone.

"Gael, is that you?" Brock asked in the dark as he leaned his head back onto his pillow. He peered at the digital red numbers on the clock across his bedroom: 3:15am.

"Listen, listen, listen! You gotta come get me, okay?" Out of breath, Gael forced his voice to whisper as loud as he could as he continued sprinting.

"What the fuck is going on, Gael?" Brock realized the severity of the situation and sat up in his bed.

Gael started to cry and his voice cracked, "I'm in some deep shit here. Can you please come get me?"

+ + + + +

Brock raced over to Gael who waited outside a 7-11 gas station. From the moment Brock pulled up, he could see that Gael had been badly beaten. His face was bloodied and swollen.

Gael ran over to Brock's navy blue Tesla and leapt into the passenger seat yelling, "Go! Go! Go!"

Brock quickly glanced into his rearview mirror to see if anyone was around or following him. No one. He hit the gas and sailed away. "Holy fuck, Gael! What happened? You need a doctor!"

Gael sobbed into his hands, "No hospitals. No clinics. They'll deport me."

Brock pressed a button on his dashboard to initiate a phone call and then clearly stated, "Call Desiree."

✦ ✦ ✦ ✦ ✦

By 4am, Brock pulled up to Bliss where Desiree was waiting to buzz them in through the waiting room.

Once inside the office, Brock saw both Desiree and Sharon in casual clothes ready to help guide Gael into the intake room. He couldn't walk without someone's help. "Who else did you call?" Brock asked Desiree in an accusatory tone.

"Don't worry," Desiree reassured him. "Betts doesn't know. She's still in Atlanta for another week or more. C'mon now, let's get you into a chair."

Gael sat in a swivel conference seat hunched over and weeping.

Desiree sat down too and faced him at his eye level. "Hey, you're home now. You made it. We're gonna fix you back up, okay? Everything is gonna be alright."

Sharon set down a glass of water on the table in front of him. When he gulped and put the glass back down, swirls of blood spun inside the glass like a mini tornado.

"I need the bathroom. I need a shower," Gael said in a broken, disheartened voice.

"Okay, we can take you to the locker rooms. We'll help you," Desiree assured him, and they did. As Sharon and Desiree gently helped him stand up and start walking down the corridor, Desiree told Brock, "Call Nova. She's the new gold ticket who's a nurse. Tell her to get over here ASAP and to bring her medical supplies. Clean up this room and give me whatever clothes you have in your locker so that we can dress him."

Desiree had been sleeping in the arms of her husband when her cell phone rang with Brock's call. This wasn't the first time Bliss saw drama, and she knew it wouldn't be the last either. When her husband had kissed her goodbye, he told her the usual: "You got this, babe."

Desiree hummed the tune "Strange Fruit" as slow and smooth as Nina Simone while the three lumbered down the Santa Fe tiled hallway into the women's locker room. They went directly to the bench closest to the showers and sat him down. Gael wiped the tears and snot off from his face with the bottom of his t-shirt, and in the instant he did so, dark bruises on his stomach and lower ribs were revealed. Desiree and Sharon shared a knowing, highly concerned look regarding the rag doll between them.

"Gael, we're gonna help you take your clothes off, okay?" Desiree said softly. "And I'll get right in there with you and help you stand. I know it's hard, but you got this." She kicked off her sandals to the wall about five feet away.

Gael reached down to his ankle and pulled out several hundred dollar bills and clenched them in his right fist with swollen, bloodied knuckles.

Desiree continued humming the most tragic song she knew. *Either hum or cry. You got this, babe.*

Sharon scrutinized every bloody line on his head and arms as she lifted his shirt up and over his head. *Punched in the left eye, scalp wounds indicate being thrown against wall or table, possible broken left cheekbone.* The lacerations to his head were still oozing blood, but his chest, stomach, and arms appeared just to be bruised. They got him to stand and undid his pants' belt, button, and zipper. As soon as his pants fell to the floor, Sharon noticed the line of blood down the inside of his left leg. She indicated with her eyes to Desiree to look down.

Desiree continued to hum in spite of wincing at the knowledge that Gael had been violently raped. *Don't you stop. You keep on going.*

The warm shower in the open tiled area that could hold five women at once soaked all three of them – Desiree under his left arm, Sharon under his right. Gael was rather inert except for favoring his left leg and clenching his money tightly in his fist. Both Desiree and Sharon wiped the blood off of his skin as best they could as Desiree sang the last three lines of her song, "The sun rots. Oh, the leaves drop. Here is a strange and bitter crop."

Brock found them and opened his biggest, plushest towel to welcome naked Gael out of the shower and into his arms as if he were a two year old. When he felt Gael's knees buckle, Sharon quickly reached down, picked him up under his knees, and with Brock carried him to a massage room where he was set on the bed.

"Buddy," Brock whispered to Gael as he took the hair tie out and Gael's man-bun fell, "We're gonna put some clothes on you, and then you can sleep as long as you like. Brock pushed away strands of brown, wet, wavy hair that fell in front of Gael's face and pushed them behind Gael's ears. He grabbed a white t-shirt from behind him, cinched it up to form the open head hole and gently placed it over Gael's head as if he were a toddler. Sharon helped thread one arm, then the other through the holes. "Lay down, buddy. Let's put some pants on you." Sharon lifted each leg while Brock pulled up his loose exercise pants above Gael's knees. As he was pulling the waistline up over Gael's penis and scrotum, he noticed that they were too pink and swollen. "Buddy, lift up, help me slip these on." No movement. Sharon reached across the massage table to grab both hips and pulled them up a few inches so that Brock could pull the pants higher. Sharon gathered the heavy warm covers from below Gael's feet and covered him up to his neck.

Gael turned on his side into the fetal position. When he felt Brock rubbing his back in large circles, he started sobbing again.

"I'm not gonna leave you, buddy," Brock reassured him. "Don't worry. You're safe now. I'm here." Brock and Sharon sat on either side of Gael until his breathing indicated that he had fallen asleep.

Brock and Sharon exited the Aspen massage room furious and full of self-reproach. *On my watch!* Desiree stood waiting for them in the front office area with another woman. Brock glanced up at the clock on the wall. 6am.

"Brock, Sharon, meet Nova," Desiree said. "She's the nurse."

Nova had just been buzzed into Bliss and used her swipe card for the first time to access the office door. Seeing Desiree in sopping wet clothes was alarming enough. Now, seeing a Hawaiian looking, second sopping wet woman made her heart thump an extra beat. *Something is very, very wrong here.* "What's going on?" Then, the man who looked like he hadn't slept in days shook her hand and thanked her for coming. *Assume the worst.*

Desiree and Sharon had never heard Brock's deep voice sound so halting and full of restrained anger. "It's Gael, he's in the Aspen massage room. Someone beat him up pretty bad… and raped him. Could you look at him… please?"

Nova did what good nurses do: without emotion, she sprang into action by barking orders at them and attending to the patient. She didn't know who they were and didn't care. She didn't know who the patient was and didn't care. At heart, nurses are leaders. "You two, go change your clothes and then Desiree, go buy some of that white diaper rash crème. And you, find me some thin, long, hard objects like a ruler and tongue depressors if you have them. If you have a first aid kit, bring that to me too. He might have broken bones. I'll check on him and do what I can," and away she ran down the hall with her blue backpack full of medical supplies. *Purpose!*

+ + + + +

Chaya, Celeste, Nefertiti, and Ying ran the office, gym, and spa without the other team leaders for the morning. All that they had needed to hear as they came in to work was the secret code phrase: 'It's Betts' birthday today.' It therefore was not weird when Desiree asked Nefertiti if she had diaper rash crème in her purse. They all knew what to do. This was not their first rodeo. Questions would be answered later.

After an hour, Brock cleared his throat twice before he quickly popped his head into the classroom and said, "Hey guys, I'm gonna have to push today's class to early afternoon; I'll find you when I'm ready. I have an unexpected meeting to attend, but if you want, you can both move on upstairs to the holding tank. Remember the rules – only your hands. No talking. Nothing fancy. In and out, okay?"

Something is wrong. "You got it, boss," David responded first.

"No problem," Marcus echoed.

Then Brock paused and added, "guys, I'm really counting on you today. Gael had an emergency, and I have to deal with it. Please help Chaya hold down the fort as best you can."

David and Marcus looked at each other and said, "Let's go find Chaya."

Brock walked quickly to the main conference room where the screen was up and closed and Betts was far, far away from the madness. He saw Nova sitting at the head of the table talking to Desiree and Sharon. "Sorry I'm late. What's the update?"

"Well," Nova began with her elbows on the table and hands held together.

Suddenly, Chaya, Nefertiti, and Celeste entered through the door and sat down at the table. Chaya admitted, "I can't stay out of this, guys. None of us can, except Ying. She's running the front of the house with Marcus and David. They'll be fine for an hour."

Sharon looked over at Brock who was holding his hand to his forehead. *He's stressed,* she calculated. *Take the lead.* "So, let me bring you up to speed before I turn it over to Nova. Upstairs in the Aspen massage room is Gael, sleeping. He's been very badly hurt and doesn't want to go to the hospital because he's undocumented. That's why we called in Nova, to help him."

Nefertiti jumped in. "Did he just come to work hurt?"

"No," Sharon replied, "he called Brock in the middle of the night and then Brock called me and I called Desiree… so the three of us have been here with Gael since about 3am. Nova, go ahead."

"You were right, he was raped," Nova reported without emotion.

Chaya, Celeste, and Nefertiti gasped and covered their mouths with their hands.

"There was some torn tissue," Nova continued, "but not as much as I expected. He claims that they wore condoms because, according to him, he lied and told them that he was HIV positive, but in my experience, we have to assume the worst. Who knows what happened exactly. He'll need testing for the next six months.

"His eye looks worse than it actually is. I don't think his socket or cheekbone are broken, but he's understandably in a lot of pain. I gave him cold packs, a shot of penicillin, and stitched and bandaged his cuts. The only painkiller I had on me was Codeine-based, so you all will need to get him something else after tomorrow that's non-addictive. I don't want him getting hooked, especially right after a psychological trauma."

Sharon's eyes squinted and scrutinized Nova. *She doesn't want him getting hooked?* Sharon noticed Nova's deliberate way of speaking, her strong square jaw, no makeup, drooping eyelids, tits up, wide mouth, straight spine – and realized that this golden ticket winner was very far from an average woman. Sharon marveled at Nova's sure-footed control amidst strangers in a bizarre situation. *Business. This lady is all business. We need to bring her into the fold. I want her on our team.*

"Now. There's his health, and then there's his circumstance. I know what happened," Nova continued. "He's gonna need counseling... and protection. You might also."

Protection? For us? Everyone struggled to decipher her code. Silence was their enemy right now as her last sentence echoed in their minds. The longer Nova paused, the more vulnerable and culpable team-Bliss felt.

Desiree whispered her question, "Just tell us. What happened exactly?"

Nova inhaled and exhaled a deep breath. She could see that all the Bliss staff in front of her were deeply saddened. "He said that there were two groups of guys, one in the first house who he called the 'Nick-traffick-pimps' and then another group who he called 'the local-John-*cabrones*'. Those are the only two names he heard, 'Nick' and 'John', but they were surrounded by other guys too."

Sharon had a small notepad, pen, and started taking notes. "How did he get to the first house? Did he go there on purpose or was he coerced?"

"Coerced. Apparently there is a well-known truck stop nearby – a place where they park the trucks – and Gael drove over and left his car somewhere nearby. He wanted to turn a few tricks, he said, and then go home."

What? Brock took this information personally. *Why the fuck is he turning tricks outside Bliss with truckers?* Brock hit his fist down onto the table. "This makes no fucking sense."

Sharon partially raised her open hand to Brock to communicate to him *Shut up. Not now.* "And then…" Sharon prodded Nova forward.

"Then it sounded like he got in a cab only to be dragged out by Nick's crew. They dragged him about two blocks away into a house where there were other teenagers. He thinks that they weren't there by choice. Said Nick's room was where they were beating him up, and that they were going to rape him, but that John came to the door and bought Gael with drugs."

Bought? Sharon was not the only one who flinched at hearing this word. "What kind of drugs? Did he say? Meth?" Sharon scribbled furiously into her notepad.

"No. Gael just saw a lunch bag, the brown paper kind."

"Was it the shape of a rectangle, like a key of coke, or smaller?"

"He didn't say, Sharon. You'll have to ask him for yourself. So next, the guys who were beating on him said that he got lucky, that he would be able to stay in Boulder, and they gave him over to a white guy named John who was fat and had a beard."

"Wait, what was that?" Brock asked Nova to reiterate what she had just said.

Nova stated the obvious in plain terms. "It sounds like trafficking, Brock. Human trafficking. Other teenagers – minors – he's 'lucky' because he 'gets to stay'. Honestly, this is way out of my league. I'm happy to help this poor guy, but I didn't know that Bliss was involved in this kind of thing…" Nova's hands pushed an invisible problem away from her chest toward them.

"We're not!" Desiree protested. "This is against everything we are about, Nova. Believe me!"

"No way," Chaya agreed, "this is not us."

Sharon put two and two together. "Did he say what the second house looked like? And was it near or far from the first house?"

"He called it a 'crack den' with a bunch of 'junkies laying around' in some rooms. Said the guys who sold the drugs were in the kitchen. Those were the guys who raped him." She paused as the unspoken question lingered in the air. She cleared her throat and intentionally spaced out her words because they were so difficult to say. "Four guys gang raped Gael. I don't know that he will ever be able to work here at Bliss. He needs a counselor – like right fucking now." Nova's index finger pointed down at the table.

Everyone waited silently as they comprehended the magnitude of what had just happened.

"Okay. I know someone," Brock offered while sharing a knowing look with Desiree, the only other person who knew about Alice. "I'll call her and get her over right away,"

Desiree shook her head "no" ever so slightly back at him.

Without talking, his palms upturned to the ceiling just enough for her to hear his thought: *What the fuck else are we going to do?*

"Who, Brock?" Sharon asked. "I don't remember having vetted any psychologist or therapist." Then, Sharon realized by the look he was sharing with Desiree, that they were keeping a secret from her. "Guys, traffickers and drug dealers who commit gang rape are no fucking joke. Do you hear me? I can't protect you if you're not honest with me. I need to know all of the details."

Brock's head hung low. "I'm involved with someone who knows about this stuff. She'll know a safe house for him."

"WTF, Brock!" Sharon yelled. "A cop?" She stood and started pacing back and forth in front of the wall of windows.

"No! Not a cop! Her name is Alice. She's a sociology professor at MSU Denver who researches the sex-slave market."

"Jesus fucking Christ!" Sharon shouted as she banged her fist on the table. "Desiree! Did you know about this?"

"I just checked her out online, not your full background check, but she looks harmless. She's just a professor. How much damage can she cause?"

"Well I don't fucking know until I vet her, do I!" Sharon yelled in frustration. Miffed, she asked, "Have you fucked her yet or where are we in this little relationship?"

Nova kept her head down, but no one seemed to care that she overheard everything. *What the hell? Should I leave?*

"Just a happy ending," Brock admitted with his head hung low.

It took every ounce of maturity for Nova to not crack a smile. While the situation was very dire with Gael, the euphemisms were laughable.

"Okay. We can work with that," Sharon said calmly and took a swig from her military-green, camouflaged water bottle.

"There's one other thing. I'm in love with her too," Brock admitted openly. *The truth is so fucking exhausting.*

Sharon spit her water out all over the table and coughed and tried to catch her breath with such labor that Nova watched closely to make sure that Sharon could recover on her own.

Brock stood and started pacing on the other side of the table. "I explained everything to her, okay? She doesn't totally get it, but I think enough that we don't have to worry about her calling the cops."

"You 'think'?" Sharon replied in a gravely voice, "You stupid fuck." She threw her water bottle across the room at the wall.

Nova cleared her throat. "Brock, call Alice and get her over here right now before Gael wakes up. Sharon, once she's here, you can talk with her directly."

Brock looked at Desiree and Sharon for confirmation, which they gave with a slight nod of their heads.

"I'll be outside Gael's room if anyone needs me," Nova stated before she got up and left.

Chapter 9: Marcus

"Which one do you want this week, sweetie?" Marcus scrolled through photos of his daughter with various cornrow hairstyles. "Do you want candy floss, a high pony tail, swirl to the side, a bun…"

Gigi's little hands grabbed her father's phone. She deftly swiped left through ten photos of herself, then decided. "This one, daddy."

"Good choice, baby. Okay, assume the position."

Gigi sat on the floor 'criss-cross-apple-sauce,' as they called it in her preschool, in between the legs of her father who sat in an armchair. For the tenth time, she was watching the *Black Panther* movie in earnest. The first time that she had seen it in the theater, she immediately remarked, "They all look like us, daddy!"

Marcus grabbed the water spray bottle from the side table and wetted a section of her hair at the top, center of her head, then combed it out. "Did you know that tomorrow is gonna be the first day of daddy's new job?" With the pointed end of his plastic purple comb, he sectioned her hair and then tapped on her shoulder to steer her attention away from *Black Panther*.

Gigi handed him a tiny pink rubber band that could double as a ring on one of her tiny fingers. "What's your new job?"

"Customer service representative," he said with enthusiasm.

"What's that?" She felt his tap again. She responded by pinching a green rubber band out of a sandwich bag full of hair ties and handing it over her shoulder.

"A really nice person who helps customers. They're gonna train me for a few weeks, and I'll start practicing what they teach me."

"Like what will they teach you? You already know how to be nice. You don't cuss, and you tell good jokes. You even hold the door open at school for stupid Noah."

You're so sweet. "I'm glad you think that, and Noah is a nice little boy. Don't be hatin' on him. Try to be like me."

"Whatever, daddy. So you don't know exactly what you will do, do you."

"I don't know, Gigi, maybe they'll test me to find out my strengths, my specialties, and then put me in one specific area of customer service." *Tap.*

"You could do people's hair, daddy. You're real good at that." She handed him another band.

"Maybe, but this is like my special gift just for you, sweetie," Marcus replied.

"If you wanna give me a gift, dad, I'll take a hover board instead."

Ha! "No way. Those things will kill you."

✦ ✦ ✦ ✦ ✦

At Bliss, Marcus' class with Brock was cancelled, but no one would tell him why. Marcus and David asked Chaya at the front desk, but even she, the loudest, crassest staff member, would not explain. "I don't know any more than you do, guys. I just recommend that you go up to the holding tank and start practicing. Ying will cover the front desk. You need to clock in 25 five-star reviews before you can move on. My advice? When you see the red light go on, head in quietly and don't talk. Remember what you learned, and follow the formula. The sooner you reach 25, the sooner you can make bank."

✦ ✦ ✦ ✦ ✦

Five Star #1

Marcus inhaled and exhaled a deep breath into his cupped hands before he opened the door to the Copper Mountain massage room. He could only see a mound of a person, feet toward him, under luxurious blankets. As a black man, he hoped that his first client would also be dark-skinned to ease him into this pool of nervous anticipation and uncertainty. As instructed, he shut the door and placed both hands on her ankles over the blankets, then slowly gathered the blankets from the bottom of the massage table and pushed them up… *nope not a sister…* and on top of the client's knees. *Hello! There she is: a white lady's Wakanda!* He could not, not grin. *Thank God she's wearing an eye cover.*

Here we go! Per the formula, he put both hands on her knees, spread them apart a little, and then slowly moved his right hand from her knee down to her black – and somewhat spotty – pubic hair. *Bald spots – that's weird.* He could see her tense up as his hand descended, then relax. What he wasn't taught became quickly apparent as he gently touched her clitoris with his upside down thumb, and she came like lightening with one long moan. *What the hell? So quick?*

The client giggled and said, "Sorry! That must be a record. It's been such a long time. Can I have one more?"

I don't know. Should I? Why not? Does anyone care? Okay, start at the knee again and slide down. This time, he touched her clit again with his right upside down thumb, then with his left hand felt her wet labia and gently pushed two fingers inside of her once. Again, she speedily came with a shiver and a moan. *Are you for real, lady?*

The client laughed out loud, "I've just been so horny, you know? I need a few more. Is that possible? Please? I'll give you five stars if you give me five more."

What? Holy orgasms, Batman! Brock never said when to stop, so I'm just giving the customer what she wants, right? Thus, without much effort at all, Marcus earned his very first five star rating.

Five Star #2

Twenty minutes later, Marcus inhaled and exhaled another deep breath into his cupped hands to warm them before he opened the door to the Breckenridge massage room. Once he closed the door, lifted the sheets, and moved his right hand down her large, dark brown, inner thigh – *finally, a sister* – he could see the pink opening of her vagina tense and then relax. *Let's begin.*

Marcus, on script, started with massaging the client's clitoris, but once again quickly realized that clients don't follow scripts. They do whatever they want to do, especially this one. So when she grabbed his hand and directed his fingers inside of her, he improvised.

With both of her hands, she pushed and pulled him in various directions.

Am I just a human dildo, sister? Seriously, this is weak. I can do better than this. Marcus semi-reluctantly allowed her to direct him wherever she wanted for several uneventful minutes. *Fuck this.*

The four hands and twenty fingers, which were acting like wild Clydesdales bucking and pronking in random directions, were forced by Marcus to gallop in unison. He pinched and pulled the ends of her butterfly winged, pink labia like reins toward him. *I'm the fucking cowboy here.* He snapped the reins downward – *let's go for a ride. Giddy up!* He yanked them downward again. In response, the beasts raced together in earnest up the grassy knoll and onto the dirt trail through the forest with legs kicking each stride and long manes bouncing in rhythm. *Hyah!* Heavy hooves thundered their obedience faster and faster at each of his commanding tugs until they charged through the edge of the woods and burst into the hot scorching sun in an open meadow full of lavender and Queen Anne's lace.

Five Star #3

A half hour later, Marcus inhaled and exhaled another deep breath into his cupped hands before he opened the door to the Pikes Peak massage room. Once he gently closed the door, lifted the sheets, and moved his right hand down the client's ultra-pale inner thigh, he could see the third vagina of the day tense and then relax like a sideways smooch. Once again, the script he was trying to follow was thwarted from the very beginning, and he had to think on his feet because, as he was about to touch the client's clitoris, she farted.

They both laughed.

"I'm so sorry! My apologies! I didn't mean for that to happen! Oh God, I'm so embarrassed!"

It's okay, lady. You're hilarious! How can I tell her it's okay? Think... Marcus decided to pat her knee like patting his daughter's back. *Understand? It's all good. My daughter farts all the damn time.*

"Are you not allowed to talk?" the client asked.

Lady, how the heck am I supposed to answer you if I can't talk? Code. Give her a code. Marcus wrapped his hand around her right ankle for two seconds, squeezed it, and then removed it.

"I get it. That means yes, right?" she asked.

Marcus held her right ankle again to confirm.

"So what is 'no'?" she wondered aloud.

That's a great question for which I have no answer because no one told me that the clients are gonna fart or talk! Think. 'No', 'no', what is a 'no'? Marcus karate chopped the air. *Well, she can't see the chop, now can she. A snap? A whistle? No, those aren't negative. Maybe a little slap?* So, he slapped her ankle… and waited for her response. He suddenly regretted his decision. *This could go very badly. Hitting the clients can't be good for business.*

"Oh! I like that kind of 'no,' but can you give me a 'no' here?" The client lowered her right leg and then leaned her bent knee over to the other side of the massage table exposing her left buttocks.

Ha! Are you for real? He smiled and playfully slapped her ass, which immediately gave him a hard on. *Oh, shit. Keep those eye covers on, lady!* Instinctively he covered his mouth with both hands as if that might help.

"Oh, that's nice. This is a five star Happy Ending, I can tell. May I have another?"

He looked to his left and right as if someone could see him.

Slap!

The client smiled and turned back onto her spine with one leg up and one leg down. "You have to do what I say, don't you?"

Marcus held her ankle. *Yes.*

"I know that you can finger me, but can you… can you… use your cock?"

God I wish, lady, but no. He slowly turned her on her side again, exposing her butt, and gently slapped it.

The client giggled. "Oh, there's no need to be shy. I won't shatter. Can you… suck my pussy?"

He slapped her buttocks slightly harder.

The client giggled and thought, *let's torture this guy.* "Can you… put your balls in my mouth and let me lick them?"

Jesus! Harder slap. His penis swelled uncomfortably in his jeans.

"Can you shove your erection in and out of my mouth?"

You're killing me, lady! Hard slap.

"Can you give me a hand job if I am not flat on my back?"

What? I don't know! I guess it's okay if I still just use my hands, right? He squeezed her ankle.

"So, if I am on all fours with my pussy in your face, you can still finger me, right? I'm just confirming."

Marcus reached down to adjust himself and then covered his smile with one hand. *I can't do this.* The thought of her doggy style was now tattooed on his mind, and his hard on hurt so bad that he squeezed his cock to relieve some of the pain. *I literally cannot do this without breaking the rules. What am I doing?* Hand to the ankle.

"Good. And if I need, and this is a requirement now, in order for me to have an orgasm, if I'm doggy style and I need to slide my ass over the edge of the table so that you can shove your fingers deep into my warm, wet pussy – and if, while I'm hanging over the edge, I hold my ankles in my hands with an upturned ass, would you still finger fuck me?"

Now he pictured this and was in real agony.

Ha! She laughed to herself. *I bet he totally has a hard on right now! Love it! Wait for it... wait for it...*

Mayday! Mayday! Marcus placed his hand on her ankle and the other hand back onto his throbbing dick and rubbed it a little. *Yes, I will finger fuck your upturned ass, and I will not drop my pants and fuck you with more man than you've ever had before.* As much as he hated to do it, he wanted to take back control, so he thought of all the reasons why he shouldn't thrust himself inside of her. *I will not assume you want my cock because I'm a professional. I follow the rules. You can trust that I won't ever cross that line no matter how sexy you are, no matter how horny I feel, no matter how hard I am, because you deserve this type of moment. You deserve to be playful and feel safe while you cum. You deserve the space to tempt me like a devil and walk away without consequences, because you're human and thereby rightfully may tell me 'no' or 'stop' at any time, anywhere, and you don't need a reason. I may not like it, but I'm an adult and will act like one. I am Marcus, and I am a professional whore.*

"Yeah!" *Oh, this guy is too much fun. Now act casual.* "Or not. Yeah, I think I'll just stay on my back." She waved him on with both hands as if saying, 'bring it on!' "Now I'm in the mood. Let's do this."

✦ ✦ ✦ ✦ ✦

As Marcus left his last happy ending client, he saw Brock and Sharon talking to two women a bit further down the hallway in front of the Aspen massage room. Alice had driven over to see if Gael could identify other missing teenagers. Marcus watched as Brock was inserting a key to open the door to the room. *That's weird, the rooms aren't supposed to be locked,* Marcus wondered. He had turned the opposite direction and was walking down the hallway toward the holding tank to wash his hands when he heard gasps of astonishment from Brock and the other women. *Huh? Should I check?* Marcus turned back and jogged down the hall to the Aspen room and went inside. "Everything okay?"

Brock hammered each of his words. "Holy fucking shit." He stood with one hand over his mouth and the other up on his hip. "Gael fucking left!" He was too stunned to even register that Marcus was in the doorway.

Sharon, head of security, implored, "Look at this! Look at this!" as she surveyed the contents of the room. "He went through all of the drawers and took everything… including the robe. What the hell."

Nova noticed a chair directly under an open window. "Why would he climb out of a window instead of walk out the door?" She peered outside and saw that the roof was scalable indeed. "Did you lock him in here?"

"No, he locked us out!" Sharon was offended. *Is golden-ticket-lady accusing us of something?* "Locks are on the inside, not the outside. We're not monsters."

Alice's stomach dropped. She clutched a thick file of missing person posters that she had been planning on showing Gael to see if he could identify anyone. "Take me over there to the house, to where it happened," Alice demanded of Brock.

Over where? Marcus wondered. *Where what happened?*

"No way," Brock stated unequivocally. "Out of the question."

"Right now there are 70 people – mostly women – who are missing right here in Colorado. I have to go – just to observe at least – because Gael saw those teenagers less than 12 hours ago. They're probably still in there."

Brock's tone indicated that he thought this was a bad idea. "And how are you going to find out if they are still inside or not?"

"I don't know, Brock," Alice responded with frustration. "I'm just putting this together on the fly, okay?"

Marcus wasn't sure if he should even be in the room or not, so he turned to walk away when Sharon spoke to him. "Hey, Marcus, you served in the marines, right?"

"Yes, Ma'am. Infantry saw gunner."

A cold chill swept over Sharon. *Glad you're on our side.* "Semper Fi."

"Semper Fi," Marcus responded with a fist bump.

Brock synthesized Sharon's question and Marcus' answer and did not like the direction of this conversation. "No. You hear me? No one else is going to be in a dangerous situation today."

Nova looked down at the empty wastebasket. "Someone should call in an anonymous tip to the police or one of those hotlines. Keep Bliss as far away from this situation as possible. Alice, what generally happens when someone like Gael escapes?"

"They'll look for him. He needs a safe house," Alice responded. "He's a liability now because he knows their location and can pick them out of a lineup."

"And if they find him?" Nova asked.

Alice threw her handful of missing person posters down onto the empty massage table. "He won't escape again, that's for sure. There's a reason why rescued victims hide their faces and voices on the news."

Sharon was bewildered. *He escaped our safe house. Why?* She scanned the room for any possible clue. "Guys, something is really wrong. We're missing a piece of this puzzle."

"It's too clean," Nova agreed. "Look, who emptied the wastebasket with all the bloody bandages? I thought we were the only ones who came and went while Gael was here."

Brock felt confused and betrayed. "No one else came in here. Just us." He walked over and looked into the empty wastebasket.

Nova looked at the papers on the table. "And where are the blankets and sheets?"

Marcus could not wait any longer. "Sharon? What happened?"

He's a gunner, Sharon reconciled. *He can handle this.* "Gael was in the wrong place at the wrong time and was beat up by these… very bad men, like ISIS-level bad men," Sharon answered in a way Marcus could understand.

"How'd he get away then?" Marcus wondered aloud.

Nova, Brock, Alice, and Sharon all shared micro-expressions of wonder, then embarrassment.

"I don't know, do you?" Sharon asked in a whisper to Nova.

"No, he never told me," Nova replied. "Anyone? Brock, did he tell you in the car ride over here?"

"No."

"Wait, he called you right?" Nova asked Brock who had now covered his face with both hands as his fingers massaged circles around his eye sockets. "From his cell phone?"

"Yeah, he did," Brock confirmed.

Nova stated the grossly illogical details that they would have figured out hours ago had they not been awoken in the middle of the night or taken care of a traumatized employee: "Guys, how could he have been gang raped *and* escaped *and* with his cell phone?"

Brock snorted like a bull and spun around. "This isn't fucking happening."

Marcus was stunned, "Whoa, he was gang raped?"

"Apparently… maybe not," Brock sneered. "I don't seem to know anything anymore."

"That's not true," Nova interjected. "There was very real trauma to his body."

"There was," Sharon confirmed. "I saw it with my own eyes. I washed the blood, piss and cum off of him myself. That guy went through some shit."

Although only partial, their perception of Gael's con inhered enough deception to mitigate their pity for him. Now, Alice refocused on the location of the houses and saving the teenagers trapped inside.

"Just tell me where it happened, and I'll call it in. At least let me make that call."

Sharon was strategizing more than a step ahead of this professor. "Anonymously. Not from your cell phone. Don't mention Bliss, Gael, no names at all, except for maybe 'Nick' and 'John'. Call from a public phone out of town."

"Okay," Alice grabbed her papers and squeezed Brock's forearm. "I'm gonna go. Walk me out and give me the details?"

Brock followed Alice to her car and waved her goodbye only because he had no other choice. Gael made him feel played and small. *I'm their leader when Betts is away, and I have totally fucking failed. This is unconscionable.* The standards to which he held himself were melting into mediocrity. Dejected and ashamed, he made a beeline for Chaya to see if she wanted to get high with him.

Chapter 10: The Hideout & The Hotline

Embarrassment is not part of Denver's broke-folk culture. Unlike the fading middle and increasingly wealthy classes, the homeless, soon to be homeless, and scratching-and-clawing-not-to-be-homeless exist in a judgment-free zone without hierarchy or accountability. Barbara, a retired bartender who never felt embarrassed, collected broke-menfolk like stray kittens. To her, it seemed they multiplied in the last decade, especially all the veterans. They dropped out of the workforce bitter and feral, with no intention to ever to return. She fed them, and when they came back around for food another day, she would ask a chore in return. It didn't matter to her if they were drinkers or mostly lazy. As long as they did a chore a day, they could stay.

In Barbara's house, the baseline of 'mental health problems' was measurably low. There was no expectation to comb or cut one's hair, brush teeth, wear clothing that fits, pay taxes, be honest, or even be kind. Nothing was weird, and everything was acceptable as long as you stayed out of Barbara's way. Leroy, for example, shuffled for close to six months between a bed bug ridden armchair in the living room and a bathroom that hadn't been cleaned in three years back in 2015. In return, all that he had to do was wash the dishes in the sink every day at 1pm, no matter how many. However, the very first day Leroy was not drunk or high was the same day Barbra decided to blend a smoothie without proper forewarning about the noise. Leroy's mind was immediately transported to Bagram, Afghanistan just before his heart attack.

Another guy, Pete, drank himself to death over the course of two years in her house. Barbara had routinely raged at him, "You'd fuck up a wet dream if you had one!" and punched him in the head whenever he passed out on the couch, "Eat something, wet-brain!" Nevertheless, she allowed him stay because every evening around sunset, having fully come out of yesterday's hangover and being only half-way to his next blackout, he sat next to her in the junk yard she called a backyard with his steel-string, acoustic guitar and earned his living by pretending to serenade his girlfriend.

Barbara's small, brick, one-story house sat on an eighth of an acre of land located a short walk to the Anschutz medical campus in Aurora, a city east of Denver. Every inch of Barbara's house and yard was stuffed with sentimental mementos of her pre-retirement life and garbage-day souvenirs she dragged in off the street from her neighbors. Piles of her random possessions filled every corner, inside and outside, until only a corn maze of pathways remained. Not one of the nine men that had lived with her over the years had used the word 'hoarder;' they weren't that dumb, but they all eventually screamed 'crazy bitch' at the top of their lungs once they left for good, including dead Pete.

Barbara had designs on Gael the first moment she met him at the #121 bus stop on Colfax Avenue. He had laughed when she insulted a suited businessman for no reason, and she liked men who laughed.

"You smell like the bad end of a harsh winter, buddy. Jesus."

"It's called cologne."

"So you pay to smell like this? It's a free country, I suppose."

Beating her to the punch, Gael had designs on Barbara 20 minutes earlier when he saw her on the #15 bus giving a five-dollar bill to a cute Mexican toddler. Gael exited the back of the bus with most of his earthly belongings wrapped up in a Bliss blanket when he saw her stepping out the front door. An hour after laughing at her joke, he was eating warm Campbell's chicken soup at her messy kitchen table and giving her a bottle of massage oil as a thank you gift for her kindness. She didn't care that it was half empty, and he didn't care that her house reeked of cat piss, for neither ever felt embarrassed.

✦ ✦ ✦ ✦ ✦

Alice earned her PhD in sociology from Colombia University in New York City. She privileged this fact above all else whenever she experienced doubt, which she rarely did. *I am smart. I am super-Mensa level intelligent, in fact. I am at least three-standard deviations above the average IQ. I can do this. To DIA!* Her logic led her to Denver International Airport because: A) it's crowded, B) it's outside of Boulder, and C) there were pay phones.

After leaving her SUV on the top floor of the west parking garage, Alice walked into the main terminal and found a group of pay phones in front of the United check-in counters. It was then that she realized paying with a debit card might trace the call back to her, so she proceeded to the ATM machine, then a café to buy an overpriced coffee and switch her bills out for five dollars worth of quarters.

Alice opened the 'Notes' app in her phone and glanced at the list. "Send a text to BeFree (233733), National Human Trafficking Hotline: 1-888-373-7888, Department of Homeland Security's Blue Campaign: 1-866-347-2423, 911." *Which one should I call? NHTH.* She spoke with a woman who tried very hard to gather more details than Alice knew or wanted to divulge. Within a half hour, Alice was back on I-70 headed west and feeling proud of her significant contribution toward balancing the scale of justice in the universe.

Chapter 11: The Interview

"Alice! You hear me?" Beth-Anne repeated louder. "There are two officers who want to speak with you."

Alice had only been in her office two hours after her phone call from a payphone in DIA to the Human Trafficking hotline. Until this moment, it hadn't crossed her mind that she could be connected with her anonymous tip in any way, nor that the police would even want to follow up with her. After all, she had reasoned, *if a lead is helpful, it's helpful. Why track me down? Why talk to me?* Nevertheless, now that they were here, she suddenly felt weak and exposed. *Plead the fifth if you have to.*

Beth-Anne, the program assistant for the Department of Sociology at MSU Denver, rolled her eyes as she stepped away from Alice's doorjamb after a preternaturally long silence. *She's guilty of something, that's for damn sure.* "I'll put them in the conference room for you." *Tits up, girl.*

"Were you at DIA earlier today?" Detective Borratto asked after introductions were made. He leaned forward onto his elbows with interlaced fingers. His appearance was very Colorado: jeans with a button down shirt *sans* a tie and jacket.

Alice didn't know whether to lie or be honest. "Why do you ask?"

"It's a simple yes or no question." Borratto's brown eyes squinted which made them look all the more weasel-like to Alice.

"Yes, I was there," Alice responded sternly. "Clearly, you already know this or you both wouldn't be here."

Borratto could see that Alice wasn't used to being the object of circumspection. *Too defensive.* "What were you doing at the airport?"

"Guys, I have a class soon, why don't you tell me why you're here. Save us all some time."

The two men in their 40's shared a knowing look, and then Detective Sontag took a turn. His style and tone were more detached and blasé. "Why did you call in a human trafficking concern anonymously? It seems unnecessary."

I knew it! "Because I wanted to avoid all of this drama, and it's my right. I wanted to help. I research sex slavery, and in the course of my work, someone told me about the houses. It's my civic duty, don't you agree?"

Detective Sontag would not be baited. "From who? A student?"

"From 'whom,'" Alice corrected. "It doesn't matter who it is. I was going to drive over myself, but then I thought better of it. So did you find the kids… the teenagers? Are they safe?"

"First, do you know what Nick or John look like?" Sontag asked.

"No," Alice replied. "No wait, that's not true. White. He said both guys were white. That's all I know."

Detective Borratto hitched onto her syntax. "Now we know that it's a guy. Thank you. Now, who is 'he'?"

"I won't say. It doesn't matter anyway," Alice declared in exasperation.

"Why doesn't it matter who your source is?" he prodded.

Who cares about Gael! The teenagers – how are they? "You still haven't told me whether or not you found the teenagers. They are the reason I called."

"Dr. Zezza," Detective Sontag skipped to the punch line, "We didn't find any teenagers. However, we did find two murdered bodies."

What?

"COD was a blunt force trauma multiple times to the eyes and head," Sontag continued. "One guy survived, actually, but he'll never see again."

Alice's words trickled out of her mouth like a faulty faucet, "The… the… the kids… were murdered?"

Detective Borratto understood her confusion. "Oh, no. Not kids. Full-grown men. Do you see why we need to talk to your student? We need to talk to the source to find out who did this."

"He's not my student. Just a friend-of-a-friend who is long gone," Alice clarified. "Can I go? I have to teach."

Both detectives pushed their business cards across the table to Alice. "Dr. Zezza, do not leave town. If your friend-of-a-friend contacts you, you contact us. Got it? We'll be in touch with you again soon."

Alice lumbered out of the conference room toward her office yoked with the weighty news. *Dead! Two!* She closed and locked the door behind her. Her breaths hastened to hyperventilation. *Cell phone – call Brock.* She rooted around her desk with shaky hands for her reading glasses and phone. *Oh my God. This is ridiculous.* Her fingers were trembling too much to effectively press the tiny buttons. *Fuck!* She tossed the phone back onto her desk and removed her glasses. *Deep breaths. Power pose.* Alice opened her arms outward and separated her feet like a starfish and took several long, deep breaths.

Chapter 12: Real Here Now

"Oh, this just keeps getting better and better," Chaya remarked in her usual sarcastic tone as she took the Pax offered to her by Brock. Her long drag from the marijuana vape pen produced a very white plume of vapor into the dry Colorado air. *This bullshit is out of control.*

Brock leaned against the back wall of the Bliss building with the bottom of one shoe bent against it. He retrieved the small, black cartridge from Chaya and took a hit. He needed to get high after Gael's escape and now Alice's news which had body slammed him like an avalanche. *Goddamn that was out of nowhere! Two murders with only two degrees of separation!* He was fearful that he might soon lose everything he had built over the last 20 years *–Bliss, my freedom, Betts, a secure future* – and as this looming loss sodomized his ego, he realized what would remain: *my sweet Alice.*

They both stared at the Rockies in shared shock for a few minutes before Chaya spoke. "I wonder if those guys can trace Gael to Bliss. Do you think they can?"

"My fucking fear exactly." Brock's confidence was at an all-time low. His cell phone dinged that he had received a text message. "It's Betts." He stuffed the phone into his back pocket after a quick glance and closed his eyes. "She says I can hire Nova."

"Good. She's solid. Hey uh, do you think those guys can trace Gael to Bliss?" Chaya repeated. Her high from the Sativa-Indica hybrid pod began to bleed into the edges of her mind. At first she felt her ears get heavy, then her eyes swell a little. "We gotta think of all the angles, Brock. Not just Gael, but the police too. Alice is on their radar now. Maybe even the FBI because this trafficking is some next level shit. You know what I'm gonna say, right? Don't make me fucking say it, Brock. You know it's what Betts would tell you to do. You fucking know it."

Brock crossed his arms in protest across his chest. "Alice has a PhD. How could I have anticipated this?"

Anger flowed like a flash flood through Chaya. "Pity that her degree isn't in 'common sense' though, right? Because then she would not have called from a place where there are a shit-ton of cameras everywhere." Chaya counted the offenses on her fingers. "Uh, let's see, they probably got her Expresstoll-pass time and location stamps, her license plate coming and going from DIA parking, her mug shot at the ATM getting cash, and her at the coffee shop getting quarters... for a toll fucking free phone call!" Chaya caught herself and took a quick breath. *Calm down.* "Sorry. I'm angry. I mean, how could a prissy lady like her even answer why she needed all of those quarters if questioned by police. I bet she has never in her life even put quarters in a laundry machine before."

Brock defended Alice's actions. "She could have said that they were for metered parking."

"I doubt she would have thought of that, Brock, she probably uses plastic everywhere she goes," Chaya retorted as if she were having an argument with her brother. "That's my fucking point!"

"I bet she would have," Brock argued unnecessarily.

"Not," Chaya repeated just to be obstinate. "My point is, is that it's lovely that you're in love, Brock, but she has got to go. She can't come over to Bliss, you can't visit her on campus. This fucking mess is bigger than falling in love. You can't associate with her at all anymore."

Associate. Brock picked up a stone and threw it at the mountains as hard as he could. "Stupidity is dangerous; I know, but I'm not just going to ditch her. There's more there, Chaya. I feel it." His high started to give him clarity and peace. "It's not like a crush in your 20s when it's hot, sweaty gymnastic sex that peters out in six months, it's more like a patient, self-assured, playful love. It doesn't take itself too seriously. It's mature and can be controlled like the knob of a light dimmer. I'm turning it up because I've never felt anything like it before, Chaya." *Not even with Betts.* "And I can't fault her. She lives in academia, not in the real world."

"Hey!" Chaya corrected loudly with an index finger pointed at Brock's face. "I don't want to defend her, but Alice's world is as real to her as ours is real to us, don't forget it. The police, they have another reality, which is also valid. The traffickers and Gael too; all of our realities coexist. I repeat: a multitude of realities coexist. This drama isn't on television, and it isn't politics where we can just dump each other into the 'clueless' pile. This is everyone's real fucking life. Real jobs. Real rape. Real slaves. Real murders. Real drugs. Real threats and thugs. It's all real, Brock, and it's all happening right here and right fucking now. Embracing reality is the only way that we're gonna fix it." Chaya backed off a bit and paused to catch her breath.

Brock didn't even try to fill the silence. He knew that he was making excuses for Alice. *Chaya's right. Although it was unintentional, Alice screwed up. The consequences are real.* He flashed back to her face behind the mask at the art gallery and then to her cumming while he cupped her.

"Look, if you can't break up with her, then you need to at least keep your distance and use enough common sense for the two of you, to protect the rest of us and Bliss. Like, use Whatsapp from now on, no emails to her university account, no regular-texting, you know. Use your brain."

"Yeah okay, I can at least keep it on the DL for now," Brock agreed.

"Promise me, Brock."

"I do; I promise." Without a smile, Brock hugged Chaya, partly because he knew accountability partners were extremely rare and therefore should be treasured, and partly because he knew it would soon be time to come clean to Betts. He couldn't be too proud. *If there is any hope of me getting out of this fucking sinkhole,* he admitted to himself, *I need all the help I can get.*

✦ ✦ ✦ ✦ ✦

Naked, Nova closed her locker at Bliss and rotated and changed the numbers on the small, metal lock. She was one of about 20 women of differing shapes, sizes, and skin tones coming and going from the locker room to the gym and spa. One woman with a towel wrapped around her waist, Nova noticed, had had a double mastectomy and was combing her hair in the mirror. *You go girl.* Nova flipped her gray, terrycloth towel over her left shoulder and walked through the long, glass door to a very steamy, open, tiled area with three different pools. She turned to the tiled showers on her left and doused herself from head to toe with the hottest water she could stand. It felt particularly satisfying to simply stand in the shower rolling her neck clock-wise, then counter clock-wise. *Fuck I'm old.*

In the dry sauna, Nova placed her towel down and sat on it without making eye contact with the other two women. *Nice. Let's sweat in peace, ladies.* Seated next to the dewy window overlooking the pools, Nova tried to relax by sitting up really straight to lengthen her spine and rotating her shoulders in small circles. *Words are on the window.* Clients had written messages on the window's interior with their finger: 'Lez' was inside a big heart next to 'You're beautiful' and 'Let it go.' *Look, they even spelled 'you're' correctly. These are my ladies.*

Nova refocused her gaze through the window to a large, brown woman in the cold pool with her back facing the sauna. About 20 feet directly above her head was a waterspout, which emptied cold water into the pool below. Nova observed this client standing underneath the weighty gush massaging her shoulders and spine like a bear scratching its back against a pine tree. Nova reached toward her and touched the foggy window with two fingertips. *How lovely you are.*

"Oh, beg my pardon. I don't know the protocol," said a naked, blond, 40-something aloud in a Southern drawl seated across from Nova. "I guess I should have sat on my towel. I left it outside."

Nova looked over at her. *Goodbye quiet Zen.* The blond was sitting teak to skin. "No worries," Nova responded. "I think it's free form. It's just too hot for me to sit down without one."

"Do y'all come here often?" the blond prompted more conversation from both women.

"It's my first time, actually. How about you?" Nova responded. *Smile and be nice.*

"I've been coming to Bliss for over four years, but this is the first year that I've come into the spa. I just couldn't handle being naked in public until now. I was too self conscious and afraid I would run into someone I know."

At this point a young, Korean woman who had been lying down on the upper, teak bench sat up and asked, "Can I join you? So what changed?"

The blond shrugged. "Me. Sorry if this is TMI, but I just reached a point when I wanted to push myself. Like, what really is the worst-case scenario of being naked in front of people? We're not in elementary school; no one is going to point and laugh. So, I challenged myself to just try it once. That was a funny day too because I wouldn't look at anyone in the eye, I wouldn't talk to anyone… I felt so rude. However, when I looked around at all the different bodies, it was like my brain recalibrated or something. I had just literally never seen so many naked women before, and once I did, my fear seemed small and silly. Childish, you know? Now, I just don't even care. It's a non-issue."

The Korean woman applauded the effort, "Good for you. You deserve the freedom."

Nova quickly skimmed the Korean's hourglass waist and plunging breasts with large, dark areola.

"How about y'all?" the blond asked.

Nova cleared her throat. "I just started coming to Bliss. I'm the reverse. I haven't been to the gym even once yet, but I needed a few hours to recharge here in the spa. Crazy week." As soon as Nova tagged on her last thought, she both regretted it and secretly thanked herself for bringing it up because she really needed to talk about it.

She knew that dangling a feeling like that in front of attentive listeners was like fanning a fire of mutual experiences and empathy. The reverse, she also knew to be true: the bigger the ego, the less listening, the less up-take, and less connection. *Mansplaining.*

"Bad week? What happened?" the blond responded on cue.

Here we go, Nova teased herself. *You did this to yourself, girl.* "No, it's just that I recently moved to Denver from New York and you know moving – it's freeing and you feel full of adventure, and then adventure finds you, and then you're not sure how long it's gonna last. I feel like I made some friends, but I'm not sure if I'm really going to fit in with them or not, or if they want me to or not, you know? It's just, a new town, new people, new me. Lots of change all at once."

"I totally get that," the Korean replied. "I felt like I was dating hard for the first two years of moving here. I was doing group-on's, volunteering, joining clubs, inviting people over for dinner all of the time. It was non-stop forging friendships. And now, I have my various crews. They are like my Colorado-family, so it was totally worth the effort, but it takes a lot of energy at first, I know."

Nova responded, "So keep on keeping on?"

"Heck yeah," the Korean confirmed with a smile. "It'll work itself out. Meanwhile, have either of you gotten a massage here yet?" she asked with a leading grin.

"No," Nova said wondering how far down the rabbit hole this conversation would take them.

"No, have you?" the blond asked.

"Yeah, they are so good. Really amazing. I was super sore for like three days after my first one. I had so many knots everywhere. Then, I started exercising and stretching out more, and the second time was a lot less painful. By the third time, it was a really enjoyable tune-up." The Korean sported a Cheshire grin as she leaned in on her last provocative thought: "Really enjoyable, if you catch my drift."

Nova assumed the obvious; *you got a happy ending!* "Can I ask you something?"

The Korean's grin transformed into a smirk. "Yeah, sure. I bet I know what you're going to ask."

The blond could see that she was missing some vital information. "What?"

I got my answer! Nova wasn't sure what to disclose. "Are we allowed to talk about... everything? Openly?"

"Why not?" the Korean rearranged her legs. "I had a happy ending, yes," she giggled proudly.

"A what?" the blond was confused.

Nova smiled at the Korean, "I'm not going to tell her; I don't know the rules around here."

"A happy ending," the Korean announced to the blond, "is like a man's happy ending at the end of a man-massage, only, this is for a woman." Both of her hands pointed at her triangle of black pubic hair.

The blond immediately sat forward enthusiastically, "No way! Are you joking? Do you mean it's a..."

"No joke," the Korean bragged. "A sweet and simple hand job. You wear eye covers; they don't talk; they just get down to business. Hands only."

Nova chuckled. "So how is it? Is it weird?"

"Not really. I mean, the very first time, yeah, I was a little nervous, but I just pictured my Hollywood crush down there making her magic, and I was good to go."

The blond held both of her hands over her mouth. "I can't fucking believe this. I've been at this stupid gym for four years working off steam, when I could have just been getting happy ending massages the whole time! Incredible! Wait." She held her hand like a stop sign. "What if they don't do it the way you want them to? I mean, what if the ending is… not ending… because you can't finish?"

The Korean wiped the sweat away from her eyes. "I don't know what everyone else does, but I just tell the lady what I want."

By her tone, it was evident that the blond was shocked. "You do? You say it? Out loud? Like instructions?"

Nova laughed. "Well, what else is she going to do? Mental telepathy? You don't tell your partner what you want?"

"Uh, no. Never. That would be weird," the blond declared her sanity.

The Korean and Nova shared a look and laughed. Nova joked, "The problem may be the team you're batting for. Personally, I don't think it's strange for anyone to discuss what they want. I mean, if the positions were reversed, wouldn't you want to know how your partner liked things?"

"Yeah, y'all are right. I guess I can add that to my 'challenge list.' First it was getting naked in public, now it's saying what I want during sex. But wait," she raised the stop sign again. "I'm married. Happy endings are cheating, aren't they?"

The Korean woman started, "I can't give you advice because I'm not married or straight, but for me it helped. Partners aren't always on the same page at the same time. It helps to get through some humps in the relationship… at least it did for me. For you, I don't know. You could just try it once, just like being nude. Just try. If it doesn't work out, no harm no foul."

Nova chimed in, "You could also just tell him straight up. I was married for a long time. I thought about sex with other people a lot. I mean, a lot. Toward the end, my husband passed of cancer, and it would have been nice to get all of that stress out. To feel someone's body, flesh against flesh, next to mine. Touch is so healing. Our bodies need it even when our minds trick us and claim that we don't. At least, my body needs it. I don't think it's always about fidelity. There are times, yes, when that's important, but other times we need to cut ourselves some slack and put our needs first."

The Korean woman clapped her hands and briefly giggled. "Okay, now we are talking more than happy endings. You have to pretend that you don't know. But… I heard that we can get laid here too. They call it a 'Happy Ever After'! Can you believe it?"

Nova no longer needed to act surprised. "Oh really?" *Nef failed to tell me all of this.*

"Oh my Lord in heaven!" the blond high fived the Korean. "Yes! How can I get one or ten?"

"I thought you were all worried about even getting fingered, now you want 'The Full Monty?'" the Korean laughed. "We have to talk to Chaya or Desiree. I heard that we can get practically anything we want. They have theme rooms too. One lady told me that they even have thrones – more than one to choose from – where a 'peasant' can go down on his 'queen,' if you know what I mean." *Ha!*

Nova could not stop smiling. "No wonder they named this place Bliss!"

+ + + + +

As Nova was exiting the locker room, Desiree caught her attention with a loud, deep shout from down the stucco-tiled hall. "Hey, do you have a minute? Brock wants to chat with you in the in-take room."

"Sure, no problem." *What's this all about?*

Seated facing each other across the conference table, Nova could see that Brock's eyes were a little bloodshot and his pupils dilated. "What's going on? Have you heard anything about Gael?"

"First, I'd like to offer you a job. The last few days have been one hell of an interview," he chuckled sarcastically, "and you passed with flying colors. I feel like we could really use you, in a variety of ways, if you'll have us. It goes without saying that helping Gael was a game changer. Had you not been here, who knows what would have happened if he had gone to a hospital. That could have been the death knell for Bliss."

"Wow. I'm happy to help. It's no problem. He wasn't nearly as bad as they can come." Nova sat with the fingertips of both her hands touching as if in prayer. *A job! No applying, no interviewing, they just see me in action, and want me. Isn't this refreshing compared to the usual bullshit of wasting my time competing against inside candidates!*

Brock zeroed in on the color of Nova's eyes, then on the particular hue of blue. *They're more gray than blue*, he estimated. *She's understated and direct. Betts will like her a lot.* "Bliss is unique, obviously. We need talented people who can exercise discretion.

Your skill set is beyond nursing; I can tell. You're a natural leader. I see the way the staff looks to you for guidance. You're a good fit with the team. So feel free to go home, take some time, and think of questions you might want to ask me."

"I'll take it, yes. My answer is yes. Thank you for the offer." Nova reached her hand over the table to shake. *Let's lock it down.*

"Well good! That was easier than expected," Brock admitted. He gave her his Hollywood smile to show her that he was very happy with her choice indeed. Then, he paused in order to discuss the real business at hand. "Now that you have verbally agreed to the offer – of exactly what neither of us knows, but we'll work it all out – I have more news to share with you about Gael's situation."

"It's a situation now?" Nova asked. "Did you find him?"

"No," Brock replied. "We haven't even tried to look for him, and he hasn't reached out to us. I could call him, but I doubt he would answer. I mean, why would he? The latest information is actually from the police. When Alice called the hotline to report the house with the teenagers, like we all discussed, the police quickly located her at her office on the Auraria campus."

"No way, really?" Nova felt confused. "But I thought she was going to do it anonymously to keep Bliss out of it."

"I know. She tried, but she didn't exercise enough caution, and they figured out who she was. Anyway, when the police were questioning her, they told her that they didn't find any teenagers."

Nova frowned. "Oh, that's a shame."

"It really is, I agree. But what took us by surprise was that the police found two guys murdered and one guy blinded who is now in the hospital."

"Holy shit. Did Gael kill them?" Nova said Gael's name as if it was a stunning revelation.

"I don't know," Brock replied in a worried tone.

"But he isn't so muscular or big. How could he take out three men?" Nova pondered aloud.

"I don't have a fucking clue, Nova. This is as much as I know. You were the one who said that we needed to protect ourselves, protect Bliss, so I knew that you would want to hear everything."

"Thanks." Nova mulled over this new information for a minute. "Brock, you picked him up, right? After it happened?"

"Yeah."

"Well, have you gotten your car detailed yet? Just in case the police connect you to Alice, do you think it would be a good idea to get your car cleaned and to have the Aspen room wiped down – I mean really wiped down hospital-clean?"

"Yeah, you're right," Brock was usually very agreeable when he was high. "And don't worry about me and Alice, she won't be around until this blows over. We'll use Whatsapp just as a precaution."

"That's prudent. Oh, and the shower. Pour bleach down the drain," she recommended.

"The showers are kept ultra clean anyway. Not a trace of him would be found there, and probably not in the Aspen room either – we have wonderful housekeepers – but you're absolutely right about my car. I'll get it detailed tomorrow morning. And as for your job, Nova, let's meet up next Monday morning so we can figure out a position description and salary, okay?"

Nova chuckled. "This is a rather unconventional hiring process."

Brock half-smiled, and with open arms said, "Welcome to Bliss."

Chapter 13: One Degree of Separation

"Give him an 8-Ball," Nick ordered Terrance, a muscular African American man dressed from head to toe in black with a shoulder holster and ankle-knife. Nick's voice was damaged and crackly reflecting a life of smoking.

A young man with brown, deteriorating teeth and smelly clothes named Forest was handed a plastic bag with a half-ounce of crystal methamphetamine, the most he had ever possessed at one time.

"I'm paying you up front as a sign of my good will," Nick declared from behind his office desk to the junkie in front of him. He sat forward attentively as far as his large beer belly would allow. A lit Parliament cigarette dangled between his fingers. *We're going to get to the bottom of this.* "What does your mama call you?"

"A disappointment," Forest replied with eyes looking down at the crystal in his dirty hands.

Ha! "You're far worse than that, boy. Must have a nice mama to not call you out for all the dick sucking you tweakers do. Now what's your fucking name?" Nick inhaled a long draw from his cigarette and then tapped its ashes into the tray. *This is as patient as I get motherfucker.*

"Forest Baker… uh, sir." Forest stood sheepishly in front of men he knew to be violent and cruel. One of John's cooks had pointed Forest out in an alley off Pearl Street to one of Nick's runners who brought him to Nick's new office. Forest was smart enough to do as he was told and not ask questions.

"I like the 'sir' part. I'll tell you what. Piece of free advice for your very predictable future: when little pussies suck my cock I better hear, 'thank you, sir' after they swallow or else they loose their front teeth." Nick laughed at the horror on Forest's face. "Awe, c'mon, I'm just fucking with you. Can't a guy have a little fun? This is me having fun."

Forest relaxed ever so slightly, but remained silent. In perpetual motion, his fingers nervously never stopped pinching the bag as if the zip lock weren't closed.

"You're not good enough to suck me off, boy. Fucking meth-mouth. Now tell me what you know. What the fuck happened? Spit it out. Every fucking detail, you hear?"

"Yes, sir. So I was there to buy some meth, and when I come in, I see a fight happening in the kitchen – a real bad one. People are running out past me, mostly crack heads, so I go to look closer. One bare-assed guy was punching the living daylights out of one of John's hired guns. Two guys were already on the floor. I think one was John. He was bleeding out his eyes and screaming, like really screaming in pain. I think the other one was dead or knocked out 'cause he didn't move. Not an inch. His eyes were gone too. All bloody."

Nick shared a 'what the fuck?' glance with his man Terrance. "Did you know this 'bare-assed guy'?"

"Nope. He ran out of there with his dick swinging, though. I know that," Forest replied.

"What color was his dick? Was it a big, black one, a teeny tiny Asian one, what?" Nick sneered.

Forest cringed. "He was white. He had long, dark hair that was up like a ballerina." He stopped talking because Nick suddenly got up and walked over to Terrance.

Forest flinched at the sudden movement and hugged the 8-Ball to his chest. His eyes darted around the room looking for a weapon within his reach.

Nick mumbled, "Let him go," and lit a new cigarette with his back to Forest. Once Nick heard footsteps out of the room and the door was shut, he answered an unspoken criticism from his right hand, "I know, I know, Terrance. I saw your look. You think an 8-Ball is too much. I get it. Sun Tzu calls boys like that a 'live spy'. Said spies ought to be paid a 'rich reward' so they don't turn." Nick's cell phone dinged four times in a row. He reached for it and said, "That's the *Art of War* right there. That's some two thousand year old gangster shit. Don't fuck with a proven recipe." He looked at his texts and laughed aloud, "Ha! Well lookie, lookie here, it's some more 'foreknowledge' from my spies. We're gonna be able to tie up this loose end and deliver the cattle by Monday after all. Feed and ice them. We're back open for business as of tomorrow. Send out our new 411."

+ + + + +

Reggaeton was blasting from the outside speakers behind White Glove hand car wash. The only workers on the books were the white, female cashier and the Spanish-English bilingual manager. Everyone else was a day laborer paid under the table. Mostly undocumented Mexicans with a few black ex-cons, they showed up at 9am and worked until the line of vehicles to be hand washed and polished was finished. They then split the till after the manager took half for White Glove.

No less than five men detailed Brock's Tesla. He walked away and chatted with Alice using Whatsapp while he waited.

Mateo's job today and most days was the inside passenger-side wipe down. The different cleaning jobs depended on speed, quality of work, and preference. Rarely were decisions made on a first-come, first-serve basis or by the manager, Julio. Instead, the day laborers worked together as a team to sort out who could accomplish which task the fastest depending on who showed up to clean that day. Julio learned to stay out of it, and let them figure it out. The quicker they could push the cars through, the more money everyone made.

Mateo specialized in the inside detailing on the passenger side. As he opened the door to the Tesla and reached down to pull out the mats, he noticed something spherical and shiny under the seat. After looking closer, a cold chill swept over him. He stopped wiping immediately, gestured the sign of the cross over his chest, and warned the other four guys to leave the passenger area as is, "*No toques nada. Voy a regresar.*"

As soon as Julio, the manager, looked under the seat, he took a photo with his phone. He then slipped on a blue rubber glove and lifted up a round piece of nickel-plated metal about the size of an apricot that had been resting under the seat. It had a spiral-thread at one end to screw it onto something and fingerprints dried in blood all over it. He quickly took another photo. Just out of morbid curiosity, Julio peered down inside the hollow threaded end to find it jammed with dried blood, hair, and what he guessed to be other human tissue. *Ahhh!* He tossed it back underneath the seat and told Mateo to leave it alone, "*Déjalo y finge que no viste nada.*"

Julio checked to see if Brock was watching his car. He wasn't, so Julio discretely took a photo of the registration inside the glove compartment and walked away. Being a manager had its perks and its responsibilities. A boon such as this cut both ways. First, he texted all the photos and details to the owner, Lupita Gonzales. Then, he walked over to Brock and had a conversation.

"Is that your Tesla?" Julio began.

"Hold on. Alice, I need to call you back. Give me a few minutes, okay? Bye." Brock pressed the red 'end call' button and gave the manager his full attention. "Yeah, is she ready?"

"No, I'm afraid not. It looks like your cleaning is going to be very expensive," Julio stated.

"Why?" Brock was confused. *Are they trying to dick me out of more money?*

"My workers found something under the front passenger seat and in order to forget what they saw, they need $500."

"What?" Brock exclaimed with enough anger and surprise that Julio took a small step backwards. *$500?* "What is it?" As soon as the question was asked, he immediately jumped to the worst possible conclusion in his mind: *Did they find a gun?*

"I don't know what it is, but it has blood and fingerprints. Don't worry though; my guys are professionals. They will leave it alone and forget everything if you can help them out, monetarily speaking."

Brock started to walk toward his car. "I want to see it."

"That's your right, but I wouldn't," Julio warned.

"Why not? It's my fucking car and you're extorting money from me," Brock almost yelled.

"Go ahead. Make a scene, make a scene." Julio invited as his eyes skimmed the distance by bouncing from one car to the next like slate skipping across a lake. "In fact there's a pig right over there. I love the taste of bacon. Don't you?"

Brock stopped and looked around, fists at his side. There had to be at least 20 workers on five different cars, and the various car owners were milling around with nothing to do except pay attention to drama. *Gael hid something there! What the fuck did they find?*

"Go to the ATM, get my cash, come back, and your car will be ready. Everything will be fine."

The only thing holding Brock back from punching Julio was his motivation to cut his losses and leave. *Run. Get out of Gael's wake.* Furious and feeling cornered, he turned and stomped away toward the ATM across the street.

Julio's cell dinged notice that he had received a text message: a dark brown thumbs up icon and the words, "Leave it."

Chapter 14: Convergence

Brock drove his Tesla directly to his remote home on Bison Drive in Boulder, which was surrounded by tens of acres of private forest. He was one of about 15 millionaires who shared this road. Once inside his three-car garage with the door shut, he opened up the passenger-side door and looked down under the seat. *There it is!* He found the weapon he had paid $500 for and decided to not get any of his fingerprints on it. Inside, in his butler's pantry, he grabbed a gallon-sized plastic bag and turned it inside out over his hand as if he were going to pick up dog excrement with a grocery bag. *Can this get any worse?*

Brock brought the plastic bag inside and held it up to the chandelier lights above his kitchen island. *What is it? A curtain-rod knob? No, too small.* The blood-dried fingerprints were very apparent, as was stray hair. *What if that hair is from the floor of my car? What if it's from the victims?* Brock rested the bag with the bloody knob down on his white, quartz counter top and looked for an open bottle of vodka in his subzero refrigerator. *What the fuck am I gonna do?*

Brock poured himself a generous glassful and used his phone to pump Barry White's "Love's Theme" through the speaker system on the main floor. *Breathe. Fuck this shit. Let's get my groove on.* He took a generous gulp of vodka and then two long hits off of his Pax, danced around for a few minutes, and sat at one of the bar stools of his kitchen island staring at the murder weapon which may or may not have DNA connecting him to two homicides. *Holy shit*, he shook his head and swayed a little. He pushed it a foot further away.

After a few minutes, he felt very stoned. He tapped his fingers like drum sticks on the countertop, then focused on the smoothness of the quartz. *So smooth and pale, like Alice's skin.* He spread his hands and stretched his arms wide, as far to his left and as far to his right on the countertop as possible, and then laid the right side of his face down gazing into nothingness.

Brock looked at his left fingers tap to the music as if it were someone else's hand. *I wish Alice were here right now.* He patted the quartz. *Right here.* He sat up straight. *I want her ass right here, right now.* He picked up his phone and video-called her.

"Hello," Alice answered as if in song.

She's sweet. "Hey, babe. You alone?" He spun around in his seat a few times.

Alice saw Brock's head with a spinning background as if they were dancing together. "I am, why?" Alice smiled with excitement of "Love's Theme" in the background.

"I'm horny, stoned, and I miss you," Brock admitted.

"That's quite a combo," Alice smiled. *Lucky me.*

"Set your phone down," Brock instructed Alice. "I want your hands free."

"What are you up to, Brock?" Alice sang.

"Well, how about some old school phone sex? I wish you were here in front of me on my countertop. I would make love to you, but I can't. So will you settle on the next best thing?"

Alice could hear his devilish smile. "I can try. Okay, what should we do?"

Brock could only see her home's ceiling on his phone now. "I'm gonna make you cum, baby, but I need your help. You have to focus, okay? I want you to hop up onto that countertop and spread your legs nice and wide. Go ahead and hold onto the edge, but nothing else, okay? Nothing else, especially not your beautiful pussy. Take a deep breath and relax. Now picture me in front of you pushing your knees a little wider. Yeah, you like it when I do that, don't you. Nice and wide for me. Do you feel your clit yet? Let her out. Relax to let her out to play with me. Yeah, now you feel her. I bet she's swelling up for me. She wants me, baby. Tilt your pelvis up a little. Now down. Think about her. Feel how she responds every time you tilt her up. Good. Focus on her. Turn up the heat. Imagine all your blood traveling to her. Now maybe you feel your lips and insides swelling. They hurt a little, don't they? That's good. That's your target. They should want me. You're focusing the energy, good girl.

"That's it, brace your arms, move your waist, close your eyes, and focus all your energy into your beautiful clit. Whatever it is you want to imagine right now, you imagine it. I could be licking your clit slow and upwards, again and again. You can press yourself into my tongue if you want. Do you want me to suck you? Picture me sucking you off, baby, just how you like it. Oh, you're so sexy, baby. Am I on my knees in front of you? Do you want my fingers inside of you? Whatever you want. I love your delicious pussy. I want to you so bad. Let me make you cum. Feel that burn; okay, push it. Keep going, baby, you got it. Lift it higher. Let it burn. That's it, you're doing it… now you can touch yourself. Go ahead, rub yourself and cum for me. I wanna hear you. C'mon, you're doing it… cum for me… you're cumming! Oh… baby…"

Alice moaned and then yelled through her long, very satisfying orgasm. "Oh my fucking God, Brock!" The aftershocks lasted a half-minute. She waited and delighted in each one which occurred farther and farther apart. She lingered her farewell for each one like waving good bye to caboose lights floating out of sight as her best girlfriend leaves on another adventure.

Brock took a long swig of his vodka and giggled every time an aftershock caused her to moan a little. *I love this woman so much. She has no idea.*

Wow. Alice blinked her eyes a bit and then jumped off from the counter and threw herself onto her couch to catch her breath. "Holy shit. Holy fucking shit, Brock."

Brock snickered, "I didn't realize that you swear so much, babe."

"It's not my fault!" Alice giggled. "You unlock my reptilian brain." She stood and picked up the phone. "It's your voice, really," she admitted. "I could listen to you for the rest of our lives." Just as she positioned the phone directly in front of her face, she heard his doorbell chime and saw Brock turn to look toward his front door, "Hold on, okay?" She heard his voice talking, but muffled.

Brock looked at the video monitor in the foyer and whispered to Alice, "I've gotta go. It's some big black guy holding Gael. Do something for me, call Bliss and tell Sharon that Gael's here. Tell her 'it's Betts' birthday'; she'll know what to do. Say 'Bett's birthday,' okay?" He punched the button to end the Whatsapp video-call.

"Brock?" *Gael!*

✦ ✦ ✦ ✦ ✦

"Membership has its privileges, don't it now," Barbara made the American Express slogan sound more like a command as the back of her arthritic index finger traced Gael's jawline. Barbara stood over Gael who was seated in his favorite reclining chair in her messy living room.

Gael wasn't surprised and didn't recoil. *Take or get taken.* Barbara wanted him to 'set her straight' as she called it. While Gael had no problem fucking or sucking whatever was required to make it through the day, he had bigger problems to deal with right now. *I gotta get that paper towel top.* His mind flashed back to spotting it on the counter during the first rape, then lunging for it right after the second. His heart raced. *Fix this, papi.* "Barbara, beautiful Barbara. I'm gonna have to take a rain check, my dear. Do you know why?"

"Don't try to wiggle out of what I gots comin' to me," Barbara warned. "I don't like that flowery talk."

"Seriously, Barbara, I just need a few hours. I have a present for you. I want to pay you back for your hospitality, but I have to go get it," Gael negotiated.

"What's that?"

"Oh, *mami* you're going to love it!" Gael squealed. "It's a car!"

"Really? Where is it?" Barbara wanted proof.

"Boulder. If you drive me over there, I can pick it up and bring it home to you. What do you say, *mami?*"

Barbara drove her 1984 Chevy Coachmen Shasta motorhome two hours west and down several dirt roads before she reached Gael's dust-covered junker. It took double the usual time since she only drove a maximum of 40 miles per hour due to the weight of all of her belongings stuffed inside the camper. The left-lane line of SUVs and trucks that passed them on Route 36 either honked their frustration or gave her the finger.

To pass the time, Barbara told Gael all kinds of stories about her family in South Carolina, old co-workers at the Smokin' Bear Lounge on the C Concourse at DIA, and friends who didn't visit very often anymore. One story was about a horny waitress whose husband routinely denied her sex. He was allergic to bees, and as destiny would have it, a bee stung him in the groin area one day. Once the wife saw her engorged husband, she denied him Benadryl and his EpiPen until he allowed her to hop on and take a ride. Another story involved a young prostitute who mistakenly left her purse with $1,000 cash inside at Smokin' Bear. "I was firing on all cylinders back in those days, so I brought the money directly to the police station after my shift, knowing that the whores wouldn't soon as go there as they would to church, and knowing that unclaimed property could be given to the finder after 90 days. I bided my time to the day and then bought myself a new tooth implant. See this one right here? That's what craft buys you."

Gael, on the other hand, passed the two hours half-listening to Barbara, half-thinking about his next move. At first, he thought about the various ways he could kill her. None of them panned out in his mind though, because every scenario attached Barbara to the car to her house. He only wanted to kill her if he could hide out at her house for a while longer. *No, better keep her alive.* Later, he considered just screwing her. Really, hiding out at her house was the safest place a criminal could find. As individuals, they were completely unattached. No one would ever find him in such a random place. *Hell, I've screwed older and uglier for less.* Finally, he contemplated starting to drive home with her and then getting off at the first exit. *She could never catch me in this metal boat, but where would I go? Where would I hide the car if she came around looking?*

Barbara took one long gander down both sides of a single-lane, empty road lined with red dirt and shrubs before she spoke. "Why'd you park all the way nowhere?"

Priorities. Go get the weapon, papi. "Barb, thank you for driving me all this way. Are you gonna be able to make it back alright? You got enough gas? I have to run an errand here in Boulder, then maybe I'll meet you back at the house later."

"I didn't just fall off the turnip truck," Barbara scolded. "I know it's time to swap spit."

Gael said an honest goodbye. "Thanks, Barbara. I won't forget you."

"Bye, Gael." As she put the camper in gear and lurched forward, she said to herself, "That boy needs a shock collar."

+ + + + +

One of the perks of working for Nick was that Terrence could sample the drugs, the girls, the boys, whatever he wanted, whenever he wanted. Breaking them in, helping them to come round, watching them successfully turn into his puppies, was, without a doubt, intoxicating at first. He trained and treated them like the strays that they were. It didn't take long before he became their go-to guy to ask for a drink of water when thirsty, a meal when hungry, and drugs when in pain. Terrence's technique was no different than any other predator. Deprive, fill the void intermittently, and keep them scared. When each one was good and ready, he never had to force. *They want me; they beg me for what I can do to make them feel good. Before me, they never floated so high.*

However, as the years passed, he felt more and more desperate for any way out of the hypocrisy. He didn't even know how to define 'monster' anymore. *Is it me? Nick? Nick's boss? The cartel? The customers? Who keeps this gun barrel spinning? When is it my turn at roulette?* Too much time had passed, too many samples had been taken, and too many bones had been broken for Terrance to be permitted to leave his life in the cartel. What he could hold over Nick about equaled what Nick held over him. It was a stalemate between dueling gentlemen whose guns were simultaneously drawn and aimed at the other. Backing away slowly was the only way Terrance thought he could save his own life.

It was a recent slave auction on the southern outskirts of Colorado that gave him the motivation to start the process of getting away… *or is it letting go?* The tears and pleas from his puppies, which he normally tuned out by getting high, were suddenly real. He could hear them now, and actually feel their fright and misery for the first time. He felt that same entrapment, the same puppy love for his boss, the same terror of stepping out of line against the cartel. *Their terror is my terror.*

After that auction, Terrance quit drinking and drugging cold turkey for in doing so he believed that he could concoct a plan to escape. *If I'm going to get out, I have to make my opportunity.* To him, his addictions and desire to feel powerful nearly drew him back in as soon as Nick handed him a joint, a pipe, or a drink, but once he realized that these were like fish hooks in his cheek, they became easier to decline. Freedom was a powerful motivator. In order to not raise Nick's suspicions, he claimed liver pain. "I gotta take a break, man. Just for a beat or two." He knew it wouldn't last very long, but he had an excuse for today, and that's how Terrance successfully played it: day-by-day.

Just before sunset after Forest's visit, Nick assembled his crew of Terrance, Boo, and Jojo in a windowless basement around a white, plastic, foldout table to discuss their next move. "I asked you to meet to preserve our piece of the American pie. Now the other night, as you know, we had to skedaddle like hot cakes out of the last house because of that boy with the bun we knocked around. Come to find out, he murdered Izzy and Eli. John, I'm not sure. I heard the boy blinded him, but I don't have confirmation as yet.

"Earlier today, I got more intel. I wanna know what you guys think. My gut tells me they're connected, but I wanna hear your thoughts. Look at this." Nick passed around his phone with the photos of the weapon, Brock's registration, and a portrait of Brock talking on his phone. Boo and Jojo took their time examining the pictures. Terrance had already seen them earlier in the day.

"Boss," Jojo asked, "What is that? It looks familiar, but I can't place it."

"I had to Google-image it for myself to figure it out," Nick admitted. "It's the top of a paper towel holder – the 'Umbra Tug'. Think about it. It fits perfectly in that boy's fist. How else could he over-power three men bigger than him? He blinded them!"

Jojo sat back impressed. "That's fucking genius, actually."

On his phone, Terrance Googled 'Umbra Tug'. *Oh, now that makes sense.* "So how is that boy connected to this Brock… Brock

Anderson?" All four tried to think of any idea that made sense. "Boss, should we look him up online?" Terrance suggested. "Maybe there's a clue in his social media. I'll look on Facebook."

"I'll Google him," Boo volunteered.

"Jojo," Nick asked, "Do you Twitter or Instagram or Snapchat or anything like that?"

"No boss, sorry," Jojo apologized. "I gotta learn that just for these moments. I know. You need that kind of information, and I'm gonna learn how to get it to you. Promise."

"Just stop, you babbling fool," Nick ridiculed Jojo.

"He's on Facebook," Terrance interrupted after a little detective work on his cell phone. *Thank you, Internet.* "Looks like he's part owner of a gym called Bliss. Not much else here. No pictures of kids, family, friends, work, nothing. Just nature photos. Looks like a fake account to me."

"Or an account for appearances," Boo added.

"Anything else on him?" Nick asked.

"He's gotta be wealthy," Boo surmised. "He has a house on Bison Drive." Boo put the address into Google Maps, changed it to satellite view, and zoomed in. "Got it. Got his big-ass house. He's rich."

"Whatsapp me that address Boo," Terrance requested. "I want to plug it into Zillow and Redfin. Let's get some photos and figure this out."

"I'll check out the Bliss website," Nick offered. "Jojo, do something useful, will ya?"

Jojo thought for a minute and said, "We need to get that weapon, that metal thing, then we have leverage on that boy, right? You want to find him, right Nick? Let's just go get the weapon."

Boo added, "Yeah. This Brock is the connection. Let's go to his house, get it, ask him where our boy is at, and bounce. We leave with intel and the weapon. Easy."

Nick shook his head and said sarcastically, "Sure. He'll just tell us everything we want to know... if he is even connected."

Terrance sat back and considered this opportunity. "Nick, I can do a reconnaissance. Watch him and his house. Maybe I can figure out the connection between them or find the weapon or rule out the connection. What do you think?"

"A stake out." Nick considered the option. "Okay. Go ahead. Whatsapp me every time there's something to report. Find a foot-trail in and out. Don't use the roads. Check for security cameras and wireless fences. I want to know everything about that house so that if we need to break in tomorrow night, we can. Don't be sloppy."

"You got it boss," Terrance agreed.

+ + + + +

"This is Bliss, how may I help you?" answered a female voice.

Alice's hands were shaking a little. "I have to talk to Sharon, right now. It's really important."

"One moment please, I'll connect you."

Alice heard the phone ring for a second time. As soon as she heard Sharon pick up, Alice started talking, "Sharon! Brock wanted me to call you."

"Excuse me, who is this?" Sharon asked.

"It's Alice! The professor. I was talking with Brock over the phone a few minutes ago and then Gael and some other big black dude rang his doorbell. He told me to call you and say that it was someone's birthday. Betts. He said it was her birthday and that you would know what to do."

"So, he's at home?" Sharon asked as she grabbed her Glock 19 handgun out from a drawer in her desk. She squeezed her cell phone between her chin and right shoulder as both hands worked to insert the magazine into the gun's handle.

"Yeah. Should I be worried?" Alice asked already alarmed.

"Alice, I want you to stay where you are, okay? Don't go to his house, and don't come to Bliss unless we call you," Sharon ordered. "I'll be in touch as soon as I get over there and find out what's going on, alright? Wait, write down my number. Text me so that I have yours." Sharon quickly shared her number and then ended the call. After she pulled her long black hair behind her head, she clicked on the 'Bliss 911' text conversation in her cell and typed, "MAYDAY," and ran out to the front office to see who would show up.

✦ ✦ ✦ ✦ ✦

Brock's mid-century, modern house full of floor-to-ceiling windows overlooked vast swaths of forested hills on all sides, yet couldn't be seen from the road below. By design, his driveway meandered like an old brook naturally carved with hairpin curves to ensure privacy and enable a safe decent in the dead of winter.

Terrence entered Brock's land from the north by foot, and laid on his stomach with binoculars at the foot of an Aspen tree to avoid detection, yet observe Brock's movements. Through the large windows to his kitchen, Terrence clearly saw Brock put something down on the counter, pour himself a drink, vape, and talk on his phone. Terrance tapped the list of Brock's actions into his text message to Nick. For the last twenty minutes, Black-billed Magpies had vocalized short glottal squeaks as if they were chatting with friends at the barbershop. Then, for no particular reason, they fell silent. *What spooked them?* Terrance wondered and looked around without his binoculars, then with them.

Terrance shifted his magnified gaze toward areas close to the house. "Well, well. Who do we have here? The fucking devil himself, I believe." Terrance watched Gael sauntering up the driveway dragging a long stick in his hand as if he were taking a leisurely walk. He still had noticeable bruising on his face. *You, motherfucker, are stupid as hell to be showing up here.* Opportunity instinctually pushed Terrance forward like a waist-high wave in the ocean shallows. Without much effort at all, he found himself creeping down the hill around the west side of the house undetected. Gael, on the other hand, seemed to want to announce his whereabouts by humming and singing "Freebootin'" from the old *Tom Sawyer* movie.

Yeah, 'life is sweet living off the fat of the land', asshole, Terrance thought as he rushed out from behind a particularly wide pine tree to grab Gael and put him in a headlock. "Hello, shithead. Remember me? Let's go say 'hi' to our friend Brock, what do you say?"

Gael pitched and kicked his disagreement, but as soon as he heard Terrance's handgun click near his right ear, he stopped resisting. They unnaturally hobbled like conjoined twins toward the front door.

"This is the second time you've threatened me, *papi*," Gael warned. "There won't be a third."

"Shut the fuck up and ring the doorbell." Terrance pushed the chamber of the gun against Gael's right temple.

Once pressed, a customized, low-octave song of bells sounded.

Brock's voice pumped through a speaker system. "What the fuck do you want?"

I want my weapon back, jackass, Gael thought.

"Hey, you don't know me, but I want to help you with this dirt bag right here who was creeping up to your crib," Terrance stated into the video camera above his head. There was a pause, and then the door clicked. Brock opened the door a few inches.

"Delivery," Terrance said. "I think you want this guy tied up for now. Am I wrong?"

"You're not wrong." Brock admitted through the crack, "Who are you and how do you know Gael?"

"I'm Terrance, and I want to make you a proposal. A win-win. Can I come in? I can't be out here in the open with this gun for very long."

"Well, I don't want you inside with a gun either," Brock chuckled as he braced the bottom edge of the door with the outer side of his foot.

"It's just for this asshole, believe me," Terrance divulged. "Let me just bring him in, and we can tie him up. Then I'll put the gun away."

Stoned and tipsy, Brock did not think. "I feel like I'm living inside the movie *Pulp Fiction*."

Terrance automatically recycled his favorite line from the movie: "That's all you had to say, negro!"

"Ha! I loved Samuel Jackson's character. C'mon in," Brock laughed and opened the door wider to let them through. "You can say that line, but I can't."

"That's very fucking true, my nigga," Terrance joked back.

"Bring him over here to the kitchen," Brock directed Terrance then surprised them both by yelling at Gael, "Sit your ass down here while I get some twine from the garage. I'm pretty pissed at you."

Terrance shoved Gael into an open seat at the table and pointed the tip of his handgun at Gael's crotch. "I'm not gonna kill you right now, but if you so much as twitch, my hand might twitch, and then you'll have no dick, but you'll still be alive... but with no dick."

Gael swept the room with his criminal x-ray vision searching for any weapon, exit, phones left laying around, wallets, drugs, keys, all the usual items. *There it is, papi!* He was elated. *I knew I would find it! This all happened for a reason, you see? I just needed to trust.* Gael closed his eyes for a moment and tried not to smile. He felt like he had won a foot race against a bunch of children and therefore shouldn't be a braggart. *After all, I am the logical winner.*

When Brock returned from his a garage with brown twine, Terrance introduced himself and explained his current mindset. "Brock, I'm Terrance, and I want to tell you some things about me. We probably shouldn't waste time, so I'll get to the point."

Brock started wrapping Gael's wrists behind his back as he listened. "Okay."

"At some point, I want you to help me get out of my current situation. The guys I work for want this guy dead or worse. They do a lot of things that I just can't abide anymore. I want out, and I think he is my opportunity. You got duct tape?"

"Uh, yeah." Brock stopped what he was doing and ran over to his butcher's pantry to fetch the silver tape roll and a pair of scissors.

Terrance took them and cut a strip long enough to cover Gael's mouth. He slapped it on roughly.

Brock could hear Gael's forced breathing in and out of his nose as he continued tying Gael's arms together and to the chair.

"Look," Terrance tried to be as honest as he could. "Not now, not today, but I want you to be my go-between with the police. I'll take Gael here and all my intel about the cartel in exchange for a new identity and full immunity. I want witness protection. That's what I want you to negotiate."

Brock cocked his head to the side and gave Terrance his million-dollar smile. "You're never gonna believe this, Terrance."

"What?"

"You're gonna love me, Terrance. I'm telling you… because I've got Gael's weapon."

"No shit?" Terrance asked in a high pitch feigning disbelief. *I know you have the murder weapon, bitch, but now I can confirm that it's Gael's. Amen!* "Yeah, sport, you can be my new BFF, no problem. Show me the money."

"It's right there on the island. Go take a look. It's gross, though." Finished with Gael, Brock pulled a chair several feet away from the table and sat down lazily with his legs wide apart.

Jackpot, motherfucker! "Is this it?" Terrance held the plastic bag with the weapon up in the air to inspect it closer. *This is too fucking easy. Nick thinks I can't roll on up in here and just ask. God damned Pulp fucking Fiction is right.*

Idiotas, Gael sneered his condescension. *I'm not going to be used as your 'get out of jail free' card, and I will rat Bliss out, cabrones. Either that or you can pay me a fuckload of dinero.*

"He's worth more dead to me." Brock crossed his arms over his chest. "Seriously. He knows too much about me. He'll just rat me out to save his own ass." Justification scaffolded by his high, Brock actually meant what he said although he wasn't proud of it. He was aware that he wanted another human being dead and was stating this to a real-life gangster. From every angle conceivable to Brock, Gael's death would be a welcome solution to his problems. He didn't want to do it himself or provoke it in any irresponsible way, but if it happened – if that was his destiny anyway – Brock would be able to start again at the top of the well instead of in the bottom of its pit.

"He's worth more alive to me," Terrance disagreed. For the first time in years, he wanted to walk away with a little integrity. "And I really don't want to kill him. I'm so tired of all that. So let's think of something else."

Gael was recalculating his odds with each conversational exchange. *We need a win-win-win.* To get their attention, he loudly hummed “Freebootin’”.

“Shut the fuck up, Gael,” Brock yelled in irritation.

Terrance pulled the tape off Gael’s mouth, but left it dangling from his left cheek. “What, motherfucker?”

Gael launched into his opening remarks. *Mr. Judge and Mr. Jury,* “Terrance, you don’t need me for the police to give you a good deal. You know where they moved Nick’s operations. Leverage that.”

Brock agreed. “He has a point, actually. The teenagers are leverage too, those sex slaves you’ve got locked up? The cops are looking for them. Do you know where they are?” *Tell me.*

“Yeah, of course,” Terrance stated as though it were insulting for anyone to think otherwise.

Gael replied, “See? You don’t need me at all. Brock, I won’t say a thing about Bliss, I promise. I’ll stay away from Colorado for good if you just let me go with that piece of metal.”

Terrance countered, “You have a good plan except for one thing: if I don’t need you for leverage, and if Brock just needs you to keep your mouth shut, then why don’t I just kill you? Save us both a lot of trouble.”

Gael recalculated his odds again. *There is no way this is a long shot!* he yelled at himself. “Because you want to turn your life around. You can’t start with a murder. You want out.”

“I already started turning it around the moment I walked your ass up his driveway,” Terrance argued for his own agency. “Maybe I was wrong before. Maybe killing you would just be a small bump in the road.”

"Okay," Gael continued Terrance's line of logic, "so what are you going to say that you did for the next few hours as you kill me, clean up the house, and get rid of my body? Huh? And if you can lie with a straight face to the police about murdering me, weigh your *cojones*. Ask yourself, are Brock's balls big enough to lie to them too? Because if they aren't, he'll eventually give you up; you know pussies like him will."

Brock launched over and punched Gael in the face. "Insulting me in my own home? We should just kill you. We can figure out what to do with the timeline later."

"Or," Terrance threatened, "I could turn you over to Nick. There's nothing more he would love than to take another crack at you. You know what I mean too, don't you, Gael."

Gael increased his odds by showing no fear. "So at least we can all agree that there's no need for you to turn me in to the police, right?"

The musical doorbell rang and then a rapping sound on Brock's front door interrupted their conversation. Brock motioned for Terrance and Gael to stay silent by putting his index finger up to pursed lips.

Terrance pushed the tape back over Gael's mouth and stood with his gun pointed down at Gael's lap.

✦ ✦ ✦ ✦ ✦

Detective Sontag and Detective Borratto passed the binoculars back and forth in an unmarked police vehicle outside the house of professor Alice Zezza. From across her back neighbor's street, the detectives were parked in the ideal location to see her between the houses and through her windows without being noticed by her.

"We are incognito," announced Detective Borratto. Since it was his turn with the binoculars, he narrated the events as he saw them. "Husband is leaving through the front door. Alice is going upstairs. She's on the phone."

"That didn't take her long now, did it?" Detective Sontag judged.

"Oh my sweet Jesus and mother Mary. Is she doing what I think she's doing?" Detective Borratto was stunned. "It's Christmas in Colorado! Ha! Get a load of this!"

Detective Sontag grabbed the binoculars and looked through them at Alice. "No way is that her husband on the phone. Call Charlie, call Charlie! He can look it up."

Detective Borratto called Charlie back at the precinct. "Can you trace the call Professor Alice Zezza is on right now?"

After a few minutes, Charlie replied, "Nope, nothing on her phone record. She must be using Whatsapp or KIK. Oh wait, now she's calling a company named… Bliss."

"What are they saying?"

"Yeah, hold on," Charlie replied and then listened on his other ear to a different phone. "They're talking about a guy named Brock. Someone is at his house. Two, two guys showed up... a 'Gael' and a black guy. The Sharon woman, at Bliss, tells the first woman, the professor, to 'stay at home'. Sharon says she's going to that guy Brock's house."

"We know where to go. Thanks, Charlie!" Detective Sontag put his unmarked vehicle in gear and headed for Bison Drive as Alice backed her car out of the driveway and headed downtown to teach.

Chapter 15: Small Group Work

Alice was in no mood to teach. Usually, she had a lesson plan that executed the course objectives through deductive then inductive activities. Today however, she was beside herself with worry about Brock's surprise visit from Gael – *a murderer!* – and the coded way that she had to call Sharon. Brock wasn't responding to any of her Whatsapp messages since their last conversation either. In fact, she realized that he hadn't even logged into the app in hours. *Is Brock safe? What would motivate Gael to return?* To make a bad situation worse, she felt like she was having a bad hair day. *I hate this,* she lamented. *I hate not looking my best and winging it!* Cancelling class was only for the adjuncts and tenured professors. Everyone else in tenure track positions like Alice had to suck it up and be responsible. Luckily, she came up with an idea on her drive over to campus. *I'm gonna put them into small groups. I can assign each group a piece of the puzzle, and let them figure out my next move. Maybe there's something obvious that I'm missing.* Once in her office, she sat down to her computer, set the stage for each group, and printed instructions.

Twenty-two of her 25 students were in attendance today. *Not bad,* she thought. Per usual, she wrote a short summary of the activities on the board and underneath wrote the word 'HOMEWORK' in big block letters and the title of a journal article. "Okay, this article is available online in Canvas in our week eight module. Read it before next Tuesday please. Okay. Today we are going to have a different kind of class. You're going to self-select into a small group, and we are going to have a mock argument over sex slave trafficking in Colorado." Several students shared worried glances with each other. "Don't worry. It should be fun, actually. Group one: I want the four toughest amongst you. If you're looking around at your competition right now, this is probably not your group. I'm looking for the most unapologetic folks in this room. Stand over here.

"Group two: I need four smart, socially adept people. I want folks who can play an intermediary role, like you could be a union representative – you can talk legalese to upper management one minute and then the next you can tell dirty jokes to your coworkers. If that describes you, sit over here.

"Group three: Over there. You like being a big fish in a small pond where everything is familiar and safe. You actively avoid challenging yourself. You're goal is to keep it easy, low risk, and maintain the status quo. Four or five of you come to this corner.

"Group four: My peacekeepers, come to this corner. I want four or five of you referees, you middle children, and you umpires right here. You know who you are.

"Group five: You're the 'snowflakes', the academic elite who are socially minded and wear their politics on their sleeves. Get over here if you post your politics on Facebook. You need to save the world."

The students looked at each other for a moment and laughed. A sophomore took pity on their professor and replied, "We're gen Z, we don't use Facebook."

"Oh, I see," Alice smiled, "I'm old. Okay, c'mon you guys. Stand up and pick a corner." No one wanted to stand up first. Alice clapped her hands and shouted, "Move it! Now! Own your spot! Five, four, three, two…" The students quickly stood and moved to the corner that best represented their personality. Alice pointed to each area where each group should assemble, "One: alphas. Two:

intelligent communicators. Three: comfort zone. Four: peacekeepers. Five: academics. Sit in circles. I'll bring you your directions."

Alice walked over to two men and two women in group one. *No surprises here.* They were all barely passing her class, yet right now looked very excited to demonstrate how much of a jerk they could be. "Okay, listen. You can all hear each other's description.

"Group one, you are the Mexican-based Sinaloa cartel; the majority of your international business is drug creation, packaging, and distribution. You are multimillionaires, but you live a very dangerous lifestyle – ask El Chapo. You move drugs and sex slaves among other things, like avocados. Your goal is to not get caught, force loyalty from thousands of employees, and make money. Here's the deal: there's been a hit on a local drug dealer in Boulder – that's you, group three – and this hit affected your local branch – that's you group two – in that they had to move to a new location. That cost to you, Sinaloa headquarters, is money and time. You lost, temporarily at least, a point of distribution of drugs and a pipeline of sex slaves from the streets into your cartel. Think about the great ROI on each slave. It's too good to be wasting days, my little drug lords. Tick-toc, tick-toc. What do you do?"

Alice shuffled the papers in her hand to the one titled, "Group 2" and read to a different circle of students. "Group two, you are the local faction of the group-one, Sinaloa cartel," Alice pointed at the previous group. "Today, right now, you have four teenagers who are your slaves: one white guy, two ladies of color, and one white lady. The police made you flee from your first brothel-slash-office. Headquarters wants you to make more money. What do you do? What are your next steps?"

Alice shuffled her papers again, and walked over to the next small group. "Group three, you are the local drug dealer who recruits teens and feeds them to the local branch of the cartel, our group-two friends right over here. You owe that faction nothing. It's all business and trade. Most days, you cook meth, and sell it. Some days, however, are special. One of these special days just occurred. You traded a bunch of drugs with your friends over there, group two, for one of their sex slaves – the guy. You bring him to your meth lab, and he goes ballistic. He blinds your local boss who is now in the hospital, and he murders two other associates of yours. You all are the underlings who ran away from the police, what's your next move? What do you do?"

"Group four, you are police detectives and DEA agents and want to catch anyone buying or selling drugs or people. You get a lead about the hit on the local drug dealer – group three here – when their boss is blinded and in the hospital. His operation, which is basically luring teens and running a meth lab, burns down. What are your priorities? What leads do you look for?"

"And lovely group number five, you are a group of concerned citizens, maybe you're college students or professors or local activists who want to make a difference and interrupt the local slave trade. You hear that all of these bad guys are somewhere in Boulder. What do you do if you can't go to the police? It may be your first instinct, but you can't rely on them. You have to figure out whether or not to help the slaves. What do you do?"

As Alice lifted her head from reading the paper in her hand, she realized that Fatou, a Senegalese immigrant, was standing with a book in her arms poised in the air ready to strike a burley, Latino classmate from group five. Eduardo's whimpers could be heard by the whole class. "Fatou!" Alice scolded instinctively.

"Ma'am, I'm just trying to kill the bee!" Fatou remarked as she lowered the book.

Alice took one long stride toward Eduardo, fearlessly snatched the buzzing bee with her hollow fist, walked over to the door, and threw it outside. "You need to be brave, groups four and five! You cannot save the slaves through fear or waiting for someone else to catch the cartel. You have to do it. The teenagers are counting on you! Everyone, go!"

Chapter 16: The Visit

> "Dr. Zezza, we're group four, the DEA agents and police," Brian stated loudly enough for the whole class to hear him. "We would shake as many trees as possible to see what fruit drops."

Detective Sontag and Detective Borratto held their badges up to Brock's front door video monitor as they pushed the doorbell a second time.

Brock pressed the 'sound on' button and told them, "Just a minute." He walked over to the kitchen and loudly whispered, "It's the police. Gael, do you want me to turn you in? Because I can. Right now. So shut the fuck up."

Gael rolled his eyes.

"Do you really think that we don't have a backup plan, Gael? That we can't turn Bliss over in less than an hour? We can if we have to, so no fucking noise, okay?"

Terrance continued to aim his gun at Gael's groin. "Brock, I'm not ready to make a deal just yet. You best not let them in. Go out if you have to."

They heard more pounding on the front door and then a muffled voice: "We just want to make sure that everything is okay, sir."

Brock walked out of his front door and shut it behind him. "Can I see your badges?"

Both detectives held them up for Brock to read. Detective Sontag led. "Hi, we're detectives Sontag and Borratto. We got a call that there were some homeless guys in the area. Have you seen them?"

"Homeless guys? Here? No." Brock shook his head.

"Okay," Detective Sontag responded slowly to Brock's lie. "If, by any chance, you have someone inside that you want us to talk to – homeless or not – all you need to do is tell us. We're happy to come inside and have a chat with him." He removed a lighter from his front pocket and lit a cigarette that had been cupped in his hand.

"…or with 'them,'" added Detective Borratto.

"No need," Brock responded. "Everything is fine." He tried to sound sincere.

From the kitchen, Terrance tried to make out what was happening on the video screen in the foyer and saw the detectives turn toward their car, then turn back toward Brock. "No, no, no, no, no," he said softly as he left Gael tied up and walked over to the monitor to see exactly what was happening. Terrance pressed the button so that he could listen in on Brock's conversation with the cops.

The detectives started to leave, then Detective Borratto turned to Brock and asked, "How'd you do it?"

"Do what?" Brock was confused.

Boratto looked at Brock with genuine curiosity. "How'd you make a woman cum without even touching her… just with your voice? I'll tell ya, I've never seen anything like that, man, and I've seen some freaky shit on this job, but today is the first time I ever saw a woman fuck a ghost. I got a little treat today for my spank bank, didn't I, Sontag." He playfully slapped his partner for verification.

"Gave me a stumpy," Sontag verified with a puff of smoke directed off to his side. "Your life is my movie, man. You should market that skill."

They're watching Alice! Brock was horrified. *Fuck you!*

Gotcha. Detective Borratto punctuated his delight at Brock's revealing facial expression. "She was just banging it and banging it like you were right there in front of her. Only you weren't, were you. You were here." His index finger pointed at the pavement beneath their feet.

Brock was caught on the back foot, and again it showed on his face.

"…and then your doorbell rang and you had two visitors," Detective Borratto continued pointing two fingers up but with the thrust of giving Brock the middle finger.

How the fuck does he know that? Brock actively tried to figure out the riddle.

"In fact, I bet they're inside right now." Detective Borratto snorted up some phlegm and spit it out off the driveway like he was launching a cannon.

Oh my God. Please let me keep it together, Brock negotiated with fate.

Detective Borratto saw that his intimidation was working, so he continued. "My hunch is that one of those guys in there knows about the murders and the teenagers being trafficked."

Detective Sontag played good cop. He loosened his tie and squinted as he spoke. "We're here to help you, Brock. We can come in right now and settle this. We know you're just an innocent bystander. But these guys, Brock," Sontag pointed casually at Brock's house, "these guys are not your friends. They are very, very dangerous thugs, and they will hurt you. Believe me, you do not want to be associating with any of them."

Brock could not see how this could end well for him or for Bliss, so he asked, "Hypothetically, what if someone knew detailed information about a drug cartel and wanted immunity and a new identity? Like they want to get out of the game and lay low for the rest of their life. What type of information would they need to give you?"

Terrance listened and watched through the small video screen near the front door and wanted to explode his gun into the faces of the two detectives and at the back of Brock's head. "No, no, no. Don't you fucking do it. Don't you fucking say another God-damned word, bro."

✦ ✦ ✦ ✦ ✦

> "Dr. Zezza, we're group one, the Sinaloa cartel drug lords. We would tell our local associates to get back to fucking business. Do whatever it takes to eliminate the threat and resume normal operations. No one is paying you to laze around. Either make bank or suck my dick."

By the time the detectives left and Brock returned to his front door, he was visibly shaken. *They know about Alice! They watched her!* His breathing was shallow and halting. *Have they been watching me too? Wait – how did Terrance find Gael? Have the cops and Terrance been staking me out?* Anger and remorse lowered him further into a psychological black hole. *What the fuck am I gonna do with these two guys? Should I call the detectives back? Is Terrance on my side? Can I trust him? Will he take Gael with him? Do I really want that fate for Gael? After all, he's just a messed up kid who was in the wrong place at the wrong time, right?* Brock punched in the code to unlock the front door on the keypad, and pushed on the handle. *Thud.* It wouldn't move. He shoved it a few times. *Thud, thud. What the fuck?* He pulled the door shut again and ran around the side of the house to enter through the back door, which he found wide open. Immediately, he looked up the hill and discovered Gael off in the distance sprinting up and away like a mountain goat. "Gael!"

Inside, a gruesome, blood-soaked scene confronted him. Terrance laid face down on the floor of the foyer in a puddle of blood originating from his neck. Brock screamed into his elbow uncontrollably. He looked at the island countertop for Gael's murder weapon; *gone*. He realized that his phone was dinging. Frightened, he looked at the front of his cell: texts and calls from Sharon. His vision blurred more and more. He stumbled toward the kitchen. Little dark, red spots in his peripheral vision appeared and populated until his sight and awareness went completely dark.

Brock awoke some time later to needles painfully piercing through the right side of his face as if he had fallen from a great height and landed face-first into an unforgiving body of water. He gulped air to breathe and flailed his arms to stave off drowning.

Chapter 17: The Clean Up

From Bison Drive at the base of Brock's lengthy, paved driveway, Sharon hiked a sure-footed path between the 70-foot tall Lodgepole pine trees with her 9mm gun in hand. At the midpoint of the hill was a clearing with Brock's expansive, large-windowed house. She pulled the bottom of her black tank top up to her face to sop up some sweat, then quickly jogged up the porch and rang the doorbell. *Silence. Bad sign*, she deciphered. *Go around back.* She lifted her heavy handgun to shoulder-level again and straightened her right elbow as she leapt off the porch and through the side yard.

After two tours of Iraq, Sharon was honorably discharged from the United States Marine Corps in May 2005. That period of her life had its merits, but she didn't miss it much. She hadn't made life-long friendships, and it didn't change the trajectory of her career. Military life was a means to an end, including learning how to shoot accurately. Target practice was part of Sharon's job as head of Bliss security. Although there had not been more than a few jilted men who tried to shove their way inside Bliss to talk to their estranged girlfriends or wives, that was a few too many to Sharon. She had to be hyper-vigilant to ensure the safety of everyone at Bliss.

Once hired at the age of 26, Sharon's initial risk assessment of Bliss clarified that the single most effective way for her to mitigate potential threats was to filter out inappropriate male Specialists. Thus, Sharon started participating in the interview process by testing them at their most vulnerable, during sex with them. Betts and Brock required presidential-level safety for clients while under Bliss' roof, so Sharon embraced her alter ego who was more docile, cock loving, and playfully naughty. It was a fun character to play during the testing process because it was temporary and with purpose. Guys who made it past Nefertiti and Celeste, but who still might not be trustworthy, typically revealed themselves to Sharon before sex. In one instance, she didn't clue in until after sex when he cracked her finger joints one-by-one, but that was an anomaly.

With almost complete certainty, Sharon could get a read on a man by either feigning an exaggerated stereotype of a sexy, Asian woman or by suggesting any number of subservient positions for her during coupling. Empathetic men who wanted to focus on her pleasure and cheer her on were never creepy no matter what she pretended. A man could be tying her wrists to a bed frame, but if he was smiling a little and at least asking 'You good?' she knew he was safe. Conversely, he could be doing something innocuous when a micro-expression or something very nuanced and ineffable would set off her internal alarm. *You're out.*

Needless to say, the rejected men did not appreciate being turned away without reason and usually without sex. They often felt cheated and let her know it through name-calling, voice raising, and sometimes threats of violence. It was as if a woman had never stood up to them directly before, which was curious to Sharon. *Why on Earth not?* She therefore felt like her work was partly charity as well. All future women benefitted from each man having been rejected and made aware that they should do better. *Just do a little better. Try a little harder. Take a baby step out of your ego and push yourself to be a little more partner-focused.*

Sharon's line of work was hazardous in multiple ways, therefore she required herself to stay in shape, spar occasionally, and maintain her shooting accuracy. While dojos were easy to find in

Boulder, appropriate shooting ranges were not. Colorado was not as red as the old days. After paying a $70 application fee, completing an extensive application with a background check, attending two meetings, and being voted in by other members, Sharon was awarded an annual membership to the Silver Miner's Gun Club... For Women. Annual dues were $150.

Silver Miner's was unique for a number of reasons. First, it was private. Members were consciously biased against any woman who "wasn't a good fit" in any indeterminable number of ways. Second, it was housed completely underground to mute the noise, and third, only women were admitted. Sharon appreciated this last detail the most because when she shot, she was so focused that she felt vulnerable to attack. She just wanted to practice without having to check her surroundings for fanatics or drunks slinking up from behind. A women's-only club ensured her this focus. The club was also more handgun than rifle-friendly, which suited Sharon as well. It had turning targets and carriages and an indoor pistol range out to 25-yards.

At the moment, as Sharon saw that Brock's sliding back door was left wide open, she was glad that she had maintained her ability to shoot and kill. She scanned the hill above her. Then, she entered through the threshold very slowly, clearing each corner in her mind like a checklist. *Holy shit!* The scene of two bodies laying face down in two different rooms shocked her. *Passed out or dead?* "Brock! Brock! You better be fucking alive!" Sharon sprinted to him and placed two fingers on his carotid artery. *A strong pulse. Thank God.* She then jogged over to the other body and confirmed death by the large puddle of blood. Room by room she checked every corner of the house until she was satisfied that no one else was inside. She then ran outside again through the back door and whistled for her coworkers' attention.

Team Bliss waited in position for Sharon's 'all clear' signal. It had taken two cars to drive everyone all the way up the steep hill to the base of Brock's driveway. Marcus let five minutes pass, as was the plan, before he got out of his car and ascended the driveway after Sharon with his handgun faced forward. He was halfway up when he heard Sharon's whistle with one high and one low tone. In turn, he put two fingers in his mouth and repeated the whistle down the hill toward the cars. Marcus returned his gun to his lower back under his pants' waistband, relieved that he could drop his guard.

Once Sharon saw Marcus exit through a grove of tall shrubs onto the driveway in front of the house, she half-jogged closer to him and lowered her voice as if they could be overheard, "Hey, Marcus. Do you have PTSD?"

"No," he answered her. "Why?" He unconsciously scanned the distance in all directions for any disturbance. *Something's up.*

Sharon paused and then clarified, "It's bad in there. Gruesome. It looks like Brock might have killed a guy, but I don't know."

Marcus furrowed his brow. "Alright." *This can't be true!*

Soon, Sharon saw the rest of the Bliss team drive up to the garage. Once they all got out, she announced to the group, "Guys. Before you go in, there's something you need to know. Brock is passed out. We need to lift him up into a kitchen chair. Also, there's a dead body, and it's not pretty. Turn around now if you don't want to be a part of this. I mean it. I don't know what happened, but this is clearly some very illegal shit. Anyway, if you're in, follow me around to the back. If you're not, now's the time to do an about-face." She turned and walked out of sight around the western side of the house.

Gael, far up on the hill behind Brock's house, watched through Terrance's binoculars as a parade of his old co-workers, Desiree, Chaya, Celeste, Marcus, Nefertiti, and Nova, followed Sharon one-by-one around the house and into Brock's back door.

The wanna-be-Pollock mural at the front end of the house shocked everyone into silence. The black man lying on the floor had clearly been facing the front door and killed from behind according to the explosive blood splatter forward. Nova, like most of Bliss, reflexively covered her mouth fighting confusion and disbelief. *Brock murdered a man in cold blood? No way.* "Brock," Nova tried to get the attention of her inert boss in the kitchen who had been propped up in a chair by Marcus and Sharon. Nova cleared her throat and uselessly paused for a response. "Brock. Brock, time to wake up." Nova walked over to him and snapped her fingers in front of his face twice. He didn't react. His eyes were mostly closed, glassy, and unfocused. "He's still out. Let's give him a little time. Sharon, I think we need to get his girlfriend over here. What do you think?"

"That professor is a fucking liability," Sharon complained. "Has been from the start, so nothing will change I guess. Chaya, call our girl Alice and give her the address, but don't tell her anything. Just say that Brock needs her."

"You got it," Chaya nodded and then mumbled under her breath as she walked away, "He needs Betts, but what do I know? I'm just an east-coast Jew." She walked out the back door and vaped until she felt high, then she called Alice using her most upbeat voice. As she heard it ringing, she smiled as big as she could because she remembered that people at the other end of a phone call can actually hear a smile. *Pretend that you didn't just see a dead body*, she prepared herself. *Pretend that Brock is fine; he's just drunk.* "Hey, Alice, this is Chaya from Bliss. How are you? Yeah, well, Brock kind of needs you right now. Do you have his address? No, no judgement, you two just started dating. I can text it to you. Everything is cool, he just seems… kind of… drunk. Do you have time to come over right now? Great! I'll text you. Just come all of the way up to the top of the driveway and then go around to the back door. Back door, okay? Not the front. See you soon. Bye, bye."

"Chaya," Desiree called to her friend as if she were serving up dinner. "Team meeting. C'mon."

"Coming," Chaya sang as she took one last vape and texted Alice Brock's address.

Gael watched the pencil-troll of red hair hesitate and exhale a large cloud of white vapor. *Is she looking at me?* He dropped the binoculars onto the ground and aimed Terrence's handgun directly at her head. Then, she turned and vanished inside. *Did she see me?* Gael put the gun in his waist under his belt, hung the binoculars around his neck, felt his pocket to make sure that the Umbra handle was still there, and then scrambled higher up the hill as fast as he could. *Time to circle around and get my car.*

Everyone except Brock assembled in the living room on the couches and chairs in front of a white accent wall with a black, brick fireplace. "I'll start," Sharon opened and sat forward onto her elbows. "We need to decide if we're gonna clean this up or not because that blood is gonna get harder and harder to remove the more time we let pass. If we clean it up, that means that we need to do something with the body. This means no police. Do we want to talk about alternatives?"

"We should, yes," Nova stated as if that was evident. "Let's consider the obvious: notifying the police."

"No," Desiree quickly declined in her deep voice. "There's too much we can't explain. Bliss, us, how do we explain why we're here? Why Brock murdered this guy? Brock clearly needs our help. He would never leave us out to dry."

"I agree with Desiree," Chaya cast her vote. "I wanna help Brock. I owe him."

"Agreed," added Marcus.

"I'm in," Celeste affirmed.

"What if he's innocent?" Nova questioned. "We are all loyal to Brock; this isn't a vote on his character, but he may be innocent – involuntary manslaughter or something. If he acted in self-defense, then this evidence would support him, not hurt him. Or, let's face it: it could be Gael. Let's talk to Brock first before we decide, or at the very least, let's look at this guy's wallet and phone and find out who he is. But a little more information is warranted before we move forward with aiding and abetting a possible first degree murder, don't you think?"

Nefertiti nodded her head in agreement. "It will take one minute to look at his ID. Let's do it. Chaya, fish in his pants for his phone and wallet, and bring them over."

"Why am I the one who has to do everything?" Chaya whined as she sulked over and crouched down next to the body. When reaching into the corpse's pants' pocket, her expression of disgust reflected a stage presence and desire to entertain her colleagues. She hammed it up as their unofficial stoner by exaggerating her expressions and using air quotes as often as she could. "Okay, you guys totally owe me a beer… and not the shitty 'locally-owned brewery' who will 'make it big next year after they're discovered at the Great American Beer Festival' kind of piss either. I'm so sick of these 'I grow my own experimental hops' hipster-motherfuckers who can't shave. Although, I don't mind a man with a beard 'kissing' me, but I digress. I want a decent fucking lager for pick-pocketing a dead guy. For real."

"Chaya!" Desiree half laughed, half yelled. "Girl, rein your shit in. This is serious. He's dead!"

"I'm either gonna laugh or cry right now," Chaya responded defensively. "I'm choosing to laugh, okay? Sue me."

Desiree gently instructed Chaya, "Just turn on the phone and look for something."

Chaya stood and pressed the button on the side of the phone. "Oh no," Chaya dramatically protested. "I'm not putting his finger on the phone to unlock it. Nef! Catch! This was your idea." Chaya forcefully tossed the cellphone across the room at Nefertiti who caught it effortlessly with one fast grab in the air.

Nefertiti wiped down the front of her clingy pastel dress as she stood up and walked over to the body. The right arm had some blood spatter that she tried to avoid. Without so much as a cringe, she carefully squatted down, pressed his index finger into place, and unlocked the phone. "Okay, let's see." Nefertiti walked back to the group with the heels of her shoes clicking against the tiled floor. "He has several Whatsapp messages from a Nick. Should I read them?"

"Yeah," a few people replied simultaneously as if the question were obvious.

"I'll go back a few messages. Terrance – I guess that's the name of this guy – says, 'In position, B arrived. B in kitchen, no sign of weapon.' What weapon, guys? Then, a half hour goes by and Nick – that's the other guy – responds, 'Terrance, where the fuck are you?' 'I'm getting nervous. If you don't respond by 7pm, I'm coming to kick your ass.' Ahhh!" She looked around for a clock on the wall of the kitchen. "It's 6:45 – what should we do?"

"We've got to write him back!" Desiree replied. "Tell him… tell him… 'All is cool. Sorry, I had to go take a dump.'"

"What?" Marcus laughed aloud. "In the woods? You're crazy, sister."

Chaya smiled as her high was peaking. "That's perfect, Dez. Fucking witty. That's how guys talk to each other, isn't it. It's all about farts and dumps. Very authentic. Right, Marcus? Especially you."

Still laughing, Marcus pawned off responsibility, "Don't look at me. That's not what I would say."

"Okay, brother," Desiree prodded him, "Tell her how to respond."

Marcus exhaled and thought for a second. "Whatsapp him back, 'All is cool. B inside alone. Just looked close. Nothing new to report.' How's that? General enough, right?"

Nova commended him, "Good job. Anything else on that phone, Nef?"

"I'll check in a minute," Nefertiti replied as she thumbed Marcus' message into Terrance's phone. *Send.*

"Okay," Nova punctuated a topic change. "If this Nick doesn't accept our message, he might be coming over here, so we can't wait any longer. Whether or not Brock did this, I've changed my mind. Let's clean up and get rid of the body. I'll find towels to soak up the blood."

"I'll find the cleaning products," Desiree stated. *Thanks for coming around so quickly.*

Marcus tried to think about how he could help best but wasn't sure. "What should I do?" he asked Sharon.

"Let's work on the body," she instructed. "We're the strongest. Let's grab a rug and wrap him up in it, but not one of Brock's expensive ones. Let's find a cheaper one in the basement. He has a guest room. Celeste, go find a hidden spot somewhere out there where we can bury him. Look in the garage, find a spade, and start digging. These mountains have big cats; we'll have to dig deep."

By the time Alice arrived at Brock's back door, everyone was working at high speed scrubbing, hauling, digging, rinsing, wiping, and mopping. The moment she realized what was happening, the toothy smile leapt off her face and was replaced with an expression of horror. "Brock!" she ran over to him in her light green sundress and stood over him. "Brock!" she grabbed his shoulders and shook him. She looked around at everyone. No one said 'hello' or spoke. It was as if they were in an eerie trance. *What the hell is going on Brock? Tell me what to do.* Her right arm seemed to be possessed as it raised up high over her right shoulder and slapped Brock hard and flat across his inert face. "Wake up!"

Brock's arms lashed out as he inhaled deep breaths. He shook his head a few times and then rubbed his face with his right hand as if to remove cobwebs. He stood slowly and half hugged – half steadied himself on Alice. "Thank God you're here," he whispered in her ear.

Cupping her cheeks, he kissed her gently on the lips and then fell into her safe embrace.

"Are you okay, babe?" Alice asked squeezing him tight. *What the hell is going on here?*

Brock pulled away and looked around to remind himself what had happened. *Terrance is dead. Shit. Gael is still alive.* His knees almost buckled under the cheap humiliation of his mistakes exposed so openly. "I must have passed out. This is madness. You have to go home, Alice. Get as far away from me as you possibly can."

"No," Alice replied as she grabbed hold of Brock's muscular shoulders to look him directly in the eyes. "I'm here. I want to help. Now you need to get it together. Everyone is here to help you, so just tell me what to do."

Brock looked at Marcus and Sharon loading Terrance into a rug and then rolling him up inside. Brock used both of his hands to wipe his face and rub his eyes. "How can I tell you what to do when I don't even know what to do?" His voice crackled with desperation.

"Okay, babe. Just start from the top. What happened before you passed out?" Alice pushed him into his seat and tried to use her most reassuring voice.

"Two detectives were here. I just went outside for like ten minutes, and this happened."

"Who came?" Alice asked as she pulled over a chair and sat down in front of him. "Sontag and Borratto?"

"Yeah, that's them," Brock confirmed. *That's right. She knows them.*

"Forty something's, one guy had lots of facial hair, skinny, the other one smelled like a smoker…" Alice described.

"Yeah." Brock continued rubbing his forehead. "That's them."

"Brock," Sharon yelled loudly to get his attention. "Who's this Terrance?" She and Marcus continued hauling the rolled rug toward the back door.

"One of Nick's goons," Brock answered at half volume, and then cleared his throat. Everyone stopped what they were doing to listen. "He's the one who beat up Gael. He came to my door with a gun to Gael's head, and then when I went outside to talk to the cops, Gael must have slit his throat. The cops were right fucking here when he did it! Right in the goddamned driveway!" *I'm so ashamed.*

Oh! A collective sigh of relief was audible among his colleagues. *Brock hadn't killed Terrance after all!* Although they had to clean up the murder scene because Nick might show up to check on Terrance, everyone now knew that Nova had been right. She alone had fully believed in Brock's innocence.

"Guys," Chaya wondered aloud while gesturing a symbol for scissors, "Should we do a little snip-snip of the ol' index finger?"

"Jeez," Alice rolled her eyes at Brock.

"What?" Chaya defended her suggestion. "Am I the only forward thinker here?"

Nefertiti reluctantly admitted that Chaya was right. "Wait. Sharon, Marcus, put him down. I'll do it. We need it for his phone." She walked over to the kitchen. "Brock, I'm gonna have to waste one of your cutting boards. Which one do you want me to use?"

Brock stood, reached underneath a counter, and produced a green, plastic board. "You'll want a butcher's knife too, I'm assuming."

"Thanks, Brock. And where do you keep your aprons?" Nefertiti opened the drawer where Brock was pointing and grabbed all of the aprons. She walked to the front door and handed them out to Desiree, Chaya, and Nova before she slid one over her own head and tied it around her waist.

Brock had placed the green cutting board and butcher's knife on the island.

"You're all welcome," Chaya stated loudly as she scrubbed pink and red circles against the wall next to the front door. "Fucking Gael, huh? What's wrong with that dude?"

"It's hard to believe that little Gael can be so ruthless," Desiree pondered aloud.

Sharon shook her head in disbelief. "Three. Gael has killed three men. How the fuck did we misjudge him so badly?"

Nefertiti hastily grabbed the board and knife and walked over to the body. She slipped off her royal blue designer high heels next to the couch and admitted, "Oh my God, I need a drink before I do this!"

"Let's all do a shot!" Chaya called out and took off her gloves. "Nef, what's your poison? Brock, I'm gonna help myself to your bar."

"Do I have a choice?" Brock joked as he walked over to the bar near his fireplace. Everyone took a break and walked over as he pulled shot glasses out from under the bar and placed them on top in pairs.

Chaya grabbed a bottle of vodka. "We need music! Brock, lets pump up Nef. Put on 'Walking On Sunshine.'" She lined up the glasses and then poured down the row each to the top.

Desiree looked at Nova who was clearly uncomfortable. "It's like she said, we are either gonna laugh or cry. Let's choose to laugh, even if it's ironically."

Nova smiled. *Okay. Suspend reality temporarily. Deal with it later.* "You're right. I'm on board now."

Brock punched the title into his phone, then smiled and planted a dramatic kiss on Chaya's cheek. "You drive me fucking crazy." He grabbed a small glass and lifted it in the air. "C'mon, everyone!"

Sharon, Alice, Marcus, Nova, Nefertiti, Chaya, Celeste, and Desiree each lifted their shot glass toward the center of their circle. They paused a second to see if Brock would toast, but when it was evident that he was distracted in thought, Nova stepped in and yelled with a smile, "May Terrence's finger be the only one Nef chops off tonight!"

"Here, here!" everyone laughed and upended their heads to let the liquor slide down.

"One more!" Chaya yelled. "Line 'em up, bitches!"

Without hesitation, the glasses were refilled and quickly chugged down a second time. *Here we go!* A space cleared for Nefertiti around the body, so she put the green plastic board down on the floor and kneeled. After reaching into the rolled rug to pull out Terrance's arm, Nefertiti gagged slightly as she produced his right hand. *This is barbaric.*

"Time for different music, Brock." Chaya declared. "Play 'Time To Say Goodbye.'"

"Be strong, Nef!" Desiree called out. "You got it, girl." To Desiree, Nefertiti, and all of the witnesses, the process of detaching Terrance's right index finger was more complicated than the simple admission that, indeed, Chaya was right; they need to unlock the smartphone. It was the creeping realization that by trying to thwart gangsters, they were becoming gangsters. Desiree was increasingly aware that holding a gun and pulling a trigger were two very different actions. *We are in the middle of some messed up shit here,* she thought as she watched Nefertiti. *I'm cleaning up blood from a murder that we are not disclosing to the police, and I'm cheering on Nef to chop off a finger. What the fuck?*

Although gruesome to everyone involved, Terrance's finger needed to be cut off or they could not rescue the teenagers. Suddenly the great room filled with the cheers of a thousand people from 2007, and Sarah Brightman's lilting, angelic voice counter-balanced the deeper, full-bodied tone of Andrea Bocelli's.

Desiree turned her head toward Chaya, "Really?"

"Terrance is saying goodbye to his finger! What?" Chaya did her best to keep a straight face.

Desiree shook her head in exasperation, "that stinky rug of organic material is not saying anything at this point." *You can do this, Nef.*

Nefertiti pushed the green plastic board underneath Terrance's hand and held it in place by his wrist with her left. "Guys, will blood spew out? I don't want to get it on me."

As a nurse, Nova felt that she should respond. "It's been long enough. The blood is coagulating according to gravity now. You should be fine."

Should be? Alice cringed.

We need the finger, Nefertiti told herself. *It's instrumental to the plan. You got this.* She looked at Terrance's hand closer. No rings. Nefertiti took a deep breath and lined up where she wanted to hit the finger – between the bottom and the middle knuckles. She practiced her swing and aim a few times, then drew the heavy butcher knife back above her head and let it fly down like a guillotine. It was a clean cut.

While half of Bliss and friends cheered and clapped at Nefertiti's accomplishment, the other half cringed as the severed finger moved to be half on and half off the green board. The winces were audible as she quickly picked up the finger to move it back onto the board.

At this point, Nova noticed how shaky Nefertiti's hands were, so she bent down with a hand on Nefertiti's back and rubbed it a little. "You did the hard part. I'll get the rest. Good job."

Nefertiti stood up and smiled to the cheers and dramatic applause from her friends. "Thank you! Time for me to wash my hands! Ikk!"

"Chaya," Nova directed, "would you get something to hold the finger?"

Chaya ran into the kitchen and wondered, *Where are we gonna put a finger? Who will carry it around? Will it be in a plastic sandwich bag shoved into one of our pockets? How long before it reeks of death?*

After Nova shoved the hand back down into the rug, Sharon and Marcus wobbled out the backdoor with the cadaver to find its final resting place. Nova put the finger in a sandwich bag and set it in the middle of the kitchen table.

"How about *that* centerpiece?" Chaya laughed. "Dinner conversation never had it so good."

After another ten minutes of searching through Terrence's phone, barefooted Nefertiti shouted and waved her manicured hand with two dazzling rings to get everyone's attention. "Hey, guys! Listen up. Nick responded and said to come back to their new location – and he sent the address! That's where the teenagers are! What should I say?"

Nova wanted Sharon for direction. "Hold up, Nef. Let me go get Sharon. She's outside with Marcus."

"Sharon," Nova began once they were all back inside the house, "Don't you think that we need to take that SIM card out of that phone and turn it off so that Nick can't track us here?"

"Not only Nick," Alice called out, "but so the police can't track him here either. Brock said that the two detectives that came to my office, came here earlier today too. So, they're keeping an eye on us. Look, I want to find those teenagers and get them out. Can we please send one last message to lure Nick away from the teenagers... maybe lure his whole team away from the new location and then we go in and rescue them?"

> "Dr. Zezza, we're group five: the concerned citizens. We would take the address of the slave-brothel, make a plan, and go rescue those teenagers."

"You are out of your mind, Alice," Chaya stated outright.

"I told you that she's a liability," Sharon agreed.

"Look, everyone," Alice stepped toward the center of the great room to be equidistant to everyone in her audience. "I know I mucked things up by calling the hotline from DIA..."

"You think?" Sharon called out angrily.

"...but I did it with the right intention. Those kids are out there in deplorable conditions. They're just kids, and they're getting raped and drugged-up and beaten. I'm not talking about some other country; I'm talking about our neighbors right here in Colorado. If you know something, do something, right?"

Chaya tried to make eye contact with someone and mumbled, "I don't think that's how the saying goes," but everyone purposefully ignored her out of courtesy for Alice.

Now that Alice held the floor, she tried to keep their attention until they agreed to find the captive teenagers. "We have to protect our own at the very least. You know why? Because if we rescue them, we rescue each other. That's the promise of a democracy. If we don't stand united with each other, we will fall – guaranteed."

Brock smiled at the floor upon hearing Alice's simplistic appeal.

Chaya whispered to Desiree, "Do all of her arguments hinge on platitudes?"

"She's an academic," Desiree whispered back. "This is probably how they talk. No shaming. You do your thing; she'll do hers. There's room for all of us."

Alice continued to enlist the support of Brock's coworkers. "At Bliss you claim to want to help women be their best selves. Well, a threat to justice anywhere is a threat to justice everywhere."

Chaya grinned and again joked with Desiree, "Seriously, MLK? I wish we were taking shots each time, this lecture would be a lot more entertaining."

"It's not just a question of moral imperative, either," Alice forged on. "I mean, I get the irony here: we are aiding and abetting a murder by burying a guy…"

Nefertiti interrupted and gesticulated wearing thick yellow dish gloves, "Not just a guy, Alice, he's a dangerous criminal directly tied to human trafficking. He's as bad as a Nazi. I have no ethical qualms with what we are doing. Maybe you do, but I certainly don't." She squeezed blood out of her sponge from the water bucket.

"Maybe…" Alice struggled to find a foothold in an effective persuasive argument, "maybe… you can donate a portion of your profit to safe houses and at-risk youth programs. Wouldn't your socially-conscious clientele feel better about where they're spending their money if they know that by using the gym or getting a massage at Bliss, they are fighting violence against women? So guys, it doesn't just make ethical sense and common sense, but it is good *business* sense. Nef, Nova, Sharon, what do you think? Are you in?" Alice finished with a hopeful tone.

"What are all of the rest of us? An after-thought?" Chaya jokingly complained.

Alice smiled. "Of course not. We all need to work together as a team. Now who is with me?" Alice walked closer to everyone and put her hand out in front with fingers spread out like a starfish.

Chaya rolled her eyes and mumbled, "Jesus, look at you."

Brock walked over and held his right hand over Alice's. "I'm in."

Geez, fine. "I'm in, you nutty professor." Chaya dramatically walked over and hovered her blue laytex glove a few inches over Brock's.

"Me too," Nefertiti smiled as her thick, yellow glove hung above Chaya's hand.

"All for one and one for all," Nova quipped as she winked at Chaya.

Sharon and Marcus looked at each other and then Sharon said, "We'll bring the muscle."

One by one, everyone formed a circle around the layers of hands.

"On my count, say 'go Bliss.'" Alice yelled, "1, 2, 3…"

"Go Bliss!"

✦ ✦ ✦ ✦ ✦

Detectives Sontag and Borratto sat at their desks across from each other in the Major Crimes and Investigations division of the Boulder Police Department after their visit with Brock. Borrato threw a sunflower seed at Sontag who was listening to a sound file on his laptop through his ear buds.

Sontag gave his partner an irritated look and then focused his attention back on the recording of an out of breath Professor Alice Zezza.

Alice: Sharon! Brock wanted me to call you.
Sharon: Excuse me, who is this?
Alice: It's Alice! The professor. I was talking with Brock over the phone a few minutes ago, and then Gael and some other big black dude rang his doorbell. He told me to call you and say that it was someone's birthday. Betts. He said it

was her birthday and that you would know what to do.

Sontag pulled the arrow to the left on the media player to back up the recording five seconds and hear it again.

Alice: Gael and some other big, black dude rang his doorbell.

Who are these guys? "Hey, did you search the name 'Gael'?" Sontag asked Borratto.

"Yeah, I'm waiting on the results," Boratto confirmed. "I put the request in ten minutes ago, so it shouldn't be long now. You get the recording of Alice's call to Bliss?"

"That's what I'm listening to right now," Sontag confirmed.

Alice: He told me to call you and say that it was someone's birthday. Betts. He said it was her birthday and that you would know what to do.

Sontag squinted and asked, "Did you catch that part about 'Betts' birthday?'"

"I did when I got the file." Boratto sat up and tossed some sunflower seeds into his mouth. "Are you thinking about her name or about the tone?"

Sontag pulled the buds out of his earlobes. "Both. It's code, right? 'He told me… you would know what to do.' So why would Brock need to send an action plan to his place of work? To a gym? And why wouldn't he just call them himself?"

"Because Gael and the other guy showed up at his door," Boratto reasoned hypothetically. "Brock must have felt threatened. Maybe he wasn't expecting them. What doesn't make sense to me is that we were just there. If he were in trouble, why would he refuse our help and simultaneously alert his place of work?"

"I don't know. Either we're not asking the right questions, or we're not asking the right people," Sontag replied. "Hold up. We got the results about Gael and Betts." Sontag double-clicked on an email attachment. "Okay, it looks like Betts is the other owner of Bliss. Brock and Betts are business partners. Oh, hello! Looks like she has served time on a prior: armed robbery. Now we're getting somewhere." He scrolled down through the text on his screen. "However, she's been in Atlanta for the last month, so she wasn't here during the time of the murders."

"And Gael?" prodded Boratto.

"Different story," Sontag headlined. "Gael was arrested in '17 for solicitation on Colfax."

"Now what is a prostitute doing over at Brock's house?" Boratto wondered aloud. "Alice said, 'Gael and some other black dude.' That means that Alice knows Gael by name but not the other guy. How would Alice know someone like Gael?"

I know! "He's the tipster," Sontag pointed in the air at Boratto as if he had just hit the bullseye in a game of darts. "Gael is the guy that told Alice about the sex trafficking. Who else could it be? That's why she called it in."

"I bet you're right. Alice called the hotline. Gael is the one who told Alice the location and the specific number of teenagers. That means that Gael knew about the location, but how?"

"Maybe," Sontag continued the chain of logic, "maybe he was there when there were teenagers and when the vics were alive. We could ask the blind guy John about Gael."

“Let’s not forget about the ‘birthday code’ at Bliss. We need to find out what that means too,” added Boratto.

“And, somehow, Brock connects Alice with Gael.” Sontag concluded their workday with plans for next week. “I’m done for the day. First thing Monday morning, if blind John is out of ICU, we should go talk to him. We also need to check out this Bliss gym.”

Detective Boratto stood and apologized to Sontag, “Sorry you had to work on Passover.”

“It’s alright,” Sontag replied. “We’re having our *sedar* tonight. Are you still going to the Easter sunrise service at Red Rocks?”

“Waking up at 3am on Sunday, yes indeed. Diane and the girls are excited.”

Sontag reacted to the time as if he had bitten into a lemon.

“Yeah, but it’s on my bucket list; I’ve heard it’s worth it.”

Chapter 18: Bliss To The Rescue

"We're scrubbing and strategizing, people," Chaya instructed as if she needed to remind her cleaning crew that they could perform two actions simultaneously.

Alice and Brock, from the stove of the kitchen, silently laughed at Chaya ordering around Nefertiti and Desiree. Alice lowered her voice to Brock for her next question because she didn't want to be overheard. "Brock, honey, you never said… why did you let Terrance and Gael inside? I don't understand. If he had a gun, you knew he was dangerous."

Brock recoiled. "Are you saying that this is my fault?" he whispered loudly. *You have a lot of nerve.*

Something is really wrong with him. "Brock, I'm just trying to understand. Maybe the hit you took to the floor has messed you up a little," Alice reasoned.

Brock snorted the irony out of his laugh, "So which part is the messed up part, Alice? When I got extorted $500 because Gael left his murder weapon inside my car? Or is it when I couldn't open my front door because it was blocked by a murdered corpse? Oh no, wait, it's when the stupid detectives told me that they watched you cum in real-fucking-time while you were on the phone with me." Brock was furious at the world for bringing him to his knees so quickly. He walked over and yanked open the door of his sub-zero refrigerator. "All of this is fucking messed up, Alice."

What? They watched me? Alice was mortified with embarrassment. *Those assholes!*

"I had the weapon literally in the palm of my hand." Brock pulled out a can of Coca Cola and a bottle of Havana Club's *Añejo 7*

Años rum. "Have a drink," he directed Alice. She strolled closer and leaned her hip against the kitchen island. Brock looked at her with defeated, blood shot eyes. He wiped some sweat from his forehead with the back of his hand as he pulled the top off the liquor bottle.

Alice paused until Brock filled two Waterford Crystal whiskey glasses with ice, rum, and Coca Cola. She gently touched her heavy glass against his and mumbled, "Cheers" without making eye contact. The cold bubbles tickled her mouth and throat. "I just don't understand any of this. Why are the detectives watching me? More importantly, why did you let Gael and some stranger with a gun in?"

Get the fuck off my back! It's enough already! Brock knew he needed to coach himself before he made a bad situation much worse. *Take a breath, Brock,* he told himself. *Wait before speaking. I have waited my whole life for someone as good as Alice. She's smart and positive. After all of these years, I'm now ready for her. She's always been ready for a guy like me, so in her mind, she's just having a fight among equals. I should too. Fight with her like an equal and don't take cheap shots. I'm better than that now. Do it. Rise to the occasion or regret it later. Answer her question.*

"I know letting them in wasn't logical, babe. My only defense was that Terrence said he wanted out of the gangster life. I was super-high and super-happy; I had just made you cum by my voice and that was so much fun. You cumming made me higher than any drug." Remembering it, he clasped Alice's drink and set it down off to the side on the countertop. He then took her by the wrist and pulled her into his butcher's pantry off the kitchen. He grabbed her by the waist and lifted her up to a sitting position on the counter. His kisses were fervent as he pushed his midsection between her legs.

The truth was that Brock felt vulnerable by his bad choices and found solace in sex. That was a familiar script, one he knew well. Hitting the marks, facing the audience, holding a photogenic pose all made him feel in control. Cumming and making someone else cum made him feel powerful. However, admitting that his decision was partially a frivolous whim not based on empathy or logic but rather a product of being high and tipsy… well that burn was too severe. *All of these people's lives have been forever altered because of me!*

The palm of Brock's hands opened and held both of Alice's thighs as his tongue lapped at her mouth like a salt lick. He slowly slid his hands under the edge of her dress and pushed forward until the tips of his thumbs and fingers touched the edge of her underwear.

Alice's clit immediately came to life and electrified. "Brock, the others…" she said when her mouth was free, but her whole body quickly fell into harmony with his.

Between long kisses, Brock maneuvered his right thumb to locate her soft nub under the top of her pelvic bone. He noticed how quickly Alice let go of him and braced herself on the counter. "Good girl. Lift your pussy up to me, baby," he ordered. He rubbed upwards once and waited for her to exhale. "Does that burn just a little?" She nodded, so he kissed her to suck and bite on her lower lip. "Good girl. I want it to tingle." Again, he pressed and pushed it upward then removed his thumb. He loved hearing her breaths change. Sometimes she held it while other times she gasped.

Brock continued to whisper in Alice's ear, "When I tell you to 'bloom', I want you to push yourself open like a blooming flower, okay?" He settled into another long kiss where she sucked on his tongue. On his next gentle rub upwards, he continued to press his thumb at the top for a few seconds. He freed his tongue and said, "Bloom, baby."

Alice focused and dropped her pelvic floor as if she were throwing opening French doors to a field of sunflowers. She pushed against the counter and held her breath, ready to cum, when Brock removed his thumb. The doors started to close, so she resumed breathing. *You tease!*

"Next one, baby, I want you to cum. Here we go." Brock entrapped her tongue and sucked on it like a baby goat. Once again, using only his thumb, he rubbed and pressed and told her when to bloom.

Alice kissed her way through the orgasm as if she were helping Brock taste it. Peaking, she grabbed his forearm and pushed his fingers deep inside of her. She gave way like hot lava erupting from a distant volcano on the horizon at sunset.

Brock smiled as the after-shocks diminished and stopped. Slowly, he withdrew his hand. "I love making you cum and listening to you cum, watching you cum, feeling you cum…"

Just then, they heard Chaya yell dramatically, "Now that we are done cleaning the foyer, we can move over to the kitchen now. Here we come to the kitchen! There's still some more cleaning to do!"

Alice hopped down off the counter and righted her dress and hair. She grinned and motioned to Brock's hard on and whispered, "What are you gonna do?"

Brock smiled his Hollywood smile as he held his cock through his pants and shooed her away. "Go, go. Don't worry about me."

Chaya continued to forewarn her interruption as she stepped closer. "We still need to pour out our buckets full of blood!"

Alice's face scrunched up as if she had eaten something sour. "Ug. I think they may know something. I'm coming! Thanks, Brock." She swiftly smooched him on the lips and walked out to the kitchen before she was seen in an uncompromising position.

In contrast, Brock hid by moving in the opposite direction through the other end of the butler's pantry and out to the dining room near the front door. He grasped the back of a mahogany dining room chair white knuckled and exhaled. *I really need to unload right now.* He headed toward his bedroom unnoticed because all of the ladies had moved into the kitchen. Inside his extra-large, walk-in closet, he sat on his bench. It was a vintage, distressed, leather bench that he typically used when he put on his shoes. *Listen.* The only noise he could hear was chatting in the kitchen. *Good.* Brock stood and grabbed a gray t-shirt to cover the expensive bench, then dropped his pants and boxer shorts to his ankles. Indecent thoughts of Alice swirled in his head as he tugged.

✦ ✦ ✦ ✦ ✦

Nearly all of Terrance's blood had been soaked up or wiped off from Brock's front door, walls, and tiled foyer. It had been a painstaking task. The last step was cleaning up the kitchen sink and counter tops, then Nova, Chaya, Desiree, and Alice would be finished. The second crew was outside digging the final foot of Terrence's grave in the post-sunset dusk of Brock's backyard. Sharon, Marcus, and Celeste took turns shoveling under the cover of a sprawling, coniferous Piñon Pine tree. Their late-arriving lookout, Brock, stood in a clearing about ten feet away from them with his arms crossed over his chest. Celeste was already in the hole spelling Marcus and Sharon.

Once the cleaning moved into the kitchen and Alice started discussing a plan, Chaya wanted to go get high with Brock again. *I can't do any of this straight.* It had been about forty minutes since the last time. Her eyes needed a moment to adjust to the darkness as she stepped out onto his grass backyard. The orchestra of bugs became louder with each step. She had offered to bring Brock back inside to discuss the night's plan with Alice, Desiree, and Nova, because no one was quite sure what to do except Alice. *And that's a train which needs a conductor*, Chaya mused.

The thick chem-lawn ended at the edge of Brock's underground sprinkler system, twenty feet from the back door, and as she stepped off the dark green grass onto the natural Colorado terrain of red dirt with patches of short grass and shrubs, she pulled out her Pax. Her last high was coming to an end, and she wanted to continue the buzz so that she kept the flow of her best-self going. *If there's ever a time for me to be at my best, it's fucking now. There's no room for error here tonight. The world is depending on me.* She then laughed at her gross exaggeration. *Eh, there's some truth to it though with these numbskulls.* To Chaya, she got in her own way more often straight than when she was high. *So maybe I'm a little too animated sometimes, so what? I'm happier, I'm funnier, and I'm kinder,* she justified her perpetually altered state of mind to herself.

Up higher on the hill, Brock stood a few feet away from Sharon and Marcus who were watching Celeste dig from the bottom of the hole. "Hey," he greeted his smoking buddy Chaya as she approached.

"You guys have made a lot of progress! How are you feeling, Brock? You good?" Chaya asked as she handed him her black vaporizer.

I'll be fucking better than good once I take a hit. "My head hurts a little where I fell, but otherwise I'm fine." Brock inhaled a long breath and held it in for ten seconds before he blew it out. "A little embarrassed is all. Hey guys, you want to take a hit?" he invited the diggers.

Sharon and Marcus walked over. They all passed around the Pax and vaped in silence for a few minutes. The sound of the metal shovel plowing into the dirt below and then flinging it up to the surface sliced through the white noise of crickets and cicadas several times before Chaya spoke.

"Are you leaving the rug on him or are we taking it back inside?" Chaya asked and then took her last long draw for the time being.

Sharon answered, "Let's just leave it on. It's full of blood, piss, and shit anyway. I wish we had some lye."

"And some face masks. Hey, Brock," Marcus asked, "Do you have baking soda?"

"Yeah. You can use that instead. Good idea. C'mon, I'll show you." Brock, Chaya, and Marcus turned downhill toward the light pouring out of all the windows like dry ice from an unnecessarily dramatic Halloween decoration.

Chaya mumbled to herself, "Fucking light pollution."

"Be right back, Sharon," Marcus assured her as he followed with heavy footsteps.

Sharon walked over to the hole and avoided the area where Celeste was throwing the dirt upwards. "What a fucked up night. Thank God I'm high."

Celeste was tired and her shoulder sore. "Is that wise?" she asked as she threw the spade into the hard ground.

"There's a lot of not-wise things happening here tonight, Celeste." *Why the fuck are you being all judgy?* Sharon pulled out her ponytail from its band and placed the black ring between her teeth. With her fingers, Sharon then combed her long black hair away from her round face and formed a new ponytail with the elastic band. "I don't think that me being high is going to fuck anything up. You can drive if that's what you're worried about. It's all good."

Celeste smiled at the irony of Sharon's statement and swung the shovel as hard as she could into the dirt below. *Yes, me at the bottom of a grave is 'all good'. True, true.* She took a few more swings and tosses as she thought about the first time she had found herself at the bottom of a pit, almost unable to get out. *I didn't make the pit alone, and I can't get out of it alone.*

Marcus jogged up the hill with two boxes of baking soda in hand.

"I'll take a turn now," Sharon offered. "You've gotta be tired."

"As history repeating itself," Celeste replied as she handed up the shovel to Marcus at the surface. *Who would have ever thought I would be digging another grave?* As they had already done multiple times that evening, Marcus and Sharon kneeled and each grabbed hold of one of Celeste's upper arms to pull her up and out of the grave. "One, two, three!" Once out, Celeste shook the dirt out of her brown mane by bending over and scratching her scalp vigorously with both hands. She wiped her glasses clean with the inside of her shirt and returned them to her face.

"Good job," Sharon said to Celeste more as an end to a conversation rather than a compliment. "Why don't you go in and grab a shower, we can finish up here."

"Are you sure? I can help you toss him in," Celeste double-checked.

"I'm sure. We're fine," Sharon confirmed.

As if she were agreeing that their conversation had finished and she was moving on to the next step, Celeste exhaled a sigh that included the word, "okay" before she walked away toward the house. "Easy does it, you two."

Sharon had already moved on in her mind to the next step like she was checking off a list. "Let's just pitch him in. It's deep enough," she remarked to Marcus as Celeste thumped down the hill. Sharon bent over and grabbed the end of the rug with black leather shoes sticking out.

Marcus mirrored her and grabbed the opposite end where Terrence's neck was unnaturally bent at gravity's will. He was too heavy to swing, but they counted to coordinate the labored toss, "One, two, three." The body and rug were heaved just high enough to fall down into the hole. Marcus ripped open one box of baking soda and sprinkled it all out from left to right. "Should we say a prayer?"

"Fuck that," Sharon immediately retorted. She ripped open the other box and sprinkled it into the hole over the end with Terrance's head.

"He was a brother," Marcus reasoned as if that were reason enough for him.

"He was also a rapist and God only knows what else," Sharon argued as she violently shook the last remnants from her orange box and then threw it down the hole too. "Prayers aren't gonna do him any good. Pray for our brothers and sisters overseas."

Marcus' head tilted to the side and nodded slightly to agree with her.

Shovel-by-shovel, Sharon started loading the pile of stucco-colored soil on top of the corpse. *Down is so much easier than up.*

As often happens when stoned people talk, Marcus and Sharon chatted about whatever was on their minds regardless of whether or not it was logical or relevant. "Why doesn't Celeste talk?" Marcus asked Sharon as he got down on his knees and started pushing the dirt into the hole with his hands. "These jeans are so ruined."

"She does," Sharon responded diffidently and with effort each time she took a downward swing into the loose pile. "The simple answer is that the heart wants what the heart wants. Logic be damned."

"That's the answer to a whole lot of questions actually," Marcus stated his truth.

Sharon stopped shoveling and thought about it for a minute from her stoned state of mind. "Yep. You get it then." In silence they continued to work down the pile of earth until the surface was flat. "I'll just toss this extra around. Can you put a ton of pine needles over the hole to hide it and make it blend in?" She threw the scoops to her left and right as hard as she could to disperse it in a layer thin enough to not be seen in broad daylight.

After a minute, Sharon completed her answer as if she had not paused and was still narrating her stream of thought. "The longer you work with us, Marcus, the more you'll see that we're all loyal to Bliss, Brock, and Betts for our own personal reasons. Our hearts led us to them, to where we are today. Celeste is an especially good example of this. We follow our hearts and fuck up our lives brilliantly. However, in the end, it's all worth it because we took a chance, played the wild card, and won. The essence of life is to believe in yourself enough to risk great defeat for great reward.

"I mean, when you think about it, do you remember anticipation? Like real anticipation… like you wait and deny yourself or are denied something for years… year after year your heart longs for something so personal, so unique to you that it leaks out as if a dam is cracking and gushing out the foamy truth. You can't stop from being you. I can't stop from being me. That type of anticipation is matched by the most rewarding completion of one's self. When the heart gets what the heart wants, there is no parallel euphoria. For me, every minute of a satisfied heart is pure, effervescent joy."

Kneeling under the moonlight, Marcus was mesmerized in his high by Sharon's panegyric on following one's heart. He looked up at her and thought, *you're fabulous*. "That's exactly it," he agreed. He hoisted himself to a standing position and clapped his hands up and down his jeans to get rid of the excess dirt. "When my wife was alive, that's how I felt. She truly completed me. Every day with her was that joy. That's why, like now, sometimes I'm nostalgic and I miss her, but that period is over, you know what I'm saying? I feel so lucky to have shared that with her, but there is this finality, like that portion or stage of my life is over. This time is not part of that time, and if the joy can happen once, then it can happen again."

"Yeah, exactly," Sharon replied as she finished flinging the dirt everywhere. "That's what I'm getting at: once a person takes that risk and follows their heart, they know that it can be done again and again."

The back porch light flickered them to distraction. They both tried to remember why they were talking about this topic, but neither was able to. Then, they each tried to remember what they had just said – because they knew it was something deep, and of import, but they couldn't. Instead they caught their breath and looked in the opposite direction of the house, up at the moon and thousands of stars. Marcus suddenly flashed back onto his interview experience with Celeste for some reason unknown to him and said, "Celeste is cool even though she's quiet. She gives great head."

"Ew, gross, Marcus," Sharon scolded. "I don't want to hear about it. Compartmentalize! Are we done?" She lifted her hand up to high-five him and change the subject to the next item on her mental list.

"Yep," Marcus replied as he slapped her hand. "Man, I need a shower."

"Me too, let's go." Sharon and Marcus walked downhill with heavyweight, clomping steps into the back of the house. The lights blinded her for a second, and then she was able to refocus on everyone in the kitchen. They took off their dirty sneakers and left them next to the door with all of the others. *No one is cleaning?* Sharon looked across the great room at the front door, and to her astonishment it was blood-free. She walked closer in her sweaty, grimy socks to inspect it and was pleasantly surprised at the absence of incriminating evidence. *Right on.*

Brock caught Sharon's eye from across the room and said, "Sharon, you and Marcus can shower over in my bedroom. Celeste is using the one in the basement. Just grab any towels you want guys. Help yourselves to my clothes too. There's a big box of Bliss promotional t-shirts right there. Take whatever fits. I can throw your stuff in the wash. Don't be shy. Take whatever you need."

"Thanks, Brock," Marcus said as he grabbed a navy blue t-shirt out of the box with the words "get BLISSed" across the front. He handed a black one to Sharon and walked down the hallway past the living room and into Brock's carpeted bedroom. The knob for the light, didn't work when he pushed on it. Sharon came in behind him and rotated the knob clockwise. Suddenly, the light increased in intensity.

"Dimmers," Sharon answered a question that wasn't asked. She walked toward the gray tiled *en suite* , threw the new t-shirt onto the counter, and then pulled her tank top and her sports bra up over her head. "Ughhh. I stink."

Marcus heard the shower water turn on. *Dimmers in the bedroom! Brock has some nice shit.* Marcus was familiar with dimmers in the dining room – arguably the nicest, showiest room in a house – *but in the bedroom? That's so boss.* He tossed the blue t-shirt onto Brock's bed and reached into his back pocket to remove his phone. He called his sister as he undressed. "Hey. Thanks for your help. How's it going? How's Gigi? Yeah, can I?" He changed his voice's pitch and sang his words to his daughter, "Hey, sweetie. How're you doing tonight? You miss me? Now don't give Aunt

Shuree a hard time. She's doing daddy a favor. Yes, of course you can help her. No problem. Okay, I'm gonna be a few more hours, so I want you to go to bed without me. When you wake up, I'll be there. Sure, pancakes for breakfast it is. Put Aunt Shuree on. Love you, honey. Sweet dreams, bye." He reverted back to his lower, staccatoed, brother voice: "Hey Shuree, Gigi can help you, but off-camera, okay? Make her a producer or camera-girl or something, but I don't want her on your vlog. Cool. Cool. I'll be home before midnight, I hope. Thank you my Wakandan general. Yeah, I won't forget. Bye."

✦ ✦ ✦ ✦ ✦

"Dear Sister Shuree," Shuree read from the email on her laptop. Her makeup was flawless and dramatic for her internet audience. "Why am I a cat person?" Her niece Gigi giggled off camera to which Shuree briefly gave her the stink eye. "Cats are self-centered and toy with their prey mercilessly. Dogs however, want to please and are excited to help. I feel like I'm stuck in cat-prison, Sister Shuree, doomed to only be worthy of attention when these clawed critters need me. What can I do? Signed, Wanna-be-a-dog-owner."

Shuree looked up to the table in front of her and addressed the camera on her cell phone directly: "First of all, no one woke says 'owner' anymore. Second, if you were actually talking about animals, this would be a lot easier. You could give away your cat and adopt a dog. Done. But what you're really talking about is your preference to not be needed or wanted by your significant other. Dogs are a great metaphor because they give so much love, but they also expect it from you too. They require training, time, and attention.

"So let's get specific: the significant others you're attracted to act like cats, and now, you feel unsatisfied. You're ready to try a significant other that is more like a dog, someone who gives you lots of attention and expresses their love regularly. Is that about the gist of it?

"Do you know what I hear? To me, it sounds like you need to be reminded that you have value, that you're worthy. Honey, I hate to say it, but you aren't going to find this in a pet or a partner. You feel undervalued because you are undervalued. Undervaluing someone is a choice. Boo on them. They should do better by you. But what's your excuse? Why are you undervaluing yourself? Why are you settling for someone who undervalues you? Stop that. Do different.

"I recommend that you incorporate play into your life. Ritualize it. Build it into your schedule so that every day you are giving yourself a gift. It could be with a fun niece…"

Gigi ran in front of the camera with her arms wide yelling, "It's time to play! Play! Play!" when Sister Shuree's cell phone rang. Gigi ran right up to it and the camera, and looked closely to read the caller ID. "It's daddy!"

✦ ✦ ✦ ✦ ✦

Marcus heard the shower stop. He removed the rest of his clothes and walked onto the tile in Brock's bathroom and shower area.

He immediately looked down at his feet as if he was angry at them. "Are you kidding me?" He asked rhetorically. "Heated tiles?"

"Brock lives large," Sharon responded as she grabbed a towel and wrapped it around her waist leaving her chest exposed. She pretended to not notice that he was nude and walked over to the mirror to pick through Brock's self-care products.

Similarly, Marcus pretended to ignore Sharon's small, supple breasts and the fact that they had had sex during his interview. *Business*, he reminded himself as he stepped under the waterfall showerhead. *Stay in your lane, Marcus.*

At the sink, Sharon kept her back to Marcus yet her gaze on him in the reflection. She could see every detail of his milk chocolate-brown body clearly through the Plexiglas shower walls as he lathered himself up. The white shampoo bubbles meandered over and around his stomach and thigh muscles as if they were riding a floatation device on the lazy river at a theme park.

"I can feel you looking," Marcus jokingly accused with his eyes closed as he rinsed shampoo from his scalp.

Ha! Sharon smiled. "Don't worry. I'm leaving. I'm gonna go look through Brock's closet to see if there's anything inexpensive that we can ruin."

Marcus sang Drake to himself as he spied Sharon leave out of the corner of his eye, "Started from the bottom now the whole team here, nigga… we just want the credit where it's due, I'ma worry 'bout me, give a fuck about you… started from the bottom now we here." He turned off the hot water and grabbed a towel to dry off. "Shit, even his towels are softer and bigger than mine." He wiped his face and then wrapped the plush towel around his waist. In the empty bedroom, he stood alone. *Where's Sharon?*

"Will you help me for a sec?" Sharon asked as if she couldn't zip up the back of her dress.

Marcus looked at where her voice was coming from. "Sure. Where are you?"

"Back here."

Marcus walked around a wall to where there was a large, semi-hidden closet. Sharon stood in front of him naked with her hands on her hips like Wonder Woman ready to fight crime. He laughed. "What's up with you?"

"I'm having trouble," Sharon grinned, "and I need your help."

"Oh yeah? With what?" Marcus' hard on formed under the white towel around his waist as he inspected the fit, muscular body in front of him.

"I'm not compartmentalizing very well," Sharon smiled openly as she approached Marcus. "Can you help a girl out? Just a quickie before we go? Just to get the nervousness out?"

Marcus met her embrace halfway. "Hell yes."

It was a little hard to kiss through their laughs and smiles. Marcus' tongue didn't want to leave until he got all of his giggling out. *Jackpot! I love sex when I'm high!* "I'm so psyched. Was it seeing me naked? Is that what turned your engine on?"

"You're so weird," Sharon smooched him.

"No, I mean it," he giggled and lifted his arms like a body builder in the air. "Was it my guns?"

"I don't know! I just feel like there's sexual electricity in the air. So are we really going to do this?"

"Right here, right now, yes ma'am," Marcus practically panted as he pulled his towel off to reveal his hard on.

"Bam! And there he is!" Sharon narrated the arrival of Marcus' penis in a way that made perfect sense in her very high state of mind.

How about that. "He did turn you on! That's good." Marcus winked and pulled Sharon in closer for a kiss. "I like him too. He's my BFF!" Marcus' hands hastily found their way onto her hips which he began rubbing.

Sharon giggled. "How about a little missionary here on the rug?" She pushed him away from her, then grabbed his hand to pull him down. She arranged herself on her back and spread her legs up and wide. "Let's bang."

Marcus directed himself inside her and then lifted her legs over his shoulders. After he pushed in the first time, he pulled out nearly all of the way. "I'm so happy!" he smiled as he slowly pushed his way back in. When he was inside as deep as he could go, he stopped moving and held himself there. "Is this where you want me?" *Hold it.* Then he swiftly pulled out and thrust back inside of her. *Hold it.*

Sharon muscled her legs out from under his shoulders and grabbed his hips. Through brute force, she pushed and pulled his hips until she controlled his angle, depth, and speed.

Sex with Wonder Woman is definitely different, Marcus realized. *She's as strong as me.* He conducted a quick internal audit. *It's still all-good though, isn't it? It is, yeah. It's totally fine. Okay, now she's making me feel better than fine.* Marcus was about to cum. *Okay! Time to take this Batmobile out of autopilot now.* Marcus shifted his weight from his arms to his knees thereby disabling a portion of Sharon's super power. "Cum with me; let's do this," he wished aloud between smiles and kisses.

Sharon arched her back as Marcus' thrust hit her g-spot, "fuck you."

"There you are," Marcus continued in earnest, reading Sharon's face and breathing. *Hold on until she cums. Hold on.*

"You go first, then I'll go," Sharon instructed between breaths. Her eyes squeezed closed tighter the more she focused.

Such a control freak. "No, c'mon. At the same time." Marcus could hear her hold her breath as he pushed to a faster rhythm, and noticed her hands directing the angle for his hips. *She's ready. I'm ready. Wonder twin powers: activate!*

✦ ✦ ✦ ✦ ✦

Ten minutes earlier, the inside half of the Bliss team had been strategizing their next move in the kitchen. "Let's work backwards," Alice had suggested as she gathered all of the aprons given to her by Chaya, Desiree, and Nova. They had sat around the kitchen island in various states of tired to exhausted. Desiree had used her forearm as a pillow for her head, and Nova had yawned unapologetically wide. "The end result is that…"

Chaya had thought that this conversation would be much more tolerable if she were high. Straight, she might not be as polite as she should be with Alice. *I know Brock likes you, lady, but you're a dangerous kind of stupid. No way am I following you.* "Hey Alice," she had interrupted, "why don't I go get Brock for this discussion." She had started walking away before hearing the reply.

Alice had put the four bloodstained aprons off to the side on the counter. *Yuk. We need to start a load of laundry.* "Sure. Good idea." Once Chaya had exited, Alice had leaned into Desiree and Nova and whispered, "Am I crazy, or does she not like me?"

"No one really likes you, Alice," Nova had tried to joke with a straight face. She was not good at staying deadpan. Instead, her smile had seeped out before the punch line was finished. *I tried.* "Just kidding. Sorry, I'm tired. We like you."

"Nobody else does though," Desiree had continued the teasing, "but we do, and that's not nothing. You got two fans in the club." She had lifted two fingers from her semi-horizontal posture laying on the countertop.

Alice had dramatically feigned embarrassment by covering her face with the back of her hand. "Why don't I make some coffee for everyone? We can't plan a good rescue with all of us falling asleep."

Once Brock and Chaya had returned ten minutes later, Alice had begun her speech again. "It's best if we work backwards. Let's figure out where we want to end up, then we can plan in the opposite direction, okay? So, we want to: one, rescue the teenagers, two, drive away safely with nobody hurt, three, we want to be unnoticed by anyone who can tell Nick or the police we were there. What else?"

Nova had added, "We don't want to leave any evidence."

Desiree had agreed, "Yeah, and we want to be prepared for whatever may happen."

Alice had seconded. "You're right, Desiree. We need a list of supplies. Brock, do you have a pen and paper?"

"Uh, yeah," Brock had said as he hopped out of his chair so fast that he nearly fell. He had jogged over to a kitchen drawer and clumsily shuffled through it until he pulled out a small notebook and a pen.

Is Brock high again? Alice had wondered. "Chaya," Alice had asked, "Would you take notes?"

"Sure," Chaya had agreed ironically. *Really? You want me to take notes when I'm high?* She had titled the page, "Bliss To The Rescue." *Play nice, Chaya,* she had reminded herself.

Celeste had walked into the house and removed her sneakers. In an unexpressive, flat tone she had asked, "Brock, do you have a guest shower I could use?" *I'm done smelling like death.*

"Of course! You can shower off in my bedroom, if you want," Brock had offered.

"That's okay. Do you mind if I use the one in the basement?" Celeste had requested looking at the dirt caked on the back of her hands.

"Absolutely. Help yourself to the towels down there," he had replied in a nonchalant voice. "Oh, but you'll need a clean change of clothes. Let me grab you some. Do you want one of our new Bliss promo shirts? They're really soft." Brock had hopped up and walked across the great room and down the hall into his bedroom.

Alice had then pulled several coffee mugs down from their shelf and put them in the center of the group along with sweet Agave syrup and low-fat milk. "Hey Brock, grab us t-shirts too." She had watched Brock return back from his bedroom and heave a cardboard box full of t-shirts into the center of the great room and then shuffle down the stairs. "Two different pages, Chaya. One is the list of what we need to bring, and the other is for notes." Alice had grabbed the full pot of coffee and placed it on a hand towel on the island. "Let's organize the discussion into subtopics: problems getting in, problems getting out, solutions, and logistics."

That's not happening, Chaya had not written anything down. *You're so annoying.*

Nova had mixed her coffee and leaned in as Desiree had sat up and did the same.

"Okay, let's anticipate problems getting in," Alice had instructed.

In the bathroom in the basement, Brock had walked through an open door and realized Celeste was already in the shower. "I've got a wine-colored Bliss t-shirt and sweatpants here for you. Thought you might like some fresh socks too." He had looked over at the shower curtain, then walked away.

Upstairs, Alice had not wanted to forget any important points. "Chaya, write these down. Nick and his thugs will be there. We could be traced or tracked, like by his phone. We need to avoid that, right Brock?" she asked as he reappeared from the basement and sat down.

Chaya do this, Chaya write that, Chaya had repeated in her mind as if she were squabbling at the playground in elementary school.

"Yeah." Brock had pulled out another idea that had been on his mind intermittently throughout the evening, "There could be a lookout or others defending the brothel. I bet they have a lookout in another building who can see the entrance and potential cops."

"Good point," Nova had agreed. She had looked over to the back door as Sharon and Marcus entered and kicked off their sneakers.

Brock caught Sharon's eye from across the room and said, "Sharon, you and Marcus can shower over in my bedroom. Celeste is using the one in the basement. Just grab any towels you want guys.

Help yourselves to my clothes too. There's a big box of Bliss promotional t-shirts right there. Take whatever fits. I can throw your stuff in the wash. Don't be shy. Take what you need."

"Thanks, Brock," Marcus had said as he took two t-shirts from the box and walked down the hallway past the living room and into Brocks carpeted bedroom.

"Okay," Alice continued. "What about getting out?"

Nefertiti set down her coffee. "We need to take three cars, right? All of us will fill two, and if there are teenagers, then we'll need a third. We should figure out who is driving."

"Marcus, Sharon, and you, Brock, right?" Desiree questioned. "Brock, are you okay to drive?"

I don't know if I would count on Marcus and Sharon, Chaya silently disagreed.

Nova calculated Brock's pause and intervened. "Brock, I can drive your car if you want."

"Sucking up to the new boss already," Chaya joked. "Don't give me that look, Nova. I'm just teasing."

Nova winked dramatically at Chaya.

Chaya wrote, "DRIVERS: Nova + anyone sober / straight." After thinking about it, she struck a line through straight and wrote above it "un-high" and laughed to herself.

"Thanks, Nova," Brock said. "That would be great."

"Or I can do it," Alice volunteered.

Chaya vetoed that idea. *No way.* In her notes, she parenthetically added, "(except Alice)." "Let's leave the Bonnie and Clyde stuff to Bliss. Nova, you drive."

After twenty more minutes of planning, team Bliss worked out a way to distract Nick away from the teenagers, and moved on to dealing with the police. Nefertiti pushed Terrence's phone toward the finger in the center of the island away from her. "As far as GPS goes, the phone is off right now. As long as it's off, I don't see how Nick can follow us. The police, however, I don't know."

Brock winced at hearing the word 'police,' remembering the state in which the detectives had seen his new girlfriend. "Yeah, they are watching Alice, for sure. I think they tapped your phone too, babe. When they visited me, they somehow knew that Gael and Terrance were here. They didn't say 'Gael' or 'Terrance' by name, but they said enough for me to know that they are watching and listening to you very closely."

Alice covered her mouth with the palm of her hand. "Holy crap, my phone too?" *You're just telling me this now? What the heck is wrong with you?*

"Voila!" Nova smiled. "There's your answer!" Everyone looked at Nova either with skepticism or confusion. "If the police tail us, Alice can call them and lead them on a wild goose chase. She could make up an emergency or something."

Chaya nodded her head to show that she was impressed. "I still don't think Nick is going to buy in to Terrance being kidnapped, but that's a good idea about the police, lady. Okay, next on the list: fleshing out a lookout."

"I think you mean 'flushing out,' Chaya," Alice corrected gently. *Why did I just do that? Why do I need to correct people all of the time? Crap. Now she's offended.*

"No, I mean I want to flesh this guy out from his lookout spot, like make him come out into the open," Chaya disagreed.

Alice tried to let it go. "It's not a big deal. Forget about it. I think you just over-corrected. Let's move on. It's just that the expression is 'to flush out' when you want to get rid of something. You're not far off though…"

"How much do you want to bet?" Chaya challenged.

"There's no need," Alice put up her hand to stop. "It's an inconsequential non sequitur. Let's just move on."

Inconsequential non blah, blah, blah. Then why did you correct me? Chaya mentally mocked Alice and turned to Brock as the authority figure in the room to settle the argument, "Tell her I'm right. C'mon professor, Google it in your phone."

"Can we let this go? We have teenagers to rescue," Alice said as if she were taking the higher ground. "There's a bigger picture here."

"You're wrong, Chaya," Celeste stated in a low, definitive voice and then took a sip of her lukewarm coffee. "'To flesh out' is to add more detail. Now, focus."

"Fine." Chaya acquiesced dramatically as if she were being forced by her mother to apologize to her sister, "I'm wrong."

Nefertiti chose her verbs carefully as if she were navigating the 38th parallel. "We can form a distraction, one that would pull the lookout's attention away. Once we know who it is, one of us can keep an eye on him.

"How?" Desiree asked.

"Well," Nefertiti continued, "I'm open to ideas. Maybe someone could walk around with a soap-board sign saying something specific like advertising for the brothel. Of course, they don't want attention, so if Nick and his guys are gone, then the lookout would call Nick. Nick would probably tell him to go deal with it directly."

"Oh," Desiree pointed at Nefertiti as if she finally understood something, "you mean those people dancing on the street corners with a big arrow… one of those people who spins signs. Got it. That would draw someone out. Good idea."

Chaya wrote, "big bozo-sign" on the supplies list.

Sharon and Marcus came out of the bedroom into the bright kitchen wearing their new Bliss t-shirts.

"Wow, nice hair Sharon," Nefertiti was impressed at the perfectly rendered Dutch braids running down each side of her head. "Did you do that yourself?"

"Thank you, thank you." Sharon posed comically to show off her braids. "No way. I don't know how to do this. Marcus did it."

Chaya clapped. "Look at this hidden talent – Marcus! Can you do mine before we go?"

"Sure. I just need some rubber bands or hair ties. I'll go get the comb." Marcus jogged back to the bathroom. *Happy time!*

Desiree glanced over Chaya's shoulder at her list and sneered, "What the fuck is this now? Doritos?"

Chaya grinned, "Cry or laugh."

For the next hour, Bliss staff and friends sat around drinking spiked coffee, putting on colorful Bliss shirts, and getting their hair braided. They refined their plan, figured out where they could track down a big sign, and assigned everyone tasks. They even hypothesized a few Plan As and Plan Bs. Then, reality set in. Brock was the first to start shutting down into zombie-mode. He stared off silently in another zone. It soon spread like an apocalyptic virus. Disquiet filled their minds. Far off somewhere in the Rockies, a wolf cried out, then a second, then a whole pack.

Almost everyone had some version of *What if this goes sideways?* in their heads. There was a genuine accounting for oneself. *Have I done more positive than bad in this world? Have I taught my children enough to get on? Have I said my peace? What do I regret? Will I be mourned? Will I be a lasting memory? For whom? How will I be remembered? What if my worst fear was true?*

Nova stood and found an empty spot on the wall. She pushed every vertebrae of her spine flat against it by positioning her feet at an angle a foot in front of her. *Relief. If I had the ability to do it all over again, I would have better posture and sit in harder fucking chairs.* She thought of her two adult sons, and how surprising they turned out. She regretted that she wouldn't be able to say goodbye to her mother. *What a trailblazer! In the final calculation, I've lived a good life.*

Chaya thought of her parents and siblings. *I should have connected with them more.* She was proud of her move across the country. *So hard, but I did it. I made my own family here.* In her mind's eye, she saw an auditorium full of women whom she had helped over the years cheering and applauding her. She blew them kisses from the spotlight on center stage as they tossed her roses and flowers of all colors.

Alice longed for a way to bring an end to human trafficking. She considered the large buckets of live, blue crab at H-Mart each Saturday morning which, if not sold, laid slowly dying until Sunday lunchtime. *Is it culture entirely that ascribes value and levels to life?*

How am I valued by others? By my shit boss? My husband? Have I seeded enough soil?

Desiree knew she was right with the world. Her choices had been deliberate. The silence among her friends wasn't surprising. *We just made a murder vanish. That's pretty fucked up in and of itself. This risk level should not be acceptable, so what makes us so different? What makes me so sure? Good intentions. Trust over time. Spontaneity. Humor. Empathy.*

Being the parents of young children, Marcus and Nefertiti could not help but think about how their kids would turn out without them. *If I die today, will I have shown her enough? Taught him enough? Hugged them enough?* Marcus saw his daughter Gigi fast-forward 20 years as a lawyer with wildly braided hair in a pantsuit arguing a case in front of a judge and jury. He presided as mayor of Denver. *There is a lot more life to live, indeed.*

Sharon used the silence to think through their next steps: picking up supplies, creating two diversions, entering, locating the target, extrication, exiting to the car, driving back to Bliss. *This is happening. Three hours from now we will be back at Bliss and be toasting our success. Semper Fi!*

Brock zoomed past all preliminary egocentric responses directly to pending doom, possible death, and spiraled down to where he often was nowadays: at the very bottom. The end. *Me = invisible = vapor = rain = sleet = When will I be mixed up with the universe enough that I'm no longer me? How many clouds are needed to scatter me to nonexistence? = I thought I could dissipate into the ether. = Why isn't it working?*

Celeste interlaced her fingers then stretched them out in front of her. Several knuckles cracked. She looked around at how each person was handling this dreadful moment. *They need Betts. Betts would straighten this whole thing out.* She inhaled deeply through her nose and exhaled slowly through pursed lips to which Brock, Nefertiti, Alice, and Nova all unconsciously echoed with a sigh. *Let the healing begin.*

Chapter 19: The Rescue

"Betts," Brock called out for his lifeline in front of his new girlfriend, Alice, and everyone else in the chaotic in-take room. His many failures of the day left him feeling false and impotent. *How is this not all traced back to me?*

Betts heard Brock's low, quavering voice. She quickly stood up from the carpeted floor and grasped his hand hoping for clarity. "I'm here, Brock."

Betts, my girl. Prompt public confession seemed to him a worthy humiliation. Certainly there were many more self-flagellations to come. He fought against his tears as he began his long apology for *being such a piece of shit.* "Betts, you're gonna hate me," his voice cracked.

Betts covered Brock's lips with two manicured fingers. *Let me rip a page out of Nova's playbook.* Leaning into his ear, she dictated her marching orders: "You are going to keep your shit together for ten more minutes, do you hear me? Go to my office and lay down. I'll be there as soon as I can. But Brock, shut the fuck up right now. I don't want to see one God damned tear in front of our staff, you hear me? Get out of here, and let's deal with your shit privately." Betts then pulled away, dramatically squeezed his hand tighter, and said loudly, "Let's find fault tomorrow. Tonight, let's just keep everyone alive. If you need to go to my office to clean up, go ahead Brock. Go."

✦ ✦ ✦ ✦ ✦

"Heatherwood Trail, west side of North 75th Street, next to Boulder Creek," Nick stated their destination as he shifted his black Escalade into reverse and backed out onto the street looking over his shoulder and past Boo who sat in the back seat.

"*Vamanos*," Boo said to Jojo and his boss Nick. He adjusted the window so that there was only a one-inch crack and lit a cigarette.

Nick shook his head ever so slightly. He did not want to learn or speak or even understand another language. *Speak fucking American.* He hated that without trying, he understood several Spanish words here and there, including this one. Nevertheless, his *English-only if you live in our democracy!* opinion he kept close to his chest. Staying in the good graces of the Sinaloa cartel was paramount, and they all spoke Spanish. He was the monolingual odd-man out, not them. In addition, he knew that all successful businesses in Colorado needed trusted associates who were bilingual. Nick accepted his stretch and his limits, so he kept his opinions to himself. Boo was fairly useless except for this one, very necessary skill. As Nick headed northwest, he asked Jojo, "You bring the plastic handcuffs?"

"Yep," Jojo responded ineffectually. "This man-bun motherfucker is gonna have his nuts in handcuffs after I'm done with him." Then, Jojo paused. "How'd you think Terrance lost his edge?"

"Shot, I expect," Nick responded. "But how the hell could that little piece of shit get the jump on Terrance?" He drove with his left hand as his right moved like he was conducting an angry Tchaikovsky symphony. "Why was man-bun even there? Tell me that!"

As Nick ranted for the next ten minutes, Boo and Jojo passionately seconded all of his main points. *Hell yeah. Fuck that. You're so right.* They feared his retribution and his predilection for cruelty. They had heard enough stories about life as a cartel member in Mexico that they were able to put Nick in proper perspective: it can always get worse. Nevertheless, they were here now, and the heat was on 'man-bun', not them, and that's how they were happy to keep it. Then, the calls started coming in. First, Boo got a call from Carmen who yelled in Spanish so loud that Jojo got goose bumps. Then, Jojo received a very disturbing call that made him wide-eyed at Boo. *Nick is gonna lose it*, they both worried.

Nick, once given all the pertinent information, had the decision of the day: keep driving and rescue Terrance, *my main man*, but probably loose the property, or turn around and go fetch the property, but possibly let Terrance die. *Man-bun won't let Terrance die*, Nick reasoned. *If there is money to be made, Terrance has value. He'll stay alive another day or two. You would've done the same thing if you were in my boots, I know, Terrance. Time to double back, double quick.*

+ + + + +

To the best of her ability, Celeste made a distracting fuss, as was the plan. She had volunteered for this job because she knew she could mentally and physically handle anything that came her way. Even though it was Boulder, not particularly known for anything nefarious, it was still a bad section of vanilla-town, and it was nighttime. This is where Celeste stood dancing in her big advertisement for Nick's brothel: under a street lamp in the middle of a rarely used intersection, directly in front of the brothel. Even at more than a stone's throwing distance, Celeste could see an elderly neighbor close his front windows and cinch his shades in reaction to her. She knew her presence was having the desired effect already. *Good.*

Instead of the fancy, six-foot long signs with handles in the back for swinging around, Bliss had to settle for the sandwich board method: one poster board in front and one in the back connected by shoulder straps. Celeste had to use whatever was available in the supplies closet, which luckily was enough. Bliss had two poster-sized, Post-It note boards that could be connected with bungee cords. Alice, who had the best, large handwriting since she was a professor, wrote the ad in clear, block lettering that could be read from far away: "Have sex with underage slaves for free. Illegal brothel this way," followed by an arrow and smiley face. In case the detectives or local police stumbled upon her, Celeste asked Alice to write another four-line ad on the sheet below the top that said, "What do we want? Time travel! When do we want it? It's irrelevant!"

Celeste put the sign over her head and looked across the street facing the two-story brick building where the teenagers were. *Now what do I do? Dance? I'm not dancing, for fuck's sake. I'll move a little like this and like that, but no fucking dancing.* Celeste swung her arms and then pointed at the building across the street.

An undocumented Mexican woman towel drying a plate and looking out her kitchen window saw Celeste and her sign. She told her four-year-old son Joaquin in Spanish to go ask this woman why she was there. "*¡Rapido!*"

Joaquin promptly ran out the door, down the steps, and over two blocks to the white woman wearing big pieces of paper. His mother watched him through her window. "What are you doing?" he asked in a high-pitched child's voice with a Mexican accent.

Celeste took one look at this adorable Mexican kid with pudgy cheeks and thought, *there's no better attention getter than a cute kid talking to a weird stranger.* "Can't you read?"

Joaquin furrowed his eyebrows. "No."

"That's cause you're an undocumented immigrant, right?" *That should piss him off. Probably won't end up literate in either language though.*

Joaquin dramatically buried his head in the palm of his right hand and slowly shook his head. "No. I was born here. I'm just four; I can't read."

"Well, that makes sense, I guess," Celeste played along.

"So what are you doing? My *mami* wants to know," Joaquin pressed on.

"Oh, your mommy, huh? Tell her that I'm advertising a whorehouse. Tell all your friends and family." Celeste started moving her arms and pointing again.

"What's that?" Little Joaquin was confused about words he did not understand.

"A place where scumbags have sex with teenage slaves 'cause they're too limpy-dick with real women their own age." Celeste watched as her little friend's eyes bulged and then ran toward a brick building on her far left. After a minute, he returned with his mother, a teenager Celeste guessed was barely 17 years old.

Joaquin's pissed off mother spoke in Spanish, and then he translated replicating her tone of voice. "My mom says that you need to leave."

Am I good or am I fucking good? Celeste pulled out one of Brock's red sashes from her back pocket. As she swayed and pointed, the red cloth brought even more attention to her and this mother-son duo. "No. I'm advertising a whorehouse. *Una casa de putas*," she said purposefully in her worst English accent ever.

The teen mother was having none of this subterfuge. She pointed her index finger and launched into a litany of Spanish that her young son translated in the same vein as his young mother: bully. "Get out, old lady. You shouldn't be here. Are you fucking crazy? We don't want commercials. You'll bring the cops. Go!"

'We.' Bingo. Celeste calmly continued her arm movements and responded in an even tone, "Ask her why she doesn't want advertising. Everyone wants advertising these days. Tell her. I'm like Facebook and Instagram all rolled up into one tight hoochie. I'm making your mama *dinero*."

"*Mami,"* the boy translated to his mother in Spanish, *"she said that everyone wants advertising, but I don't understand what she is advertising. She thinks she's making you money*."

"Putas. Las niñas de Terri. Dile que ella tiene que decidir. Ella puede quedarse y morir, o chingarse."

Little Joaquin pointed his index finger up at Celeste's face and yelled menacingly, "You have a damn decision to make: you can stay and get a bullet through your head or you can leave and go fuck yourself."

Celeste cringed and felt a cold chill go up her spine. *What a shit species we are. This kid is doomed right from the start*. Just at that moment, a gunshot sounded from the building in question. In an instant, the teenager backed away, grabbed her phone out of her back pocket, and spoke with gestures so animated that Celeste needed no translation to understand. Celeste peeled off the front-and-back Post It note sandwich boards, threw them to the ground, and sprinted to her Prius two blocks away as fast as she could.

✦ ✦ ✦ ✦ ✦

The bass beat of MIA's "Paper Planes" pumped through Sandra's wire ear buds and wagged her head to and fro like a happy Rottweiler puppy. She relished feeling as powerful as a gangster by dancing with more neck rolls around the room in her red-checkered Vans high top sneakers. *Don't fuck with me!* This downtempo hip-hop music spoke to her old, Hispanic soul of 15 years. With a loaded .22 Ruger pistol in hand and a dark hoodie covering her hair, Sandra's fancy footwork glided her over to the bathroom. In the mirror, she dramatically played to her imaginary audience through deadpan poses and pointing the handgun at random targets. *I'm a mighty bad ass. A fucking killer. A baller. A winner.* She pushed her hoodie back a little to more fully see her drawn-on eyebrows and black lips sing along with the song, "Everyone's a winner now, we're making that fame, bona fide hustler making my name."

Sandra continued slithering down the hallway to the music. At the first open bedroom door she sang, "All I want to do is" and pretended to shoot her gun four times, then finished singing the chorus: "and take your money." At the second open bedroom door, she noticed a red headed woman with two thick braids wearing a red shirt outside the window peeping in. *What the fuck?* Sandra yanked her black, Stranger Things hoodie back and the right ear bud out to let it hang from the wire to the left speaker. Shoulders offensively wide, she strutted toward the freckled stranger. “What the fuck are you doing, *Roja*?”

Chaya pushed in closer to look through the window and decorative, steel bars, “Hey. Are you a slave?”

“A what now?” Sandra asked as if this stranger were crazy.

“A slave of the sexual kind,” Chaya clarified as her eyes zerod in on the semi-lit figure of a woman.

Sandra lowered the tip of her gun to face the floor. *She's got no game.* “I'm a teenager. Go away.”

“Yeah, yeah, yeah. That's what I mean,” Chaya explained. “You got kidnapped, right? Stolen from your parents?” She felt like she was making slow headway.

Sandra's sarcastic tone sounded typical of many teenagers trying to be annoying, “Uh, no.”

“Okay,” Chaya gave up and took a step backwards to view the whole side of the building lit by street lights. “Well, is there a whore house in this building? We're trying to save some sex slaves.”

Ha! Now it's clear. “You're looking for Terbear,” Sandra yelled through the windowpane. “But he isn't here.”

“Come again? I'm pretty sure he's not the guy I want, my little head-banger, but what's his name?”

“Terry-Bear.”

“Nope. That's not… wait. Terry, is he a big, black guy?”

Sandra talked to Chaya as if she had a mental problem. “Yeah, Terr-*ance*. Terry. Terbear.”

"That's the one! Yeah. Me and my friends are rescuing you right now!" Chaya was excited for the breakthrough. "Listen to me, my friends have gone through the window upstairs…"

"Shit." Sandra put her ear bud back into her right ear and jogged away with her pistol held at shoulder height. "All I wanna do is…"

✦ ✦ ✦ ✦ ✦

Five minutes earlier, two blocks away from Nick's new brothel, the three cars with Bliss staff in matching Bliss t-shirts waited for Celeste's signal. Marcus had braided everyone's hair except for Desiree and Nova whose hair was too short, and Nefertiti who simply preferred to leave it down. Marcus knuckle-bumped Chaya who sat next to him in his Prius. "We got this. We're ready."

"We are," Chaya replied as she adjusted the visor so she could better see her braids in the tiny passenger mirror, "but I don't know about everyone else."

"That's it. I see it!" Marcus exclaimed.

"Where?" Chaya flipped the visor up and saw Celeste off in the distant intersection waving a red scarf. As planned, the two cars pulled forward and down the alley beside the brothel.

"Ready?" Nova asked Sharon as she got out.

Sharon cocked her gun and nodded.

Nova nonchalantly walked down the east side of the two-story, brick building to the front door and tugged on it. *Locked.* Sharon stayed three yards behind Nova with her gun held against her chest pointing upwards. Nova looked back to Sharon and shook her head "no" slightly, then continued around the other side of building. Since all of the windows had decorative steel security bars, she lowered herself down on one knee and pretended to tie her sneaker so that she could look up at the second floor windows on the west side. All of them had bars except one on the second floor. *Gotcha!*

Sharon circled back behind the building, and once she saw Nova motioning in large waves with her hand for the group to follow her, Sharon said to Brock, "Time for the ladder."

✦ ✦ ✦ ✦ ✦

"Terry-Bear."

"Nope. That's not… wait. Terry, is he a big, black guy?"

Sandra talked to Chaya as if she had a mental problem. "Yeah, Terr-*ance*. Terry. Terbear."

"That's the one! Yeah. Me and my friends are rescuing you right now!" Chaya was excited for the breakthrough. "Listen to me, my friends have gone through the window upstairs…"

"Shit, negro, that's all you had to say!" Sandra put her ear bud back into her right ear and jogged away with her pistol held at shoulder height. "All I wanna do is…"

"Oh, no, no, no, no, no! Hell no!" Chaya felt the adrenelin shot like she was about to undrown herself. She yelled and banged her hands on the black bars as the girl with the gun ran away deeper into the apartment. *Go!* Chaya sprinted over to the ladder screeching, "She's got a gun! Watch out! She's got a gun!" The alley, however, was empty except for the ladder under the spotlight of a street lamp leaning against the window Marcus had broken open. Everyone in the Bliss coterie had gone up and inside the second floor. *Shit!* At this moment, when Chaya's gaze climbed the ladder to the open window, her world slowed down to less than half time. Her hearing turned off; she was deaf to the ensuing gunshot. However, her sight intensified and extracted the main detail she needed to know: she lasered in on a tuft of long, black hair that violently waved like a flag out of the window for a half-second and then quickly disappeared as if to signal the start of a drag race. *Nef!*

✦ ✦ ✦ ✦ ✦

Nick downshifted and raced back to the brothel. *No one steals my fucking property.*

Jojo instinctively raised his open hands above the dashboard as a gaggle of geese crossing the street in front of them came into focus. Wildlife interloping on residential space was common in Colorado. The western side of Colorado Springs, for instance, butted up against Pike and San Isabel National Forest where bears coming out of hibernation could be seen regularly pawing through unsecured trash cans this time of year. In Estes Park during the fall mating season, moose regularly would cross streets and occupy open space to feed on tall grass and tree branches. For this reason, Jojo prayed that the geese would move because he knew that Nick would rather see feathers fly right now than slow down. *Please, please, please!*

"Don't be such a pussy!" Nick yelled as he pressed on the gas pedal.

✦ ✦ ✦ ✦ ✦

Keesha awoke to the sound of glass breaking somewhere down the hall. She quickly sat up on her sheet-less mattress and listened closely. *Footsteps. Whispers.* Sandra's voice was distant but indisputable. *She's talking with someone.* There were other voices, however. *Men, women! Who are they?* Keesha covered her mouth with her hand, forcing herself to not call out for help until she verified that the voices were not from Nick or Terrance. She stood and tiptoed over to the door to better eavesdrop. Keesha heard Destiny yell for help from another room and an unfamiliar voice responded. *Holy shit!* "I'm in here!" She beat her fists against the locked door. "Help!"

"You're gonna be alright!" a man's voice said loudly through the door.

"Unlock my door! Get me out!" Keesha demanded. She heard several voices discussing breaking down her door.

"What's your name, sweetie?" a woman asked.

"Keesha. Keesha Jones. Can you get me out of here?"

"Hi Keesha, I'm Alice. We're working on it. Back away from the door."

"Just find the key!" Keesha urgently directed her rescuers in a high pitched voice. Now she could hear more people talking to Destiny and Luz. "C'mon! Get me out of here!"

Brock immediately told the others, "I'll go look downstairs," and he jogged down the dark hallway and down the stairway. At the bottom, he noticed a girl dancing as if she hadn't heard them break in. *Thank God.* Then, he saw her gun. *Hide!*

Marcus felt around the top of the door jam and found a small key to the padlock. "Found it! I got it!" He yelled to Desiree and Nova down the hall, "Feel above the door! The key is above the door!"

Brock found a closet near the front door and quickly got inside. He cracked the closet door just enough to not be seen but to still keep an eye on the stairway. The armed dancing girl sounded like she was talking to someone. *Do not move*, he instructed himself. *Do not make a fucking sound. Let her go up the stairs first, and then you can surprise her from behind*, he plotted.

Desiree, Marcus, and Alice unlocked the padlocks one by one and opened the bedroom doors to the strong smell of urine. Locked inside each of the three rooms were scared teenagers and little more than a mattress, a plastic bucket, a box of tissues and a pile of power bars next to bottled water. Desiree noticed that the small windows had been spray-painted black. "It's okay. I'm Desiree," she reassured a black girl who did not look older than 15. "We're here to help you get out. C'mon." Alice and Marcus had similar conversations simultaneously.

"Hallelujah!" Keesha yelled.

Through the small door opening, Brock heard the dancing girl in a hoodie yell, "Shit, negro, that's all you had to say! All I wanna do is…" and witnessed her running upstairs. He slammed through the closet door and ran after her across the front room and up the stairs two-at-a-time. Her silhouette was outlined against the bright light from the broken window directly in front of them. *Get her!* "Hey!" he screamed.

Two rapid-fire noises occurred so close to one another that they sounded like a loud truck trampling over a pothole. A millisecond after Brock yelled, his ears were assaulted with the deafening blast of a gun. The silhouette forcefully bucked backwards at him.

Seconds before, just as Sandra had run to the top of the stairs, she came face-to-face with Nefertiti standing on shards of glass. Sandra had hardly calculated that the window was broken when a man yelled at her from behind, "Hey!" Truthfully, Sandra was frightened. She was the only one left protecting the house and was caught off guard. Entranced in her music and surprised by the red head downstairs, now, strangers were flanking her at both sides. Fear pulsed directly from her heart to her trigger-finger. *Bam!* Her whole body was immediately thrown backwards one foot from the force.

As the silhouette in front of Brock spun around from the force of the gun, he lunged forward full of adrenalin. The heel of the gun collided with his head, cutting his scalp open. He then felt a powerful punch to his eye. Footsteps banged down the flight of stairs past him as blood flowed down his eye and cheek.

Sharon screamed and ran down the hallway, "Brock! Nefertiti! Are you okay?"

"Here!" Brock called out. Marcus and Sharon ran down the hall to find Nefertiti lying face-up on a filthy carpet full of broken glass.

"Nef's shot!" Sharon yelled. "Help me! Chase the shooter!"

“I’ll go,” Marcus yelled as he glided down the stairs with his gun at the ready. Once down, he saw that someone had run out and left the front door open. “All clear down here!” He ran back up the stairs and looked at Brock long enough to see all of the blood. “You hurt, man?”

“I’m okay. Help Nef,” Brock said in a hoarse voice. *Fuck me.* He pressed his palm against the open wound above his forehead.

The next ten minutes were the most challenging for everyone at Bliss. They were rattled. What little euphoria they felt upon unlocking the ‘bedroom’ doors and knowing that they were indeed saving three teenagers was erased with the shock of the gunshot and then the knowledge that Nef had been hurt, or worse, may be dead. Only Nova was unparalyzed. “Get out! Right now! Sharon and Marcus, grab Nef! Move it! Move it! Alice and Desiree, get the teenagers out of here! Go out the front door, forget the ladder, and go back to Bliss! Brock, go! Now! Get to my car!”

Chapter 20: The Aftermath

"You're a warrior, Nova," Brock rasped gratefully from his seated position in the office chair. His voice, normally so deep and smooth, had been beaten down to a crackling whisper barely audible through the loud sobbing and yelling in the conference room.

Sharon pushed a handful of tissues onto the blood that continued to drip from Brock's scalp and down the right side of his face. His left eye was swollen and turning purple. With Sharon's other hand, she pulled her handgun out from underneath her back waist and laid it on the long oval table a few feet away from Nefertiti's head.

"Did you hear that?" Brock repeated with admiration, "I said you're a warrior, Nova."

Nova ignored him and maintained focus on treating Nefertiti's gunshot wound on her left shoulder. "Alice," Nova yelled her stern order, "I can handle this one, but you have to calm those women down. Check where the blood is coming from and put pressure on it."

"Okay. Okay. What am I doing?" Alice was out of breath. Her hands shook violently from the traumatic preceding events.

"Alice, focus," Nova tried to calm her. "They look hurt. We need to know if there are any other gunshots or knife wounds on them. Anything life threatening."

"Okay. Okay. Okay," Alice repeated, nearly hyperventilating, as she approached the three crying teenagers huddled in office seats in the corner.

Nova turned her attention back to Nefertiti lying on the conference table in front of her. Lacking proper medical supplies, Nova pulled off the blood filled towel from Nefertiti's arm and quickly took off her own button down shirt, and pressed it on the wound.

"Desiree, go get me more towels from the gym. Chaya, I need my medical bag. It's in my locker. Combination: 10-14-2!"

"You got it!" Desiree yelled.

"10-14-2!" Chaya repeated. Both Desiree and Chaya started toward the closed door of what they called 'The Intake Room'. "10-14-2. 10-14-2…"

Suddenly, the door burst open. With so much adrenalin still pumping through all of their veins, guns and knives were instinctively drawn to steel against whosoever had come upon them. The young women screamed; everyone was ready to pounce and attack as they had been doing all evening.

Although disoriented and only able to see out of one eye, Brock reached out his bloodied right arm toward the door. It was Betts and her handgun was pointed directly at Nova. As best he could, he loudly whispered, "Stop Betts! No! This is Nova!"

Betts' shoulders and straight arms slowly lowered. Her tilted head straightened.

"Nova," Brock rasped, "This is Betts."

Chaya didn't skip a beat. "Well this is an epic introduction."

Nova had heard Betts' name mentioned by all of her new friends at one time or another. They seemed intimidated or worried, but in such a way that they clearly respected her. Nova had surmised that they wanted to please Betts, *but why?* Thus, Betts was more of a general idea of a person than a fleshy attacker. Now, meeting such a legendary icon in person was underwhelming precisely because Betts had a gun. *Basic is not attractive. You look weak.*

Betts quickly lowered her gun and pointed it at the floor after she saw the look on Nova's face. *What have I done? Shit, I almost shot her.* "What the fuck, guys? I'm sorry. I'm sorry, Nova. Please forgive me."

The adrenalin pulsing through Nova's body made her want to reach out and violently grab Betts by her throat. *How dare you? Where have you been?* she wanted to demand as if Betts owed her an explanation. *Why have you let your team flounder helplessly without you?*

Betts calculated Nova's ever-powerful presence. She watched as Chaya and Desiree ran out of the in-take room. *Chaya is marching to Nova's orders.*

"Welcome home, Betts!" Chaya yelled sarcastically as she passed by. "10–14–2."

Betts returned her gun to her purse and went directly to whom she calculated needed the most first aid: Nefertiti. "Let me help," she half stated, half requested Nova.

Nova's eyes darted back and forth with Betts' as though they were two equally matched wild beasts. Nova had to talk herself out of smacking Betts across the face. *Be gentle, now. Be calm. Violence is the adrenaline talking. You can work this out later with her.* "Press on this. Hard."

Without hesitation, Betts pressed the shirt as hard as she could against Nefertiti's arm so that blood oozed up through the cloth and between her fingers. "Nef, mama, are you awake?"

Desiree and Chaya ran back into the room, "Here you go. Here's your bag."

"I have to wash this blood off my hands," Nova announced. "Desiree, look for a two-centimeter long ammonia inhalant to break under Nef's nose. It'll look like a little piece of white rope. I'll be right back!"

Nova ran out as Desiree rummaged through Nova's medical bag for anything that looked like a tiny rope. *There it is.* "Okay! Got it! Now what do I do?"

Betts instructed her, "Put it under Nef's nose and break it in half. It'll wake her up."

Sure enough, within one second of smelling the blast of ammonia, Nefertiti awoke to a pain like shattered glass shanking her upper left arm. Reflexively, her working arm punched away the source of the pain as hard as she could.

Brock cried out, "Betts!"

Nova reentered the in-take room just as Nefertiti slammed Betts directly in the middle of her chest. Nova ran around the conference table to see Betts on the floor with the wind knocked out of her.

Bett's eyes were open and panicked as her hands were grasping at the air aimlessly. Her chest heaved even though no air was entering or exiting. *I'm dying! Help me!*

"Bett's!" Brock yelled again. *Why is everything going wrong?*

Nova quickly kneeled down and saw the fright in Betts' eyes. Nova gently soothed Betts by grabbing one of her hands and cooing, "It's okay, Betts. You're okay. You'll breathe in just a second. You'll get your wind back. It's coming. Here it comes."

Hhhhhuuuuuuuaaaahhhh! Betts inhaled like she had just cheated death. Eye to eye, she felt fear swirled in the elation of oxygen transfer directly through her gaze into Nova: *my warrior princess.* Just at that fragile, critical moment, when Betts' feelings of gratitude intersected with idolization, she gripped Nova's hand tight as if she were floating away and Nova was her only tether.

"I'm happy to help, Betts," Nova cooed sincerely and then looked to her left and right to see if anyone was paying attention to them. No one was, so she lowered her voice and yanked Betts' arm closer. Her whole upper torso jerked forward until her face was within inches of Nova's. "But if you ever point a gun at me again Betts, I will make you beg me for forgiveness."

Betts' reptilian response was unequivocal: she quickly put her lips on top of Nova's in supplication. Continuing to signal her beta status, Betts then pulled away before her alpha did. This entire evening was all very unexpected for Betts. As soon as she had received the "MAYDAY" text, she flew back to Denver from Atlanta as quickly as she could. She knew better than to call or follow up with more texts. *And now this.*

"It's okay," Nova said loudly to be overheard. "Take your time. I gotta help the others, okay?" Nova stood. "Nefertiti, let me see that arm."

Betts did not take her eyes off Nova. *Damn.*

"Did I just punch Betts?" Nefertiti asked Nova as she sat up. "I feel like my left arm is dead."

Nova looked down at Betts on the floor who was returning her gaze like a puppy. *Mercy, we need to lighten the mood.* "You did. You knocked the old girl out flat," Nova joked. She winked at Betts to get back into the game.

Nice. "Who you calling 'old'?" Betts replied with a wry smile and a side punch to Nova's calf. Slowly she regained a normal cadence to her breathing. From the floor, Betts pushed Nova out of her mind and scanned the room full of her top employees – bloody, scared, hurt, some crying – and then feared the end of Bliss. *Who are all of these people? What the hell happened?*

"Betts," Brock called out for his lifeline in front of his new girlfriend, Alice, and everyone else. His many failures of the day left him feeling false and impotent. *How is this not all traced back to me?*

Betts heard Brock's low, quavering voice. She quickly stood up from the floor and grasped his hand hoping for clarity. "I'm here, Brock."

Betts, my girl. Prompt public confession seemed to him a worthy humiliation. Certainly there were many more self-flagellations to come. "Betts, you're gonna hate me." Brock fought against his tears as he began his long apology for *being such a piece of shit*.

Betts covered Brock's lips with two manicured fingers. *Let me rip a page out of Nova's playbook.* Leaning into his ear, she dictated her marching orders: "You are going to keep your shit together for ten more minutes. Go to my office and lay down. I'll be there as soon as I can. But Brock, shut the fuck up right now. I don't want to see one God damned tear, you hear me? Get out of here, and let's deal with your shit privately." Betts then pulled away, dramatically squeezed his hand tighter, and said loudly, "Let's find fault tomorrow. Tonight, let's just keep everyone alive. If you need to go to my office to clean up, go ahead Brock. Go."

Brock proceeded to stand and leave without saying a word to anyone. *Humiliation number two: I'm not worthy of acting like a boss. I need to just get out of the way like a newbie.* Once he was in the hallway, he saw Marcus and Celeste walking toward him. *Pull it together*, he ordered himself. *You want to know how the last steps turned out. Focus on that. Focus on them.* "Hey. Is everything okay?"

"Depends on your definition of 'okay,'" Celeste responded.

Jesus, don't make this so hard, Brock wished to himself and kept walking past them.

Inside the in-take room, Betts regained her composure and clarity. *It's time to clean up Brock's mess.* "Chaya!"

"Yes?"

"Who are all of these people?" Betts looked around and let her line of sight fall on a pale redhead.

"Hi Betts, I'm Alice. I'm Brock's friend. These ladies are in our care for the night. I know a safe place for them to go in the morning."

Betts stood silently judging Alice and trying to comprehend the situation for a minute. *Brock's 'friend' and minors. In my building. Nef is shot.* She couldn't make it add up. "What happened tonight?"

Desiree, Nova, and Alice all shared knowing looks with each other. None of them was ready to tell Betts the whole truth. Chaya spoke first. "Betts it's a long story and we are exhausted, so can we just tell you tomorrow or Monday? Can I reschedule tomorrow's massages and put these three in our massage rooms to sleep?"

Betts nodded.

"Desiree, let's show them where the showers are and give them a change of clothes. Alice, c'mon. You need to help us."

The in-take room slowly emptied except for Nefertiti, who was still seated and bleeding from her shoulder, Nova, who was assessing

Nefertiti by moving her arm around, and Betts, who was assisting Nova. "How bad is it?"

"Fucking bad," Nefertiti winced in pain.

"Nef, you're lucky. It went clean through you," Nova said. "and missed your major nerves and arteries. I can wrap it up. You can actually go home."

"Good," Nefertiti grunted through the pain. "My wife can come and pick me up. I'll call her. Betts, go ahead. I know that you need to check on Brock and everyone else. It's okay. Go."

"Okay, mama," Betts said to Nefertiti. "I'll talk to you after a good night's sleep. I can see that you're exhausted. More much later, okay?" Then, Betts directed her attention to Nova. "Thanks, Nova. Looks like Brock was right; you are a warrior."

Chapter 21: Sleep Tight

War and liquor aside, in Betts' experience, men rarely sob. They cry sometimes, but they do not allow themselves to sob. Thus after the teenagers were settled and Nefertiti was stabilized and on her way home, Betts entered her high ceilinged office for the first time in many weeks looking for Brock. By the way he was seated on her leather couch with his head in his hands and right leg bouncing restlessly, she knew he was in crisis. She realized that whatever had happened, whatever she had missed these last few weeks, had been extraordinary. *Bliss and Brock need me.*

"I fucked everything up," Brock admitted through tears. "Really bad, Betts. I'm so sorry. Without Nova, I don't know what we would have done. It's all my fault. Everything. You have to forgive me. I feel like total shit." Brock bent until he broke and sobbed uncontrollably.

Betts handed him a box of tissues and sat down in the corner of the couch next to him with her feet tucked under her. She let him cry it out. He eventually settled down with his head on her lap facing her in the fetal position. *Babe, we're stronger than this. What spooked you so bad?* She placed a pillow under his head and tucked the throw blanket tight so that his arms were constricted. Her mind was filled with tens of questions that she knew had to wait until the morning. Betts unbuttoned the front of her blouse and unhooked her bra from the front at her sternum. She released her left breast out from under the cloth bra cup and let it lay in front of Brock's sad face.

"Do you remember our first time, babe?" She combed his hair away from his forehead. "How you made me cum in six different places?" Like an infant rooting for milk, Brock's lips found her warm breast and sucked on her artificially high nipple gently. "What a pair we make." Her large brown areola was covered with Brock's mouth as he squeezed his eyes shut slowly sucked harder. "We're in hot water, I can see, so I'm going to fall asleep with you. I need energy for tomorrow to clean up this whole mess. Let's just remember our first time like a Netflix movie and fall asleep together like old times, okay? Everything will be better in the morning."

Brock's hand birthed its way out from under the cover to reach up and gently kissed her breast. Then exhaustion fully enraptured him; he disengaged and succumbed to sleep.

"Twenty years ago," she remembered out loud as she combed his hair back, "only within hours of meeting you on that chairlift, we were in my secluded mountain cabin laughing and strategizing about Bliss. Do you remember?" Betts felt Brock startle with a body twitch. "You were there from the very beginning – so handsome and no gray hair. Not like now, old man." Betts smiled to herself and leaned her head back onto the couch with eyes closed. "You taught me so much. You practically created Bliss. Do you remember? We went back to my cabin after skiing and I spilled some wine..."

> As Brock was stepping out of the shower in the guest bedroom in Betts' rental cabin, he heard a short scream, so he threw on the white terry cloth bathrobe hanging on the door and ran down the stairs out to the living room. He saw Betts pulling a square cushion out from the seat of the long gray couch. "Are you okay? What happened?"
>
> After taking a longer-than-necessary stare at the glistening wet man in front of her, Betts continued unzipping the cover around the square seat cushion. "Oh, I just spilled some red wine on it by

accident. Sorry for the scare. I'm just going to throw this into the washing machine."

"Thanks for letting me shower here," Brock said while combing his fingers through his brown wavy hair. "I'm glad we're hanging out. This is nice." He looked at Betts in her pajamas and had to turn away when he saw that she wasn't wearing a bra. Her nipples were long and erect. "Any chance that I can throw my clothes in there too?"

"Better than fair, I'd say," Betts replied with a killer smile. "Actually, I'll throw my stuff from today in there too. Unless you're against co-mingling."

Brock returned her smile, "Nope, I certainly don't mind. I'm all about 'co-mingling.'"

Betts and Brock filled the washing machine with the cushion cover and the day's sweaty ski clothes.

"So you said that you're opening up a business. What kind? What do you do?" Brock watched her start the machine and pour clothing detergent into the small drawer at the top.

Betts smiled broadly at the thought of sharing her business idea. She pressed the 'Start' button and the engine hummed. "I shouldn't tell you. It's illegal," and walked out of the laundry room into the kitchen.

"I'm intrigued! Is telling me illegal or is the business is illegal? Wait, I'll guess. Intercontinental drug dealer?" he quipped.

"No," Betts laughed.

"Communist spy!"

"No!"

"Gimmie a hint," Brock cooed as he leaned on the kitchen island.

"Okay. I'll tell you my business slogan, and you try to guess the company."

"Okay, shoot," Brock's eyes absorbed the natural beauty of her softened left nipple protruding through her thin nightshirt. Her long black hair swooped around her shoulders like a scarf and fell over her right breast, halving the frequency of his longing glances.

"Well, it's less like a slogan and more like a motto. It's: Maximize the maximum number of orgasms by women, for women. Wait, no. It's: The maximum number of orgasms for the maximum number of women, by women, for women."

Brock smiled with raised eyebrows. "I see that you have a very refined mission statement."

"Shut up! I'm still working on it, but you get the gist," Betts grabbed a can of cashews from the counter and set them on the island in between them.

Seeing the nuts made Brock's mouth water. "It's about orgasms and lots of maximizing, right?" he summarized with a toothy smile. "So my guess is that you want to own a sex shop full of vibrators."

"Close, but no. Something way better than that." Betts went to the refrigerator to retrieve a plate full of various cuts of cheese and salami, a container of hummus, and crackers. She laid the food next to the nuts and sat down on a barstool.

"Brock, has it ever crossed your mind that women don't get enough orgasms?"

Without pausing and in a serious tone he agreed with a nod, "Yep. Every day."

Through her facial expression, Betts asked him to be forthright. "No, really."

"I'm telling you the God's honest truth, Betts. I've been with a lot of women, a lot. And I can tell you first hand that they are a pretty unsatisfied bunch. Not with me, of course," he joked. "I know how to satisfy people, but in general."

"Oh, yeah? What's so special about you?" Betts cooed.

Brock leaned in with his dazzling grin and retorted, "Well, I guess if you're going to share your illegal business idea with me, I can share mine. This is a safe space, right?" Brock joked as he pointed at the perimeter of the kitchen island as if it was a large circle of trust.

"Be serious," Betts giggled and threw a cashew at his chest.

"I want to maximize the number of orgasms for the maximum number of women. For women, by a man." Brock beamed as if he were on stage in front of a cheering audience.

Ha! "Touché!" Betts laughed aloud. "Well, since we seem to be kindred spirits, I'll spill the beans. I want to open a type of brothel for women. Only, there isn't a word in English yet for it. I'll have to invent one. It'll be a place where clients can be anonymous and get their groove on safely. Since they are paying for it, there won't be any strings attached. Strictly business. Strictly fun-business. I'll hire the best lovers around and pay them top dollar. Everyone wins. Everyone's happy."

"That's not gonna work," Brock disagreed shaking his head a bit. "Nope. I thought you said you want to maximize it."

"Buzz kill! I do," young Betts replied.

"Well, the women you want are so much more nuanced than that. You know this! Why am I telling you what you already know? Think about the long game, like if you were coaxing a friend who has never gone downhill skiing to suddenly spend upwards of $300 to go with you to Aspen. You're asking them to do something that everyone claims is fun and amazing… but might actually kill them – and they have to pay handsomely for it."

Betts considered her blind spot. "Keep going; I'm listening."

"Well," young Brock continued, "I've tried to persuade out-of-town friends to ski – continuing on with my metaphor because it's equally as fucking hard to persuade the non-believer into actually having sex – and the hardest part is getting them to commit despite the numerous drawbacks. The *idea* of sex or downhill skiing is fun and easy; these activities already have great face value. Everyone knows that. However, so many obstacles before the reward are discouraging. They have to use up vacation time, ride in bad traffic on I-70 for hours, rent expensive equipment, and pay for an over-priced lift ticket. With all of those obstacles, why should anyone even try?"

"Okay, I'm with you so far," Betts replied, "So how do you persuade them?"

"Well, I certainly don't try to sell them on snowboarding the black diamond trails at A-Basin, you know what I mean? I break down the steps for them." Brock started listing by counting on his fingers. "I tell them to hydrate and do squats a few weeks ahead of the trip to help them prepare. We buy half-day tickets instead of full day. We don't drive and ski on the same day; I make a fun weekend out of it. I take them to someplace like Eldora in Nederland so we can avoid crazy crowds and I-70. And we go to the bunny hill, where I teach them to 'pizza' slowly, step by step. Then it builds exponentially from there. They acclimate at their own speed. At first, however, you have to give a lot of thought to onboarding. That's gonna be your key to success."

"One of them." Betts' face muscles relaxed and softened except for her eyes, which seemed to be studying something unknown, and she fell into a kind of trance.

Brock waited by tossing cashews into his mouth and sipping his wine. Her concentration seemed intensely intimate and private, yet he felt as though she allowed him to witness her in this vulnerable state. His nostrils flared as he forcefully willed himself to look down at his drink and away from her thin, revealing pajamas.

Betts continued to stare off into an unknown memory, silent and inert, as if she were trying to solve a puzzle. After 30 seconds, she came out of her hypnotic state. "Sorry, I drift off sometimes. I'm aware of it."

"No, no worries. I'm talking too much," Brock apologized with a chuckle.

"Not at all," Betts said as she reached her arm across the granite counter top to give a small squeeze of reassurance to his hand. *Electricity*. "As a matter of fact, you make a lot of sense. I need to build in steps up a ladder. Women, in general, are a bit more risk averse, I'll give you that. If I want to appeal to a broad range of women, I need to think about specific ways to gain and grow their trust..."

"...and give them a process, a formulae, or a kind of curriculum so they can learn to 'pizza' first." Brock smiled a full mouth of sparkling white teeth again.

"Yeah." Betts lifted her wine glass in the air in front of him. "Cheers."

"Cheers to you, Betts." They looked into each other's eyes for good luck. *Ping!* the glasses sounded. "Ever consider a business partner?" Brock only half-joked.

Betts sipped. "There's something that you should know about me if you're considering partnering up."

"What's that?" Brock smiled.

"I'm not like traditional women. I'm not risk averse," Betts flirted.

"'I hadn't noticed' said the guy you just met who is naked under a bathrobe," he flirted back.

Betts leaned forward onto the countertop exposing her cleavage. "Should we fuck and then talk business or the reverse?"

Brock winced. "No. Sorry, that's not what…"

Betts was surprised and suddenly stood up straight. *Have I been misreading him?* "Really?"

"Really," Brock said convincingly as he stood up as well. "I don't want to *fuck* you, Betts, and I don't want you to *fuck* me. We're more sophisticated than that, don't you think? I don't want to just 'pizza' with you."

Betts felt like he had posed a challenge – one she wanted to win. She teased him by moving around the island to stand in front of him and lifted her V-neck pajama top from the waist up-and-over her naturally large breasts. The sheer cloth arranged itself above her long brown nipples as her arms returned back down to her sides.

Brock could not control his hard on which protruded through the opening of his bathrobe in his seat, but his mind was made up. "You're stunning, Betts. So inviting, but I still don't want to fuck you. I think you can handle more than a bunny hill. C'mere." Brock curled his forefinger cheekily toward himself.

Betts sauntered over and stood closer in front of him, tits still out.

Maintaining eye contact, Brock put his right thumb into his mouth to wet it, then pulled it out and wiped his saliva off onto the very tip of her left protruding nipple. He could see it glisten and harden in the light. Brock then leaned in inches from her chest to gently blow air at her wet areola.

Without thinking, Betts clasped her hands behind her back and arched her bosom into the tender warmth tickling her. “If this is not fucking, I’m glad we’re not fucking, but I’m not going to stay on autopilot for very long, Brock,” she admitted breathlessly.

“You can and you will,” Brock ordered. “I haven’t given you permission to touch me,” he whispered seductively.

Challenging him further, Betts shimmied her pajama bottoms over her hips so that they fell to the floor, exposing a small light blue thong. “I hereby give you permission to touch me and to fuck me.”

“Thanks, but no. Let’s elevate this to a higher standard, Betts. I can ski a green diamond trail anytime, anywhere, with anyone.” Brock considered his options.

“Am I a green diamond?” Betts asked leaning her right hip against the island counter and holding her left hand on her other hip.

“You’re not and that’s the point. I won’t fuck you because you deserve better and are capable of so much more; I can tell.”

“But maybe that’s what I want,” Betts lifted her arms and pulled all of her hair behind her shoulders.

Brock watched her large breasts sway naturally as she moved around. “Not tonight. Another time though.”

Betts was impressed that he spent so much time on verbal foreplay. *Very good. You’re getting me in the right mental mood first. That’s advanced for most guys in their twenties.* “What makes you think there will be another time? That's a bit cocky."

Standing, Brock reached around to her back shoulder blades and gently separated her long black hair into two fistfuls and pulled them forward over her shoulders. As if they were two upside down paintbrushes in his hands, Brock tenderly swept the two tufts of hair across both of her nipples. "You may be right. There may not be a next time. I have a feeling, though, that at some point you're gonna require some fucking." He noticed her nipples had relaxed into a softer shape.

"I'm requiring it now."

"No you're not. You only think you want that. Look at how ripe you are for something more. Look at your beautiful breasts." Brock brushed her nipples again with her hair and watched them harden again. "See that? You actually want me to *make love with* you," Brock cooed.

Now Betts winced and took a step backwards. "No thanks." Her black hair fell out of his hands. She pulled her pants back up and her shirt down. "I'm not looking for marriage, Brock. I just wanted to have a little fun. You're a good looking guy, I'm a good looking woman, we spent the afternoon skiing together, and here you are in my cabin –naked and sexy. This doesn't have to be complicated." Betts reached out for her nearly empty glass of wine and finished it.

Brock thought about it from her perspective for a moment. *Why doesn't she want to make love? Why seduce with a cheap strip tease act?* Her behavior seemed so incongruent for what he believed to be a sophisticated, wealthy businesswoman. “Can I ask you something, Betts?”

“Sure,” she replied fully covered with arms crossed in front of her chest.

“Have you thought of a name for your company?”

Betts smiled a toothy grin at him again, “Bliss.”

“That’s an awesome name. I love it. Should I open us another bottle?” Brock walked behind her and then stopped to rub her shoulders and neck. “I hope this is okay.” *No response.* Brock pushed both of his hands, open fingered, into her hair and massaged her scalp. “I know that one day you’ll misbehave badly enough for a proper fucking, but right now – you’re too damn perfect.” He could literally see her posture relax and shoulders droop. He expanded his fingers to press at the edge of her face and rub, then back an inch and rub more, then back another inch so that his fingers bridged her from ear to ear. “I won’t do it when you want it, though. You’ll get it when you deserve it.” Brock pressed and rotated his thumbs into her upper neck in small circles. He saw her shoulders relax even more. *Very responsive.* “You’re so sexy, Betts.”

“Thank you, that feels great,” she replied. *When I deserve it*, Betts recounted his words. “There’s a chardonnay chilling in the fridge if you want to switch to white.” Betts felt his hands recede, and then a kiss to the top of her head. *He’s sexy and sweet.* She exhaled a deep breath and then stood, taking the two used glasses with a little merlot at the bottom over to the sink.

Soon, the chardonnay gurgled as he poured new glasses. “Cheers.”

Betts lifted her glass and touched his gently, “Cheers.”

Suddenly, a soft gentle beeping music played. Betts looked at Brock, “Cushion cover is done.”

They spent the next 15 minutes wrestling the cushion cover over the square cushion. “I can’t get this thing on!” Brock snickered at how complicated a simple task turned out to be. “This is like putting panty hose on an elephant! Why do they make the covers so tight?”

Betts laughed and tried to help. “Okay, you hold the cover open, and let’s slip it in little by little.”

“That’s what she said,” joked Brock.

They worked the stuffing in inch-by-inch by squeezing the foam and yanking the cover over it. “Ahhh, finally! It’s in!” Betts yelled.

“Now just keep squeezing so that I can zip it shut,” Brock instructed with a pained voice. *What a struggle!* The cushion cover was designed in such a way that the flaps of the seams hid the zipper. “I can feel the little sucker, but she won’t come out.” He tried again to feel for the little metal zipper, grip it, and pull to no avail.

Betts laughed. “Do you know what this looks like? Look from this angle.”

Brock laughed. “Like a clit, I know! I’ve been trying to not think of our little vagina here which is giving us such a hard time,” Brock chuckled. He gave it a playful smack with his open hand and chuckled.

“So if it were a real clit, would you slap it like that?” Betts joked. “That’s your problem: you don’t know how to handle it.”

Brock loudly guffawed. *Like I said, you don’t want me to fuck you tonight, babe.* “Oh, well, let’s see,” and instead of trying to pinch it with a downturned right hand, he turned his hand over and pushed his middle finger under the seam and his thumb above it to feel for the hidden zipper. Once found, he pushed his middle finger and thumb in a little deeper, angled it down, and then slowly pinched and pulled it out.

“Yeah! You got it!” Betts laughed.

“Well my manhood was on the line,” Brock congratulated himself on a job well done. “I didn’t want you to think that I don’t know my way around a zipper.” He threw the cushion on top of the sofa and pulled Betts into his embrace. Both of his hands found their way onto either side of her face when she leaned in and kissed him.

Their kisses, at first soft and nibbling, turned more fervent. They blindly stumbled toward the moonlit bedroom. Betts loved how soft his lips were. They cushioned her gentle bites. Inside, the skylight in the ceiling exposed each tuft of Brock’s chest hair, every sinewy muscle, his broad shoulders, and well-apportioned, circumcised cock.

Betts happily laid on her back. “Look at you. I don’t care what you do with me. You can make love to me or fuck me or whatever you want, baby. You’re gorgeous.”

"Do you mean it?" Brock asked as he playfully gripped her wrists and pushed them over her head.

"Why, what do you have in mind?"

Brock lunged his tongue into her mouth again and then moved his kisses from her lips over to her earlobe. "How many places can you cum from? Can you cum from your tits?" he whispered as he bit and wagged his tongue over and around her lobe.

Just the sexy question alone whispered in his deep voice was a turn-on to Betts. "I don't know," she admitted with a grin. *No one has ever asked me that question before.*

By her groans and movements, Brock gauged what she liked. His hands cupped her breasts that hung to the side and pulled them toward the middle of her chest. *Licks: no reaction.* "I want to show you some of your own magic." His thumb and index fingers then pinched and pulled her nipples upward and outward.

Betts felt her clitoris swell, so she arched her back in response.

Okay, pulling works. Brock let go, then pulled again a little harder on both of her long nipples and heard her ecstatic moans. "Feel it in your clit," he whispered. *Pull.* "C'mon baby," *pull*, "you can do it, cum for me in your tits, baby." Brock could not wait any longer to take as much of her right breast into his mouth as he could and suck on her. *Let the pain guide you.*

Longingly, Betts tilted her pelvis up to brush herself against his cock.

"No baby. Don't touch it. Please. I'll use my mind, and you use yours," and Brock wiped her breast along his cheek before he put it back into his open mouth. "Through here. You have the magic."

To Betts, learning to cum from her nipples was a great feat of mental engineering. She had to lay the pipeline from her clitoris out to her breasts inch by inch each time Brock turned her on and cheered her on. She focused her thoughts on the burning sensation on the tips of both breasts and her swollen clit, then pushed it outwards through the new pipeline.

Soon, Betts had had her very first nipple orgasm. It pulsated up from her clit and out through the pipeline. Her nipples felt like they were a giant hawk's wings flapping in unison en route across a foggy lake lined with trees at sunrise when a small fish jumps out of the surface to catch an insect and the hawk glides on its two wings low and fast and aims at this meal of a fish; and with absolute certainty she opens her talons and snatches that fucking fish like the breakfast that it is.

Brock was pleasantly surprised by the sensitivity of his lover's newfound erogenous zones. His lips and tongue retreated off of Betts' breast to compliment her. "Wow. Very impressive. That was almost too easy for you, wasn't it. Let's try somewhere else and see what you can do."

At dawn, Nova made the rounds to check on everyone who had not gone home: Desiree, Brock, Alice, the teenagers, and Betts. Nova hadn't slept all night long; she kept alert to any possible danger like the police or Terrence's gang or Gael. *What a fucking mess this has been since I won that golden ticket. What a curse.* She gently pushed open the tall wooden door to Betts' elaborate office to find Betts and Brock sleeping on the couch. The digital clock on the wall displayed 5:30am. The office was clearly customized to Betts' personal preferences and vastly different than the rest of Bliss' interior design. It was the first time Nova had seen it.

Nova's gaze reached up to the far corners of the ornate high ceiling, which had Italian-style vaults as if it were a church naive. Indeed the luxurious fabrics on the walls and opulent stone pillars all aptly reflected homage to Tuscany. *I wonder what Betts did there for it to warrant such an expensive commemoration?* A mammoth window covered the entire west wall and overlooked the Boulder Valley. *Same view as the conference room.*

The day's easterly sunlight streamed across Betts' and Brock's peaceful retreat. Nova noticed that Brock was cocooned in fleece blankets and rested his head on Betts' lap. In contrast, she was seated and still dressed except for her unnaturally large, naked, left breast full of silicone which hung just inches from his face. *Ha!* Nova grinned and stared at the artificial breast for a moment before she quietly pulled the door closed. *That is funny.*

Brock awoke with a start when he heard the door shut. As his eyes lazily opened to a blurry, dimly lit world, he saw a breast. *Suck it.* His left hand reached up and held it steady by cupping and squeezing it. The thick scars underneath made him remember that it was attached to Betts. *I'm so glad you're home, Betts. I missed you. I've needed you. I love you.* He guided and manipulated the silicone to push her nipple where he wanted it: between his teeth.

Betts arched her back in sleepy pleasure as her clit awakened from its slumber. She looked down at Brock who was energetically wiggling out of the blankets and grabbing at her bosom. *Good morning.* While her nipples would never return to their pre-surgery level of sensitivity, they still had enough nerve connections to have fun.

Brock sat upright and held her face, then kissed her parted lips to find her tongue and haul it into his mouth as if he was playing tug of war. *Off with this.* He ripped her blouse apart so quickly that four buttons popped off. They both sucked on each other without a care in the world.

Betts' hands eventually found their way onto his thighs and up to his swollen cock. *Feeling wanted never gets old.* As familiar lovers, they did not need to say anything. They knew all the next steps to undressing and caressing and lying in the middle of the office on the antique, Italian carpet.

Brock's transition inside of Betts was slow and deliberate. Like looking at one's own reflection in the mirror, they moved and adjusted unselfconsciously. Sometimes, at these beginning moments, the lines blurred such that they didn't know whether he was inside of her or she was inside of him. Both felt true. Movements were coordinated and shared interdependently. He fully slid in as far as he could go and stayed in deep with slow, gentle pushes at her core.

Betts' eyes reflexively closed, as she moaned without inhibition. Together, they pulled and pushed each other in that negotiated rhythm which changed and evolved until...

The sudden arch of her back and eyes squeezed shut told Brock that he had found her g-spot. "Baby, cum with me." He thrusted slightly faster into her deepest part, "C'mon. I need you." The urgency soon kicked in. Brock reached his right thumb down to rub her clit in small circles, and as soon as he felt it, they came together loudly and without inhibition.

Exhausted and having forgotten that they had individual bodies, Brock stayed inside of her. They rested and then slept in each other's arms in a slumber so satisfying that twenty minutes refreshed them as much as an entire night's sleep. Brock finally awoke still on top and inside of Betts. He smiled and moved his penis ever so slightly inside of her. *Hello. You awake?*

Betts' eyes immediately opened as she grinned.

Brock giggled and moved it again which then made her giggle and him grow a little more.

"Do it again," Betts half-requested, half-laughed.

"If I keep doing it, by the laws of nature, you know we're gonna have to cum again." Brock kissed her smile with full tongue as his hips slowly pushed forward again. He felt her pelvis turn upwards to welcome him. "Good, babe. I'm glad you want me again. I want you too, but you know that you've made a big mistake. I can't make love to you until you've been properly disciplined."

Chapter 22: One Step Forward

"Hope House."

"Hi, this is Alice from last night. I just wanted to check in and tell you that the three girls are safe and sound. They're still sleeping." Alice tapped her pen on the conference table in the in-take room.

"When will you be bringing them in?" a female voice asked Alice on her cell phone.

"I don't know. Should I wake them up? I don't know what to do. I don't know if it's dangerous here or not."

"Where are you?" the voiced asked.

"We're in a building. It's a company's building. I mean, it's physically safe and locked and everything, but there are these people – these bad men and then there's the police looking for us. I just don't know if anyone knows that we are here or not."

"If you are questioning the safety of these kids in any way, Alice, please wake them up and drive them over here. It's better to err on the side of caution, don't you think? I'll make sure that everything is ready for them. And once you get them here, we'll know that they're physically safe. They need to get checked out and call their parents, those sweet kids. There's a lot to do. Okay?"

"Yeah, okay." Alice agreed. "I'll bring them over ASAP. Thanks. Bye."

Desiree walked into the in-take room and set a hot cup of coffee down in front of Alice.

"Oh my God, thank you," Alice said gratefully as she looked over at the clock on the wall: 7am.

"No problem," Desiree replied with a closed-lip smile of understanding. "I'm going to need a few more of these to get through today with only four hours of sleep last night."

"Tell me about it. I got stuck and slept in the waiting room on the stupid couch until a housekeeper with a swipe card came in. Hey, where are the kids?" Alice drank eagerly from her mug.

"Up in the massage rooms, I believe. Why? You taking them over now?" asked Desiree.

"Yeah," Alice responded, "I'm still worried about Gael and Nick and God-only-knows who else."

"Just tell Betts or Brock first, okay? They'll want to know," Desiree recommended. "Go check her office for them. Nova made the rounds earlier and said that they were asleep in there. You should probably wake them up if you're leaving."

Alice took her coffee with her as she proceeded down the hallway. Before Alice even knocked on Betts' office door, she could hear Brock moaning and grunting inside. *What? Brock is having sex!* She leaned her forehead on the door and listened curiously. She could hear up-tempo thrusts and whimpers, but also the down-tempo, slow talk. *Yes, this is definitely sex! I didn't think that he meant he would have sex with her within the same day as me!*

In the back of her mind, Alice heard the song, "You Can't Always Get What You Want," by the Rolling Stones. Hurt, Alice turned her ear to the door and focused on Brock's voice. She noticed that his tone with Betts was nothing like how he had spoken to her on the phone or in his pantry last night. With her he was sweet and selfless, even encouraging, but now he sounded harsh. Alice was in disbelief at hearing him growl, "You have no idea how much trouble you're in for leaving me here all alone, Betts." *What?* Both of her hands squeezed into fists. *This is bullshit. Fuck you, Brock.*

Alice ran away down the hallway and up the stairs to the massage rooms where another surprise awaited her: Nova seated clumsily on the floor. "Hey! Have you been here all night with them?"

"What's wrong?" Nova asked as if she had just been woken up. "Why are you running? Is someone here? Is everything okay?"

Due to Nova's slightly slurred speech, Alice realized that Nova was probably a mix of sleep-deprived and drunk. "No, I'm sorry. It's not like that." Alice sat down next to Nova on the floor. "No police, no gangsters. I'm just pissed at Brock."

"Don't tell me," Nova smiled broadly because she was confident that she knew the punch line to this joke. "You went to Betts' office and saw her big, fake tit hanging out. I thought that was some funny shit, actually. This Brock. This fucking Brock is supposed to be such a big man according to all the Bliss staff, but he's so little. He's such a small man compared to her."

"You're exactly right." Alice felt over-stimulated with information. *Small, tiny man. Asshole. Cheat.* She took a seat on the floor next to Nova.

"Her. Betts. The famous Betts," Nova continued by stretching the irony out of the word 'famous.' She rubbed her eyes to wake herself up a little more.

Alice looked down and noticed a bottle of vodka and a red, plastic cup next to Nova on the floor. "Are you drunk?"

"Are you stupid?" Nova laughed.

Damn that answer was fast. Alice crossed her arms over her chest, unhappy with how this entire morning was turning out. *I am right; she is kinda drunk.* "I'm not stupid, but you seem drunk. Sorry. Didn't mean to offend."

"Why, because Betts is wasting her time, letting some piss-ant suck her tit?" Nova slurred angrily. "Like a fucking baby? He needs to suck her? My new friend? I'm the warrior. That's my tit that I should be sucking."

Yeah, this makes sense. "So, she's your new friend?" Alice's furrowed brow dissipated into a smirk as she continued to put two and two together. "Well, your fucking new friend is – guess what, wait for it – fucking my new fucking friend. They're not just sucking, warrior-Nova, they're fucking. Actual fucking is taking place. I heard them."

Nova acted astonished. "No way!"

Alice disclosed what to her was fairly scandalous information: "Yep. Full blown, hard-core fucking. He's talking dirty to her and everything."

Oh my God, is this woman for real? Nova laughed out loud. "Oh, well, if he's talking dirty," Nova replied sarcastically, "then I have nothing special to offer her anymore. I may as well make like a tree and leave." Nova grinned. "Leave. Leaf. Leave it," she sang to the tune of Michael Jackson's 'Beat It:' "Leaf it! Leave it!" She was so happy with herself. *See how hilarious I am!* "Do you get it? I have so much to offer that lovely lady. Get it?"

"Drunk Nova is a little weird," Alice admitted with a grin.

"So? You're boring and plain," Nova retorted without thinking. "I'm sorry. Have a drink, girl." Nova offered Alice the plastic cup and bottle.

"Yeah, I won't say 'no' right now." Alice poured less than a shot into the cup.

"It's okay. I'm plain too. I just admire people like Betts more. She's the opposite of plain."

"So, you're gay then? And you like Betts? I did not see that one coming." Alice guzzled down the contents of her cup.

"It's not every day that a gorgeous woman tries to shoot me dead. I'm intrigued by her indeed," Nova professed. "But I hate her for getting off on Brock."

"Yeah, me too. I'm so mad at them right now. Everyone talks about her like she's legendary," Alice said in a half reverential, half ironic tone. *Is she though?* "But I don't know what to do about Brock. I feel like ever since I met him my life has changed irrevocably, like I can't go back. There's no rewind. Like I just created a unique alternate universe for myself. I can't undo it, but I also don't know what's gonna happen next."

"Oh my God, I know exactly how you feel; it's like we're past the point of no return. For me it's because I found a Bliss golden ticket. Yep, you're looking at the golden ticket winner," Nova pointed her thumbs at herself proudly.

"Yeah, that's why you work here. Brock told me," Alice replied nonchalantly.

"Come again?" Nova was confused.

"Brock said that you found the golden ticket. That's how they hire people," Alice replied as if this were common knowledge.

"What?" Nova could not have been more surprised. *No one mentioned anything about that, and I've put my life on the line for them!*

"'Part gratitude, part attitude.' That's what he told me," recited Alice.

"Are you absolutely shitting me right now?" Nova asked rhetorically, suddenly feeling very sober, awake, and angry.

Suddenly, the Aspen massage room door opened in front of them. Luz poked her head out and rubbed her eye, "Hey. I'm worried about Terrance and Nick. Are they gonna find us here? I wanna leave and go to the safe house and call my mom."

"That's my cue," Nova said as she stood. "Time for everyone to go home, especially me."

"Yep. Let's go, Destiny." Alice stood up. "Let's wake the others and hit the road." *Onwards. Forget about Brock for now.* "Nova, I'm sorry. I don't know what to tell you."

"No, it's fine," Nova stated flatly. "You have nothing to do with the golden ticket. You and I are just innocent bystanders who got sucked into this vortex they call Bliss."

"It's gonna be okay, Nova. I'm sorry, but I gotta run. Just cool off. Rest today and talk to Brock about the golden ticket on Monday, okay?"

"Yeah." Nova reached out to Alice for a quick hug goodbye. "Thanks and drive safe."

"Me? What about you?"

"Taking RTD, the Flatiron Flyer, and leaving my car here," Nova assured her.

"Finally, someone making some sense!"

Chapter 23: Sunday

"'Harrowing.' I said yesterday was 'harrowing,' mom." Nova repeated herself louder from the tiled floor in the center of her apartment. She laid flat on her back with her knees bent up. A frozen bag of peas covered her eyes and forehead.

"Can you just put the speaker closer to your mouth?" Nova's mother Mary Ann requested. "You kids nowadays have forgotten how to even talk on the phone because you text so much."

"Mom. I'm 46. I'm not Gen Z. I'm not even a millennial." Nova rolled her eyes and then moved the base of her phone closer toward her mouth under the bag of peas. "Anyway, Dad loves those Bitmojis. You shouldn't be sharing a cell phone if you don't want all of my texts."

"I know. He likes how young it makes him feel. The grandkids are telling him to add some wrinkles to his avatar, but he thinks that if his Bitmoji is bald, that that's old enough. Anyhoo, so what was so harrowing about yesterday? I thought you were looking for work."

"I found a job, actually. That's why my day was so harrowing," Nova admitted.

"Really?" Nova's mom walked around her expansive wrap-around porch of a newly renovated Victorian home so indicative of Saratoga Springs with a watering can. No less than ten colorful flower arrangements were hanging from the porch ceiling.

"Yeah. I almost got shot."

"What? Don't tell your mother stuff like this. Do you want me to have a heart attack? This is why I told you to take your guns." Mary Ann resumed watering the flowers.

"Mom, it was just an accident. Betts wasn't really trying to kill me in particular, she was just pointing her loaded gun at me."

"What is wrong with those Colorado people? I just heard about that Florida girl who flew over there and bought a gun and killed herself in the mountains. I mean, what is going on these days? And who is this Betts?"

Nova chose to ignore her mother's big picture questions. "She's my new boss, mom. I work in Boulder at a gym called Bliss, but I live in Denver. People are normal here, just like in New York."

"Oh, for goodness sakes, Nova. What kind of job have you gotten yourself involved in where your boss carries a gun?" Mary Ann set the watering can down and sat in a white Adirondack chair.

"You don't want to know, ma," Nova admitted.

"You're right. I think I don't. You're more than grown now and can take care of yourself. I don't need to know what I don't need to know anymore, *capisci?* Every conversation with you these days is like a pending heart attack. I'm just gonna trust that you're gonna take care of yourself." Nova's mother paused and shared the silence before she moved on articulating a truth they both needed to hear out loud: "Nova, I know you need to live your life the way you couldn't these last few years. I know what you gave up. Believe me, I know. I gave up a lot too; every married, Italian woman does. So, now go. You're free. Spread your wings, Godspeed and all that, but just tell me about the best 10% of your life from now on, *capisci*? With love? Can I say that with love from New York?"

"Yes you can; thanks for the boundary, mom. I hear you loud and clear, and I take it with love, from Colorado. Oh! Did you put 'ICE 1' next to my name on your cellphone?"

"Yes, stop worrying about the small stuff. Go live the life you always wanted. Bye, bye kiddo."

"Love you. Give dad a hug from me."

"Will do. Love ya too." Mary Ann set her cell phone down and wrapped her pink, manicured nails against the arm of the porch chair to think better.

Nova twisted and cracked her back on both sides before she removed the frozen peas and sat up to meditate. Just as her hangover abated and she started to find some Zen, her cellphone dinged twice. "Oh, Mom." The face of her phone, however, revealed that it was not her mom. Nova smiled. *The big tit!*

Homecoming was never so sweet as after last night's seemingly endless cleanup and rescue. Upon arriving to her tiny house tucked up in the small mountain town of Lyons, Celeste celebrated by playing her phone's 'happy' music list over her wireless speaker. Tommy James and The Shondells' "Crimson and Clover" played as she slow danced with her fifteen beautiful cats. "Hi, cuties! Did you miss me?" They surrounded her ankles with their tails in the air and loudly meowed the return of their queen. "Mommy missed you too!"

Brock dragged his reluctant legs up his three porch steps and psyched himself up to open his front door. It took a full minute for him to tap the six-key security code into the keypad and push the door wide open to nothing and no one because while his foyer was immaculate and free of stain, his memory of it was not. Sweat droplets ran down the side of his face, and his breathing labored. He tried looking past the memory of Terrance's corpse toward the kitchen, but then there was the image of Gael running at him like a crazed lunatic with a raised knife. Brock turned back around and looked out across the beautiful mountains, pulled out his Pax vaporizer, and took a long drag. *To get a mile away, you have to get a mile high, man.*

Across town, as soon as Marcus entered his apartment door in the early morning hours, Gigi ran over in her purple, footed unicorn pajamas to hug and kiss him. "Daddy's home!" Down on one knee, he held his daughter like the precious salvation that she was. Thankfully, he had remembered that it was Easter amidst all the chaos of the previous night and bought a pastel-colored basket full of chocolate bunnies and yellow marshmallow candies. His sister Shuree tried to downplay her greeting. "You're late, bro." She did not rise from her sleeping position on the couch in the living room. "Happy Easter, ladies. I'm so grateful to have two super amazing Wakanda-women in my life. I love you two." Marcus first kissed his daughter, then walked over to the couch and kissed his older sister on the forehead. "Let's get ready for church."

High on vapor-courage, Brock finally entered his house through the back door. The sunrays from the skylight above angled down to spotlight Terrance's half-index finger and phone still sitting on the kitchen island. *Fuck, more incriminating evidence.* Then he looked over at the pile of blood-spotted aprons and clothes on the counter in the corner. *Goddamnit.* Once again, the panic started to bubble in his stomach. *It's just a thug-stump of dead cells*, he reminded himself. He slowly crept up and inspected it as if it could blow up at any moment. *You won't be pulling any more triggers. This is over. I need this whole fucking week to be over.*

Nefertiti awoke in her marital bed, in great physical pain, but emotionally gratified as soon as she realized that Chaya had returned her back to the safety of her home. "Yeah! Mommy's awake!"

Nefertiti rubbed the sleep out of her eyes. Peach flavored Greek yogurt and granola sat on a tray beside the bed on her left as a very exciting game of Shoots and Ladders between her three children and wife took place on her right. "I'm so glad to be home. I missed you guys!"

Brock, still sore and bruised from the last 24 hours, sat down at his kitchen island thumbing through the photo gallery in his phone. He found a lovely photo of Alice with her face in the wind and zoomed in closer. *You're so beautiful, babe. What the fuck are you doing with me?*

Nick hooked the right side of Bliss' ladder, which was leaning up against the side of his now empty building, with both of his hands and violently yanked it down to the alleyway pavement with a roar of frustration. Jojo and Boo stepped back wide-eyed. The steel toe of Nick's right boot repeatedly kicked the rungs of the ladder as he screamed, "Fuck, fuck, fuck!" Jojo and Boo turned and walked away out of respect and self-preservation.

Celeste cooed at her furry friends, "Life is good, my sweeties, isn't it." She sat in the middle of her home flanked on all sides by felines waiting their turn for a glove-brush massage.

In the Silver Miner's sound-safe viewing area of the shooting range, Sharon led a meeting about last week's statewide, school shut down. "All in favor say 'aye.'" "Aye!" several women chimed simultaneously.

When Barbara looked through her front window at the dirty car parked in front of her house, she realized that Gael was fast asleep on her porch under his Bliss blanket. "Reprobate. You're good for one thing only."

Feeling happily high, Brock called Alice. To the tune of the French nursery rhyme "Frère Jacques", Brock sang to himself: "Please pick up, please pick up. Alice, it's me. Don't ignore me."

Once Alice had arrived at Hope House, she silenced her phone and focused on settling in the three freed young women. The first few hours were both heart warming and breaking as Luz and Keesha surprised their jubilant families with phone calls. Destiny, however, checked in with her social worker. She didn't have any family to call. Alice gave Destiny her cell number and told her to call if she needed anything. "I need a cell phone," was the teenager's response.

Brock took another hit off his Pax and texted Betts, 'Loved waking up in your arms this morning. Every time with you is as memorable as our first.' Then, he second-guessed how she would take it. After all, she had left her office extremely angry. *C'mon, Betts. You know I gave you exactly what you wanted.*

Betts stood alone in her office in a sweaty, red, green, and white, biking outfit looking at the valley through the window. She clenched her right fist and admired her cracked and bloodied knuckles. She started thumbing a message to Nova when she received Brock's. *Ignore.* 'Nova, Betts here. I think I owe you a new shirt and a drink… or 20 :) Can I meet you at your place at 4pm? My right hand needs first aid.'

Suddenly forgetting her headache, Nova entered the enlightened path after seeing Betts' text. Nova squealed and danced from her meditative position on the floor.

Brock checked his texting app again. *Why aren't they answering?*

+ + + + +

"You're back in town early, Fun Girl," David stood and kissed late arriving Betts on the cheek inside the brightly colored Boulder Dushanbe Teahouse. David wore his usual jeans and well-worn t-shirt advertising a local brewery while her tight biker's outfit evoked indecent thoughts in David's mind.

"Fun my ass… David." Betts tone was flirtatious. She knew he hated hearing others use his name, so she said it to goad him.

Your ass is fun, David volleyed in his mind as he reviewed the curve of her backside.

"I'm too busy to be fun," she baited as she removed her helmet and CamelBak and shoved them under the café table. The high ceilings and white noise from the early-afternoon crowd required them to lean in toward each other in order to hear each other properly.

"You're my boss now, technically, so…" David started. He marveled at how he saw the fourteen-year old Betts every time he looked at her. *Those aren't her wrinkles. That's not a gray hair. She doesn't have dark circles under her eyes. I can still see the real her.*

"Technically," Betts grinned. Her eyes swayed back and forth over his hair and slightly chubby cheeks, the flecks of gold in his blue eyes, and his slouching posture. "But life isn't always technical."

"Well, technically, I want to be appropriate out of respect for your position." David grinned, reached over and snapped the bottom of her biker shorts as if the elastic hem was a rubber band around her lower thigh. He then lowered his voice and leaned in further, "But if you use my name again darlin', you'll feel a slap across your ass so hard you'll never forget."

Punishment wrapped in an invitation, va-va-voom! Betts' slight grin immediately revealed her inner thoughts. *Acknowledge the line*, she told herself. *You knew he didn't like hearing his name.* "Sorry. It won't happen again." Simultaneously, she was still sore and satisfied from Brock this morning. *Flirt and move on, no more today.* Under the table, she pulled open the Velcro on the wrist of her right biking glove, but she couldn't slip it off. The scabs on her knuckles from this morning had painfully bled each time she had made a fist and broke them open. Now, the blood glued her glove to her right hand. *Just leave the glove on.* "Why is it so crowded in here today? Why is everyone so dressed up?"

"Happy Easter, Darlin'. I ordered you your favorite tea, by the way." David motioned toward the server who was delivering two small teapots. His head sweetly dipped to the side. "Hope that's okay."

"Absolutely." Betts lifted the white porcelain lid off and smelled the fragrant Jasmine Pearl steam rising up off from the tea. "I love it when friends are proactive."

"Thanks," David told the server as he added two large spoonful's of brown sugar into his mug of chai.

"How is work?" Betts asked hoping for some unbiased insider information about her staff.

"It's different than I expected," David honestly stated. "My wings are clipped at this low level, as you know, but uh, you got something good here. I see what you're building, and I'm starting to understand. Not to sound like a big brother, but I'm proud of you.

You've really made something out of yourself. I think you're helping some women in a unique kind of way. They seem… I don't know exactly what I was expecting, but they surprise me. They're really confident and grounded. Rooted." He sipped his chai and returned her gaze.

"I'm so glad that you appreciate our clientele. And thanks for your kind words. I was hoping that this would be mutually beneficial. A little bit further up the administrative chain though, and it's crazy. That's why I had to come back early." Betts tried to sound casual.

"What happened?" asked David.

"I don't know exactly," Betts admitted with a chuckle to seem understated. "I wanted to ask you if you knew anything."

"Me? No, I just do my job." David replied. "Trouble always seems to find me, but I try my best to avoid it."

"I don't know what he did, but Brock is at the center of some broken bicycle spokes," Betts surmised.

David pointed his fat index finger at Betts. "There. I might be able to help with him. Did you know that Brock has screwed half your staff?"

"So what? So have I. You've nailed a few yourself, by the way." Betts wiped her forehead from left to right. "And lest you forget, we are in the sex business. It's my job to hire people who enjoy sex. Like you, I might add. That they act like rabbits is far from a revelation. If you're making guacamole, you might as well rub the avocado into your hands."

"That's not a thing," David chuckled.

"To make your skin soft."

"It's really not a thing."

"I know, but it could be if you repeat it," Betts laughed at herself.

"Nope. Not happening," he smiled.

"Whatever. Avocado really hydrates." Betts feigned indignity. "So, Brock."

David offered all that he knew, which was not much. "Yeah, Brock, he seems like a good instructor, so far. I heard he has a new girlfriend. A professor."

Betts contemplated this for a moment. "I've met her, Alice; she's no secret from me. Kind of basic, but hey, it's his choice. So does everyone know that he's dating her? I thought they just got together recently."

"I think news about Brock travels fast among the women at Bliss," David guessed. "You asked me to keep a third eye on him, so as your oldest friend-from-the-inside, I'm telling you what I know: nothing really."

"Yeah, no worries. I just wanted to check in with you first." Betts sipped her Jasmine tea and then asked cryptically for public consumption, "Hey, uh, if I find out that Bliss needs to suddenly 'renovate its exterior,' if you know what I mean, is that something you would be able to help me out with?"

David sat back in his seat and decoded the message. "Depends on the size of the job, the manpower, and the time."

Betts sat back too and crossed her arms in front of her chest considering the logistics.

David scrutinized her gloved hands. "Jesus, Betts, look at your knuckles. I can see that you're bleeding from here. Should I ask?"

"If you want," Betts chuckled and looked around the large open dining room.

"I'm not going to. You usually make an effort to hide clues, what gives?" David worried.

"You said my name." Betts leaned forward with a grin and changed the topic. "Lucky you, my biker shorts don't have a belt."

✦ ✦ ✦ ✦ ✦

"You haven't asked me how I did this to my hand." Betts blindly reached into the treasure trove of Nova's mind and rooted around for anything that fit her grasp. She needed a summary of what had happened in her absence, so she had texted Nova from the teahouse, went home and showered, then drove east. They sat facing each other on the black, leather couch in Nova's apartment living room overlooking lower downtown Denver, both exhausted from having had less than six hours of sleep. Betts' swollen, right hand rested palm-down on a couch pillow between Nova's crossed legs.

Nova half smiled and looked closer through her trifocals at the tweezer tips she was pinching on Betts' right hand. Without proper cleaning, Nova knew the small wounds would become infected. "I know how your hand got that way. What I don't know is how you could go on all day long as if it's nothing when it's obviously painful."

Betts reasoned, *either she doesn't expect any backstory, or she knows but doesn't care about Brock. Either way, how unexpectedly progressive!* "Pain is relative. You've had surgery, right? So you know." She generally motioned to her chest. "It's the same thing: the scars can be the same, but electing a boob job is different than not having a choice, you know?" Betts mind flashed back to the first time she saw the scars on her black and blue chest and exhaled a deep breath.

"I guess I'll reserve my sympathies for Brock then." Nova smiled at what, to her, was a clear reference to breast augmentation. She was not sure to what degree she could be informal with Betts, her new boss. Everyone else had bonded all day yesterday, but Betts was not a part of that so she refrained from poking fun at Betts' fake breasts. Instead, she wondered, *What does Betts know?* Betts had arrived at the end of all the action and had almost shot her on accident. *Why did she come all the way to my apartment?* "So is there anything else you need, or just a little first aid?"

"Are you inviting me to stay for a drink?" The mere fact that she asked in addition to how she asked clarified the situation to both of them.

Coquette! Nova tried her level best not to smile. "Oh, I don't drink. Five years sober."

The record scratch reverberated through Betts' brain. *Whoops.*

Ha! "The look on your face!" Nova's smile finally escaped; she was proud of herself for delivering a punch line without breaking her expression. *I did it!*

Betts, in deadpan, slowly shook her head 'no.' *Really?*

"C'mon. Yes, of course alcohol is a good idea," Nova came clean. "I should have already offered you a glass. So sorry."

"I got a fright just then. I was like, 'no wine? No vodka?' I would have never made it through the last three years without them!"

"I know!" Nova laughed. "Me either." She stood and walked over to her kitchen. "I have a white chilling in the fridge, is that okay?"

"Chardonnay?" Betts asked.

Does it matter? "Rueda, actually. It's a little bitter. Would you like to try it?"

"Sure, why not." Temporarily a lefty, Betts tossed her long, dark hair over her shoulder and looked around the expensive but undecorated apartment.

Nova walked back over with an open bottle of Naia from northern Spain and filled two short glasses. "Cheers."

"Cheers! Thanks for letting me drop by," Betts remarked and took a sip.

Back in position on the couch, Nova pinched another tiny piece of black thread caught in Betts' index knuckle with the tweezers and pulled it away from the raw wound. "So go ahead, I think you want to ask me something," Nova lightly flirted.

"I hear that you won the golden ticket," remarked Betts.

"That's not a question." Nova wiped the little flecks of plastic and dirt off of the tweezers onto a tissue.

"Are you glad that you won the golden ticket?" Betts jokingly rephrased and took a sip of her Rueda. She was confident that she would hear the inevitable answer: *God yes, thank you.*

"I don't know yet." Nova maintained her focus on cleaning the small circular, red wounds on several of her knuckles. "Sorry if that sounds rude or ungrateful." She put down the tweezers and picked up the Vaseline and cotton swabs.

What? "Well, it does sound a little like that, yes. It's worth a lot of money, you know. I, myself, came up with the golden ticket idea. Why should only the rich get massages and pedicures?" *...and Happy Endings and Happy Ever Afters...* "There's tons of working class folks who are on their feet eight hours and more every day. Who's giving them foot massages? Who's cleaning under their big toe nails? And the aching back muscles some women have, don't get me started. They deserve at least a hot tub to float in each day after work. Did you know that university English as a Second Language instructors have to teach double the number of classes as composition instructors for the same salary? Why? They both have master's degrees! They're both teaching English for Christ's sake!"

"That's an oddly specific complaint on behalf of the working class, Betts." Nova dabbed one end of a cotton swab into Vaseline.

"Oh, I just hate the way the university exploits my niece. She's the hardest working kid I know, and they pay her peanuts. But you get my point, don't you? The golden ticket is supposed to be like winning a small lottery."

"Well, I get that you intended to do something nice for people who might need it the most, yes. And if intentions built a yellow brick road ahead of me, I'd be skipping with a Scarecrow right now. However, in reality, it's much more complex than that."

"Really?" *She wants to lecture me on the complexities of good luck?* Betts started to question the premise of her visit. *I could have hung out with Chaya or Desiree to get the low down.*

"Betts, I'm not trying to pick a fight. But, do you understand just how illegal and how dangerous your line of work is? I've only been working at Bliss one week and many people have been put in jeopardy, including me obviously. Forgive me for not understanding what it is that you do as a business owner, because we just met, but how come your staff who purport to love and respect you so much hide critically important information from you? Is it fear? I don't know.

"All I know is that I felt like I had to step into a very high level leadership role because critical decisions had to be made quickly: those girls needed to be rescued, people needed first aid, half your staff was high or drunk while we…" *How much should I share all at once?* "The list goes on and on. I felt I had no choice but to just jump in and work, help, do whatever was needed, fill the dearth, and get the team through. But that's not how this lucky golden ticket is supposed to go.

"One of them should have called you. Who was I to call you up and tell you anything? I didn't know who you were until you were pointing a gun at my face. Thanks for that nightmare, by the way. Betts, this golden ticket has changed me forever, and this is only week one. My God, I wonder, what will my life look like after a year – if I survive?"

"If you survive? What the hell! Let's back up. Clearly, I see that you're processing. I'm very, very sorry that I just burst in armed with my gun last night, but Nova, that's what people do when they're defending their property or their business or family. Look at it from my perspective. I get a 'MAYDAY' text out of the blue, seemingly so, and I get on the very first flight back here and taxi my ass all the way to Boulder, directly to work. No pee breaks, no apologies to cancelled meetings with clients, and then I hear crying and high-pitched voices as I'm coming in. Of course I grab the office gun and kill the safety switch. These people are my family, so please accept my apology. I really never meant to frighten you. Why don't you just tell me what I missed, because nobody has told me what happened. Everyone just left this morning, including Brock, without telling me anything."

You're laying it on a little thick here, my dear. Nova glanced down at Betts' bandaged right fist. "Well, for the record, both Alice and I swung by your office to talk to you. When I saw you, it was at sunrise and you were… asleep." *With your fake tit out, by the way, but that's none of my business.* "However, by the time Alice came by to talk to you about the teenagers, you and Brock had gotten, were getting… busy. She heard you guys, freaked out, and left with the kids to Hope House. So don't blame us, okay? We – your 'new friends' – checked on you and tried to talk to you."

Betts fell silent as truth's weight pressed its load down. *Where were my people? Why were Nova and Alice the responsible ones? If Alice is upset, then Brock is going to be even more upset.* "Got it. I hear you. Thanks for checking on me this morning, and for this."

Betts took that better than expected, Nova noted. She finished taping the gauze and declared, "Of course. You'll be fine."

"I meant thanks for your honest accountability," Betts corrected. "You know, we've had many, many golden ticket winners, but none quite like you." Betts briefly contemplated leaning in and kissing Nova, but realized that her timing was off. Nova was not finished airing her grievances.

"Yeah," Nova continued, "about that, I've been told that this is how you hire your staff."

Ha! "That's total bullshit. I've given away ten times that many tickets, thank you very much. It's just that some feel so grateful that they end up working for me, but no, not everyone. Some. I thought that you may have been one of them, but maybe not."

Sensitive much? "I'm on your staff for now, don't misunderstand me. This may all turn out positively in the end, and I hope it does. I just can't let the excitement and adventure of moving to Colorado put me in a position – toward the end of my career that I've worked so hard for – where I lose ground financially, emotionally, or lose agency or integrity. Do you know what I mean?"

Betts could not help but smile with every muscle in her face. "I sincerely hope that you recognize that you can have all of the above. You deserve to have both excitement and integrity. And what's adventure without agency? That would take all of the fun out of it. I, for one, would certainly never ask you to settle for less, Nova."

"Well, then you understand me perfectly: I'm not settling this late in my life for the bottom half of Maslow's hierarchy, girl, not with my relationships and not with my work." *Finito!*

Betts affirmed her agreement, "I get it. I'm just stunned to hear that you think working at Bliss is settling for 'the bottom half' and is 'unsafe.'"

Even through Betts' tough exterior, her pain was evident. "You're hurt," Nova verbally nudged like a mother horse's nose to her newly born calf.

"I am. I just can't believe that my staff, with whom I have built so much trust over so many years, didn't come to me. I don't get it. Can you just tell me what happened, because I can't sort through this blind."

To give her the complete story, Nova invited Betts out onto her porch where they stood overlooking the swarm of locals and tourists navigating the farmer's market in front of Union Station. Nova walked Betts through her first interactions at Bliss and how she met Gael.

"We all took him at face-value and assumed that he was honest, but he just lied to us and used us. He got some first aid, a good night's sleep, and took off. Luckily, I encouraged Brock to get his car detailed and that's when Gael's murder weapon was found."

Betts' jaw dropped. *Murder?* "Was Gael murdered or raped? I'm confused."

"My bad, I'm sorry. Gael got mixed up with the local drug cartel, and one night last week he killed two guys. He punched them in the eyes first with a metal thing. Really gross stuff. The third guy, John, is blind from Gael, but alive in the hospital. So Brock drove Gael to Bliss the night he got raped, but at the time, Brock didn't know that anyone had died. Gael hid the weapon under Brock's passenger seat. So yesterday morning, Brock found out about the weapon. In the afternoon, Gael showed up with a Sinaloa cartel thug named Terrance. Why Brock let them inside his home is beyond me."

Betts gulped the last of the wine in her glass and then asked in a measured tone, "Are you telling me that Gael, a new Bliss employee, murdered two men, and blinded a third guy, and that Brock knew Gael murdered and hospitalized them, and that Brock actually had the murder weapon in his possession, and he *still* opened his front door to Gael?" She could hardly meet Nova's gaze. *How humiliating.* She almost felt dizzy. *Fucking idiot.*

"I'm sorry, Betts. Let's sit." Nova motioned to her deck chairs under the shade of an umbrella. "Once Gael and Terrance were inside the house, Brock told us that he tied up Gael. Then, the police came, so Brock went outside to talk to the police. At this point, we have deduced that Gael got out of the rope, grabbed a knife, and slit Terrance's throat. Gruesome, I know. Right in Brock's foyer."

"Holy shit, Nova. Is this is a fucking joke?" Betts leaned forward eager for every word. *How can this be?*

"I wish. That's what I'm trying to tell you. It's bad. All of us at Bliss got the 'MAYDAY' message, and we assembled at Brock's house to help clean up the mess."

Betts stated the obvious conclusion: "Which must have involved a dead body."

"Correct." Nova paused. Even to her, even though she had lived it, this story sounded like a lot to swallow in one bite. *What have I gotten myself into?* "So, we call Alice, Brock's new girlfriend who you met, and bring her in to deal with Brock who had passed out. The thing you need to know at this point is that Alice researches sex trafficking, okay?"

Betts rolled her eyes and stuck out her lower jaw. Her head slowly swung 'no.' *There are no words left to say. Brock, you better have one hell of an explanation for all of this.* She grabbed the bottle of Rueda from the table and poured herself another glassful.

"So Alice comes over, see's dead Terrance – we figure out from his phone where they are keeping a house with teenager sex slaves – and this is when Alice convinces everyone to rescue the teenagers. We had had a few drinks and were like, 'Sure! Let's go after some sex slaves tonight!' And that's what we did, believe it or not. What could go wrong? We cleaned his house, top to bottom, spick and span. We buried the body in his backyard. We got our hair braided the same way, I shit you not, and made a rescue plan. We even cut off one of Terrance's fingers so that we could use his cell phone."

Betts could not believe what she was hearing. *Have they all gone mad?* She finished her glass of Rueda and poured herself a third. *I need something stronger; wine will never take away this much sting.*

"At first, everything was going according to plan: we distracted all of the thugs and their lookout, found a way in up a ladder and through a second floor window, and then we even found the teenagers. Great. But then, come to find out, there is some other teenager guarding the sex slaves and this girl has a gun. She shoots Nefertiti and knocks Brock in the head with the gun handle. That's when we all just high-tailed it out of there back to Bliss. And then there you were, another gun blazing in our faces."

Betts did not respond immediately; the lump in her throat was too painful. Instead, the intimacy of sharing the silence grew. She looked out past the glass railing toward others on their porches like she was skimming her Facebook feed. *Do not cry.*

Nova reached over and squeezed Betts' left hand. *Tits up, girl. We got this.*

Because Betts was avoiding getting emotional, she stayed silent and squeezed Nova's fingers tighter.

Nova stood, still holding Betts' hand, and pulled Betts up to a standing position for a long embrace. *We're gonna get through this.* Nova's left hand rose to the back of Betts' neck while her right pulled Betts closer from the small of her back.

Unconsciously, Betts further burrowed her face into Nova's neck. *Brock and I have failed everyone.*

Neither of them rushed. Nova held Betts and thought, *it's gonna be okay if we stick together; this is Brock's fault. You weren't even here.* Betts held Nova and thought, *I could murder Brock right now I'm so angry. Thank God for you, my warrior.*

Nova pulled away slightly and kissed Betts' inviting lips with just enough tongue to taste her. Nova then backed off to measure her effect on Betts. *I'm game. Are you?*

Chapter 24: Accountability Partners

QUESTION: Dear Sister Shuree, My mom doesn't give me the respect I deserve. What should I do?

ANSWER: You immediately need to increase the value of yourself, your work, and your decisions by placing your instinct above all else. People who don't recognize your value cannot judge you objectively. Unplug from whatever it is that you think you're getting from your mom. All that you need to hear right now is already inside of you, so listen to yourself more. Meditate if you have to. Picture her walking her sorry butt up to the highest, furthest seat in the bleachers of your life. You're Payton Manning in your stadium, and she is just a speck.

+ + + + +

In her home office, Alice clicked on the YouTube video of Sister Shuree so it would stop. *She's right. Let's do this.* She texted Brock and asked him to meet her in a public place in downtown Boulder because she wanted to prevent herself from fooling around with him and encourage herself to say what needed to be said. Intellectually, she knew she had to break it off with him even though this was in direct opposition to her heart. *Why did you have to be so stupid, Brock? Why don't you understand how delicate relationships are?* Alice pulled her car into a nearby parking garage and then walked to the spot where Brock sat on a wooden bench staring out into space. As if greeting someone at church, Alice politely remarked, "Happy Easter," as she sat down beside him.

"Oh, is that why everyone is so dressed up today?" Brock looked around the pedestrian mall at the tens of Boulderites shopping and hanging out on Pearl Street before his eyes swept over her like a fast breeze. *She's cold. Distant.* Brock braced himself mentally. The six brick-lined blocks were home to dozens of local restaurants and shops. It was old Americana at its finest with flower beds of tulips, peace lilies, and multicolored hyacinth surrounding the foot of every tree. This afternoon, there were street artists juggling fire, a zany woman dressed as a Bronco's fan who danced wildly through the crowd, and some high school students playing the cello badly for tips. Blond toddlers in frilly, pastel clothes climbed on large rocks as their parents thumbed their cell phones and dragged along the family dog. "How are the girls? All settled in?" Brock failed at sounding sincere.

"They're about as good as can be expected," *Moron*, "traumatized, but relieved the ordeal is over. Their lives will never be the same. I'm going to spend more time with Destiny, the tall one, like as a big sister or aunt. She needs clothes and a cell phone, so I'm going to bring those around to her tomorrow."

"You're kind. You're always so kind. Yeah, none of us are going to be the same again after that." Brock took another quick glance at Alice who continued to stare straight ahead.

Of course you're thinking about yourself. Alice halted her negativity. *Chill, girl. Chill. Say something nice.* "Thanks, Brock, for helping me rescue them." She finally turned and met his gaze. "I really appreciate you and the Bliss staff getting on board. You all literally saved three lives yesterday. Literally. I'll never forget last night for as long as I live." Alice refocused on a server filling up two dog bowls with water just outside a café to their far right. "How is Nefertiti doing? Is she okay?"

"Honestly, I have no clue. I just wanted to give her and her family some space today." Brock leaned back and crossed his legs. "Nova said she was fine and sent her home last night, so I'm assuming that she's just at home recovering."

Instead of stating the obvious, that he absolutely should be checking on his coworker who was shot, Alice moved on and purposefully let the words dribble out of her mouth: "Yeah, I didn't see her this morning – when I was walking around Bliss – looking for you and Betts." Her pauses spoke for her. *Connect the dots, Brock.*

"This morning? You were looking for… us?" Brock started to clue in.

"Yeah, before I brought the girls to Hope House, Desiree thought I should check in with both of you, as the bosses, and yeah – you two were busy, so I just left." *Very busy.*

Like a fierce crack of lightning ripping through a dark sky, Brock suddenly realized the implication of Alice's phrasing. *Jesus. So this is what's going on.* Brock's hand covered his mouth momentarily. *Bad to worse, worse to unrecoverable.* "I fucking hate myself right now, Alice. I was open with you last week about her, but that doesn't absolve the fact that I didn't discuss… my interaction… with you first. Ug. You have every right to be pissed."

Alice was momentarily baffled. *Okay, let's mince words.* "Do you think I'm angry at you because you didn't talk to me about having sex with Betts before you did it? Is that why you think I'm mad?"

"By the look on your face, I see that I'm wrong. Again." Brock sat up and crossed his arms in front of his chest.

"Don't do that," Alice held him accountable and denied him an out.

"What?"

"Don't play the victim. You don't get to twist this around. I'm the one who had to knock on a door and be ignored because my lover is fucking someone else! Do you have any idea how embarrassed I felt? How humiliated? I'm a full-grown woman being treated like I have not been treated since I was a teenager. No one disrespects me like that nowadays. I am reliable. Do you understand that I'm a professor? That I'm professional? No one makes me wait for a meeting. People show up on time because we are adults. They don't ask me to do anything illegal either like clean the blood of a murdered guy off your walls. If I'm acting like a twat, my friends tell me. And, they expect me to do the same for them. In fact, my friends donate their time to my causes and my whims, as I do to theirs. I have eyes on me, and I have an impact on the community. I'm accountable, not that you would know what that means."

Defensive, Brock tried to placate her. "I'm sorry, okay?"

"Brock, I got locked in your Goddamned waiting room over night last night and you didn't even notice. Nobody did! I even texted you for help. I mean seriously, Brock. I had to go to the bathroom on your Ficas tree. Did it even cross your mind to check on me at all? Clearly not. And when you saw my text many hours later, why did it not occur to you to respond – like, acknowledge my feelings at all? What is wrong with you? Not you, not anybody is going to treat me like a snot-nosed teenager anymore. Adult Alice does not accept this low-level bullshit. You either treat me with the respect I deserve or I'm out."

Brock rubbed his throbbing forehead. *This is so bad.* "Can I explain?"

Don't let him. He's gonna suck you back in. Stay strong! "You can try, but I don't think that there is anything you can say to me that will make sense in my world. I'm monogamous – except for you, but generally speaking I'm loyal. I get respect, and I give respect because that's what fucking adults do. You were the first guy that came along and excited me to fool around in over 20 years. Me! Breaking the code of loyalty! The problem is that I just didn't realize how little sex meant to you. It's nothing. It's just another biological function to you like spitting as you jog."

Brock turned and faced her. *She has to believe me.* "No. That's not true at all, Alice. Sex is very meaningful to me. With you, fooling around is so delicious and refreshing, I can't begin to tell you. I feel like we are just getting started and now you want to kill it. Alice, you have to give me another chance. Please."

Stay strong. "No, I don't, and I'll tell you why: I'm not like your clients. I can appreciate that there are all kinds of women out there in all different kinds of relationships. I'm not so naïve to think that everyone needs to think or behave like me. That being said, I'm just not that."

"Not what?" Brock's remorse melted into defensiveness.

"Not one of your clients. Not that kind of woman."

Brock could withstand Alice's jabs that he was immature, but making fun of his clients was an insult worth righting. "What kind of woman is that exactly?"

Alice continued her rant. "The kind of woman who can allow her lover to be with other people. I don't want to be with others, I want you. Only you. I'm open minded, but for the life of me I cannot understand why I would want to share you or why you would want to share me. This is who I am, Brock. When I heard you in Betts' office, I just wanted to cry. You were sharing something so personal with her that I felt betrayed. If you can't put me first now, when will you? Ever?"

Brock argued back. "I'll have you know that over half of our clients identify as being in monogamous relationships. Do you know why they come to Bliss? Because it makes their monogamous relationship better and therefore last longer. Also, your worldview could be more inclusive and relative. Lots of women learn to manage their relationships like a volume dial or dimmer switch. They know exactly how much energy and time to give the various people in their lives. Bliss is just a safe and private alternative for what they already do. And our service menu is not simply sex. Lots of women just enjoy a flirt and a drink, sexting, the list goes on and on – way past your imagination. It's not about sex, it's about women's sexual agency." Brock took his vape pen out of his back pocket, but before he could use it, Alice stopped him.

Alice placed her hand over his, pressing down toward his lap. "And that's another thing. Do you have to be high or drunk all of the time? Can't we enjoy each other's company sober?"

"You don't need to feel ashamed about getting high. It's legal now. Everyone does it. You have to get rid of that old sneaking and shaming mindset."

"I don't want to get high, Brock! And I don't want you to get high. Not right now. I just want a sober conversation where level heads prevail. Clearly, had you been thinking straight this past week, Bliss would not have been so far compromised. But no, all of these lives and livelihoods are at stake simply because you were high."

Brock stared *fuck you* at Alice. "So what is the main issue here, that I like to get high or that I screwed Betts? Pick one so I know which argument to poke holes in first."

"You're gross. Grow up. Stop reacting like a child and own up to your choices. You chose to be high practically 24-7 this weekend and let Gael into your house. A known murderer!"

"You don't understand how it went down. It wasn't just that I was high. Terrance had Gael subdued. I was joking with Terrance, he didn't seem like a bad guy, and I had no idea that the police would come. You have to understand this point: Bliss is in the unique position that we have to keep everything on the down low. You know this. By letting them in, I was trying to deal with the situation without involving the police. That was my only play."

"Was it?"

"Yes! What else was I supposed to do? I had the murder weapon. Gael was obviously looking for it. If he had been alone, I would have called Sharon and not let him in the house. But Terrance was there holding a gun to Gael's head. He had the situation under control. Terrance even told me that he wanted to get out from under the cartel. He wanted witness protection."

"He did?" Alice was curious.

"Yes, he was asking me if I would be a go-between with the police. He was ready to give up the criminal life."

"Huh. Well, while this information helps, guys like him are exactly the problem, Brock. The nature of your work involves you with reprehensible people who do reprehensible things, which make them need a completely new identity to get out. On the flip side, I'm an educator and a feminist and will defend my sisters' ability to choose whatever they want for themselves – abortion, contraception, sex, any type of job, what have you – but do not turn around and pretend that your stoned decisions don't have consequences. The consequences are very real to the people around you, people like me. I honestly thought that you loved me, Brock. I was even thinking about divorcing my husband for you."

Brock wiped his face with both hands. *Maybe we're both right. I made the best decision I could, but it still hurt her and everyone else. God, I totally fucked this all up.*

Alice realized that Brock was not arguing back anymore and tried to decelerate her anger by explaining her motivation like a professor. "This amount of truth being shoved down anyone's throat tends to be a choking hazard, I know. Most grown men would, rightly so, be upset to know that they have caused such pain unintentionally. Truth tends to crack doubt across our shrine of self-understanding. Confrontation makes us question the ripple effects of thousands of decisions that could have been given pause and a second critical thought. Seriously Brock, one's soul is not lost simply due to double-checking on a decision or questioning its plausibility from a new angle – namely an angle that is not one's own. Self-reflection is good."

Brock felt blank. He did not know how to win Alice back.

"You know Brock, as I get older, I see a pattern when I attempt to be empathetic. When I try to understand someone else's reality –

even if it is a silly guess – my emotional attachment fades away like a Chinese lantern being cast off into the sky at dusk. Empathizing is healing yourself, one better-decision at a time."

Brock ached. He had been shutting down emotionally for over a week now, so there was no way that a last beat-down was going to revive him into a new reality. *Broken can always get more broken, just break the last half in half, then break that half in half, and then another half, and another...* Brock registered that he was at a very important crossroads as the high from his edible hit him. *This is it. I can either keep doing the same thing that I've always done, or...* Brock took a moment to honestly try to empathize with her. He closed his eyes and visualized his spirit lifting out of his body and floating down into hers. He imagined looking through her eyes down at her wedding band. *What does this mean to her?* The palm of his hand found the top of her thigh and braced it tightly as he opened his eyes. "You know Alice, I've never been married. I've never even been in a monogamous, long-term relationship before.

"When I'm home, I literally do not need to think about coexisting or getting along with anyone. I can just do what I want, whenever I want. The life of a bachelor is a hell of a lot of fun, actually. I don't have to compromise or share; it's great! Well I thought like that up until now. Before you, with my money, and let's face it my looks, there's just so much power and excess. I lie to myself that all the energy I put into work, into Bliss, justifies the recklessness, but it doesn't.

"Kids, pets, grocery shopping, family meetings, braces, car-pooling, plants, and tooth fairies don't even cross my mind because the privileges and freedom are just so much more enticing. You see, your frame of reference, Alice, is not my frame of reference. I'm just grasping at straws to even guess at words that describe your married life, because I really don't know. I've never carved a pumpkin or held a sick kid. I don't even know if that stuff is fun or worthwhile.

"That's why I left the murder weapon on the kitchen island out in the open, Alice. No one comes to my house unannounced. No one even lives within miles of me, and frankly, no one has wanted to be monogamous with me before. You're the first. It's so sweet, actually. I didn't realize how nice it would feel to have someone say that they want to be exclusive."

Alice mirrored his smile. *There's my sweet man.*

"You're right, Alice. From your perspective, I'm not acting like I want you. You're the complete package and have high expectations on all aspects of your life; I get it. My life is tailored just for me, and yes, admittedly, that's based on a high degree of self-indulgence. So what do I need to do to repair this? How can I keep you? Keep us? I'm not ready to give up."

Without hesitation, Alice revealed the essence of her desire: "Earn me. Get high less and be monogamous with me. Completely monogamous. No clients and no Betts, not ever again." Alice crossed her arms stealing herself against the inevitable pushback.

Brock did not have to decide. For the first time in his life, he acquiesced to another's will as if falling backwards into welcoming arms. It struck him as odd that the bachelor life, which he had painstakingly constructed and enjoyed, was so easily demolished by the miraculous relief that Alice had given him another chance to love her. "Okay. I will."

"Really?" Alice asked with surprise.

"Of course, Alice." Brock could not help but smile wide and grasp her hand. "I don't want to blow this second chance, so if that's what you want, you got it. I want to earn you."

Alice returned his smile and placed her other hand on top of his.

Brock wanted to kiss her so badly, but he held back. "You have to do something for me too, though, babe."

"What?" Alice wondered, playfully circumspect.

"Divorce your husband. Start moving toward the life that you actually want and stop settling for 'pretty good.'"

Alice was surprised at how the conversation turned like a hairpin against her.

"You can move in with me," Brock offered with a hopeful smile.

Alice laughed out loud. "C'mon. Seriously? This is too fast. In your world, fast means decisive. Fast is nimble. Fast is good. In my world, fast is a big, red flag. If I'm going to consciously uncouple from my husband, it's going to take time and maturity."

"Okay, slow gear. Less pot and only sex with you. I want to be that for you. Just, at your own pace, get yourself ready for me too, babe." Brock squeezed her hands again and leaned in closer to her ear. "You take the lead and I'll follow. I'll follow you anywhere, I swear."

✦ ✦ ✦ ✦ ✦

"Question: Dear Sister Shuree, I have a bad habit of following advice from the wrong people. How can I tell the difference between people with good and bad advice? Good question! Here is my answer. Advice from anyone is never more than itself: it's inherently subjective. However, to increase your odds of getting helpful advice, look for: experience, expertise, intelligence, and empathy.

"Like me, for instance. I earned my BA in Psychology and my MA in Clinical Counseling from Cornell. I'm a Licensed Professional Counselor and Marriage and Family Therapist in the state of Colorado. And, my private practice is located in Cherry Creek if you want more specific, long-term help.

So now that I established my ethos, I'll tell you what you already know: if your car's 'check engine' warning light is on, don't go to the dentist, girl. Please don't do that. Have some sense now. Get it together.

"The very fact that, as you claim, you ask the wrong people for advice means you didn't want to get the right advice. Now why would that be? I'm not exactly saying that you bring it onto yourself, but I am saying that you can't con an honest man. Think about that statement right there. What is 'an honest person'? An honest person will call bullshit on you because they are willing to be held accountable as well. Only those who are hoping you will overlook their pile of feces will so quickly overlook yours. That's why we all need good accountability partners.

"Accountability partners help us make our own bullshit more palatable. They help us cut it down into little, itty-bitty, bite-size pieces so we can digest our own self-loathing. And once we take a few bites, we can course-correct and move in a more positive direction. So I'm sorry to feed you this bitter truth, but you need to find one person in your life who tells you what you don't want to hear and then listen, girl. Listen real good."

+ + + + +

"Mary Ann Gambino! How the hell are you? 'It's been a minute,' as my granddaughter would say," Steady warmly greeted his oldest and dearest friend, Mary Ann. He opened his long arms wide to squeeze her tight into his embrace. "You look divine, as always. Love the lipstick!" The two friends hugged between the renovated carousel and the mesmerizing 'Spit and Spat' fountain in Congress Park in Saratoga Springs, one of the few economically thriving cities in upstate New York. Its fame was broad based: horse races, ballet, SPAC, mineral springs, and Skidmore College. Its infamy, however, was singular; Saratoga had a long and intriguing history of gambling, thievery, and murder. Many multigenerational Saratogians like Steady and Mary Ann therefore had connections to crime in one form or another. Tainted by family name only was not a big deal to the locals. However, having only two degrees of separation from organized crime put Steady and Mary Ann in a different league of locals.

"Hi, Steady, so good to see you." Mary Ann admitted happily in his arms. Her thick black hair cascaded out of a black beret down her shoulders. "It's been too long, but I'm so glad we're finally getting together now. I've missed you so much."

"I know. Me too, Hon." Steady squeezed her shoulder tight. His short gray beard, baldhead, and tall, thin frame were accented by the punch of blues and lavenders in his suit and bow tie. Dressing impeccably was his brand.

"Should we assume the position?" Mary Ann motioned with a smile to the bench near the twenty-foot long, rectangular 'Spit and Spat' fountain.

"Absolutely. You know an old queen like me needs to sit more often these days. Let's smoke and dish about life. Tell me everything." Steady pulled out a cigarette from his pocket and lit it with a heavy, metal, flip top lighter. His gaze momentarily fell to one stream of water flying through the air. Each end of the fountain had white marble statues of a young, bare chested, Roman man blowing water out of his mouth at the other. One was named Spit and the other Spat. Steady sat to her left and loudly flipped his lighter open again to light her cigarette. "You're still smoking, I see."

"Eh." Mary Ann sounded as if she was indecisive.

"Girl, you have your own pack. Own it already," Steady scolded.

Mary Ann chuckled and exhaled a white plume of smoke upwards toward the maple trees. "You're the only person I smoke with, Steady. I don't smoke. I'm not a smoker, but I know that when I'm going to hang out with you, I go buy a pack. God I love this. I love our friendship; I love this town. And, of course, I love the excuse to smoke."

"Awe, that's so sweet, hon! I didn't know that you did that for me. I love you too. And, I still love this town as well. Our roots are so deep. I've always enjoyed having a sense of place, of being so grounded."

"Me too, for the most part. I miss having my kids here though. Nova left, you know, out to Colorado."

"Good for her. I hope she smokes a shit ton of weed."

Mary Ann tossed Steady a disapproving look. "So I told her to apply to the hospitals out there, but she didn't want to. Now she's got some kind of job at a gym. Something health-related, I don't know, but she's in some kind of trouble."

"Oh, no! What's going on with my girl?" Over the decades, Nova had grown up around Steady. She was as close as family to him. As adults, they occasionally crossed paths at LGBTQ events and fundraisers around town. He liked her bossy attitude. *Full of piss and vinegar, that one… at least until her husband got cancer.*

Mary Ann took a long drag from her cigarette and brushed some errant ashes off of her lap. "Don't give me that worried look, Steady. I can tell already that you're going to be judgy."

"What look? I'm not giving you a look. You, however, are feeling guilty about something obviously. Do tell."

"Don't. I hate feeling bad."

Steady exaggerated his disapproving expression for dramatic effect. "Let's not play coy. Out with it already." Steady crossed his legs and leaned in.

"Okay. Here it is. I think Nova got mixed up with a violent job, and I'm a little concerned. Yesterday, she told me that her boss pulled a gun on her and almost shot her."

"Holy shit! Did she bring her firearms with her out to Colorado?"

"No. She gave them to me to put in our safe."

"Well, what was she thinking? She needs a gun! We all need guns! Fuck, you and I would not even exist if it weren't for our fathers and uncles fending off the other gangs. You couldn't run illegal gaming in this town in the '50s without guns… and bribes to the police… and alcohol for the gamblers." Steady laughed deeply like a productive smoker. "My girl Nova knows this. Anyway, what did you say to her?" Steady waited longer than necessary for a response and then realized there was more to her story. "Mary Ann. What did you tell that girl."

"She's not a girl," Mary Ann corrected. "She's practically 50 and shouldn't be getting herself into these predicaments. I told her not to tell me anything more, that I don't want to know. It's too stressful. I'm old now."

Steady gasped dramatically. "No. No way. You cut her off?" He was stunned. He picked up a stone from the ground and threw it at a goose that was getting too close. *Fuckers.*

"I wouldn't phrase it that way. I just told her, 'Godspeed. Live life the way you want, but don't tell me everything.' I don't need to know everything. I said it with love, from a good place. She told me that she understood."

What the hell? "Where are your fucking mom-genes, Mary Ann? Seriously. How can your daughter tell you that her boss almost shot her dead, and your response was, 'Don't tell me more?' How is that coming from a loving place?"

"Boundaries are good. No?" Mary Ann felt sheepish.

Steady stared at her as though she had just lost her mind.

"I know, I know." Mary Ann lowered her head down into her right palm.

"Get it together. That's what you do when you're a parent, Mary Ann, you know this. We have to rise to the occasion."

"Wow. That's a heap-ton of shame," Mary Ann complained as she sat back up.

"I'm what kids today call an 'accountability partner.' It's a good thing, and it's real; you can look it up. I saw it on Miss Sister Shuree's vlog this morning."

Mary Ann huffed and pretended to strangle an invisible person.

"Did you actually think your job was ever going to be over? You don't just get to turn it off like a spigot, whenever it suits you. Put on your big girl pants and help her."

"I'm not a horrible mom." Mary Ann picked up a stone and threw it at another goose that was hungry for bread they did not have. "Go, stupid geese leaving shit everywhere."

"Of course you're not a horrible mother. You're just full of self interest and egocentric tendencies," Steady teased as he lit another cigarette.

Mary Ann lit herself another cigarette as well. "Life is a lot. There's more than just my progeny to deal with."

"Really? At our age? We're rich, and we're retired. We should be gambling and having tea parties at Mrs. London's with our grandkids."

"Nova is her own bird, and she can fly. I taught her well. She's very strong."

"Be less witchy! Do you hear yourself? If nothing else, Nova needs your emotional support, but she may need some physical protection too."

"I don't really know the situation or her involvement, but she didn't sound scared. All I know is that she works at a place in Boulder called Bliss."

"Bliss, eh? Weird name for a gym, but it's Boulder: hippy-dippy. Do you want me to send a few guys over to check on her? These are the perks, after all, of being the children of gangsters. You know our fathers would insist if they knew the circumstances."

Mary Ann suddenly grinned and sarcastically provoked Steady, "Finally you offer to help. Jesus, already. Making me beg."

"Oh my God, you didn't beg!" Steady was surprised.

"I shouldn't have to ask, is my point. You should just offer."

"Jesus." Steady lowered his baldhead into both of his hands.

"Quicker, is all I'm saying. Offer to help quicker."

"Did your edibles just kick in, love?"

"You're not so steady these days, are you Steady? You're kind of emotional." Mary Ann laughed with a deep belly chuckle and a few strong smacks to Steady's back.

"And people say I'm queer," Steady teased.

Chapter 26: Monday

Early Monday morning, eager to jump back into work at Bliss, Betts tackled her first order of business: she entered Brock's six-digit front door code and went in without knocking. "Brock!" For good measure, she slammed the door closed and listened. *He better be home.* "Time to get up!" Dressed in a business casual jeans and a button down shirt, she marched through his house into his bedroom. *Wake up, it's time for an intervention.*

At the moment Betts entered, Brock was awoken from a sound sleep. "Hey!" *Fuck off, Betts.* He rolled over. He suddenly remembered yesterday evening when Brock had no answers that could satisfy Alice, and she broke up with him. For the past two days he had been feeling like *a worthless piece of shit*, but now, it was confirmed. Brock felt cornered and angry.

"Get out of bed, Brock. We need to talk," Betts demanded. "Now." She stomped away to the kitchen where Terrance's finger and cell phone laid on the counter top. "Is this for fucking real?" Horrified, she inspected the evidence closer. "Christ, Brock," she mumbled. After a few minutes, she heard a shower start. Two of her fingers firmly pressed between her eyebrows to ease some of the pressure building in the center of her forehead.

From inside the shower, Brock yelled his question as if he was accusing her of something, "Why are you here?"

Betts, pissed off, trudged back to his room and turned into his expansive, marble bathroom. "What?"

Brock continued to shower. "Why the fuck are you here, Betts?" Brock knew that when Betts didn't respond to his text yesterday that she was angry. *Fuck off already.*

"I'm livid at you, Brock," Betts said to the blurry figure through the glass shower door.

"Oh, you're mad at me? That's rich," Brock argued from inside with a sarcastic chuckle. "You wanna punch something again? Would that make you feel better? Don't blame me for giving you what you want."

"That's not what I'm talking about," Betts clarified and shook her head. *Idiot.*

Brock continued on his diatribe as he soaped up and rinsed off his tanned body. "I know you sometimes like it rough. My willingness to be that, to do that, makes me sexy. And yet I didn't hear any fucking safe word yesterday morning. But then, you lose it and go nuts." Brock turned off the running water and stepped out of the shower naked. He angrily dried himself off with a dark purple towel in front of her. "I'm the one who was here when the shit hit the fan. I've been putting out fires and dealing with crisis after crisis while you're off wining and dining clients. Your response? Temper tantrums."

Betts was confused by his self-depiction as a victim. *According to Nova, she was saving the day.* "Say whatever allows you to look at yourself in the mirror, Brock." Agitated, Betts wiped her face from her forehead to her chin. "I'm here to discuss your poor choices, your behavior, your acting out."

"Well, I want to discuss yours! Where the fuck have you been?" He wrapped the towel around his waist and started combing his hair in the mirror.

Betts ignored his toned body. "Doing my job. How about you doing yours? Because as others tell it, you hired a murderer, are dating a sex trafficking researcher, *and* endangered our staff by having them bury a fucking body – criminal evidence – in your freaking backyard." Betts' hands were on her hips.

Brock walked past her into his closet and put on some boxer shorts and faded jeans. He threw the damp towel as hard as he could at his bench-seat. "I know it's fucking bad, Betts." He agreed as he exited the closet zipping up his fly. He started making his bed bare-chested. "I've been kicking myself repeatedly for days now. I know I've messed everything up, but in my defense, you've been MIA. I don't know what the fuck has been taking you so long to get back to town and check in with your responsibilities here. Meanwhile, I've been coping alone."

"Not well, obviously, because you haven't been coping *alone*," Betts mocked.

"Alice? Fuck off! You're not jealous of her," Brock defended himself. "She broke up with me last night anyway, so what's the real issue?" He picked up several pillows up off from the floor and tossed them hard onto the head of the bed.

"We both know what you, off the rails, looks like." Betts crossed her arms over her chest.

Brock stopped and took a deep breath, then walked over to her. "What? Tell me, Betts, this should be good."

Betts searched his face. "This." She held up the plastic sandwich bag with Terrence's finger. "It looks like a finger thoughtlessly left on a kitchen table. It looks like Nefertiti's gunshot shoulder. It looks like you exploiting our staff in order to satisfy the whims of your new ex-girlfriend. Everyone took all of that risk, and now Alice just walks away? Well, maybe she's not so stupid after all."

Brock almost slapped Betts across the face, but instead leaned in and asked with a sneer, "Who wrapped up your hand, babe? Nova?"

A micro-expression of surprise escaped over Betts' face.

"Yeah, I know. I knew the minute I met her that you two would get along. Did you tell her how you messed up your hand? Did you pretend that you couldn't fix those tiny little scabs yourself so that she could do it for you?"

"This is off the topic. You're trying to deflect the conversation." Betts suddenly recognized just how defensive Brock really was. Like someone desperately trying to not drown, he was grasping to pull down anyone within reach.

"Wait, let me guess. You let Nova believe that you punched me and messed me up, right?" Brock chuckled as Betts stood silent. He grabbed a t-shirt and stretched it over his head and semi-hairy chest. "It doesn't fit your boss-image that you put a few holes in your office walls, does it." Brock's face was only inches from Betts. He grabbed the collar of her button down shirt and pulled it toward him. "Worried that your new lover will know you were having a temper tantrum… baby?"

"Fuck off, Brock," Betts sneered as she tried to push him away.

Brock slightly yanked her collar closer toward him. "Did you fuck her left-handed after she wrapped up your right, Betts, or did you use a strap on?" Brock let go of her collar and pushed her away with a grunt not dissimilar to a wolf growling.

Betts quickly took a step backwards. "You're out of line and way more fucked up than I thought."

"Says the ex-convict," Brock provoked by poking at her weakest point. His eyes stared intensely into hers. *Fuck you!*

Impulsively, Betts' cocked her right arm and punched him in the jaw as hard as she could. Rapid punches would have continued had her knuckles not made her recoil in pain. "Fuck you!" Betts yelled as she looked down at her hand to see four bloody circles that rose to the surface of her bandages. She stepped back and vigorously shook her hand in the air to lessen the pain.

After his cutting words provoked the requisite response from her, Brock rubbed his face with his hand. "Betts, I didn't stick my cock into anyone except you this weekend, okay? I'm sorry that this has gotten ugly. You know I love you, but I love her too. One day we are going to be together again when the timing is right. Why is it so hard for you to make room for her? It never was a problem before."

"Shut up with your half-assed apologies, Brock. This is me trying to help you not fall down the rabbit hole, and what do I get in response? Malice." Betts felt so frustrated.

"Oh, this is you *helping* me? Your inattention and violence are supposed to be helping me? In what universe? No thank you." Brock stormed out of his bedroom and through his kitchen in bare feet.

Betts followed him and sat down at the kitchen island in front of Terrance's phone. She placed his finger in the sandwich bag down next to it.

Brock grabbed the old coffee grounds out from his espresso machine and banged the handle against the inside of his waste paper basket. "Do you want coffee?" he asked in a more measured tone without looking at her.

"Yes," she replied, reluctantly civil.

Where do we go from here? Brock wondered as he poured coffee beans into his grinder and pressed the button. They both let the mechanical noise fill the gulf between them. When the machine stopped, he turned to her and remarked, "Betts, I love Bliss. We created it together. As pissed off as I am right now, the company needs both of us."

Betts stood and walked over to his dishwasher and pawed around to find two coffee mugs, which she set on the counter near him. "I'll admit that the staff are closer to you now. I may have cultivated them with each new onboarding, but for whatever reason, they end up in deeper relationships with you in the end. I can admit that."

Brock's phone dinged the arrival of a text message, but he ignored it. *Is Betts trying to meet me half way?*

"Nova shared with me yesterday all that has happened these last two weeks," Betts continued. "I am starting to see, from her more objective point of view, that Bliss is a dangerous place. Well, it shouldn't be, but it can be. The margin of error for us is razor thin. One bad hire rippled outwards like a freaking bomb. Everyone has been affected. We need to build in another level of security into hiring. Not the usual stuff, I mean we need very thorough background checks, credit checks, criminal record, references, some personality profiling test that can weed out all of the Gaels out there. Whatever we need to do, let's just do it. I am not letting everything we have built come crashing down just because of one idiot."

Brock finished playing with the coffee machine and turned to face her directly as it dripped out into the two small espresso mugs. "I'm sorry I brought up prison. I just wanted to hurt you, and that's not kind."

"Well, you did. I'm sorry I punched the wall yesterday… and you," Betts stated reluctantly.

Brock looked down at his bare feet as the toes of his right foot touched the tip of Betts' manicured toenails in her sandals. "Please check in more often the next time you leave. Create room for us to communicate with you when things aren't going well, because sometimes it's like I need to prove that I don't need you, so I don't tell you about the small stuff. Then, work blows up, and it's too embarrassing to tell you the much larger problems. Can you just communicate with me and everyone more?"

Betts opened her left hand palm up. "Yes. I'm still in shock, but I know one thing – we're never gonna fix this divided. So are we good enough to forge on?"

Brock placed his right hand inside hers and squeezed when his phone dinged a reminder about the text. "Good as gold." He let go of her and glanced at his phone. *Gael! Holy shit!* "Betts. It's Gael!"

Irritated, Betts crossed her arms over her chest. *What does this murderer have to say for himself?*

"Holy fucking shit. He wants $100K. He's blackmailing us, the little prick!" Brock's mouth hung open. They held each other's gaze in mutual frustration over this never-ending drama.

"Goddamnit!" Betts squeezed her right fist until the pain in her knuckles was so strong it calmed her down and made her take a deep breath.

"I can't believe this," Brock mumbled and then asked without sarcasm, "We can't give him a dime. You know that, right? He'll just keep milking us." Brock took the two full, little mugs out from the espresso machine and gave one to Betts.

More blood soaked through each of Betts' knuckles up through the white gauze. "Yeah, I agree. We need to right this runaway train. We need to protect Bliss any way possible."

✦ ✦ ✦ ✦ ✦

"At twelve o'clock we have mashed sweet potatoes, at four o'clock there's chicken breast. It's breaded. And at eight o'clock is my favorite: brussel sprouts with bacon. You got your plastic cutlery on the right side of the plate and your pop is on your left. You good?" asked the young man delivering cafeteria food to the ICU patient.

"Straw?" John asked as his hands tentatively pushed forward. Once his fingertips reached the plastic food tray, they followed the edges of it around the left and right corners. He heard two more sets of footsteps enter his hospital room and stop. *Too quiet for medical staff.* It amazed him how acute his hearing had become after he was blinded.

"Yep," the worker assured him. "The cup's got a plastic cover and the straw is poked through. Anything else?"

"Who's here?" John asked him as a reliable witness.

"We'll help him out. No worries." Detective Sontag interrupted and directed his comment to the nurse.

"Looks like the police wanna talk to you. I'll be back in an hour for the tray, man."

Sontag walked close to John who was seated upright in his hospital bed and waved his right hand in front of John's face to verify if he could see through the bandages or not. "Wow, life must really suck for you right now." He noticed that John's hands immediately formed fists.

Boratto noticed the fists as well. "Hey, you're not cuffed to the bed, so that's something."

"I have a feeling that he's not a flight risk," Sontag joked.

Boratto introduced himself so that John could connect names to the voices. "Hey, John, we're detectives Boratto and Sontag; I'm Boratto. We have been assigned to find out who did this to you. We heard that you don't have orbital fractures, but that your eyeballs got popped. On top of that, the morgue has two of your buddies, so I'm hoping that you can help us out and bring yourself – and them – some justice."

"Justice." John spat out the word like he was punch-lining a joke. His fat hand nervously pulled at his unkempt beard. "You can bet there will be justice."

"John," Boratto continued, "Just tell us who did this to you. Was it Gael or a big, black guy?"

"Big, black guy? You just said my two guys were down in the morgue, now which is it?" John's right hand gesticulated directly at his cup of soda, which fell forward onto his blanketed lap. "Fuck. I fucking hate this! Can you help me?"

Boratto grabbed the plastic cup and righted it as quickly as he could. "There's some left inside. It didn't all spill out. Do you want me to leave it on the tray, or..." Boratto slowly returned it to the empty corner of blind John's tray. He tapped it loudly three times. "It's right here."

Blind John blew air through his puckered lips like he was blowing out a candle. "This is my fucking life now thanks to Gael. He did it. He blinded me and killed my men."

Boratto and Sontag smiled at each other and knuckle bumped.

"Do you know where we can find Gael?" asked Sontag.

"Sucking dick in an alley, I imagine," John replied.

"Got it: you don't know. Before we go," Sontag continued, "Do you know women named either Betts or Alice or a guy named Brock?"

"Barak Obama?"

"No," Sontag chuckled, "Brock is a white guy – good looking – owns a gym here in Boulder with Betts. He's dating a lady named Alice."

"Nope. Never heard those names in my life," blind John stated unequivocally.

A nurse named Sophie leaned on the ICU front desk watching the two detectives exit blind John's room and walk down the hall to the elevator. She fished her phone out of the pocket of her pink scrubs and texted Nick in Whatsapp, "Police just left John." One minute later her phone vibrated Nick's response, a Bitmoji of Nick lying dead and above it, a car's red gas meter on empty.

Once they got back into their white SUV, Sontag brainstormed out loud before he put the car in gear. The air conditioner roared on high as usual. "Okay, so blind John is at the losing end of a blunt force object. Gael is his attacker. Alice finds out about the sex slaves from Gael, how?"

"Research?" Boratto took a guess.

"But who introduced them?" Sontag wondered aloud. "She's a professor and he's a scum bag. Her research isn't better than ours. She wasn't hanging out with blind John and conducting qualitative interviews for some ethnography."

"By process of elimination, then, how else would a guy like Gael be connected to Alice? It's gotta be Brock," Boratto surmised. "There's our chain of information: blind John, Gael, Brock, Alice, hotline."

"Let's find Gael, then, through Brock. I know we're right. Blind John is our witness identifying Gael for both murders, and I bet Gael will want to narc Blind John right back if he can get his sentence reduced. So we just need to pay another visit to Brock and get him to tell us where to find Gael."

"This time, though," Boratto said as he started the engine. "Let's put the pressure on Brock at work. Let's go to Bliss."

> "Dr. Zezza, we're group three, the local drug dealers. You said that our boss is in the hospital and that two of our coworkers were murdered, so we would just hide and wait to see what happens. Basically we would do nothing and lay low. We think that group two will get the heat from both ends and explode."

"Hi," Sophie greeted the uniformed police officer seated outside John's door in a soft voice. She entered his hospital room after the detectives left. "Hey, John, I'm Sophie." From her pocket she produced a nickel colored, Umbra paper towel topper and placed it in John's right hand to hold. The EKG machine attached to John started beeping wildly. The police officer turned around to look at them. Sophie saw his chest rise and fall with each deep breath. *He's scared, poor thing*. "It's okay. Nick says 'hello,'" she said slightly louder than a whisper.

Blind John rolled the chunk of metal around between the tips of his fingers until he knew what it was and calmed down.

Sophie made herself look busy by inspecting the bag of saline dangling from the IV pole and pretending to take notes in his chart. "Is there any message I can pass on?" She took the piece of metal back out of his hand and slipped it once again into her pocket.

The regular-paced beeping revealed John's relief. "Tell Nick to find Gael." John replied in a lowered voice. "Detectives are looking for him too."

"How is it going otherwise? Loosing your sight is really traumatic," Sophie sympathized.

"I'm never gonna see again," John admitted the obvious haltingly, almost ready to cry. Feelings of betrayal triggered pain at the inner corners of his empty eye sockets. "This is true torture." John put his hand over his mouth and pretended to slightly cough.

Sophie squeezed blind John's right hand and felt him squeeze back. "I'm gonna hit you with a little truth: We're all stronger and braver than we think." She let go of his hand and pulled out a capped syringe from her scrubs pocket. "You hang in there, okay?" Sophie took the top off and slid the needle into John's IV line, pushing a cocktail of cyanide and arsenic up inside. "I'll pass along your message to Nick. Everything is gonna work out in the end. You'll see. Nick's got your back."

Exiting the hospital to look for her car in the expansive parking lot, Sophie quickly pulled off her fake ID, shoved it down into her purse, and put on a baseball cap. She listened to Nick complain at the other end of her cell phone.

"No shit, Sophie. That's all he had to say? Nothing else? Just 'find Gael?'"

"Yep. I deposited the money into his checking account too. We're all good," Sophie reassured Nick.

After Nick got off the phone with Sophie, he called Jojo, Boo, and Sandra into his latest 'office' – an old RV that he parked on a desolate back road near a trailhead.

Sandra wore her usual white t-shirt with her 'Stranger Things' black hoodie wrapped around her waist. The left hip pocket of her baggy black pants bulged with her cell phone and headphones.

From his seated position at the RV kitchen table, Nick shook his head disapprovingly at Sandra standing in front of him. He smacked his lips insultingly at her drawn-on, too-thin eyebrows and dramatic black lips. "You look like a fucking clown." *Ugly Latina.* Nick had reached out to what he liked to call his 'spies' to find out if the police were looking for Sandra after she shot someone. Luckily, she was not on their radar. *You live to choke on my dick another day, fea.* He growled at her: "Sit the fuck down."

Sandra's resting, zombie-bitch face rarely changed, even at a moment like this *when I just might get my fucking brains blown out today.* Happy moments were rarely-if-ever happy for her. On Sandra's ninth birthday, for instance, her father was high on cocaine and stabbed her mom to death before her very eyes. For this reason and numerous others not uncommon to broken families, frightening moments were also not so frightening to her. Numbness was her armor, and nothingness her shield. *You can't kill it, if it's already dead, motherfucker.*

Nick's voice roared as he paced inside the trailer. "Tell me how the mother-fuck we got shook down, Sandra. How?"

From the living room, Jojo's stomach growled loud enough for everyone to hear. He remained seated next to Boo with his head down.

"I was outnumbered," Sandra admitted flatly.

"Bootsie!" Nick turned and yelled at the far end of the RV. "Get out here. I want you to hear this."

A fit, middle-aged, clean-shaven man in a black t-shirt, jeans, and steel-toed Timberline boots emerged from the back bedroom and slowly swaggered over to them as if he were cashing in a winning bet at the race track. He was the lightest-skinned and least tattooed Sinaloan member that Nick had ever met. This scared him slightly knowing that the guy was probably used as a mercenary or for other special missions where he had to blend in. Unlike Sandra, the Mexican half-smiled a 'hello.'

Sandra's eyes immediately fell to his well-defined, muscular buttocks.

Jojo's stomach growled 'hungry' again.

"Guys, meet Bootsie," Nick announced. "He's my new associate. If Terrance comes back, and I hope he does, he still has a place with us. But for now, Bootsie is going to fill in. Bootsie, this 'clown-ess' is Sandra. She's a cat with nine lives apparently. Over there is Jojo and Boo." *Fucktards*. Nick grabbed and lit a cigarette from a pack on the kitchen table.

Small time, Bootsie thought. *Easy. This is my speed.* "Right. Outnumbered? You said you were outnumbered." Bootsie gave

Sandra his full attention in unaccented English. He studied her C-cup tits and looked for the nipples, then inspected her puffy lips very closely as she spoke. *Zooming in. I see saliva. I see black lipstick and pink insides. I see your tongue. How do you use it? How do you like it? I see you, girl. I see behind your armor and behind your game. Do you see me? Do you see me seeing you?*

Sandra dispassionately recalled the chain of events, but as she was talking, she became more and more mesmerized by Bootsie's gaze. "I was dancing with my headphones on and doing a security check when I saw this *roja* in the window. Bitch says that they are 'rescuing our property.' So I sprint upstairs, ready with my pistol, when a high-class, Asian lady is coming in our window. I popped her, like you know, of course, but then a white guy – high-class too – is coming up from behind. I have the re-coil, you know, and that gives me the power to just pistol-whip him in the head. On my right, in the hall with the rooms, I heard lots of people and saw them running toward me. There was a whole group of them. What could I do? I just got the fuck out of there." Sandra had to forcefully yank away her shared gaze with Bootsie. Instead, she eyed the pack of cigarettes and red lighter sitting next to a very full ashtray. She knew better than to ask Nick for one right now. *What the fuck is going on with this Bootsie?*

"What does your gut say right now?" Bootsie asked provocatively.

"My gut?" Sandra suddenly felt naked the moment she made eye contact with him again.

"About who they were. You said 'high class' twice. If you had to guess, what would you say?" Bootsie prodded.

Sandra stopped to think about it a minute. She thought of their faces – the redhead, the Asian, and the guy. *Blackish.* "Blackish. Like the family on Blackish; they seemed regular, nice. Only they weren't black. They were white folk. Definitely not in our type of life. I think if they were really trying to steal the girls, then they're probably from some not-for-profit. Do-gooders, maybe. Nobody that we have to worry about."

Suddenly Nick jumped at Sandra and grabbed her face and hair with both of his fat, sweaty fists. "You do not tell me what to worry about, cunt!"

Just as predicted, Sandra wasn't frightened – not when he grabbed her face and mushed it in five different directions, and not when he slammed the side of her skull repeatedly down onto the table. *Can't kill dead, stupid. Can't kill dead.*

Chapter 27: Barbara's Hideaway

Gael, like everyone in Colorado, lived as close as he could to the resources he needed. Those with money paid for a view – and quite a spectacular view of the Rocky Mountains it was indeed. The working class, in contrast, increasingly needed a reasonable commute and affordable groceries, so this meant moving closer to city centers and light rail stops with park-and-ride. For the most destitute, however, resources equated to a meal, urgent care, and a place to relieve oneself without getting arrested. Unfortunately, because Initiative 300 – a measure meant to reverse the seven-year urban camping ban – did not pass, the homeless existed illegally, mostly loitering in downtown Denver near Coors Field and Five Points or around the state capital building where dinner at the Denver Rescue Mission was only a walk or a free 16th Street bus ride away.

In spite of measurable reality, in Gael's mind, he was far from being homeless and refused to sleep at a shelter downtown. Simultaneously, he had about as much use for a view of the Rocky Mountains or a short commute as he had for an avatar or a podcast – which meant none. He was his own kind of man, an early 20th century kind of man. He had never printed anything to paper or looked at a screen on his dashboard to reverse his vehicle. Gael rolled his own joints and paid for everything in cash. Social media was for suckers. Sadly for him, he was twenty-seven years old and had nothing in life but his beautiful hair, his name, and one potential grift which promised to support him for several years if he did it right: he was going to blackmail Brock for the knowledge that Bliss was a front for a women's sex club. This information, in combination with his ingenuity and a bed at 'Barbara's Hideaway,' as he liked to call it, was his single best shot at funding a semi-normal life. Ever.

For Gael, blackmailing Brock was a logical solution because it was easy and low risk. He had already done the hard work. *It's time to get paid for it, papi. So why isn't Brock texting me back?* Brock's unrequited communication frustrated Gael to his core. He paced back and forth on a strip of carpeted path in Barbara's backyard as she watched him through her small kitchen window. *Brock lives in a multimillion-dollar house*, Gael reasoned. *He has money to spare... enough to change the lives of several people for generations. But what does he do? Does he share it? No. Hoarders! They fucking hoard their savings as the people around them starve and struggle. Little Susie needs a $25,000 private school to make it into the 'right' college. My wife is gluten-free. Careful, Tommy is allergic to peanuts. Micro-greens are only $5 an ounce – what a bargain! Would it kill this millionaire to hand over a few thousand to folks who really need it? That's fucking entitlement, papi.*

Gael finally decided to call Brock as he continued to pace back and forth with a lit cigarette in one hand and his cell phone in the other against his ear. "Pick up, pick up, pick up."

Watching Gael through her kitchen window, Barbara discerned that he was very agitated as he poked at the air with a cigarette perched between his fingers. Gael's brown, wavy hair hung down to his shoulders. He had appeared on her front porch yesterday, *like a flaming bag of dog shit.* Since he was exhausted and contrite, she allowed him to stay for a few more days to "rehydrate. But then you got to go. I'm not running a dog-hotel here."

"Brock, man, did you get my message?" Gael asked.

Barbara overheard Gael yell into his phone. She pushed her greasy white hair back behind her right ear so that she could hear him better.

Gael was confident in his justification. "One hundred thousand isn't that much to keep Bliss a secret, not for a player like you, big Brock."

Well, well. Looks like reprobate Rapunzel has a blackmailing con job going on here. Barbara grabbed a pen and small piece of paper and wrote: 'Bliss' and '100k.'

"I don't care about Betts. I'm talking to you, Brock. Whether you consult with her or just take money out of your savings, I don't give a shit. I just want one hundred thousand dollars in cash in a gym bag by tomorrow, 3pm. I'll call you and tell you where by 2:30pm."

Barbara added to her note, 'Betts - Brock, 2:30, drop-off.'

"Stop lying, Brock!"

Barbara listened as Gael continued to yell angrily into his phone.

"You fucking have it. So what? So you had to clean up your house. *Pobrecito*. Do you think I give a shit about how you were inconvenienced, *papi*? That's the story of my life, but you – I bet you didn't even clean one inch of your own walls, did you? Oh, no. Not one drop of that black guy's blood ever got near your perfectly manicured nails, did it. I'm right, aren't I; I knew it! That's why you need to pay, because you're so fucking rich and entitled. You think you're above getting your hands dirty. Literally. You're running an illegal brothel, bro. You think that you're above the law. I'm so sick of self-absorbed pricks like you, so you're gonna pay one way or the other. Your choice."

"You and me both," Barbara muttered to herself. *Gael hit the jackpot!* She scribbled: 'brothel – illegal, black guy – blood.' By the time she looked up, he was putting his phone into his back pocket. "I'm sick of self-absorbed pricks too." She picked up her cell phone and dialed zero for the operator in order to ask for Bliss' number.

A deep male voice said, "The service you have attempted is restricted or unavailable. Please contact…"

Barbara looked down at her phone as though it were on fire. "What the fuck is wrong with this world?"

✦ ✦ ✦ ✦ ✦

Sandra came to with her head and arms sprawled out on the RV kitchen table. When she sat up, she could only see out of one eye. The right side of her face felt wet with blood and sore. Bootsie handed her a bag of frozen peas and carrots, which she placed directly on her swollen right eye and cheek.

"So you were saying that you were out numbered and that you thought these people were with some not-for-profit. Is that right?" Bootsie pressed on as if nothing had just happened.

Sandra slowly nodded her head in agreement.

"They were high class, you said. What did you mean?" Bootsie asked. He was now sitting across from her, and Nick was pacing and smoking near Boo and Jojo.

Sandra saw double of everything. *Focus, girl. Bootsie asked you a question.* "Well, they all seemed surprised and a bit scared. They weren't bad-asses or nothing. And almost all of them had the same type of t-shirt. They looked like they should be on a float at the Pride parade."

Bootsie and Nick were surprised to hear this description. "What do you mean? What did the shirts look like?" Bootsie asked.

"They were all different colors, like a rainbow of colors, and all the shirts had the word 'Bliss' on the front in big, swirly letters. It was like a logo, but the way it was, was real classy and swirly." As she said it, Sandra realized that she should have led with this information.

Nick recognized the name and immediately blew a puff of smoke through the hair of his mustache and beard. He flashed a smile at Jojo and Boo and stated what they had already pieced together with Terrance several days ago: "Brock Anderson's gym! What a small, fucked-up world." Nick passionately shoved his cigarette out in the ashtray between Sandra and Bootsie. "Road trip, boys. Let's go."

✦ ✦ ✦ ✦ ✦

By late Monday afternoon, less than 48 hours after the teenagers were rescued and delivered to Hope House, several sets of eyes were monitoring Bliss' front and back doors. Betts stood behind Sharon seated inside the Bliss security office. The dashboard in front of her had dozens of buttons with names next to them like Entrance 1, Entrance 2, Gym, Bar, Office, Exit 1, Exit 2, Exit 3, Exit 4, Cave 1, Cave 2, Cave 3, Lux Naughty rm, GOT rm, Red Carpet After Party rm, Steampunk Vic Goth rm, Roman Bath rm, Obs Deck rm, Zen Balance rm, and Ninja Warrior rm.

Above the dashboard of buttons which remotely unlocked doors were ten different television monitors showing live security camera footage of the Bliss exterior. Some cameras were motion sensitive, while others continuously recorded everything.

Sharon pointed up at screen number three. "See, Betts? Those are the detectives I was telling you about: these two guys in the white SUV across the street are Sontag and Boratto. They're the one's who questioned Alice after she called the hotline, and the same ones who visited Brock at his house when Gael slit Terrance's throat."

"So they're often a day late and a dollar short," Betts summarized from her standing position behind Sharon's swivel chair. "Good to know."

"And now look over here, behind the police by a few cars. See that Jeep? There's four guys in there who have been staking out Bliss too." Sharon pointed at the image of Nick seated next to Bootsie behind the steering wheel.

"That's not good." Betts inspected the other monitors closely, then pointed to one on the upper right. "Who is that woman? Do we know her?"

Both Sharon and Betts looked more closely at an elderly white woman who lumbered her heavy body forward with a pronounced limp. The woman's wooden walking cane was withstanding quite a bit of pressure each time she pitched to her right and leaned on it. Because she was walking up to the Bliss front door so slowly, Betts was able to zoom in and get a good look at this stranger's very wrinkled face. "I've never seen this woman before. Is she one of our clients?"

"Nope," Sharon replied. She picked up her office phone and dialed the extension for the front desk. "Chaya, listen to me. Get a pic of this old lady's ID and text it to me as soon as she comes in, okay? If she doesn't have ID, she needs to leave. But first, get her talking. Betts is with me in the control room. We'll listen. Find out as much info as you can, okay?" Sharon put the phone back down onto the receiver and switched out the image of the older woman from the upper right screen to the larger one directly in front of them.

The camera's angle was from over Chaya's right shoulder to the chest and head of the elderly, hunched woman with a long nose. Her stringy, white hair hung flat against her head and down to her braless bosom. "Is this Bliss?" she said into the opening at the bottom of the Plexiglas.

"Yes, ma'am," Chaya replied happily. "What can I do for you today?"

"I'm looking for," the woman reached deep into a pocket on the side of her loose fitting dress and pulled out a small piece of paper. "Brock and Betts."

"What's this regarding?" Betts and Sharon could hear Chaya talking to the black and white image of the older woman. A few years prior, they had installed a microphone in the ceiling light of the front door for just these types of occasions.

"A little bit of this," the woman responded as she dramatically scanned the office behind Chaya. "And a little bit of that."

"What's your name, friend? Can I see some ID?" Chaya pressed on. "We're a secure facility, it's nothing personal. Everyone is required to show ID."

"I don't need ID to get in, Red," the old woman scoffed.

"Sorry, but I'm under strict instruction. No one comes in without an ID. At least tell me your name. I'm Chaya."

"Ain't that sweet as diabetes: a redhead named Chaya killing time at the front desk. And yet, they didn't even tell you about the magic password, did they."

Sharon, Betts and Chaya were all confused. "What password?" Chaya asked the old woman.

"The one that gets me through this door and into a meeting with Betts and Brock without ID."

Sharon said to Betts, "She's bluffing." Sharon pressed a speaker button down so that her omniscient voice spoke directly to the strange woman with a limp, "Cut the crap, grandma. We can't help you without ID." Sharon let go of the speaker button.

"Okay, if that's how you want it," the female visitor said casually as she turned around and hobbled slowly toward the door to exit.

Betts leaned over quickly and pressed the speaker button down and said, "What's the magic password?" Betts, Sharon, and Chaya were all curious. Betts shrugged dramatically at Sharon and let go of the button.

The old woman grinned and turned back to Chaya who could now see that the visitor was missing several teeth. The woman lurched forward onto her walking stick toward the Plexiglas separating her from Chaya and said with gravitas: "'Gael.' Now, open-fucking-says-me."

Betts immediately reached up to several small headphones hanging on the wall of Sharon's security office and grabbed two. One, she handed to Sharon, and the other she wove around and into her right ear. She then texted the staff, "CODE BLUE." She then pressed the microphone button and spoke to her staff, "Headphones everyone. Testing 1, testing 2. Hit me back when you can hear me. We are live. Testing 1, testing 2. I repeat, we are live..." As Betts awaited confirmation that her key staff had all put in their ear pieces, she texted David, "GO TIME. Renovate the exterior. NOW."

Chapter 28: The Deal

Jada's mission today was to take her little titties and fat belly to her motherland, Puerto Rico, dressed as a Bronco's fan, so she did not put on a bra and let her kinky, black hair *do it's natural thing. Let's go!* The penetrating sun on the street made her sweat and hurt her eyes, so she put on blue, heart-shaped sun glasses and got down to business. Jada outfitted herself for today's *mile-high mission* with blue sequined platform boots and matching cape over a tight, coral orange onesie not dissimilar to those worn by the Blue Man Group.

Each afternoon when Jada got stoned, she took on a new, important mission that would save the universe from itself. *Thank God for me.* Some days her mission was to pile rocks on top of one another to make cairns in Boulder Creek next to the public library, other days it was to walk around the block backwards to turn back time to the beginning of her weekend. Although locals found her attention-grabbing weird, she was harmless. Today, her assignment was to dance to the song "Tomboy" all the way to Puerto Rico in her mind, which equated to boogying down the middle of the street. *Not a problem. My little titties got this.* Jada turned up the volume in her headphones and swung her skinny hips in rhythm as she sang along with Princess Nokia, "Who dat is, ho? That girl is a tomboy. My little titties and my fat belly!"

Sontag momentarily stopped biting into his sandwich. "Jesus, look at this. Juicy Jada is in a dancing mood today. We've got our own private stoner party with Bronco's greatest fan."

Boratto laughed. "No way. Her crazy couldn't even get through security into the stadium."

"Oh, watch out. She sees us," Sontag chuckled just before he shoved a ciabatta roll into his gaping mouth.

Jada watched Sontag and Boratto as she danced toward Puerto Rico. *That girl is a tomboy!* As she swiveled closer to their car, she realized that they were cops. *Fuck! Run little titties! Run fat belly!*

"Nope, wait. There she goes. She's moving on." Boratto watched her as she danced down the street past them. He looked into his rearview mirror at her, then at a Jeep full of idle men two cars behind him. *Why are they waiting here?* Then out of the upper right corner of his rearview mirror he noticed two men dressed in dark suits walking with purpose down the sidewalk toward them. Their black hair was shiny and neat. *Italians. Something is not right.*

Nick and Bootsie became statues as a beautiful, Puerto Rican dancer pranced and jumped around on the street in front of their Jeep in bright, shiny Bronco's colors. "What in God's name?" Nick's voice trailed off in confusion.

Jada's eyes scanned the four sets of eyes looking back at her. *Yeah, ho! Who dat? Who dat? More police! My little titties and my fat belly!*

Nick turned to Bootsie and said, "Fuck it. We're going in. Too many crazies out here." They both got out of the Jeep, gave the dancer a nasty look, and then crossed the street toward Bliss.

Jada glanced up and saw two more business men that looked like FBI walking toward her. *Who dat up in the north?* Then, Jada's paranoia really set in. *What are they all doing here? It's a sting!* As she gyrated around, she started to feel more and more sick to her stomach. *Save yourself, save the universe, Jada!* Her upbeat dance morphed into a survival, protective spell that she put on her chest and stomach to summon a safe passage. Then, she broke down the fourth wall by rapping directly to an imaginary audience: "Shit is going down, yo. All the way up from Mexico, all through my heart in Colorado, all the way down to Puerto Rico. She's back like a boomerang, killer karma. Back like a boomerang, killer karma."

✦ ✦ ✦ ✦ ✦

The beautiful Arab-style door opened in front of Barbara, but she hesitated walking through. Desiree was on the other side waving her in. "C'mon in. I'll bring you to the bar to meet Betts and Brock. I'm Desiree."

"Hi," Barbara said with a hint of a southern accent. She stepped through the threshold into what looked like the hostess station at the front of a very dark restaurant. Most of the light was artificial save two large skylights. "A bar is a good meeting place. They're gonna want a drink once they hear what I'm about to say."

"Do you drink?" Desiree asked.

"Course. Who doesn't?" Barbara leaned on her walking stick heavily as she labored down the three, carpeted stairs into an elegant bar area with many small, round tables for two and one very large dining room table in the middle. The chairs stood out to Barbara above and beyond the ostentatious and opulent interior design. The seats around the big table were normal enough, but all of the others around the intimate café tables had a back and sides so high that they curved around over the chair like a protective nest. Only two people sitting directly across from each other would be able to see the other in this type of chair. "Who decorated this place?"

"We value privacy here," Desiree understated. "They're called 'Cocoon' by Skipper Furniture. Aren't they cool? They're on little wheels, so you can move around, and they have lights and speakers inside."

"It's like a room inside a room."

"Exactly. It's helpful in this big open space. Our clients love them to really relax and build intimacy with a friend," Desiree affirmed as she pulled out a regular chair at the end of the large wooden table for Barbara.

Barbara turned and aimed her generous backside at the chair before she let herself free-fall with a loud thud. "My knees are arthritic."

Not going to have you sit in a cocoon, then. Desiree smiled in amusement. "Can I get you a drink? You're gonna want something strong when you hear what they have to say too."

"How could they possibly have anything to say to me?" Barbara ended her sentence by striking the tip of her walking stick down against the carpet for dramatic effect.

Betts and Brock entered the bar from a hallway on the opposite end.

"I'll take a sip of your best scotch," Barbara replied quickly while keeping her eyes on Betts and Brock.

"Me too," Betts stated loudly with a welcoming smile as she confidently approached Barbara. Her long dark hair was pulled back today highlighting her long neck and artistic necklace.

"Make it three, please," Brock tagged on.

"Of course, coming right up," Desiree replied.

"Not the 15 either," Betts directed, "Go get the 30 year, single malt Balvenie. Hi there. I'm Betts and this is Brock." She knew better than to reach her hand out to shake, so she just sat down.

"I'm Barbara. So what do you do here in this bar? Kind of strange to have a bar at a gym, don't you think?" Her probing skepticism was transparent.

"Not strange at all. We can rent the space out for parties and host special events like our annual gala. It's coming up this weekend, actually. That's when we wine and dine our clients, introduce new staff, and generally keep everyone very happy. You should see this place all dressed up." Betts looked around at the corners of the room and center of the table as her memories of raucous parties from the past decorated every inch of the room. "She looks plain now, but our festivities bring out the best in her. She's dazzling and loud and fun."

"Are you still talking about the bar or your daughter?" Barbara pretended to be confused.

Brock laughed loudly. "Well, I guess Bliss is like our daughter. We are proud of her and how she's grown; how she's helped so many people."

Not missing a beat, Barbara added, "how she's made you rich."

Knowing that the only reason they were sitting with Barbara was due to her connection to Gael, and knowing what a murderer and blackmailer Gael is, they cringed. *Lady, we are showing you as much hospitality as we can. Let's not go low so quickly.*

"Tipped my hand, didn't I," Barbara realized.

"Here you go," Desiree sang as she took three heavy, crystal glasses off her tray and set them on the table. Then, she poured each of them two fingers of some very fine scotch and left the bottle.

Barbara grabbed a glass and lifted it high into the air to make a toast.

Betts and Brock looked at each other with a slight shrug and lifted their glasses too.

"My enemies never drink, but my friends always do, so let's drink this lovely scotch, so I can tell the difference between the likes of you." Barbara's toothless smile and silly toast made her audience of two smile.

After she swallowed, Betts returned her glass gently to the table and focused on the matter at hand. "Did you know that the police are looking for Gael? So are a bunch of thugs outside."

Barbara made a throaty growl after the alcohol landed. "Why? What did that shit for brains do?"

Suddenly, both Brock and Betts heard Chaya in their earpiece. "Houston, we have a problem. Some guys named Nick and Bootsie are here and want to talk to Brock. What do I do?" Do you know these guys?"

Brock put up his index finger in the air to Barbara to pause the conversation and replied to Chaya, "Ask them who our mutual, black friend is."

"Sorry, Barbara, we have some visitors," Betts said in a low tone.

Chaya replied, "They said Terrance."

"Okay, have Desiree show them into the bar," Betts permitted.

Barbara sat up a little straighter knowing that they would have company. She watched as Betts and Brock moved their hands away from their earpieces and refocused on their conversation with her.

"So Gael is a wanted man," Betts restarted.

"And he is blackmailing you," Barbara countered. "Idiot just can't do right. I bet you want him out of your hair, and I'm willing to make a quid pro quo."

Betts and Brock looked at each other. *We can at least listen.* "Okay, let's hear it."

"I know what y'all do here, and I'd like some action on the regular, if you get what I mean, and I don't want to pay for it. You let me come here for free, and I'll take care of your problem."

Just then Desiree came in from the hallway and walked past them toward the door. She pressed a button and the Arabic door swung open from the lobby.

"Who the fuck did the cat drag in?" Barbara asked as she stared across the room at one middle aged man with a black doo-rag over his head in jeans and a leather vest over a Harley Davidson t-shirt and a younger, handsomer man in a white t-shirt and jeans who looked by his muscles like he was trying to hide the obvious: *he's a bandit.*

✦ ✦ ✦ ✦ ✦

"We've got some movement," Boratto announced as two of the four men from the black Jeep got out and strutted toward Bliss. "They don't look like they're going to exercise."

"No way. Does the biker look like he's carrying?" Sontag wondered out loud.

"Boulder's not Denver," Boratto reminded his partner between bites of his sandwich. "Open carry isn't a crime. We need to find a plausible in."

"And look at Juicy Jada back there. She's having a complete stoner melt down in front of those two guys." Sontag watched Jada in his side-view mirror move too quickly toward one of the men who in turn, opened his arms wide and tried to back away from her rhythmic advances. "He's got a gun. Front left."

"Let's see where they're headed." Boratto smashed up the paper wrapper that had been around his sandwich into a ball and put it in the garbage bag in the back seat. Using the various car mirrors, he watched the two suits finally get past Jada, cross the street, and enter Bliss.

"This is no coincidence. There's no way it makes sense to have this many guns at a gym. Let's put some pressure on them and flush them out." Sontag picked up the police radio and said, "This is 924."

"924, go ahead."

"Requesting backup, over."

✦ ✦ ✦ ✦ ✦

When the Bliss front door opened, Chaya was standing behind the Plexiglas with her hands on her hips like she was about to scold the next visitor.

The two men quickly scanned her billowy red curls and Ruth Bader Ginsburg t-shirt that said, "Women belong in all places decisions are being made." *Bitchy, but non-threatening.*

"Can I help you?" Chaya said as though they were bothering her.

"We're here to speak with Nova."

"And you are?" Chaya demanded more than asked.

"Friends of the family, so to speak. Tell her Steady sent us."

Chaya maintained eye contact with the visitors as she pressed the button on her earpiece to activate her microphone and sang a line from one of her favorite '80s movies, "Hey Nova, It's Johnny Cammareri." She paused long enough to hear someone laugh at her joke, but no one responded. "What? No one's seen *Moonstruck*? Two Italian, mafia-looking dudes are at the front door for you, Nova. Said Steady sent them."

Nova sat up and looked at Betts with surprise.

One of the gentlemen reached up to brush his five o'clock shadow with the back of his fingertips. In doing so, the pistol on his waist was revealed to Chaya.

"Is that supposed to intimidate me, bucko? You're not the first sinister-looking dude to come through here today, so save the scare-tactics for someone who gives a care."

Nova looked at Betts in front of Barbara, Nick, and Bootsie. "It's gotta be my mother. They might be helpful right now, under the circumstances."

Betts pressed her microphone's on button and told Chaya, "Let them in. Desiree, round three."

"It's your lucky day, boys." Chaya opened the entrance to the waiting room. *Click!* "Take the revolving door to your right."

✦ ✦ ✦ ✦ ✦

Sontag and Boratto walked over to Bliss' entrance and showed their badges to Chaya through the thick plastic window.

"Great. It's the Tweedles," Chaya quipped to herself. "Bliss is like the fucking ark today; all the beasts coming in two-by-two."

Boratto knew how to handle ornery people: make a joke. He elbowed Sontag and claimed his name proudly, "I'm Tweedledee."

"Hey!" Chaya was in no mood. "I make the jokes around here, buddy."

"We just want to chat with Brock. Let him know that if he let's us in and chats with us, we won't have a bunch of cops clog up traffic around your building."

"You're not getting in here without a search warrant." Chaya turned on her microphone and asked, "Sharon, Sharon, please verify. Are cops surrounding Bliss?"

Betts, Brock, Nova, Chaya, and Desiree, all listened intensely for Sharon's answer.

"Affirmative."

Chapter 29: The Summit

Betts knew better than to smile even though she was secretly euphoric and terrified to see what would happen next. *Keep your street-face on, girl.* A bar full of unknown, untrustworthy folks felt like a shot of adrenalin directly into her vein. *The best defense is a strong offense,* she coached herself. "Trust me when I say that we are all here for the same reason, so have a seat everyone. Let's get down to business." Betts raised her open palm toward the long, dark mahogany, table in the middle of the bar. There were no customers or bartenders around during the day, so in Bett's mind it was a logical place to meet.

In mixed company, Nick looked more like a biker than ever before. He felt out of place and nervously pulled on his beard. *Where is the exit? Hallway dead ahead, okay.* He looked at each person in the room threateningly as he slowly approached the table and sat a few seats away from Barbara.

Following his lead, Bootsie also stared menacingly at the strangers before sitting as well.

The two Italian men took a seat nonchalantly opposite Nick and Bootsie. The broad shouldered one in a navy blue suit coat wiped some crumbs off the seat before he sat down. The tall one loosened his silk tie after he sat. They both eyed the $1,000 bottle of Balvenie in front of them and licked their lips.

Betts looked at Barbara at the opposite end of the table who still held her walking stick in an arthritic hand as if she were a witch on a throne. Betts was flanked by Nova to her left and Brock on her right. *I'm ending this today.* "First, introductions. NOT in attendance are Detectives Boratto and Sontag who are planted outside these very walls with another twenty cops." Betts suddenly saw the whites of everyone's eyes. "Don't worry, I can get you all out of here safely. We have tunnels. My name is Betts and these are my colleagues Brock and Nova. Brock and I own Bliss."

Much to everyone's surprise, the door from the kitchen behind the bar swung open and fifteen well groomed men of varying ethnic backgrounds walked out one by one. All were wearing yellow hard hats. David, the shortest among them, led the line across the room and out the door where all the visitors came in.

Barbara immediately knew who these men were and reflexively muttered, "Damn, Betts. You're a Goddamn genius," as her gaze lingered over various muscles in the parade.

A slight, naughty smile escaped Betts' lips. "And these guys are my Specialists who will create a diversion for the cops outside. It's like I have my own, very good-looking, little army. And in front of me, is my new friend Barbara." Betts' index finger swirled an imaginary soupspoon around her cauldron of bad guys as she said, "Barbara knows where to find our one degree of separation."

Everyone glanced at each other with continued confusion as to how they all could be connected.

"Who?" the broad shouldered Italian asked puzzled.

Barbara then roughly stated, "Fucktard," as if it were his name, and then clarified, "Gael."

Nick leaned in immediately and poked the table twice loudly with his fat index finger. "Prove it."

Barbara rummaged around in her purse for a painfully long half a minute and pulled out the Umbra metal piece and black binoculars she had stolen from Gael before she left the house. She tossed them like dice indelicately down the table in front of Nick.

"Holy shit," Nick said to Bootsie as he grabbed the piece of metal before it fell off the table. "She knows Gael, alright. How did you ever get this? This is what he used on three of my associates. Dead associates."

Barbara was visibly shocked as she slammed her walking stick down against the floor. "Gael murdered a man? Three men? And you couldn't tell me that little gem, Betts?"

Betts ignored Barbara and turned to Nick, "Sorry, who are you?"

"Nick and Bootsie, Sinaloa Cartel."

Brock kicked Betts under the table. *Holy shit, we are in so much trouble.*

Barbara had never heard of the Sinaloas and therefore had no idea that they were the largest and most powerful drug traffickers in the Western Hemisphere. Had she known their predilection for violence, rape, and murder, she never would have returned their earlier skepticism through mimicry: "Prove it. Neither of you looks like a beaner."

The broken fire hydrant of Spanish words that burst out of Bootsie's mouth shocked everyone except Nick. Not only did he speak so fast that they knew he was a native speaker, but he was also so loud and dramatic with his tone that they actually thought they could understand him. He clearly directed several insults at Barbara. Then he translated a cleaned up version: "In other words, I got my name, which is Bootsie by the way, when I was fifteen because I kicked a policeman in our village to death. He refused to get paid off, so I refused to take my boots off his living body. Is that 'beaner' enough, old lady?"

"I'm Nick," he pushed onward. "We're looking for Gael and one of our missing associates who owns these binoculars." He unconsciously pulled them a little closer.

"Terrance," Betts stated nervously. "I'm sorry to have to tell you, but Terrance is dead, Nick, and I have some proof to share as well." Betts pulled out the finger in a baggie and phone from her bag under the table and pushed them down in front of Nick.

Nick stood up violently upon seeing the finger forcing the chair legs to screech their retreat. "You did this to him?"

Nova interrupted with her arms waving, "No, Gael. Gael murdered Terrance at Brock's house."

"And you have his finger, why?" Nick wondered furiously as he sat back down.

"To turn on the phone," Brock shared sheepishly.

"Cold but practical," the Italian with the tie stated.

Nick did not care for unsolicited opinions and normally would give a beat-down to anyone around him who couldn't mind their own business. However, he decided to show discretion until he assessed the risk level in the room, so he asked, "And who the fuck are you two?"

"Petey and Sams. La Cosa Nostra." Petey loosened his tie again as he looked directly at Nova and smiled, "Steady says hello, by the way."

Wide shouldered Sams removed something wrapped in cloth from his inner coat pocket and laid it on the table. With two hairy fingers, he pushed it down to Nova. She uncovered a pistol with a rainbow stripped handle. Nova laughed as she shared a knowing look with Betts. "Yep. That's Steady."

"He's worried about you, and now I see why," Petey shared. "This looks like one of our Cosa Nostra meetings, so let me know what I can do to broker peace here. No one needs to give the police outside probable cause to enter. It sounds like you all just want this guy Gael dead. Easily fixed. Am I right?"

"Not entirely," Nick snarled reprovingly at Betts' end of the table. "We're owed restitution for our property that was stolen by a bunch of people wearing Bliss t-shirts."

Brock, Nova, and Betts turned crimson due to a mixture of being called out and anger at the messenger.

Petey read the room. "Looks like they don't deny it. What did you all steal?"

Everyone patiently waited for the answer.

Nova could not, not be offended that Nick – *a sex trafficker, no less!* – would want restitution. *Are you fucking kidding me, asshole?* She wanted to jump across the table and punch him in the mouth. *But you've got to manage the message,* Nova instructed herself. *Mom will hear all about this eventually.* She decided to strike a more measured tone. "The girls have been returned to their families."

Nick smoothed down his moustache and beard with an open hand. "I will wipe the shit off his boots with your face if you're not careful."

Petey intervened. "You want restitution. Heard loud and clear," he affirmed. By the looks on their faces, Petey realized, this was not business as usual at Bliss. *They're out of their element.*

"Betts. Back home, we offer a lump sum or a percentage over fixed time."

Or a knife to the jugular, Betts fumed. *I have to pay this lowlife?*

Petey leaned forward and nudged Betts. His eyes intensely flicked back and forth between hers. "I'm going to say this in as nice a way possible: It's just the cost of business amongst us thieves."

Dick. But Betts knew he was right. *If this can all be over*, Betts reasoned, *and Bliss can be left alone, I should just pay it and move on.*

Reacting to the prodding facial expressions of Petey and Sams, Nova leaned over and whispered in Betts' ear, "Offer Nick something."

Exasperated, Betts reluctantly admitted, "I haven't a clue what to offer you, Nick," *you trafficker of children, seller of drugs.*

Sams broke the next long silence with a deep, Brooklyn accent. "How about a drink?"

God yes, Brock agreed. "Desiree," he clicked the 'on' button on his earpiece. "Can you bring out four more glasses? Thank you."

Sams continued negotiating as Desiree entered and poured four more crystal glasses with golden scotch. "You know, you all are in the same town, and what a fucking speck of a town this is. There's no room for anybody here, so you have to give each other room, space to conduct business, so to say. Stay out of each other's way, you know what I mean? What's that adage, Petey, 'good fences makes for good neighbors?' So the two of yous need to build a nice, tall fence. What do you say, Nick. You can be flexible on the restitution, right?" Then he said to Desiree as she walked away, "Thanks. Take a sip and think about it, Nick. These guys aren't narcs." *They're small time.*

"No. We are not," Brock quickly said with exaggerated conviction. "You do not need to worry about Bliss or us or our staff ever meddling in your business again."

Think of the staff, Betts told herself. *They need a safe exit.* "I'm open to hearing a reasonable number, Nick."

After Nick knocked back the expensive scotch as if it were a shot, he scribbled a number on his cocktail napkin and passed it over to Betts upside down.

Sams took a slow sip and then put the heavy glass gently down on the table with a satisfied shake of his head. "That's amazing, thank you." He watched the paper slide across the table.

Betts took a look at the number in front of everyone. "Okay. Deal. Let's trade cell numbers so I can get it to you." She reached across the table to shake his fat hand firmly and did not let go first. *Fucker.*

Everyone nodded their approval. Sams and Petey winked at Nova. "That's how Sicilians do it. Well, we can do it lots of ways, but we like it when people can walk away of their own volition, like all of yous. Nick, Bootsie, thank you for being reasonable. Now, regarding the matter of Gael, since your crew suffered the worst, Nick, you get dibs on him. May I recommend something painful and simultaneously undetectable?"

✦ ✦ ✦ ✦ ✦

As Sontag and Boratto spoke with Chaya at the entrance to Bliss, the door to their right opened, and a peloton of strong men with yellow hard hats walked through and out the door. "What is this?"

Fucked if I know, Chaya thought to herself. She played it cool even though she had no idea why all of the specialists were wearing hard hats. "That's not your business," she barked. "Mind your own."

"We'll be back with that search warrant," Sontag said to Chaya. "Anyway, Brock can't stay in there all day. He's got to come out eventually."

✦ ✦ ✦ ✦ ✦

"So, this is a real nice place you got here, Betts," Petey complimented after enjoying the last of his drink. "Real nice." Now that the negotiations were finished, all of the visitors began to relax and calculate the high quality of their surroundings. *Futuristic, privacy chairs? Tunnels? $1,000 scotch?* "But how do you make so much money if your bar is closed in the afternoon? And Nova, Steady said you're a nurse. What's a nurse doing working at a bar with no customers?"

Betts knew that she could not bullshit any of them, so she did not bother trying. "Gentlemen, Bliss is a bordello. A house of ill-repute. A brothel." She said it as if she had to keep stating synonyms until Nick could understand.

"She's the madam," Barbara said wagging her crooked thumb at Betts. "And those boys that just strutted through? Them is the bait."

All four men were wide-eyed and smirking with disbelief.

Betts felt excited to brag about her great idea realized as a profitable business. “It’s a bordello by women, for women. It’s very different than anything you men can possibly imagine, but it is your wife’s wet dream. Our clients are from all over the world. They travel to Colorado for skiing and sex. Safe and healthy, consensual, bespoke, sex. They get as many orgasms as they can handle given to them by the gender and orientation of their choice in the manner of their choosing in their dream-like setting.

“I teach them to want it and how to maximize their experience. Our clients don’t just get laid, gentlemen, they get schooled. They move in stages, challenging themselves more and more outside their comfort zone over whatever length of time is comfortable and reasonable to them. Once they move from exercising, to the spa, to Happy Endings, and then to Happy Ever Afters, the sky is the limit, really. It’s a totally curated experience so that they walk away with a heightened sense of agency and with their bodies humming away unapologetically.”

“No way!” Bootsie laughed in disbelief. “Is this for real? Happy Ever Afters? How does it work? Woman don't want to fuck a stranger.”

“Like hell we don’t,” Barbara muttered under her breath.

Sams chimed in, agreeing with Bootsie, “They don’t even want to fuck, do they? Most of them? They like to ‘make love.’” He giggled like a young girl.

Petey chuckled in camaraderie, “And there is no way that they pay for it. No way.”

"No," Nick agreed as he took it all in. "And that young blood must be charging you tons to fuck ugly, old, rich ladies. There's no way that this is a profitable business."

"And where do you find the women?" Bootsie continued to challenge aloud. "You can't advertise. And then when you find them, how do they not run at the mouth to all of their girlfriends? In a town this small, the police would find you out in the first six months."

Within minutes, the tone of conversation had changed from the threat of potential violence when they first met each other to provoking Betts' and Nova's ire with their misogynistic bile. All four guys were on the same page: *a brothel for women was simply impossible. It could not exist. Female clients did not exist. Safe, consensual, bespoke sex did not exist.*

"Tell me something, Nick," Betts started. She had them right where she wanted them. "Since we don't have to beat around the bush anymore, how much do you charge your clients? Do you charge by the amount of time or the act?"

"Both. It depends on the situation," Nick stated like a proud businessman in front of the whole group.

"For the sake of argument, just ballpark the cost of a blowjob for us," Betts requested.

"Twenty bucks," Nick replied quickly.

"Oh really?" Petey added, "Out in Vegas they charge about $50. Safer product, I guess."

Brock could almost hear Betts' punch line. *Wait for it... wait for the question.*

Betts purposefully let the pause last longer than it should. She took another sip of her smooth scotch. *Wait for it.*

Finally, Bootsie was on the hook first. "Why, what do you charge here at Bliss?"

Betts and Brock looked at each other and grinned. Brock then disclosed their price. "For that, we start at $250 but can go up as high as we need to in order to curate the exact experience that the client wants. And satisfaction is always guaranteed or the client gets her money back."

Now, everyone around the table sported toothy smiles, including Nick who yelped and smacked the tabletop with a flat hand. "Woo hoo! That's some rich pussy!"

"Wait, satisfaction is guaranteed? How do you mean?" Sams chuckled.

"Well, isn't that obvious?" Brock asked with an air of condescension.

"No, no it's not. What do you mean?" Sams guessed.

"Well, they define their own experience, but typically it involves orgasming at least once." Brock sipped his glass. He was surprised at how slowly they were processing the concepts. "I mean, if that was what they wanted. They don't all measure satisfaction the same way. We work with them ahead of time to define their goals."

The scotch that nearly spewed out of Petey's mouth directly at Bootsie's face could have started a bloodthirsty murderous affair. Instead, Petey took one for the team and nearly choked himself to death keeping it down. *Define their goals?* He had never heard a more ridiculous business plan in his entire life. *And yet, here we are choking on $1,000 scotch in a gorgeous, costly bar. The money had to have come from somewhere.* When he was finally able to breathe and talk, he croaked, "Define their goals?"

Brock chuckled, "It's just good business. How do you know if your clients are happy with your service if you don't measure outcomes? It has to be quantifiable. How else do you get repeat customers? You can't be investing in recruiting new clients all of the time. That's dumb and expensive."

Bootsie put his hand up like a stop sign. "Wait. You mean to tell me that you count orgasms?"

"Absolutely, if that was a goal. Sexuality is nebulous, though. More often than not, a woman has a defined goal like, 'to feel good about myself' which is measured by the presence of whatever makes them feel good or the absence of whatever makes them feel bad. It's weird. Some women want to laugh and be heard, others want to dominate and control a bottom, the permutations just never end. There's too much variety to have one goal with one price point, so we have price minimums and have to talk it though with the client after that. We figure out a price specific to that woman's ideal experience."

Betts underscored Brock's point. "In other words, if we don't know what they want, not only could we set the price too low, but we also would fail every time. There are no assumptions at Bliss. It's not like for men, not even a little."

Bootsie was intrigued. "So what is the highest number of orgasms one of your boys ever gave at one hook up?"

"You see," Brock smiled at the pedestrian question, "You're still thinking in this very traditionally male way. That's why Bliss is so profitable: because woman are surrounded by a bunch of doofuses."

"Now I know that you're not calling me a doofus." Bootsie leaned forward in earnest.

"No, no I'm not," Brock stammered. "Not at all. I just mean that you need to ask more creative questions. All men need to. It's not about the highest number – which is ten by the way – but location, length, pacing, combinations…"

The goofy smiles returned to their faces as they all digested his last four words: *location, length, pacing, combinations? What the fuck is he talking about?*

Sams smiled and took the opportunity to make a joke. "No problems with length at this table, I'm sure."

Brock laughed, "Not length of a man, time! 'Length' meaning how long is the client's orgasm."

Now, Nick took a turn like challenging the premise of their business model was a game. "Okay. What if it were some Ethiopian who had her clit cut out? You can't guarantee anything for her."

Nova burst out laughing. *There are so many things wrong with that, where do I begin?*

Brock flashed his Hollywood smile and tapped his forehead. "Think about it: location, location, location."

Petey thought he solved the puzzle and explained it to Nick in plain language. "They fuck her in the ass."

"Oh my God, guys," Betts reacted without thinking. "How can you all be so…"

"Choose your words carefully," Brock mumbled in a low voice.

"…ignorant about the female body?" Betts was stunned and felt sorry for them and their lovers who, without a doubt, were not fully satisfied. "You know that we have many erogenous zones, right? With clients who are victims of FGM, rape, or other traumas, we have special experts who are therapists. They have very different personal goals. Basically, take everything that you think you know about women and turn it upside down."

"And then fuck her in the mouth," Sams joked with a belly laugh.

Bootsie high fived him and said, "Good one!"

Nova, Betts, and Brock cringed with an awkward smile.

"So, uh, where do they do it? Can't be this bar."

"We're done, right?" Betts asked the group. *Because I'm done tolerating the chauvinism at this table.* "Would you like a tour?"

Nova picked up the gun and pushed it into her back waistline. *I'm done with this shit.*

"One bad guy to another?" Petey complimented Nova, Betts, and Brock, "This is such a fucking baller idea. I can't believe that no one has thought of it yet."

"Oh, but we have," Betts self congratulated. Despite not trusting these men, her pride pushed her to brag and show them what a legitimate, safe bordello should look like. "We've thought of everything. Come, I'll show you a room. Then you all need to go."

✦ ✦ ✦ ✦ ✦

Back in the SUV, Boratto watched the construction workers trying to set up scaffolding. Sontag stood outside the passenger seat taking long pulls from a cigarette. The 15 men in hard hats were moving around metal piping and wood boards, but it seemed fairly disorganized and chaotic from Sontag's perspective. One man, the shortest one, was barking out orders to the others who were desperately trying to understand what to do, but the number of times that they were getting in each other's way was too obvious.

"These numb-nuts don't even know how to set it up. They aren't fucking construction workers." Sontag threw his cigarette down violently.

"Jesus," remarked Boratto from inside the car. "They're all in there right now. Gael is probably in there too."

"Has anyone seen him today?"

"No, no one has seen that little prick."

Chapter 30: Monday Night

"Follow me, everyone. This wing is where our clients bliss out," Betts invited as she walked toward the hallway at the other end of the Bliss bar. "We have a standard gym and spa, but on this side, off from our bar over here are our theme rooms."

Full of curiosity, Nick, Bootsie, Barbara, Sams, Petey, and Nova all followed Betts and Brock down a long, blue tiled hallway. Would you like to check one out?"

"Sure," Petey replied for the group.

"Let's show them the luxury naughty chambers," Brock said as he unlocked a door with a white plastic card. He pulled the red velvet curtain quickly to the right. In the center of the room was a circular, red leather bed with a high headboard also made out of red leather except for the hollowed out center where there were vertical, metal pipes.

Nick was genuinely surprised from top to bottom. He never expected his day to turn out like this. Tens of thoughts were spinning around in his head like a blender: *Poor Terrance; that fucking Gael, he is dead by tomorrow; restitution is good, that was unexpectedly easy*; and: "Are all of your rooms this expensive? You must have paid a fortune for that bed."

Betts shook her head. *Actually, fucker, that's none of...* "Actually, we recouped our investment within the first few months. It's our most cost-effective room."

"This one automatically comes with the S & M toy bar," Brock stated. "You see the rods at the head and foot of the bed? They're built in really well. The bed was expensive basically so people can tie or handcuff each other in, but other than that, this room is just a regular hotel room."

"So you're playing a long game," Nick calculated aloud.

"Yeah, but sometimes," Brock admitted, "they're not so popular, so we change them out. Like, we all thought that a secret agent room would be a hit, but it was a total bust. The ladies do not care about 007."

Betts explained further, "After that, we made sure to do a lot of research on exactly what our clients wanted… even if they didn't know exactly what they wanted, we realized that we have to ask questions in different ways or from different angles to really understand them so that we can curate the rooms correctly. Otherwise, we're just burning green."

"Like what do you mean?" Sams asked as he watched Barbara approach the bespoke bed and then press down a few times on the mattress.

"Well right now," Brock said matter-of-factly, "we're working on a tactile room for the tree hugger crowd. They want to wipe their palms on tree bark and regain their natural finger sensitivity."

"So," Bootsie was honestly confused, "They can't feel? People pay to touch stuff? Why? I don't get it."

"Well, tree bark is just an example," Brock explained. "I guess the idea is that we're all 'fingerblind' from under stimulation."

"We have a lot of nerves under our fingertips," Betts continued, "or so I have learned, and nowadays we don't touch much except the cell phone and keyboard all day, so our nerves are kind of sleeping. And Bliss is all about waking everything up – our nerves, our bodies, our mind – so we're trying to make a room that encourages and enhances tactile sensation. It's a quality of life issue."

All four men were smiling again, but none more than Barbara. She limped back to the group from the bed to joke. "What's this now? Fingerblind? What are they gonna do in that room, finger-fuck? You both are bat-shit crazy if you ask me. No offense. I still want my membership though. A deal's a deal."

Brock walked over and gently lifted Barbara's left hand. "May I?"

"May you what?" Barbara's bark was definitely worse than her bite as she willingly complied with Brock's whim to cradle her docile purple, arthritic hand.

Brock gave her instructions. "I'd like you to close your eyes, and then I'm going to put your fingers against my beard stubble. Is that okay with you? Do I have your permission?"

Barbara giggled. "Go ahead, weirdo, but at my age with my arthritis, I pretty much just feel low grade pain all day. But you can try to make a finger-seer out of me." She noticed how warm his flesh was as he held her hand up to the right side of his face.

"Close your eyes," Brock coaxed her in a sweet, slow voice. He held her contorted fingertips at the base of his right jaw and slowly pulled them diagonally across his beard stubble.

Everyone watched as Barbara reflexively inhaled and exhaled a deep breath. Only Brock could see that she also had goose bumps.

"Okay," Barbara smiled and opened her eyes as she pulled her hand away. "I don't wanna be fingerblind no more, that's for damn sure. I want more men like this when I come to collect."

Nick squinted, "So what is this deal that you two have going on?"

"It's about Gael," Betts revealed. She reached over and turned up the lights to kill the ambiance. "He is trying blackmail us," she shrugged. "Barbara knows where he is. She's going to help us take care of the situation."

"No, no, no, no, no." Nick shook his head. "We all agreed that I would be taking care of Gael. He's mine."

"Then come over to my house," Barbara replied. "You take care of him like these guys said." She aimed her thumb at Petey and Sams.

"He lives with you?" Brock asked as if he discovered a new level of crazy.

Betts was having none of it. She turned to Brock in front of everyone and accused, "Isn't that the pot calling the kettle black."

Nick interrupted and said to Barbara, "Bootsie will follow you once we get out of here. He'll get the job done – for all of us." He made meaningful eye contact with Betts, Nova, and Brock. "Thank you for putting my Terrance to rest. That was decent."

Nova could tell that Nick was attempting to be nice and did not approve of the direction this new relationship could take. *You're still a human trafficker, asshole.* "I'm not sorry that we rescued those teenagers," Nova reflexively admitted like a snarky teenager.

No sooner had the words escaped her mouth than Petey's open hand smacked Nova upside the back of her head as if she were a petulant child. "Shut the fuck up, you. Nick, ignore her. Barbara, thank you in advance for allowing Bootsie into your home. Betts, let's move on. I can't wait to see more."

Nova's face went flush with embarrassment. *What the fuck?* She waited for Betts or Brock to defend her, but they both just turned and walked out of the room with Petey in tow. *You assholes!*

"Let's move on," Betts said as she turned and quickly exited the naughty chamber. *Nova, you overstepped there. You're gonna have to suck it up right now.* "Well, I think it's time to head to the tunnel." *Time for all of you to get the fuck out of my house.*

Ha! "This place is amazing," Sams simultaneously congratulated Betts while trying to move on from the topic of having to tell Mary Ann that her daughter stepped out of line. *Nova should be ashamed of herself right now.*

Everyone followed Betts and Brocks to the locked door at the far end of the Pueblo Wing.

As she lurched along behind everyone, Barbara felt excluded. "These rooms are too fancy for me. You're so focused on rich folk that you forgot about the rest of us lot."

Brock responded by wagging his finger at her. "Not true. All people who identify as women are welcome. We have a room for more mature women that may not be fully mobile, not unlike you, and our water room is another popular option so that you're not fighting against gravity. Hell, we even give a steep discount if someone just wants to hang out in the room alone."

Bootsie couldn't resist. "Better watch out, Barbara, they might start asking you about 'your personal goals.'"

"Oh, I got me some goals alright," Barbara admitted with a sly smile, "and they're all real personal."

Everyone chuckled.

"I don't know how you advertise, but don't send anything to my wife, okay?" Sams joked. "I don't want her getting any ideas about 'personal goals.'"

Betts faked a broad smile and offered her hand to shake with each of the men. "This has got to be the strangest meeting I've ever had," she admitted honestly. "I hope I never see any of you again, except, of course, you Barbara." Betts winked dramatically at her. "Just go on through, follow the hallway into a basement and up the steps. You'll be in the 7-11 across the street. Just say that you're a friend of mine and the manager will let you through. Good luck; I hope the cops don't see you."

"Fuck them. They can eat a bag of dicks," Nick growled. "Hey Betts, you've got my number so that we can coordinate payment."

"Yes I do." *Asswipe*, Betts silently insulted him.

Then Nick paused a moment and said, "and if you ever need anything, just ask."

"Thank you, Nick," Betts lied. *Honor among thieves, my ass. No way will I ever call you, buddy.*

Petey squeezed in one last joke. "And Nova has our number if the Mexicans can't help you. Us Italians will get the job done." He grabbed and vigorously shook Nick and Bootsie's hands to underscore his joke then turned to Nova more straight faced and pointed at her as he gave his final command, "Call your mother. Bye, guys. Good meeting everyone."

Chapter 31: Bitter Pills

As soon as Betts and Nova were inside the office, Betts shut her door and locked it.

"That was humiliating!" Nova yelled at Betts. She was fuming. "I got bitch-slapped in public like a child! A child!" *So mortifying!*

Betts made a beeline to her small bar to the right of the large window. After their guests left, Betts tasked Brock to work with Desiree, Sharon, and Chaya to finish planning the big gala. Little had been organized thus far due to the drama of the past week. Now, Betts hoped, they could buy the decorations, hire a caterer, and find a tarot card reader in the next few days. *I'll help them tomorrow,* Betts thought. *Right now, Nova clearly needs to be my focus. One step at a time.*

"And I'm just supposed to just power through that?" Nova continued ranting as she paced. "And walk around like nothing happened? You should have defended me, Betts!" Nova needed to release all of her frustration. She impotently scanned the various objects in Betts' office calculating whether or not she should pick one up and hurl it against the wall.

Betts calmly poured herself a chardonnay and kept her back facing Nova as she pondered whether or not to apologize. *I'm not actually sorry, but it would calm her down.*

"This is total bullshit. I have literally put my professional reputation and life on the line for you, your staff, and your company, and this is how I'm repaid?"

Betts turned to face her. "I'm sorry, okay? I can see that you're really upset. Look. I didn't slap you, the fucking Italian mafia, who is apparently related to your family, did. And by the way, when were you going to share that little tidbit with me?"

Nova thought Betts was missing the main point. "How am I supposed to know that they were going to show up?"

"Your mom didn't tell you?" Betts wondered suspiciously.

"No, I had no idea. Really. The last time I spoke to her, she actually wanted me to stop telling her the gory details about my life."

"What gory details?"

Nova had stopped pacing and was now directly in front of Betts pointing at her. "Like you, my new fucking boss, pulling a gun on me."

Betts was exasperated and let out a loud grunt as she rolled her eyes. "Yeah, because you're so helpless! That whole situation was not my fucking fault and you know it. Why are you telling your mom about that shit anyway?"

"That's what she said. 'Don't tell me the bad stuff, only the good stuff,' so I didn't say anything else." Nova retreated to the minibar and poured herself vodka in a tall, thin glass.

Betts took a seat in the corner of the couch where she had slept a few nights earlier with Brock on her lap. She pushed her shoes off by the ankles and then crossed her feet under her legs to be comfortable. "Well, that's more appropriate. You can't tell your eighty-year-old mother about real life. They're too old."

"Stop." Nova walked over and sat down facing Betts sideways on the couch. "Don't tell me what's appropriate between me and my mom. You don't hardly know me. She obviously had a change of heart. She was worried about me, so she had Steady send for Petey and Sams to check on me. She did the right thing in the end. I'm beginning to think that I'm wrong, actually. Maybe older folks are better at handling reality than we are. They're detached, ya know? Maybe they think more clearly."

"I don't know about that," Betts disagreed and took another sip of wine. "Think more clearly than you, maybe." Betts winked at Nova. "That was a joke." *Too soon, apparently.*

"Well, if it weren't for Petey and Sams basically running the meeting and brokering the peace, what would you have done? You were as pissed at Nick and Bootsie as I was, and you know it."

Okay, so we are not ready to decelerate this argument yet. Fine. Let's drag out the carcass into the sun so we can all stink to high heaven. "They didn't run the meeting. Please." Betts was offended at Nova's interpretation of events. "I did most of the talking."

"Except for the most important moment when you needed to negotiate the compensation. You didn't want to give him anything. They had to tell you to do it, and then I had to insist before Nick turned the whole meeting into a bloodbath."

How dramatic. "It wasn't ever going to be a blood bath, Nova. You're exaggerating so much."

"Am I? I was looking at that stupid rainbow gun like I might have to pick it up on the quick and shoot Nick."

Betts snorted her denial out her nostrils like a bull. "You're so dramatic!"

"Betts, did you not understand the weight of that moment? How are you not calibrated at the same level of self-preservation as the rest of us? How was that not a scary mother fucking moment? I was actively contemplating how I would grab my gun and aim it quicker than Petey or Sams at Nick. It was going to be on me if that moment went sideways."

Such hyperbole from a hypocrite, Betts silently protested.

Nova could see that Betts was unsympathetic. "Well, those are my true feelings. And feelings are feelings. This is my reality, so you can either try to understand it or whatever," Nova disputed.

"Then for the love of God, why did you mouth off to him?" Betts asked Nova. "Why am I in trouble and you're not? You're so debased and humiliated right now because you got a little slap to the back of your head, but if you claim that our lives were on the line and it was me who might have screwed everything up, then why would you have ever taken that same risk and mouthed off to him?"

Put that way, Nova silently fumed at her lost argument. *Fuck! Goddamnit. Did I really do that? What was I thinking?*

"I may have made a mistake, but you made it worse. Don't be mad at me when you're actually mad at yourself," Betts mumbled.

Nova shook her head from side to side and them mumbled in defeat, "But you weren't publically humiliated and then everyone acts like nothing happened."

"Again, get over it. We didn't act like nothing happened, we acted like you had received your just desserts." Betts gulped her wine until she had an empty glass.

"My just desserts," Nova repeated sarcastically. "You know, you sound like an asshole."

"I've been where you're at, Nova. You don't think I've had my fair share of comeuppance? Public humiliation? We all have, okay? It fucking sucks to make mistakes especially being a leader. When people count on you and you let them down, you feel repelled by your own reflection the next morning. I choke on the bitter pill of my own hypocrisy about twice a day, but this is the muck of life. I gotta swallow it down and move on, just like everyone else."

Nova turned her head with a sigh and looked out the window to the full moon that gently lit the Rockies.

Betts reached out with her left hand and put it on Nova's warm thigh. "You're right about your mom. And me, okay? I didn't want to commit to giving that shit-for-brains a dime. Nick is scum of the Earth."

Nova took a sip of her drink and made eye contact with Betts again.

Betts was glad to see that Nova was calming down. "Nevertheless, Petey and Sams were right, I eventually got it. We had to make it work. You were right to push me. There weren't any other workable solutions other than paying him off."

Nova grasped Betts hand and brought it up to her lips to kiss. "Thanks for that. For being big like that, willing to listen, and to humble yourself. For everything. I'm sorry I lost it."

Betts smiled wide and toothy which made her high cheekbones stand out. "Let me tell you something, Warrior Nova. Bliss would not have survived without you this past week. Brock would have absolutely run us all right off the cliff. No doubt in my mind." Betts rubbed Nova's hand. As the larger problems were resolved, very small details appeared to Betts. *How deep are Nova's palm lines? What symbol do they make? Does she push when I pull? Can I interlace my fingers with hers? Will she squeeze me back?*

Betts set her glass on the windowsill and then took Nova's vodka. "Can I finish this?" She upturned the glass until it was empty, then set that cup on the sill as well. “C’mere you.” She leaned forward and gently touched the tip of her nose to Nova’s. *Rub up. Rub down. Rub left. Rub right.* She couldn’t wait to kiss Nova any longer. Like driving through a long, dark tunnel, both women quickly shed the argument and charged forward toward the light. Betts’ mouth automatically parted and reached for Nova’s soft, thin lips.

Before Betts totally relaxed, she broke away for some pillow talk. “This is real nice. The other day was nice too.” *Nice? Why are words failing me? Our sex was spectacular!*

“It was,” Nova said in a markedly lower voice as she smooched Bett’s big lips and leaned back again.

“It was,” Betts repeated as soon as her lips were free. “You know, I’ve never been with a squirter before.”

Ahhhhh! “Oh, no? Sorry. I should have forewarned you the other day.” Then, Nova realized something wonderful. “I must seem like the goose that laid a golden egg to you then, eh?”

Betts smiled from ear to ear. “In more ways than one, indeed. Your life is my fairytale.”

“Ha!” Nova grasped both of Betts cheeks and tipped her head a little for another short make out session. This time, she was more probing with her tongue because she wanted to see how Nova would respond. *Will you suck me like you need me?* Betts did.

Like the centripetal force of a tornado swirling her around and out of control, Nova felt Betts pulling her in to more than a kiss and certainly more than a job. There was something so familiar with every cellular detail of *this fucking stunning woman* that her attraction grew with each interaction. Nova’s fingers found their way through Betts’ long, dark hair. Nova gathered it gently into a mass and then pulled it straight up hard and fast. *Yank.* Their lips were jerked apart.

The grin on Betts' face revealed a thousand secrets. She would, no doubt, spend the remainder of her days telling *beautiful Nova* each secret one-by-one that ran through her mind at that precious, special moment. Each strand of hair on Betts' scalp was tugged straight up above her head almost high enough to pull her out of her seat, but not quite. She was instantly launched into a dream-like state. *It's perfect. This is fucking perfect. Warrior Nova is perfect.*

Nova watched Betts find peace in her compliance. She noticed how Betts' shoulders and eyelids relaxed. Nova gently lowered the rope of hair until it fell back down over Betts' shoulders. "C'mon, get up," she invited with a peck on Betts' cheek. As Betts stood, Nova could see that her nipples were hard. *Righteous.* Nova reached up with both thumbs to feel them and also leaned in for Betts' lips that she wanted again. "I'm jealous of this shirt. It's closer to you than me. Can I take it off? I gotta feel you."

"Babe, you can do whatever the fuck you want," Betts admitted, still buzzing internally from the hair-pull.

"Oh yeah?" Nova giggled. "What can I do?"

"You can just take me whenever you want in the middle of the night. Have at it. It's okay when I'm sleeping. You just get on in there and do your thing. It's all good." Betts laughed at herself.

"Do you hear how rapey that is?" Nova laughed in astonishment as she unbuttoned Bett's shirt and pulled it off of her. "You weirdo, allowing me to take you in the middle of the night. That's internalized sexism right there."

Betts jokingly slapped Nova's left arm, "You know I'm joking! Ish."

"Oh my God, take your bra off already. I gotta get at them."

Betts laughed at how silly Nova was. *What a kid!*

"What's this?" Nova was suddenly serious and lifted Betts left breast to examine the scar underneath.

"I had an elective double mastectomy," Betts said matter-of-factly. "And reconstruction, obviously."

Can Betts be any more badass? Wow. No wonder she wasn't worried about Nick. Nova lifted Betts' other breast and scanned that scar as well. "So did your mom have breast cancer? Is that why you had it done?"

"Yep. She died when I was nine. My aunts all passed away too." Betts smiled. "I made the right decision for me. Frankly, reconstruction with nipple preservation was my best option if I wanted to continue feeling, you know?"

"Holy shit," Nova exclaimed. Her thumbs gently, almost medically, touched the front of Betts' nipples. She watched them change shape as they hardened.

"Can you feel like you used to? Like, 100%?" Nova wondered.

"No, but I practiced to increase the sensation as high as I possibly can. It's a trick of the mind." Betts grinned. "You can see for yourself if you want."

Oh yeah, my love, I certainly will. Nova pulled Betts' left nipple up and out as she squeezed the right nipple forward and into her mouth. Nova licked and sucked as hard as she possibly could. After a few minutes, she felt all of Betts muscles tighten like a board below her. *Go, baby.* Nova sucked in a rhythm that made sense to them both.

With other lovers, Betts always experienced a half-millisecond of doubt before cuming, like a self-conscious double check, *should I go through with it?* Right now, however, there was no hesitation. It seemed to Betts as though she were biking down the trail next to I-70 at 50 miles an hour. Surely if she tried to slow down and break now, she would fly over the handlebars and crash, so she rode like the wind.

Nova looked at a very satisfied Betts breathing hard, still with her eyes closed. *I love the post-cum moment. Is she gonna take a deep breath? Yes! There it is. Peace.*

Betts' voice was raspy as she complimented Nova. "Fuck you're good at playing me like a violin." Little earthquake reverberations hit her several times. *Damn, there they go.* Betts changed position and pushed Nova back. Her fingers pulled Nova's shirt out of her jeans and up over her head. She then found the back of Nova's bra and unhooked it. "Thanks, that felt great."

"You're welcome. You like my little boobs?" Nova laughed. "They're small, I know."

"Compared to me, yes, but not that small. Just right. Let me see. I need more of an up close look." Betts knelt on the floor in front of topless Nova who was seated in her jeans. Betts put her hands on Nova's thighs and slowly spread them wider and wider until she couldn't push them any further. She leaned her nose in toward Nova's vagina and inhaled deeply from her nose. *Nice.* She pressed her thumb against Nova's clitoris through her jeans and circled it a few times. She looked up to see Nova brace her hands against the seat of the couch and close her eyes in earnest. *Gotcha, girl. Moving in that direction.* Betts reached up and unbuttoned Nova's jeans and then pulled them down and off with Nova's help.

"I don't want to be bare-assed on your couch, can I pull down this blanket?" Nova asked.

"Of course, babe. Be comfortable," Betts agreed. She watched Nova lay down the blanket and sit on it, however the expression on Nova's face revealed her discomfort. "What's the matter?"

"I need a pillow or something for my back." Nova looked around for a pillow.

"Do you want to lay flat?" Betts asked wanting to get rid of Nova's pain.

"Actually, yes, but not on this couch. I need something hard, like your floor. Is the floor okay?" Nova asked.

Betts briefly flashed to her recent lovemaking session with Brock in the very spot that Nova was laying down the soft, gray blanket. Then, Betts remembered when Brock had turned her over to take her from behind. Remembering that made her clit swell and pulse again. She looked at Nova, naked, sitting on her ankles. *So fucking gorgeous.* "Look at you," Betts cooed at her lover in a soft voice. "I love your dark nipples." Betts reached over and fondled them with her fingers as well as with her gaze. "You're so natural and unassuming."

"Now see, there's where you're wrong," Nova teased as she leaned in to smooch Betts' lips. "I am absolutely assuming that you're gonna lay me back and have your way with me."

And that is exactly what Betts did. To say that she made love with her mouth and fingers like the professional that she was did not, in fact, do her justice. Their lovemaking became a series of expected and unexpected performances based on each other's reactions and responses. Together, they built a paranormal, almost supernatural experience that was far more than the sum of their desire. It must have been divine intervention that scripted their congress. How else could they explain how Nova's body yielded to and was awakened by Betts' touch? How else were they to understand the peculiar thirst Betts had for a unique liquid she had never tasted before? How did Nova cum so many times? How did she know just the right amount of pressure Betts needed to make her go limp and acquiesce? In a world full of musicians who needed to read sheet music in order to play, Betts and Nova had finally found a jazz partner who could improvise with joy.

Around 11 o'clock later that night, Betts and Nova awoke from their post-sex slumber. Betts positioned herself onto her bent elbow and looked down at Nova who was laying flat on her back. "Hey, I forgot to ask you something."

"What's that?" Nova responded as she rubbed her tired eyes.

"Do you want to be my date this Saturday to the gala?"

"What would I have to do?"

"Dress up, that's it. A suit is fine."

"In that case, absolutely." Nova pulled Betts down to kiss her pillowy lips.

Betts smooched Nova and then pulled away. *Time to break the news*. "You know that this party is for the clients, right? And so, what we do, we allow each client to bring one new person on board that they think will want to be a member of Bliss. Each year, every member of the inner circle can, if they want, onboard one more person for a discounted membership. It's our draw. Most people can't afford Bliss indefinitely, so when they recruit new clients, they pay ten percent less."

"Wow. Really?" Nova was surprised. She sat up topless and faced Betts who was also topless. "So do you mean that if I recruited ten clients one year after the next, I could have a free lifetime membership in ten years like my golden ticket?"

"Not completely free, but a very steep discount, yes. You get it. The gala is our way to persuade and explain our services. We get all dressed up, give them delicious food, free drinks and entertain them."

"Wine and dine, I get it. That's what the clients want. Okay." Nova was sensing that there was more to this story.

"Actually, to get them to put down a deposit, I've got to hit them with a lot more than that," Betts admitted. "We try to make them laugh and feel horney at the same time."

"Okay, so how can I help?" Nova wondered.

"Nothing. You don't have to do anything. Just schmooze. But, I have to be transparent about my show. It's a little bit fucked up. It includes Brock…" Betts paused and then finished, "…mind-fucking me."

Nova dramatically contorted her face to display her confusion, and then roughly rolled on top of Betts, holding her down with her arms above her head. "Are we really going to have this discussion after last night? I kind of think you're mine now." Nova smiled and kissed Betts' neck. She swiped her small nipples against Betts' silicon breasts that faced up instead of hanging to her sides.

"Nova, we're just demonstrating our product. At the end of the day, giving people orgasms is our brand. This is part of my job and

Brock's job. I want us to be together, but in all seriousness, I have to have certain freedoms with Brock."

"Like having sex with him? No." Nova blew a raspberry onto Betts' neck.

"Like promoting Bliss." Betts laughed and gently pushed Nova off of her to sit up. "I'm serious. This is a deal breaker for me, Nova. Bliss is my baby, and this is our most effective marketing campaign. I don't want to fix what ain't broke, as they say. Do you know what I mean? But I need you on board. I need a break from all of the drama."

Nova could see that Betts would not budge on this issue. *Then negotiate.* "Well you sleeping with other people – in any shape or form – is a deal breaker for me." Nova watched for Betts' reaction.

Betts toothy grin revealed her happiness, "Why Nova, are you asking me to be exclusive?" She giggled at the idea. "You're so part of the tribe."

In self-mockery, Nova put her hands together as if in prayer and asked in a silly juvenile voice, "Will you go out with me and only me?"

Betts smooched Nova's lips. "So sweet. Fine, babe, only you. But you just gave yourself more work."

Chapter 32: Tuesday

"Numbnuts is here," Barbara alerted Bootsie in a low voice as her kitchen light flicked on. She set her green glass half full of cheap vodka down on the arm of her outdoor chair to look closer at the bright rectangle of her kitchen window. She could see Gael holding a glass under the water faucet. *That'll be the last drink you enjoy, shit-for-brains.*

Bootsie took a long draw from his plastic straw as he looked askance at the dilapidated house and small kitchen window. He sat next to Barbara in her so-called backyard that to him was unequivocally a junkyard. Barbara had mixed for him ice, lemon juice, and vodka in a dirty Mason jar. He figured that drinking from a straw might mitigate her dirty germs to some degree. He looked up at the light streaming out into the darkness. *Game on, guey.*

"*Soy yo!*" Gael sang to himself as if he were lead singer Li Saumet in Bomba Estereo. Music from the evening piped through his brain and out his mouth. He had been out dancing. *Por que no, papi? I'm gonna be rich manaña!* After filling his glass with tap water, he guzzled it down.

"Gael, is that you?" Barbara yelled loudly knowing full well that it was him.

Gael turned out the kitchen light and peered through the window out at Barbara who sat drinking with a man. *Must be Save A Stray Day again. Don't worry, Barbara, my Lazy boy chair is gonna open up real soon.* "Yeah, it's me. I'm going to bed."

"And by that he means the arm chair in the front room," Barbara clarified to Bootsie in a low voice. "He's barely house-broken." Then, she increased the volume of her voice and yelled to

Gael, "feel free to take the fan out of my room if you want it. I'm going to sleep out here tonight where it's cool."

After finishing his vodka and learning about how Barbara had her tooth implants completed inexpensively in Costa Rica, Bootsie stood and said, "Remember, you were just giving a homeless man a place to crash for the night. Hide this after he wakes up." He picked up and shook a portable green oxygen tank a little for emphasis. "You have my number if you need it."

"I won't. I can handle myself, but thanks anyway. Mind the path on your way inside."

Bootsie did not need to tiptoe inside Barbara's slummy house because Gael left the volume of the black and white television on high. An infomercial for a wearable towel blared through the tiny, messy home as Bootsie looked around for the fan. As expected, he found Gael fast asleep on a tilted back armchair in the living room. The fan sat in the corner directly facing him at full blast. Bootsie loosened the cap on the tank to allow some oxygen to leak out, then he set it directly behind the fan. As he exited, Bootsie lit himself a cigarette and then left the rest of his pack of Parliament cigarettes and red lighter on the small table next to Gael.

+ + + + +

"Breaking news today live out of Aurora, Colorado." The gaggle of local press tried to stay out of each other's camera shots of a chalk outline of a body around a black, burned spot on the pavement. A cracked sidewalk and overgrown front lawn on the opposite side of the street were the only available areas for the camera crews due to all of the first responder vehicles covering the rest of the block. "Local authorities have just confirmed to 9NEWS that a person burned to death after blowing up around 8 o'clock this morning. A neighbor, Chet Miller, witnessed the event and immediately called 911. Chet, tell us what happened."

The news camera panned wider to include a bearded hipster with a wine colored beanie hat standing next to the young, freshly shaven reporter. "The guy walked out from that house across the street this morning and lit a cigarette. I remember because he wasn't vaping, he had an actual lighter and an actual cigarette. It was the weirdest thing. I was just watering my tulips, glanced over, and then bam! It sounded like a boat's sail catching a gust of wind, you know? The next thing I see is this huge fireball and the guy running around and screaming like crazy. He must have been in tons of pain, man."

"What did you do?" asked the reporter.

"I immediately ran over to him and was like, 'Stop, drop, and roll!' but he was completely freaking out. He tripped off of the curb and fell. Hard. Cement always wins, man. He didn't get up after that, so I threw all the water from my can at his head and called 911."

The camera zoomed in to the reporter's face again. "Police say that identification has not yet been made, and it may take a few days before they are able to determine the cause of this bizarre occurrence. Back to you at the 9NEWS station."

"Thank you, Mike. In other news, three local teenagers were recently discovered to have been trafficked for sex here in Colorado, then mysteriously rescued from their captors and brought to Hope House..."

✦ ✦ ✦ ✦ ✦

"You look very lesbian," Mary Ann confirmed to her daughter.

"Mom," Nova said exasperated at the image of her mom's face on her cell phone, which was leaning against the bathroom mirror. She wanted to video chat with her mother tonight to show off her new outfit, but was now regretting this decision. "That's not a compliment. That's not even a thing."

"But that's what you're going for, right? You said you like Betts," Mary Ann clarified as she held her cell phone closer to her face.

"I do, but I'm not dressing to look like a lesbian; I just am a lesbian." Nova played with her short hair and pushed it around and sprayed some product on it to keep it in place as she continued chatting. Nova thought she pulled off the hipster persona fairly well for her age. She wore a white t-shirt and dark gray suit. Tonight was the Bliss gala and everyone was dressing up for the celebration.

"Well, technically you're bi," Mary Ann corrected.

"Ma!" Off camera, Nova squeezed the final drops from a plastic bladder of chardonnay she had removed from its box earlier. Her glass filled up, and she threw the empty bag into the trash. *This is not my finest moment.*

"Okay, okay. Define yourself. You're a lesbian, and you look very lesbian. Good job, that's all I'm saying, sweetie."

Nova was suspicious. "Holy shit, ma, what are you doing? You're being a little too affirming."

"I'm making you feel better about your outfit. Now tell me what shoes you're wearing."

"My red, checkered Vans." Pleased with herself, Nova spun around in the mirror.

"Great! Good idea. Very Ellen DeGeneres."

"Jesus, mom. Is that the only lesbian you can think of?"

"No, there's Portia, and I know you too," Mary Ann joked. "And Stacy, your first love from college, of course."

Nova started rubbing the stress out of her forehead and eyebrows.

"Don't touch them! They'll smear!" Mary Ann instructed.

"Ma. What is with all of the attention today? Usually you're so..." *Don't say 'self absorbed.'* "...busy." Nova drank her wine and listened.

"Well, since you're asking, Steady called me the other day. Said he might stop by this afternoon. He scolded me the last time I saw him. Said that moms 'still protect their kids even when they're grown', so I asked him to send over those guys to check on you. Hope that went okay. Steady said that they think you're perfectly fine. Sounds like they met Betts and really liked her too. Said that you're in good hands with her."

Ha! "More like she's in good hands with me, Mom." *Let's get that straight.*

"Probably true, you've always been an alpha, like me. Now honey, I'm just going to say it: I never do not want to know everything about you, okay? I screwed up. Please forgive me."

"Wow, Mom. By your weird double negative and halting affect, I take it you really are sorry."

"I am, sweetie."

"Well, thanks. That's big. I know I'm grown and should have it all figured out by now and make totally healthy choices all the time, but the truth is – I need you. I'm always going to need my parents. In fact, Steady understated the amount of help Petey and Sams gave me and my friends, actually. Frankly, without them there..."

"I heard my name!" Steady yelled dramatically as he entered Mary Ann's kitchen as if it were a stage.

Nova could see Steady kiss her mother on the cheek and then talk directly to her through Mary Ann's phone.

"I also heard you still have a smart mouth, young lady," Steady scolded Nova.

"Sorry, Steady." Nova was contrite.

"What did she do now?" Mary Ann asked Steady in confusion.

"Nothing. I'm just teasing her." Steady changed the subject. "Look at you, girl! All dressed up! Another fund-raiser?"

"In a matter of speaking," Nova qualified. "I'm going as Betts' date. It's a client party at her company. What do you think?" Nova spun around with her hands up in the air.

"Marvelous! She's lucky to have you, and I'm not joking. Enjoy, darling," Steady wished as he exited off screen.

"Thanks you two." Nova felt satisfied. "Okay, I gotta go. Love you both!"

"Hey! Last thing." Mary Ann wagged her finger at the phone. "If you're going to break the law, don't get caught, okay?"

"Wow, that's very Saratoga-esk, life advice, Mom," Nova laughed. "Love you. Bye."

Chapter 33: Gala Night

"Are you ready?" Nova asked Betts as she closed a handcuff attached to Betts' left wrist around the opening in the Royal Throne chair. *Click! Click! Click!*

Betts closed her eyes, inhaled a deep breath, and tried to relax as Nova buckled her down. It was, in fact, a very effective parlor trick, so Betts performed this signature show every year.

"You got this," Nova cheered her on. "It's your brand. Only you can do this. Only you are uniquely qualified. You're fucking amazing. And fucking hot." She let her middle and index fingers slowly trace a line from Betts' ankles up to her inner knees and then higher up her thigh toward her thong underwear. Nova looked up at Betts' high cheekbones, fat lips, and closed eyes. *Goddamn perfection.* "You're such a baller, Betts," Nova admired. Marcus had braided Betts' hair up and backwards Dothraki style, a silky, curvy waterfall of French and Dutch braids. This polished effect alongside her billowing, red dress with a wide queen's collar rendered Nova breathless and wanting. She pushed on the swollen area between her legs and then loosely closed another set of handcuffs around each of Betts' ankles pinning them to the throne.

Nova roughly lifted Betts' dress up above her knees and then attached Betts' right wrist to the throne as well. *I smell you, Betts. No matter how long you shower, I can still smell you.* Nova looked down at Betts' open legs and inhaled deeply. Her underwear was masked by a mound of billowy red cloth and chiffon. "You smell awesome. So alive." Nova pushed the dress higher and then Betts' knees as far apart as the throne would permit. *God I wanna fuck you.*

It wasn't only Betts who was performing; Nova had to get her there by talking her through it. *I have a new found respect for Brock.* "Look at you, all tied down," Nova said in her deepest, bedroom voice. "Legs spread. There's so much I could do to you right now." Nova's thumbs pushed harder into the flesh on the sides of Betts' knees. "I so want to fuck you. You better be ready. Let me see you lift your clit. Aim her high." Nova picked up a long black feather off from the floor and playfully caressed Betts' inner thighs. Nova could see Betts' hips tilt further upwards. "Do you want this little feather? I bet you do. My tongue wants to float over your pussy too…"

Chaya's round face and beautifully Dutch braided, red hair poked through the heavy stage curtain and peered at them. "You kids almost ready?"

Betts kept her eyes closed, focused and intentional. However, both of her hands ungripped the chair and gave Chaya a double middle finger.

Nova was on her knees and silently gave Chaya a 'thumbs up' sign with her hand as she continued fluffing Betts.

"Every time," Chaya mumbled her complaint as she shook her head. "It's not like we have 150 guests waiting or anything." She quickly yanked the curtain back in place and gave the DJ the cue to turn down the music slowly. *They're here for me anyway, not you, Betts.*

Nova could hear the volume change and told Betts, "I'm going to put your eye mask on. We're gonna start. Are you ready, my love?" Nova pulled the black eye covers that were dangling around Betts' neck upwards over her eyes. Nova placed the tip of her thumb on Betts' bottom lip and wiped it a little to see her teeth, *just the way you like it.*

Betts arched a little and clenched the handles of the chair. *Ready.* She nodded her head.

"Hi, I'm new. I'm supposed to ask for a person named Betts?" the young Arab woman said with a questioning tone as she removed her ear buds. She stood at the threshold of the Bliss bar looking in past the bouncer where she saw tens of people dancing in front of a small stage with a closed red curtain. Most had drinks in their hand. Suddenly, the volume of the music lowered and in its place was a new, overlapping sound. *Breath? Breathing? What's that? Moaning?*

The Bliss bouncer for tonight's gala was Marcus, who was more than happy to take on the role since his sister, Shuree, was hired on at the last minute to dole out advice as though she was a tarot card reader. The last thing he wanted was to be working the clients in front of her, so he was more than glad to stand guard in the waiting room outside the bar. The look of confusion on the Arab woman's face was trying to connect with Marcus for answers. "Don't ask me. I just work here." The next sounds over the speakers were even more clearly a woman in the throes of an orgasm. *No, this is not weird at all.*

There was whimpering and fast breathing which then evolved into elongated moans. Marcus smiled big, slightly embarrassed at the confused Arab woman. *Stay professional.* "Can I see some ID first?" Marcus already knew exactly who she was: She was Fatima, a Gen Z Arab who Chaya called the 'hot butch lesbian unicorn.' "I don't think that that's what a unicorn is," he had remarked to Chaya. Marcus understood her point though, and in short, gave Fatima props. *Muslim. A lesbian Muslim hired to fuck women for money. Badass, this one.*

She would soon more than fill Gael's place at Bliss. They didn't know it yet, but Fatima would eventually turn out to be one of their most accomplished Specialists.

Fatima objected with a disgusted face above the whimpers and loud moans. "I showed them at the entrance already."

Spicy is good, you'll need that here, Marcus thought. *But know your place. Respect our ways.* Marcus pretended to be tough. "If you want to work for Betts, you better start by respecting how much she cares about security. There's a new push for a higher level of safety around here. Someday it may be yours she's worried about, you feel me? So out with it."

"Yeah, yeah, whatever, bro." Fatima quickly produced her Colorado driver's license that Marcus feigned to cross-reference with a paper list. "You're gonna have to wait a minute for her."

"Why, where is she?"

Marcus returned her license. "She's coming. Literally."

Marcus and the visitor turned and looked through the door to the stage with curtains that slowly started to open as the sounds of the female orgasm being piped over the speakers increased in pitch and volume. As her climax hit its peak, the curtains fully opened to reveal Betts handcuffed to a throne with Nova kneeling on her right side whispering in her ear.

The crescendo of Betts' orgasm over Billie Eilish singing "Bad Guy" made the crowd scream and cheer with delight. The audience of over one hundred stood and cheered as Betts finished, out of breath and sweaty. Collectively, they turned to one another and high fived and laughed like they had just unexpectedly inherited a fortune.

"Mother Nature is right there. Center stage," Marcus smirked and pointed through the door at Betts.

"God damn." The Arab woman was genuinely impressed. She looked to where Marcus was pointing and saw another woman kneeling next to the throne stand up and wave to the crowd proudly as if she had just won a foot race. As she was bowing, two stagehands rushed onto stage and quickly unlocked all four handcuffs for the woman in the red dress. Then, the woman stood, wiped the sweat from her upper lip, and waved to wild applause from her audience. She blew double handed kisses as if she had won an Oscar. Then, two very muscle-bound men who looked like security guards with earpieces escorted her down the stairs.

Fatima noticed two women in the crowd who looked to her like news anchors curtsy with deference as if the woman in red truly was Mother Nature. The crowd cleared a path for her as she walked toward Nova. The song changed to "Oh Baby" from LCD Soundsystem. Then, an older Japanese woman with spiky white hair in a pantsuit held out her open hand in which Betts placed hers. The older woman kissed the back of Betts' hand as if she were the pope.

Having reached her final destination, Betts walked into Nova's open arms and smooched her in front of everyone.

"Drink, your highness?" Nova joked as she held up her glass for Betts. "You were awesome. I don't want you to be thirsty, my queen. And while I'm just a mere knight, I want to do everything I can to make you feel comfortable."

Betts smiled and chugged it down. *Yes, my knight, my warrior Nova.*

"That was outstanding," Nova complimented seriously. "I have so much to learn from you before I die."

"Before you die?" Betts laughed over the loud crowd. *You drama junkie.*

"Yeah, Betts, I'm gonna die first, okay? Not you," Nova yelled loudly over the techno music. She pulled Betts closer into her embrace.

"Oh really? Why is that?" Betts leaned in. *This should be good.*

"Because I won't be able to bear losing you, babe, so I have to die first," Nova cooed like the lover she was and placed a small kiss on Betts cheek.

Awe, she's sweet on me. "I love you," Betts admitted. *Telling her is the right thing to do, always.*

"I love you too, babe," Nova replied as she kissed Betts lovingly on the center of her lips. The room spun around them as if they were inside the eye of a tornado.

From across the room, Fatima asked Marcus in disbelief about what she had just witnessed. "Holy shit. Who the fuck is that again?" *Wow, a real public orgasm without any help. Now she's kissing another woman. I can't believe this fucking job. Who are these people?*

"Meet your new boss, Fatima," Marcus shouted proudly above the noise.

At hearing her name, Fatima's expression resembled a gangster who was ready to fist fight. "Never call me that. I'm Phoenix," she said with dignity and purpose. *How can he ever understand?* Then, her expression softened. "Sorry. I just need you to use my true name. Never call me by my birth name. Anyway, you were saying? That's my what?"

Islam on the DL; got it. As a matter of principle, Marcus felt it was absolutely unfair that some people could pass while others, like him, could not. He could never not be black. However, this particular situation was a very rare exception to the rule. *If I were an openly gay Muslim woman who looked like a hot skateboarder, I would pass as non-Muslim too. Sure, I have an unfair share of black man-specific problems, but honor killing is not one of them. I don't have to worry about my own brother jumping me in the middle of the night like a pussy and then bragging about it the next day to the pats on the back of family, friends, and neighbors. Fuck that shit. I got your back girl, no matter how mean you are to me and no matter how much you push me away.* "Welcome to Bliss, Phoenix. I'm Marcus, and that woman in the red dress is Betts. Our boss." He extended his hand to shake. "Nice to meet you."

Phoenix shook his hand and admitted with a grin, "This is not what I expected."

"Yep. Sounds about right," Marcus chuckled. "Hey, you're not the only newbie. My sister is in the corner over there. Her vlogger name is 'Sister Shuree.' She's new too. Feel free to go chat with her. Give yourself time to feel out the room. I wouldn't interrupt Betts right now though. Her fan club will take a while to mellow out after that performance, but then you can approach her later." Marcus looked around to see if he was being overheard and then tacked on a little advice. "Just be inconspicuous and observant. Take mental notes. You should be counting cards as you play. You feel me?"

Phoenix entered the bar and walked around the long way toward Sister Shuree by following the walls instead of walking through the center of the gigantic room. The dark, wooden bar flickered with shadows from thousands of candles in brass candelabras on the tables. On the walls hung large clan banners featuring various angry wild animals with threatening fangs, teeth, horns, and antlers. Phoenix' mouth watered as the smell of delicious, hot *hors d'oeuvres* wafted through the air. Bacon wrapped dates filled with parmesan cheese were at the table to her right. *What better way to pass than to walk around with bacon.* She filled a small plate with three of the non-*halal* appetizers and continued weaving in and out of the crowd of Bliss clients and staff.

Even though the lighting was dim and she was a bit far away, she noticed how the crowd in the room's center was an eclectic mix of different ages, ethnicities, orientations, and clothing styles. All types of men and women were here except, notably to her, Arabs. She could hear Spanish and Chinese being spoken amidst plumes of laughter from all parts of the room. It was festive and brisling with energy. *This is awesome.* A beautiful red headed woman who seemed to be wearing a blue medieval peasant dress walked across the stage and spoke into the microphone.

"And that's how you do it, ladies and gentleman, please give a round of applause to our hero, the one and only Betts!" Chaya was so proud of her Dothraki braids that she positioned herself from different angles as if she were modeling. *Hopefully someone will take a photo of me.* She saw Nefertiti wearing a white, shoulder sling to her left, *no, she doesn't have enough hands to take a shot.* Desiree was behind the bar helping with the drinks, *no, she's too busy as always.* Brock was hugging Alice in the middle of the crowd, *ew, don't smell her hair.* Nova was leaning against a table to her right, *no, she's only focused on Betts. You guys, do I have to do everything*? Chaya reached into her bosom and pulled out her cell phone in front of the audience, turned around, and posed for a selfie with everyone in the background. As soon as the audience realized what she was doing, they screamed and shouted with their arms in the air.

Chaya then returned her phone next to her left breast, lifted the microphone out and waved its wire in circles to unwind it from the stand. A stagehand quickly ran across the stage to move the stand out of Chaya's way. "Thank you for participating in this special night. Team Bliss wants to welcome you, our beautiful clients, to our annual celebration of everything blissful. That selfie was epic. You guys are awesome. And Betts' performance shows you that we know what we're doing, ladies. We just wanted to prove it to you. In the flesh. What she did, my friends, is called a 'mindgasm.' It's sex at the Olympic level. That was fun to watch. How about you? Was that any fun?" The audience screamed and clapped. "Did it make you a little horney? Give you a little stubby, guys?" Her fans roared again at how she had dug into their mind and knew their little secret. "Thank you, glad you enjoyed it too. Have a seat. Be comfortable. We're all about the comfort here, aren't we," Chaya giggled. "Would you mind if I got comfortable too? As if I haven't already, am I right?"

With the tone and timing of a seasoned comedian, Chaya made her audience laugh through self-deprecating jokes and insights unique to someone in the trade. "So, if you're new to Bliss, I'd like to introduce myself. I'm Chaya, and I work for Betts and Brock, who co-own Bliss. I have a couple of different jobs, and one of them is to teach. Bliss clients can sign up for my class called, 'Mind Body Conversations' where they learn to 'mindgasm.' Teaching this class comes pretty naturally to me, because I'm like Betts: I never remember not knowing how to do it. In fact, that's how I first met Betts so many years ago here in Colorado. Birds of a feather, I guess.

"You see, I come from a very traditional family where masturbation was prohibited. Even the mere thought of it was a sin. But the funny thing is that I also don't remember 'discovering' masturbation. Masturbation and mindgasms just have always been part of my bodily functions. But just to keep it in perspective, I've met very few people like me and Betts who don't remember their first time, so I think I'm in the minority here. Actually, let's take a poll. How many of you remember your first wank? Raise your hands."

The majority of people in the bar raised their hands and looked around at each other. "Okay, that confirms it. Betts and I are weirdos." The audience laughed with Chaya. "I'm the sicko. It makes me wonder if it was nurture instead of nature that made me this way, you know? Like, what type of baby was I? Did I play with myself all the time? Why? Because I had to have started masturbating before my memory started, otherwise I would remember it, right? So I'm just picturing me as a little four month old having a good old time in my crib. 'You're going to Ferberize me, mom and dad? Okay, I'm going to self-soothe in the creepiest possible way as payback.' Most babies suck their thumbs when they're left to cry themselves to sleep. Oh, not me. I had an altogether different methodology." Chaya paused for effect. "Apparently. What babies do that? I'll tell you what kind: fucked up little babies do that." Laughter filled the room again.

"Just kidding, folks. Moms and dads in the audience, you cannot fuck up your kids psychologically by letting them cry themselves to sleep. Well, not major psychological damage at least." Chaya laughed at herself. As a stage whisper she clarified, "They will just feel abandoned and never fully trust you, but who cares? No, I'm kidding. I swear I'm kidding. Think about all those families with three and four kids. You have to be organized if you're in a big family. Parents have to divide their attention thoughtfully. You can't be in four places at once. God only gave you two hands. So, you have to help the kids have a schedule. It makes sense. You're helping little Noah with his homework at my baby Chaya bedtime. He was the first-born, and he's male. You've invested so much in him already. Why would you rock a baby girl to sleep when she won't even remember it? There's no reward in that. But little Noah getting a good grade in math, now that might make the difference between a four and five star retirement home. He could end up an engineer or a doctor. You've got to choose your investments wisely, parents, I understand. No, the real psychological damage that makes a full-grown woman masturbate in public without touching herself is far worse than baby Chaya crying herself to sleep.

"What confuses me though as I try to be my own psychological detective, is how come no one was like, 'Put an extra diaper on that baby before she touches herself to death.' Oh no, not my family. Instead, I bet my siblings were laughing their fucking asses off at the baby masturbater. I can see myself as a toddler probably humping the arms on the sofa or the corners of coffee tables. And there were my six sisters and brothers. Laughing and laughing at funny baby Chaya with a vagina problem."

Chaya looked accusingly at the audience, "Maybe I had an itch, okay? Maybe that's how it all started before my memory. I bet I just had a little a diaper rash." Chaya dramatically started itching her vagina, which made the audience erupt with laughter. "And I just had to get some relief. I bet it was those God damned cloth diapers. They don't take the moisture away from the skin like those expensive store diapers do!"

Chaya feigned a moment of awareness and resolution. "I can't believe that I'm just now piecing this all together. So let's see: because I wore cloth diapers, I got a rash. The rash made me itch. Itching the itch made me feel good, so I kept itching. Then an itch became a rub, which turned into humping sofa arms in front of my siblings who would point and laugh at me."

Now Chaya added even more drama by pointing directly at the audience. "Oh, my God! You represent my family! And Betts and I are still doing it! We're still crazy babies itching for a laugh!" Some women in the audience were giggling so hard that they were crying.

Chaya paused for dramatic effect, then walked around a little, chuckling to herself. "Mindgasms. Can I be honest? They're fun in public – especially when the public does not know your having one. By the way, if you're ever using public transportation and the person seated across from you looks like they are taking a dump by the expression on their face, like it's insanely red and swollen, you should walk away. Just walk away, people. She's mindgasming. And, hey, let's face it – when I teach you how to do it, you will try it in public at least once. Guaranteed. I know you will. You know how I know? Because I've taught tons of you how to do it, and you all go out with your new superpower and mindgasm at the library, the grocery store, at meetings, wherever, and then you come back to weirdo Chaya and tell her every last, delicious detail."

The audience cheered with pride at themselves.

"Yes, you should be proud of that ladies. You're learning new things here at Bliss, aren't you. You're taking care of yourself and, though it seems counter intuitive, your strengthening your partnerships and marriages. Did you know that there is a *Journal of Sex and Marital Therapy*? They have a journal for everything nowadays. So I was reading this article in *Psychology Today* that cited this sex journal, and it had some really interesting facts. I want to test you. Let's find out what you all know – or don't. By a show of hands, what percent of American women masturbated in the past year? 90%? 80%? 50%? 30%?"

Many people from the audience cupped their hand around their mouth and yelled out the answer they thought was correct.

"Thirty eight percent. Can you believe it? Only 38%. We have got to increase that number, ladies. And gentlemen, you too. You need to do your part. You need to cheer us on more. We can do some amazing shit if more people just cheered us on, don't you agree, ladies?"

The clapping from the audience was resolute.

"Okay, next question: Which race masturbates the most? White, black, Asians, Latinos, Pacific Islanders?"

Again, answers were shouted out at equal frequencies by the audience.

"It's white people. They are more likely to do it." Chaya pointed and laughed at some groups in the audience. "Oh, look at them. My black clients are like, 'I bet that's not a statistically significant sample of research subjects. I disagree with those findings.'" Chaya laughed along with the audience.

"Let me hit you with some more truth. You know which group of women masturbate the most? The ladies who are involved in a sexless relationship. In fact, this article I was reading, 'Masturbation in the United States,' said that 'one of the best predictors of masturbation was a relationship that lacked emotional intimacy.' It makes sense, right? Because sex involves two things: physical proximity and emotional closeness. So this is how Bliss is helping so many women. We keep the gears oiled. Then they turn and turn and turn."

Chaya saw that a stagehand had placed a rum and coke on a small table on stage, so she walked over and took a few sips. "So I don't remember learning how to masturbate, mindgasm, nor do I remember what propelled me to have a whole constellation of them in one sitting. Oh, you don't know that word? It just means that our orgasms are like M&Ms… you don't have just one. I mean, you could, but you shouldn't. It's best to toss them into your welcoming mouth in groups, groups of three, sometimes four, or if you're feeling energetic, five or six. That's a workout, isn't it ladies? Yeah, a fun way to burn calories! That last one is like climbing Mt. Everest, isn't it. Damn, we're violently shaking like we're having a seizure, sometimes drooling… oh, it's a glorious mess that last orgasm." The audience responded with another explosion of laughter as Chaya dramatically pretended to be holding a jackhammer.

"So I like to call them 'constellations,' like each one is part of a picture. They are more than the sum of their individual parts. Most days, for me, it's a triangle. Three beautiful stars holding each other's little star-hands. Three is beautiful. And fulfilling. Don't get me wrong. Three is awesome. But every so often, I create Ursa Minor, or in layperson's tongue, 'The Little Dipper.'

"'The Little Dipper' has five stars." Chaya held all five fingers of her left hand wide in the air. She then poked at the air in the shape of a dipper as she counted, "One, two, three, four, five. Five and up takes a bit more stamina, ladies. I won't lie. There is a significant difference between three and five orgasms. It's hard enough on our own, but if we are with a partner, we need a lover who is super focused. They've got to know to glide you through numbers one, two, and three without stopping.

"Ladies, if your partner is a guy, you have to tell him that as soon as number one is done, we only need ten seconds. He should not go anywhere. He should not think, 'ok, she had one, now it's my turn!' No! In order to reach three or five – and this is not even the Holy Grail people – you need a lover who is aiming from the beginning to give you five. Now, this is where lesbian lovers are so great. They already know this. They start giving head with a plan, and the plan is: one, two, three are going to be grouped together. Then I'll give her a bit of a break to catch her breath and start again with a previously unemployed technique. She knows the last two are hard, and she knows she got to help you, so she goes for something new: new technique, maybe new location. Guys, you've got to make friends with lesbians. They have so much to teach you." Chaya took another sip of her drink.

"Now for the more advanced clients in the room, I want you to aim for Ursa Major, 'The Big Dipper'. They both have the same number of stars, five, but I call the advanced move Ursa Major because it's like liftoff. You slide and glide smooth and hot into outer space where you're weightless and floating." Chaya laughed at herself and her dramatic voice that she spoke closer on the microphone.

"Oh, God. If you think one orgasm is good, how about two? At the same time! In two different places!" Several men in the audience whistled their approval very loudly over the applause and cheers. "Ladies, you and I are thinking about the clit and the g-spot right now, aren't we, but the men are not. You know why the men are going nuts right now, don't you? Because they're all thinking of a different location." Chaya paused, leaned into the microphone as if she were going to whisper a secret, and loudly yelled, "Gee, I wonder where that would be? Yep. The ass." The audience roared. "I know what you're thinking. It takes a one to know a one. So predictable." Again, Chaya paused dramatically in order to hit her punch line harder. "I also know that we both have asses, motherfucker, and we both can Ursa Major."

Laughter roared throughout the bar. The women in the audience screamed while some men shouted, "No!"

"Hey, don't knock it 'till you try it, boys. You don't know. How does anybody know anything until they try it? Really. I hated coffee as a teenager. Now I drink it every morning. I used to hate wine in my twenties. Now I drink a bottle every freakin' night. I do. I'm shameless, I know. I need to grow some self-respect. I used to hate pot, now I enjoy it immensely. Colorado rocks!

"I'm not pushing drugs; I'm really not. You know your limits. Follow your limits. But what I am trying to say is that mindgasms, cumming in constellations, or from new-to-you locations – you can learn it all too. That's what we do here at Bliss: we teach and entertain you. We're the sex-ed teacher you always wished you had had. Thank you for your enthusiasm, folks. I'm so happy that you, like me, want to celebrate the female orgasm. Thank you for coming out tonight. I want you to enjoy yourselves. Any questions you have can be directed to anyone wearing a Bliss lapel pin. Thank you, and I'll see you in class soon!"

✦ ✦ ✦ ✦ ✦

DJ Shadow rapping "Nobody Speak" pumped out of the speakers as Chaya, very pleased with herself, strutted off stage and into the crowd toward Brock. "Picture this. I'm a bag of dicks. Put me to your lips. I am sick. I will punch a baby bear in his shit." The audience was going nuts. Many people high-fived her. *Nailed it, again.*

Brock squeezed and then let go of Alice as Chaya finished her act. "I've gotta go congratulate her. Excuse me for one second." He was so happy that he felt like the world was in slow motion. As he moved through the crowd toward Chaya, the women looked at him like ravenous wild animals in heat. *No, no, and no.* The men smirked and knuckle bumped him to show respect. He strutted along the wall until he met Chaya. They bear-hugged. "You were great! Really funny!"

"Yeah? Are you sure?" Chaya played coy.

"A total hit. C'mon. Come say hi to Alice," Brock encouraged.

That's a hard 'no.' Looking for an out, Chaya saw Phoenix standing nearby with a small plate in her hand. Chaya zeroed in on her new co-worker. "Hey wait, isn't that Phoenix the unicorn?"

Brock turned and looked in the direction Chaya was pointing and saw his newest employee. "I don't think that that is what unicorn means." When he had offered Phoenix the job a few days ago, he invited her to the party to observe the clients, but nothing more.

"Hey, Phoenix," Brock smiled as he approached. Passers by patted him on the back. "I'm glad you came. Did you see the opening act?"

"I did, yeah. Betts is pretty amazing. I can't believe that she can do that." Phoenix set the plate of bacon wrapped dates down on a nearby table so that she had a free hand to more easily hold her rum and Coke.

Brock replied slowly and deliberately with a half smile. "How she can do that." His voice trailed off as if he were contemplating a deep theoretical issue. "We are superheroes, Phoenix. Her superpower is mindgasming, and mine is bushwhacking her a path to it. Well, at least I used to." He laughed at himself. "Now she has Nova and I have Alice."

"Oh, okay. So, you two used to be together?"

Chaya intervened. "It's complicated. You're Phoenix, right?" Chaya extended her hand out to shake. "I'm Chaya. I work the front desk."

Brock laughed. "Are you kidding me? I can't believe that you introduce yourself to people like that, especially after that performance."

Chaya smiled at Phoenix, "Well, it's not untrue. I'm the one who will let her through the front door each day. I sit at the front desk."

"Phoenix," Brock started. "Chaya is so much more than someone who presses a button and does clerical work behind a desk."

"Clearly," Phoenix smiled at Chaya. "You're funny."

"And she saves women's lives every day, and I am not exaggerating." Brock put his arm around Chaya and pulled her in close. "You are looking at my vaping buddy, my accountability partner – AKA office jokester who will never let me take myself too seriously – and of course one of our best instructors. She has saved my ass on more than one occasion, and… little known fact… she's an excellent painter."

Chaya and Phoenix shared a knowing look communicating that Brock was probably drunk, high, and fairly exhausted. *Play along*, they thought in unison.

Phoenix spoke first, challenging Chaya. "Really? Oil or acrylic?"

Oh, we're gonna go there, Chaya silently whined, *in the middle of a raging party, we are going to get academic? What is this – checking to see if I know my art?*

Phoenix saw Chaya's reaction and decided to poke the bear a little harder. "You don't have a preference, do you. In fact, you don't even know the difference in drying times or how oil retains its color better, do you."

Chaya turned to Brock and said as a stage whisper, "I guess I shouldn't tell professor here that I painted my most recent piece in pig's blood."

Brock immediately choked on his laughter.

Chaya knew an exit when she saw one. She turned to Phoenix and said approvingly, "I like you, girl. You're annoying, but you got spunk. I got your back. Don't forget that, okay?" She walked away happy, and then quickly turned back to shout and point a finger-gun at Brock, "Hey thanks, man. Love you to the moon."

Brock tilted his head back to finish his expensive scotch. As he swallowed it down and lowered his head again, he noticed the expression on Phoenix's face. *Concentration. Fear. Surprise. What's going on?* Brock looked to his left and right as if he should be able to see what was so obviously bothering her. "What is it?"

Shhhhhh! Phoenix put her index finger to her lips and then listened closely.

Brock looked around at the floor and tried to listen too. *But to what? Fucking loud techno music?* "I hear a lot of stuff," he yelled at her, "but I don't know what I'm listening for."

"The perpetual state of manhood, I know," Phoenix slammed, "It's hard being you."

What did I do? Brock wondered in confusion. A male fan passed by and yelled at him, "You're amazing, man! You'll have to share your tricks with non-clients too!"

Brock was slapped on the back twice in admiration. He waited anxiously for Phoenix to stop *being weird.* "What the fuck is going on?"

Phoenix finally composed herself and grabbed Brock's upper right arm and half-dragged, half-pushed him through the crowd toward the bouncer Marcus.

Because Phoenix was so rough with Brock, a deep male voice called out at them in an Indian accent, "What's your safe word, Brock?" to a cacophony of laughter from anyone within earshot.

Phoenix stopped, let go of Brock, and rushed over to the Indian man who had called out. She grabbed and squeezed his balls and penis until he was frozen with fear. Invoking Billie Eilish, she sneered, "You're a real tough guy, but I'm the fucking bad guy. Watch out, and don't ever disrespect Brock again."

From out of nowhere, Betts appeared smiling in her red outfit and Dothraki braided hair. Her red lipstick perfectly matched her clothing for a very dramatic effect. "Abhinay, so good to see you." She leaned in to give him an air kiss on each of his brown cheeks.

Phoenix quickly let go of Abhinay's crotch and stepped back the moment Betts started to lean in.

"Abhinay, I'm sorry about this. I think that there has been a misunderstanding," Betts stated matter-of-factly.

"No, no, no, no, Betts. The young lady is right. I shouldn't have been making a joke at Brock's expense." He turned and called out to get Brock's attention. "Brock! Sorry, man. I was just kidding."

Brock made a thumbs up sign with his hand. "It's all good."

"We know you were, Abhinay," Betts replied. "I'll find you later, okay? I need to talk to Phoenix right now." Betts turned to Phoenix, pointed toward the door, and sternly said, "March."

Betts, Brock, and Phoenix exited the bar into the waiting room past Marcus.

"What the fuck was not clear about your instruction to 'observe'?" Betts accused in a loud voice.

"Yeah," Brock admitted in exasperation. "What happened in there, Phoenix?"

Marcus rolled his eyes. *Jesus. You're here less than 30 minutes and have already managed to piss off both of your bosses? You gotta give to get, girl. C'mon. Don't be basic.*

Phoenix crossed her arms over her chest defiantly. "Bliss has a big problem."

"Oh yeah?" Betts asked sarcastically. "How would you know?" *Guessing the obvious doesn't sound profound, zygote.*

"I heard a man planning something," Phoenix responded cryptically. "In Arabic." She did not see any reason to candy coat her message. "You have a problem with the Arabs."

Betts, Brock, and Marcus looked at each other with *déjà vu*.

Stoned and tipsy, Chaya danced down the secret hall full of theme rooms away from the *thump! thump!* of techno music playing in the bar. The further away from the bar she was, the less she could hear the music until it faded out completely. She did not, however, stop dancing. She was so happy that her performance was a hit. *Life! Love! My friends! So much to be grateful for! Orgasms! Choice! Ability to make money! To those who influenced and changed me, I'm here today, whole and broken, in small part because of you. I was not created in a vacuum, so don't give me shit.*

Chaya turned left and headed toward Betts' office. The closer she came to the door at the end of the hallway, the louder the hip-hop music became. Suddenly, the door opened to a loud party full of women with Nova and Desiree dancing close to the door.

Chaya entered the room and yelled, "I'm ready to get my bliss on, ladies!"

Nova greeted, "You made it!"

Shanon grinned as she danced. "It's about time, lady!"

Desiree, who was dancing with her husband, yelled, "Get on in here! The party is just getting started!"

About the author:

After working in higher education for over two decades, Becca is currently embracing a career shift and writing fiction full time. She hopes that *With Love* is the first in a trilogy of Bliss adventure novels.

Made in the USA
Columbia, SC
15 December 2019

84910837R10262